The Book of Galahad

by

Susan D. Cook

First published in 2004

PUBLISHED BY
PAUL MOULD PUBLISHING

Library of Congress Cataloging-in-Publication data

Cook, Susan D.
The Book of Galahad / by Susan D. Cook
p. cm.
ISBN 1-58690-016-1 (alk. paper)
1. Galahad (Legendary character) --Fiction. 2. Europe--History--476-1492--Fiction. 3. Knights and knighthood--Fiction. 4. Arthurian romances--Adaptations. 5. Quests (Expeditions)--Fiction. 6. Grail--Fiction 1. Title

PR6103.O667B66 2005
823792--dc22

2004063508

ISBN 1-58690-016-1 (USA)
ISBN 1-904959-07-5 (UK)

Printed in Great Britain by
CLE Print Limited

Prologue

Galahad awoke early, roused from a light sleep by the low, cheery voices of the serving women as they passed by the hall on their way to begin the first tasks of the day. He pushed back the cloak that covered him and stood up carefully, trying not to disturb a man who had rolled close to him in the night. His dog sprang up, too, instantly alert to his master's movements, and Galahad quickly hushed his excitement with a raised hand. He picked his way cautiously among the sleepers in the Great Hall, the dog following with surprising care for its size, until both reached the wooden doors that were pulled to, but not barred this past night, for no attacks were feared. Slowly, the boy pushed one door open and slipped through a gap just wide enough to admit his body sideways. The dog followed, forcing it a little wider.

Outside, it was not quite dawn, and the two figures were but barely discernible grey shapes moving swiftly across the environs of the stronghold. The dog trotted eagerly back and forth across the boy's path, sniffing the ground. Galahad lifted a hand to pat his massive head as he passed before him.

"Freedom today, Samson," he whispered.

He smiled a blind smile in the darkness. Today marked twelve years since his birth. Such remembrances were not usually distinguished in the course of life here, but today he was officially entering manhood, and he knew that recognition of this was planned by his family. This was why he had arisen so early - to escape his mother and grandfather for as long as he dared. At least, he thought, they had spared him lessons today. There would be no tutoring by his solemn teacher, Brother Conlaed, no being forced to learn to read (why he had to be literate when his grandfather was not, he did not see). Sometimes he felt that Brother Conlaed was trying to turn him into a monk himself, the way he interjected lessons on monastic discipline at every opportunity. Even though Galahad had never made an effort to learn Scriptures, his tutor repeated them at such length and frequency that he had unwillingly absorbed more verses than he could number. Still, he had to concede that Brother Conlaed was more rational and entertaining, when he chose to be, than most others of his grandfather's household.

He walked on, past the small buildings where his mother and grandfather had their private rooms. He was nominally supposed to sleep in his grandfather's quarters, but he preferred the Great Hall and the company of the regular men, and he had never been commanded to forsake this choice. He came towards the gate, and saw the figure of the night guard. It was Mark on watch tonight, he knew, so he had only to ask for secrecy, and he would wink him through. He came forward jauntily and was almost upon the man before he realized that Samson had stopped in his tracks. Galahad pulled himself up short, suddenly aware of a shadowed figure that stood in his path. The man put out a hand and laid it on his shoulder. Had it been pitch black, he could have told from the grip that it was his grandfather, and though even now he did not look at the hand that detained him, Galahad could sense the presence of the dark tattoos that traced a pattern across it and up the arm, signifying indescribable evils.

"You are out early on your special day, grandson."

King Pelles leaned forward, and his necklaces swung down into Galahad's face, leather and gold, hung with symbols of the gods that were supposed to be forgotten.

"You, too, my lord," replied the boy, attempting stoutness. Pelles laughed.

"I see you are becoming aware of your manhood. It is well. But what secret lure does the forest hold for you that you should shun your kin to seek it?"

"You knew." It was not a question, or even an expression of surprise. His grandfather had ways of fathoming the lives of all his subjects. Galahad glanced down at the bag of rune stones swinging from Pelles' belt. Pelles laughed again. The mixture of brown stumps and yellowing ivory that comprised his teeth, and which had terrified Galahad as a young boy, were thankfully but dim shadows above the lighter grey of the old man's beard.

"May I go?"

"I see no reason against it. You are leaving childhood behind, Galahad. You will face the adventures of a man's life soon, and you must learn to control life before it has you by the throat. Its claws are sharp - yours must be sharper." He drew his own long nails across the boy's neck by way of illustration. Galahad swallowed. His grandfather might have been called a madman for his attitude, were it not for his terrifying clarity.

King Pelles stepped aside from the gate. Galahad pushed on through without bestowing his intended pleasantry on Mark, Samson clinging closely at his heels. Even the wolfhound, who would have killed anyone who threatened his young master, was a cowed cur in the presence of Pelles. Galahad made his way down the gentle slope that elevated the stronghold above the surrounding countryside. His freedom had a bitter taste now that it was detected, but he shook himself free of his resentment, determined to make the most of it. At least he had not met his mother.

It was almost two miles to the edge of the forest, but he and Samson strode quickly to the young trees at its perimeter. Some were coppiced for the use of the people - they shot up groups of long, thin trunks, reminding him of his grandfather's fingers. Amongst them stood the ancient oaks, broader than the circled arms of two men together. Their glossy green leaves caught the rays of early sun which penetrated the canopy of the forest. Samson snuffled around, busy, but ready for the commands that would lead to an adventure. He stopped frequently to mark the trees.

As Galahad made his way deeper, he heard scuffles as small animals, mostly squirrels and mice it sounded, fled at his approach. It was the only power he possessed as of now. He moved on, touching the branches of small trees, pulling off a leaf here and there and tearing it up before casting the pieces before him and watching them tumble to the ground. It was a childish act, but a comforting one. Samson started sniffing and growling low in the undergrowth. Galahad turned aside to the spot to see what had disturbed him. He pushed the dog away with some effort, and peered down. Hidden amongst the bracken was a woven basket, a coney trap, and inside a coney cowered, petrified by the feel of Samson's hot breath.

"Leave, Samson," said Galahad sternly. The dog lay down reluctantly and put his head upon his paws with a great sigh. Galahad stood up, debating what to do. It was clearly not a trap set by one of his grandfather's men, and other folk had no hunting rights in this part of the forest. He should set the coney free and destroy the trap, or wait for the poacher and terrify him when he realized that the king's grandson had discovered him. Then he felt for the slim dagger in his belt; it was his only weapon, and perhaps not enough of a deterrent to a man desperate to escape mutilation or death. He dismissed that notion. And then, he might - yes, he would do just that. Turning from the basket, quivering from the shaking of the creature inside it, he motioned Samson to his side and strode on. It was a small victory over the adults who controlled his life.

He felt happy that he had been able to show some act of magnanimity and defiance, here where reality was hushed. The ever-growing wood, impervious to any demands save those of its own cyclic life, made time seem irrelevant. Here Galahad was not any one age; at times he felt was a little boy again, free to make believe he was an elven prince or a dragon slayer; at other times he was a man, and king, pondering soberly on the welfare of his subjects. It seemed to him that all the Galahads he had ever been or would become somehow existed in this wood, because no matter how often he came, no matter what had grown or died, it was in spirit the same place.

He jumped over a rivulet that emerged from the cover of some low bushes to cross his path, and journeyed on. Around him the mismatched chorus of birds grew as pigeons, blackbirds and songbirds both announced their presence to the new day and grumbled about Galahad's own arrival in their domain. Samson sent a flock of low-perching sparrows indignantly into the air as he bounded noisily under their tree. He swung back towards his master, his mouth stretched in a canine grin; his idea of adventure, at least, was being fulfilled. Galahad wandered on, lost in a blessed absence of thought, until his path eventually took an instinctively circular bent and he neared the edge of the forest, close where he had entered. He paused at the break in the trees, reluctant to set himself upon the path of return. Then he drew himself up. He was twelve; he could face his home. Putting a hand on Samson's solid back for reassurance, he set forth towards the stronghold.

When he climbed the slope to the keep, he was relieved to see that only a regular guard was in the vicinity of the gate. Exchanging a brief greeting, Galahad went on into the grounds. Now there was activity everywhere. Fires were being lit to roast meat outside; women were carrying food or slops destined for the men and beasts who sustained the life of the household; others, sleeves rolled up to reveal arms stained reddish-brown to the elbows, were staggering with armloads of dyed wool to the work shed where it would be woven into rough cloth to fit the household's other bodily needs.

He came to the stables where Drystan stood, talking amicably with Brother Conlaed. Drystan was Pelles' combined head horseman and master-at-arms, perhaps the most important man below the king himself. He was no longer young, but his dark, wiry frame had stood the onslaughts of time. He was a Pict, and a most dangerous one at that, for the natural wild viciousness that characterized his clansmen had been coupled with the precise ruthlessness imposed by a military education supplied by the old Romano-Briton units that had colonized the great northern wall. He had been astutely selected, like all of King Pelles' chief men.

Now, though, he was laughing with the monk over some matter. Both stopped as Galahad passed by. Drystan clapped him on the back and then tousled his hair. Galahad grinned -

he knew that Drystan was especially fond of him, despite the bruises he gave him at training.

"A man now, heh? So you'll be drinking the warrior's mead tonight, or catching the eye of a girl?" He nudged Brother Conlaed.

"I thought perhaps we might hold a service to remember your mortal body and immortal soul," the monk said, but the twinkle in his own eyes told the boy that he too was teasing. Galahad was grateful - he knew they were softening the ordeal of his formal family celebrations.

"Make me a monk tomorrow, Brother," he grinned. "Today I'll be a man."

The two men laughed as they watched him walk on, a little more jauntily.

"I remember the very day of his birth," said Drystan, shaking his head, "for he was not in this world but a moment when the king sent me to fetch you to watch over him. 'He must be from the Isle of the Scots,' he said to me, 'for only a monk bred there is able to talk with the angels and the fairy folk together.' And so he sent me, all the way West, across the Isle of the Scots itself to Aran, that barren rock where you lived." He paused in his tale to let Brother Conlaed begin to remember his own past life in his homeland.

"And I tell you," he continued, "I'll never go to sea again. Six days we were on that boat, three days going and then three returning, and I thought that by the time we reached land my guts would have been choked out of me into the sea!" He clutched his stomach and grimaced. Brother Conlaed chuckled sympathetically.

"I seem to recall not a few threats to cast me into the sea also," he smiled.

"Aye, well, I'm no saint, and that was a sea stirred by demons if I ever saw one. And I recall a monk that did not take too kindly to all those days on horseback to Pelles' land, and kept bemoaning his sore arse to his God!"

"The Lord has a way of creating equals," said Brother Conlaed.

"Well, you've been a good friend, even if you can't take to the battlefield beside me. But I'll never know what happened to the luck of the wee folk that you were supposed to bring to this house. I've never caught you talking with a single one," he sighed.

"It would take a brave fairy to face a Pict, now, would it not?"

The master-at-arms drew himself upright in agreement.

"And more than a Pict to face her without wanting to murder someone," he muttered to the monk darkly. Both men looked to where Galahad was approaching his mother's rooms.

Elayne was sitting on one of the benches outside her small home. She held a spindle in her hand, and was idly spinning out yarn. Beside her sat Morgain, her old nurse, watching her carefully and trying to engage her in trivial conversation. Two younger girls occupied the other bench, chattering easily as they wound yarn and teased wool. Morgain looked up and smiled as Galahad approached.

"Well, the young lord, at last! Greetings, honey child." The girls giggled, and Galahad grimaced. She had always called him that on account of his golden brown hair, and even though he was continually embarrassed to hear the endearment uttered in front of others, he never dared object - she had brought both him and his mother into the world, and exercised the authority that only a nurse can have. She had also been Pelles' concubine, and even the king treated her with respect.

Galahad took her proffered hand and leaned to kiss her. Then he turned to his mother, sitting quietly, staring forward at a scene she envisioned within her.

"Mother," he said, and kissed her cheek dutifully. Something inside her stirred and she comprehended him. Her eyes lit up. They were as beautiful as ever, he thought, a hazel green that shimmered to gold and jade in the sunlight. The rest of her face had been beautiful once, too. He remembered that, when he was young, he had thought she was a fairy woman, like the ones in the tales he heard in the Great Hall. She had nearly always been lucid then, as well, and she had made him the centre of her life. There was not a day he could recall of his early years when the figure of his mother had not been hovering about him, the fount and guardian of his happiness. He hardly knew when it had changed, but one day he realized that her beauty was worn thin: her exquisite skin was pale, no longer touched by swan's feathers, but with sickness, and her cheeks hollow. Her dancing eyes were finely lined, and her mind - he knew where it had gone, to a place beyond his memory.

"It is the day he turns twelve, a man," the nurse was prompting her. Elayne put a hand on his arm.

"So handsome, beyond all others," she murmured, "and soon you will be him." She placed her spindle down, and drew him to her suddenly, pulling his head down to her shoulder and stroking his hair. Galahad steeled himself; there was something in her embraces of late that made him uncomfortable. He did not wholly understand, but he knew that she did not always touch him as a mother touches a son. Morgain came to his rescue, gently removing Elayne's hands, so that he could straighten up. He ran a hand through his hair and stood awkwardly.

"How is my hair today, Morgain?" Elayne asked, putting her hand to her own tresses which hung loose down her back in the manner of maidens, though it was an almost equal blend of rich brown and grey.

"It is smooth as a rose petal, child," she responded gently.

"Do you need me today, mother?" asked Galahad. He wanted to help, but at the same time he had an irrepressible urge to escape.

"I do not know - wait, there is a feast tonight, for you, I think. Yes, for you." Sometimes, prompted by inexplicable trivia, she recovered herself for long periods of time. Let it be now, thought Galahad, let it be for good this time. It was his great unanswered prayer, the longing, as Conlaed would have said, that schooled him in faith. "But there was something else. I had it..."

"Here, child." Morgain reached beneath the bench and handed a sheathed dagger to Elayne. She in turn held it out to Galahad.

"This is for you, because it is yours, at least, it was his." She stumbled towards confusion once more. Galahad and Morgain held their breath. On the next bench, the two young girls carried on their conversation discretely, so used to these scenes that they did not even have to pretend nonchalance.

Elayne began again. "It was all he left behind, so it belongs to you, as his son. Take care of it - none can match its workmanship here."

Galahad drew the dagger from its plain sheath. Now it was his turn to be momentarily confused. The dagger gleamed in the rays of the climbing sun, dazzling him. He stared at it. The hilt was carved with a dragon on one side, and a cross on the other, which was inlaid with jet and amethyst. He turned it back. Blue glass glinted from the eye of the dragon, and its body writhed in gold down the handle.

"It is wondrous," he said at last. "I will keep it - for you," he added. He could not bring himself to pretend that he would keep it for his father. Elayne returned her melancholy smile.

"Then one day I will have my champion," she said. "But for now, you are a young man, and you do not want to spend your day in the women's quarters. Come to see me when you are readied for the feast. Let me arrange your clothes. Will you do that for me?"

"Yes," Galahad promised.

"You will remember that all day, will you not?" asked Morgain. It was her way of coaxing Elayne to hold herself in this world.

"Could a mother forget her son on the eve of his manhood? I will remember, if he will not forget his mother."

"Never," Galahad promised, though he was thankful the interview was over. He bent to kiss her briefly again. When he stood up, he noticed that the two girls on the other bench were eying him with great speculation, not to mention rather alarming smiles. He left hurriedly.

When he passed the Great Hall again, he heard the men talking animatedly, and smelled fresh bread and cheese. He had forgotten that he himself had not yet eaten that day. He stole a meal from a serving woman on her way inside, and ate hungrily as he strode on.

Drystan was leaning against the stable, eating his meal alone. He rarely associated with the general melee of Pelles' men; instead his woman usually brought him his portion to the stable. He was ruggedly set in his ways; he shunned most Britons, though he was held in great respect by them, and changed his women only as often as he changed the king's horse, though with much less emotion.

As Galahad began to pass on by, Drystan stopped him with a low call.

"How is my lady today?" he asked roughly.

"Well enough," replied Galahad. He had never quite understood why Drystan should show so much concern for his mother, and yet refuse to go near her. To cover his thoughts, he held out the sheathed dagger his mother had given him. Drystan drew it from its scabbard and whistled though his teeth as he held it at arm's length.

"It's a rare piece," he said. He examined the blade, spitting on a tarnished spot and rubbing it clean on his tunic. "Weightier than your old knife. It'll need a different technique, too."

"It will?" said Galahad, not too doubtfully, since he did not want to contradict. At Drystan's nod, he drew out his own knife and handed it to him. Drystan held each loosely in his hands, bouncing them up and down gently. Then he quickly tossed Galahad's old knife back to him; Galahad was used to this, and caught it swiftly by the hilt.

"Now, you see how much thicker this handle is, and how the blade is flatter and curves down from the centre line?" He ran a finger down the knife. "You'd naturally be tempted to arch down with it, to make use of the weight advantage, but then you'd leave yourself vulnerable for an upward thrust." He grew more animated, always pleased to demonstrate his expertise.

"But you have to learn to thrust straight with this knife. It'll not get stuck, because the blade isn't flat. Here, swap, and you try."

Galahad obeyed, though he was nervous. Drystan was never bested in practice, even by men half his age, and the more cocksure ones invariably ended up with salutary scars. He held the new blade for a minute, feeling its weight and gauging the force he needed. Then he held it back, and after a pause, leaped forward at Drystan, who jumped aside and knocked his arm up, throwing it further than Galahad had anticipated. He put Galahad's old blade up towards his ribs, but the boy parried, swinging the Pict's arm sideways. Drystan grinned.

"Good," he said. They exchanged a few more thrusts and parries, always with Drystan gaining the upper hand, before the older man stepped back and put his arm at his side.

"You did passing well," he said, "but you'd still be dead if it wasn't me you were fighting. Now, follow me." He began to guide Galahad through the use of his new dagger, making him perform the same moves again and again until his arm ached with tension and the hilt began to grow hot in his grasp. At last, he let him go.

"It's a noble blade," he said in dismissal, "even if its last owner was less than noble. Use it for something worthy." Galahad looked quizzically at him, but Drystan had already turned back to the stables and was shouting at a young serving boy.

Complete freedom, Galahad decided by the end of the day, was not as exciting as it sounded. There were currently no suitable companions of his age at the keep, and Samson was less than the ideal fishing companion, though he had been willing enough to join in a swim after drenching his master so much that he had given in to the inevitable consequence of angling with a large and exuberant wolfhound. Still, Galahad was not complaining, and he was whistling contentedly as he and Samson wandered back towards his grandfather's building, where his better - and dryer - clothes were stored. He knocked, and hesitated before entering. His grandfather was there, hunched over a small table, examining runestones. A small bottle stood at the edge of the table. Pelles glanced up.

"Are you preparing now, boy?" he asked.

Galahad explained that his mother had asked to assist him. He turned away and opened the small oak chest that contained his and his grandfather's clothes. He selected a cloak, a blue tunic and his other pair of leather leggings, which were newer than those he wore now. He pulled his rough tunic over his head.

"You must make allowances for her," Pelles was saying suddenly. "It is not a question of blame or fault. She consented to the will of our ancestors, in ignorance of the sacrifice necessary to fulfill it."

Galahad paused inside his shirt, unwilling to pull it off and look his grandfather in the face. The old man sighed, and he heard him walk away. Hastily, he switched tunics and leggings, and grabbed a cloak. On his way out, he glanced at the table. The vial was gone, but the runes were still there. He scanned them idly - he knew a little of their import, though they did not interest him. Brother Conlaed had instilled a scepticism of such things, though Galahad would not admit it to his grandfather. They seemed to bode ill, whatever Pelles' question had been.

Elayne was thankfully still lucid when he entered her room. She was sitting on her bed, with several brooches cast about her. She stretched out her hand to her son.

"Show me your cloak," she said. "I have to choose just the right brooch for it."

Galahad held out his dark blue, woollen cloak. Elayne studied it for a moment then turned back to the brooches.

"This one!" she said triumphantly, holding out a large, bronze disc, beaten with knotwork. She drew the cloak across

Galahad's shoulders, pulling the cord at each top edge to meet in the middle of his chest. Then she fastened them together with the brooch. She patted it, and made Galahad step back.

"You will look worthy tonight, son," she said. Galahad bowed his head in acknowledgment. "Will your mother do you justice herself?" she asked, almost coyly. Galahad looked at her.

"You appear very well tonight, mother," he said, truthfully, for Morgain had worked hard to restore as much of Elayne's beauty as was possible. Her hair was braided with golden threads, which hid the grey and drew attention away from the lines in her face. Amethysts about her ears and neck warmed her skin colour. A soft green tunic fell gently over her lighter underdress, caught in with a loose belt of bronze rings that subtly emphasized a figure, at least, unravaged by her life.

Elayne smiled at his answer.

"Then shall we go?" she said. She stood, and held her arm out to him. He took it awkwardly. She was the same height as he was, but it felt strange to behave as her social equal. He was wrong to be ashamed of her affliction, he thought suddenly. Now he was a man, he would resolve to honour her always.

The light outside was fading, and torches were being lit to show the path to the Great Hall. Dark shadows scurried about the courtyard, calling out orders and greetings. The night breeze brought the pleasingly greasy smell of the gargantuan hog which had been roasting outside for the entire day. Now, both doors of the hall had been thrown open, and as they approached, they could see the glow of the fire that burned in the centre. Pelles' men had filled the hall; some were milling around talking, others had found places at the benches to rest as they drank their ale. They turned in acknowledgment, bowing their heads as Elayne and Galahad made their way through to the table at the head of the hall, set upon a dais. Galahad escorted his mother to her seat and sat beside her. A serving girl slipped forward and filled their cups with wine, a drink too foreign still for most of the men, though the Romans had brought it up north generations ago.

A gradual hush rippled through the hall, signifying the approach of Pelles. As he entered, he halted on the threshold to mark his presence. Tonight, he had clothed himself as a king. His crimson tunic hung to the ground, and animals danced at the hems in red and gold thread. A broad gold circlet bound his hair to his temples, and thin braids hung down among his hair and beard. He was flanked by his personal guards, large and vicious men who intimidated everyone in the keep save Drystan and Conlaed. They carried their swords upright before them. As the king proceeded into the hall, all rose in honour. He did not take any palpable notice of the obeisances offered, but walked forward, his eyes fixed upon his family who also stood for him. He took his place and looked over the group.

"Tonight we make a feast intended to mark our grandson's transition to manhood. The honour of the evening is first to him. Yet we have other business also. Morvidus has sent his kinsman to treat with us concerning his homage. They are arriving as we speak."

Galahad looked up, as surprised as some of the other men. Morvidus was an under-lord to Pelles, who claimed the title of king for his own demesne, and had been refusing his homage offerings, asserting his land to be sovereign. Any delegation from him would be unlikely to be cordial.

"But first," continued Pelles, "let us drink to the health of Galahad. May he witness and learn great deeds from those assembled in this hall!"

The men cheered and lifted their cups. Galahad grinned, unable to restrain himself to a more sober acknowledgment. Elayne looked across at her son and, catching his smile, raised her goblet, too. His grandfather made no further gestures.

They had barely begun their meat when a commotion was heard coming from the direction of the gatehouse. It grew louder, moving towards the hall, and many men checked the position of their daggers without pausing in their meal, while serving men began to take down the weapons hung around on the walls, and lay them in readiness against the sides of the hall. Pelles took no notice, and called for more wine.

All at once, the doors opened, and two guardsmen announced the arrival of the expected deputation. Without waiting for a formal invitation, a man stepped forward between the guards and halted for a moment, as Pelles had done, before striding towards the dais. Galahad could see why he had been sent; he was a span above the head and shoulders of most men there, and broad as a coracle. Behind him, some of his men stood glancing defensively around the room. He advanced purposefully through the hall, until Galahad could see his face illuminated clearly by the great fire. He waited for Pelles to speak first. The king sat for a few moments, looking closely at him. The man did not falter in returning the gaze, though his fingers twitched almost imperceptibly at his side.

"Does Morvidus think it not fit to come himself to treat with his overlord?" asked Pelles pleasantly.

"King Morvidus," the man replied with emphasis, "needs must guard his land and rule his people, but he has sent me, Kathel, his cousin, to give you word that he is willing to parley for a revised tribute in return for acknowledging him as sole ruler of his lands."

"Indeed? Well, he makes his request at a time when we are disposed to be merciful, this being a celebration for our own family. Lady Elayne, bring forth the cup of honour for our guest; let him sit here, beside us." Pelles stared hard at Elayne, who rose gracefully. She went to a small serving table where a glass chalice stood upon a cloth of embroidered linen. Elayne gently wrapped the napkin up around the delicate stem as she carefully picked it up. It was one of the most precious objects Pelles owned, older than the king himself, cast and etched with a craftsmanship that was lost to this generation. Galahad looked in his wonted admiration at the vines that wove their tendrils about the cup; catching the firelight, they glowed strangely blue tonight. The light refracted dimly onto his mother's face, dancing around a visage which was pale and impassive. Kathel came forward to take his place; Galahad suddenly felt small and boyish again in comparison to this bear-like warrior. Elayne handed forward the cup, and he grasped it by the bowl with both hands, obscuring the goblet as he lifted it to his lips. Galahad, beside him, saw that as he placed it down, his lips were unmoistened; he knew what he feared - poison from the hand of a man rumoured to be a necromancer.

Kathel sat down, and turned to Pelles.

"Did we drink to a treaty, then, King?" he asked almost jovially, relieved that his message had been so calmly received.

"A feast is not the time for politics," replied Pelles. "Come, eat first. But I think you will soon have little to complain of." He leaned forward and took some pork from his own trencher, passing it to Kathel's. "That you may see I do not intend to poison your food," he smiled. The man was hungry; he pitched in, and his own men relaxed as they saw him, and turned to the benches themselves, where Pelles' men were grudgingly offering food as the servants hurried to bring them more dishes and to carry their swords away.

Galahad watched the man eat. He was attacking his meal with some gusto; it was rare to eat any better than at Pelles' court in this remote, northern country. Yet he was not absorbed in it; he was watching the behaviour of his men, and throwing the odd word in reply to Pelles' pleasantries. Then, suddenly, he stopped still. His eyes grew wide, and he made a small, strangled sound as he fell forward into his meat. Galahad recoiled, and Kathel's men jumped to their feet, but Pelles' retainers were quicker, and surrounded them, hands to their daggers. The women present fled to a corner of the hall. Pelles began to call for a healer, quite calmly, as a heated discussion erupted between the two sides.

But Galahad barely comprehended what they were saying. He was staring at the giant felled beside him. His face was slack, his mouth grotesquely pushed to one side across his meal, which began to spill and trickle down to the floor, joining a small pool of urine which had escaped from the dead man's bladder. His hands were swollen and a mottled blue-white in colour. Then Galahad looked across at his mother. She was sitting quite still, staring serenely ahead, as if she were oblivious to events around her. Her hands were folded neatly in her lap, smooth and white. He focussed hard on them for a few moments, then glanced back at the fingers of Kathel. Then he knew.

As the diplomatic quarrel grew, no one noticed Galahad rising and starting for the door, cautiously at first, but breaking into a run as he made his way down the hall. He pushed the door open, and found Samson at his side as he bounded out. He ran across the courtyard until his stomach retched so much that he had to stop and vomit by the corner of a hut. Samson sniffed the vomit curiously, but then followed Galahad, who had set off again. He reached the main gate, and with barely a nod at the sentry, stepped outside. He ran out to the east edge of the hill that jutted out from the corner of the keep, reigning over the shadows below. He stopped and stood there breathing heavily, trying desperately not to let fall the tears that hovered in his eyes, because he was a man.

He clenched his fists at his side, and felt his new dagger. The sensation stung his hand.

"I will leave," he hissed at the darkness. "I will leave, and I will be avenged. I hate you, I hate you that you made me, and left me here." He shuddered as he tried not to think of his father and Elayne, doing - what the beasts of the field did - to create him.

"I am a man, and I will be avenged," he said loudly, to the wind. Then he sat down on the grass, buried his face in Samson's soft fur, and cried.

Chapter One

Guenevere gazed round at the men seated before her, posed stiffly in their best clothes. They had left their lands to play the reluctant part of courtier, as was customary at the dawn of the new year. Arthur was proud of his great alliance with the lords of Britannia; he saw this confederacy as an army of God, but there was hardly a man among them, as she reckoned it, that was not a murderer, an adulterer or a rapist. They saw their power, for the most part, as a sign of their divine right to trifle with the lives of men, not a great commission to rule as saints. However, she let none of her thoughts show upon her face as she sat serenely playing her own part, the exquisite consort of Britannia's chief ruler, Arthur, the Regissimus, highest of kings. She turned her attention back to her husband, who was announcing the business of the court. He was beginning to show his age, she thought. He still had the body of an active warrior, and no stoop detracted from his imposing height, but he had a grizzled look about him. The grey in his hair and beard were about to overtake the chestnut brown, and his flesh was beginning to look weary of the bones it covered. He could appear younger, if he willed himself to present the image of an eternal king. He had never learned to wholly conceal his true self. Even now there was a faintly discernible, unseemly edge to the eagerness with which he reiterated the goals he set forth with the coming of each new year.

"...and we know that, as soldiers of Christ, we shall pray continually to be met with such enterprises as shall honor both him and our kingdom. Some are new to our fellowship - they are right welcome - and some have labored in it for many years, but we are brothers in God's service."

Guenevere had always thought that he should invoke the Deity a little less often in his speeches - it was so awkwardly incongruous in addressing these warrior-lords. However, it was not her duty to give advice, and so she sat, year after year, wincing inwardly at his excessive expressions of piety.

"As is our custom," he was continuing, "we turn to our advisor, Merlin, for his sagacity in guiding us towards our destinies."

Arthur sat and nodded to Merlin to arise. He was an old man, and his heavily creased face was beginning to sag, yet his authority had not fallen with it, and the entire court straightened themselves, in hope or dread of hearing a proclamation that might help their star to rise, or send them on a quest that would leave their lands vulnerable and their lives in jeopardy. Merlin smoothed his beard, which hung, braided, down the front of his long, purple tunic, matching the thicker grey plait which fell down his back. His pause discomforted those anxious to hear him, as he had intended. Without moving his head, he looked around, noting those who had something to fear.

"To those that have the wisdom," he said, "there are many ways in which man's destiny can be traced, be it in the heavens appointed by God, or the more humble signs he places upon the earth."

He held up his hand and cast a handful of runes upon the table. Forgetting themselves, several men leaned forward, craning to get a glimpse of the stones, but Merlin swiftly swept his hand across their prophecy, snatching them up and out of sight once more. Assured of his impact, he continued.

"As I searched for the answers that would guide this fellowship of rulers for the coming year, my questions were continually brushed aside. All individual endeavors, my divinations tell me, are to be regarded as nothing, for we have reached a defining moment, perhaps the apex of this brotherhood, that will see a great quest for those among us who will be judged worthy."

Arthur became visibly excited; many of the courtiers looked relieved, having no hopes or worries of being selected for special honors.

"The stars are moving in the heavens, as of old, to portend a message. There is one who is to come into the midst of this fellowship and change its face forever." There were faint sounds of stirring outside the hall. Merlin strode past the men to stand by the central fire. He raised his outstretched hands, and, of a sudden, the fire hissed and glowed blue. Several servants waiting around the edge of the hall clutched amulets and pressed themselves against the wall. Into the blue light stepped a young man.

"I am Galahad, kinsman of King Pelles of the north," he said. "I am come to join the fellowship of King Arthur's men."

Many of the warriors forgot their roles altogether, and the hall erupted in a babel of questions, challenges and appeals to the king who had himself arisen and was staring intently at the young stranger. Only four people remained calm: Galahad himself, who stood boldly staring back at the company; Merlin and Guenevere who kept their places and looked on impassively; and an older lord who drummed his fingers lightly upon the table as he considered the newcomer. At last he arose, and with a commanding gesture, silenced those around him.

"Kinsman of King Pelles," he said formally, "you come from a worthy line indeed, and yet you are young to claim such a place among us. Feats of arms and leadership are what join us here. What have you to lay before our king?"

The question gave Arthur a chance to resume his royal stance. He seated himself and, clutching the arms of his chair, leaned slightly in the direction of the young man.

"We welcome you in the name of King Pelles, who, as Lord Launcelot says, is a good ally of ours. To what degree are you his kinsman?"

"Not of the first degree of closeness," replied Galahad, "but close to the female line." His voice was low and soft, yet determined, as if he had been trained of habit to be self-controlled.

Arthur looked at the young man. He was a little above middling height, lean and muscular. His hair, a honeyed brown, fell to his shoulders where it lay neatly trimmed. Although he was speaking as a man, he still exuded youthfulness, and there was little evidence of facial hair. He was attired for traveling, with good leather leggings and a thick woollen cloak, but his clothes were evidently of good quality, if serviceable. He wore several rich rings upon his fingers, gleaming with newly cast gold and polished glass. Galahad withstood the scrutiny, his face composed into an attitude of deference, though his eyes held a hint of disdain.

"All of suitable degree are welcome to venture in our alliance, but, as Launcelot has said, each has to demonstrate that such a place has been earned. Have you fought in the northern wars between King Pelles and Morvidus? Or have you tried yourself in Armorica?"

"I have taken my part in the affairs of King Pelles," said Galahad dismissively, "but I come to claim a place through proving myself in a quest undertaken in your name."

"Galahad, kinsman of Pelles," interrupted Merlin, with an emphasis on the word 'kinsman', "you see that there is but one place unclaimed at this table. It is a seat for those who would do great deeds. Do you mean to try it this day?"

Another warrior rose to his feet, slightly ponderous, yet with a presence that warned against thinking him past being dangerous.

"My king, you cannot let him sit blindly in that place of death! Merlin knows, perhaps better than most, what fate has befallen those who have attempted it!"

"Lord Bors is correct," said Arthur. "This seat is reserved by divine appointment for an unsullied warrior of Christ who is to grace our fellowship. It was conceived in a vision by our Lord Merlin. Those who have tried themselves in it have died that very same night - seasoned warriors, eager sons of kings, and even a monk. All were mysteriously and miraculously struck down before they might sit there a second day."

"He who takes that seat," interjected Merlin, "must be a man whose life is set on one sole purpose, one who is sure of his destiny." He looked coolly at Galahad. "Are you a man of single mind, are your thoughts of pure and sacred intent?"

Galahad returned Merlin's gaze. He considered the old man carefully. At last, he turned and made his way around the table. He drew the seat out and sat himself down in it, laying his hands upon the table.

"I will try my destiny," he said, simply. Those on either side drew their chairs away from him.

"Merlin," said Arthur, "is your vision related to these happenings? What insight can you give us?"

Merlin strode before the throne and bowed.

"My king - and my lords," he said. "I would ask your leave to tell you a tale of divine and mystical import, from the days when the King of Kings himself walked upon this earth."

"Tell, counsellor," replied Arthur. "We have need of understanding."

Merlin walked around the table and towards the fire, his features softening into a more relaxed attitude as he took the role of bard. He warmed his hands before the dancing flames, once more returned to their familiar orange hues, before turning to face his audience.

"The story begins in the holy town of Jerusalem, in the last days that our Lord was to live among us as a mortal. He had come to Jerusalem, his own city, to celebrate the Passover. He sent his most trusted disciples, Saint Peter and Saint John, to prepare a room in which they might feast together. As these men readied the room, not knowing that this would be the final night their Lord was to spend among them, the door opened, and the blessed Virgin stepped in. Though it was nigh thirty winters since she had borne and suckled the Christ child, she still wore the bloom of youth. Her hair, the hues of darkened amber, fell to her knees; her skin was white as alabaster, save for the blush of her cheeks, as soft and ruddy as the first roses of summer. Her eyes were as blue as glass, and shone with the holy light within her.

"The disciples bowed low as she approached, but, in her virgin modesty, she bid them quickly arise and to do her no homage. She proffered them a parcel, wrapped in silk.

"'Take this for the Passover. It has come from the courts of King David, to whom my son is heir.'

"She laid the gift upon the table and left. The disciples reverently unwound the silk, and a cup rolled gently into their hands. Saint Peter held it aloft, and both stared in wonder, for it was a vessel the like of which they had never before seen. The base and stem were of pure silver, and were cast in the likeness of a tree whose roots spread across the base, while a gnarled trunk rose up the stem. The bare branches spread out and upwards to encase a cup of crystal finely etched with the symbols of an ancient language, and so bright they could scarcely look upon it for more than a few moments. It is said by some that the tree was a likeness of that very one which was hewn down to make our Lord's cross, which had stood since the time of King David awaiting its doleful fate.

"This cup it was that our Lord used that last supper, which touched the lips of our blessed Saviour and all of his holy disciples, save Judas, who was sent from the room beforehand lest he profane the sacred vessel.

"Great was the lamentation among the disciples when our Lord was taken to be crucified, and who could tell or show the grief of his maiden mother who had lived to feel both the agonies of his birth and of his death? Yet she remained the handmaid of the Father. As she lay in prayer and weeping upon her pallet, the Angel Gabriel returned to her.

"'Holy Mother, whose praise shall be to everlasting with that of your son! Take heed of my words, for this is the last task that the Lord Almighty shall require of you in his service. You are to take the cup of David, the Holy Grail, and give it into the keeping of the man who shall tend the body of your son. Arise, as your son is to arise in his resurrected glory!'

"In meekness and wonder, Mary arose. As she did so, her maid came to her chamber, to give her tidings that a worthy Jew, Joseph of Arimathea, had taken claim of the Christ's body. Following her vision, she carried her precious gift to his home and placed it into his hands.

"For two and thirty years after our Lord's Passion, Joseph kept the Grail faithfully, never suffering another human hand to touch it; it is said that were the unworthy to come even within sight of it, they were struck down mortally.

"In this time, Joseph was constrained to leave Jerusalem to join in war against the unbelievers. He was given a vision in which it was revealed to him that he should never again return to the land of his fathers. Heavy of heart, he resolved to keep the Grail safe. One night, in the quiet hours, he stole from his home and journeyed to a hermit's dwelling, where other men never visited, and left the Grail in the keeping of this holy man.

"Great were the adventures that Joseph and his men met with as they journeyed across land and sea, battling in the name of God, and many were the heathens they brought to belief by the sword and the Word. And, at the last, when Joseph was hoary with age and in the final years of his strength, and his band had dwindled to but a few, they came to our lands.

"As he lay dying, Joseph rehearsed the story of the Grail to a scribe, a holy young monk, and bid him let it only be known to the wise ones of the kingdom. The whereabouts of the Grail has been hidden ever since, the knowledge belonging only to those whom God wills, who are themselves instructed to keep it a secret until they encounter the one who is worthy to recover it. Some, it is said, have been waiting for many hundreds of years, kept alive by a miracle until the days of the Grail have come. It is also said that the descendants of Joseph of Arimathea walk yet in this land, the offspring of his son who journeyed with him, and a beautiful Briton princess who became his bride.

"It is four hundred and fifty years since Joseph came to this realm; the time, some say, that the purpose of the Grail is to be fulfilled. Are we, perhaps, in the company of those who will fulfill it?"

Merlin finished, his arms held open in question and anticipation. The warriors sat, still spellbound by his recitation. Guenevere, too, sat still, a polite smile barely raising the corners of her mouth. Yet inwardly, she was thinking rapidly. What could his purpose be? Merlin held to Arthur's Christianity even less than the men from the remote parts of his kingdom. His skills and power derived from the old ways. He would not care to further it except for pragmatism. Whom did he want out of the way?

Around her, as the other men recovered, they began to turn to Arthur, waiting for a lead in their reaction. His fingers were white from gripping his chair, yet his countenance showed a restrained joy. He surveyed the company.

"It is, as you know, a day for which I have long hoped; a day in which we shall see the fulfillment of a great quest in the name of the Lord. It remains now to choose whom we shall find worthy to undertake the task of finding the Grail. Even I am willing to put my kingdom and duties to one side in the holy task before us."

"My king," said Guenevere, interrupting smoothly, "we know that none are as suited as you to go forth in the name of God, but surely you have already been appointed to serve here, to keep this realm safe from the unbaptized barbarians, and to guide the Grail questors - whoever they may be - from your throne."

"My lady speaks true," said Launcelot. "None could hold this kingdom together in your absence."

Arthur bowed his head.

"I acknowledge your advice," he said. "Yet it grieves me that I cannot actively pursue the Grail. Who, then, Merlin, shall go?"

Merlin looked across at Galahad. The young man rose.

"My kinsman, King Pelles, has always maintained that he is of the stock of Joseph of Arimathea. I claim my place by blood and honour, to prove myself worthy of a place at this table."

"Let us first see if he still breathes on the morrow before we give credence to such claims!" said Lord Bors, eyeing the newcomer with suspicion.

"Launcelot," said Arthur, "you are my warrior of greatest prowess; you must lead the search."

"Lord Launcelot's is a name I have seen clearly in my divinings," said Merlin. "Indeed, he should go."

Launcelot did not reply.

"I claim a place," spoke another quickly, a younger man, distinguished by his softly curling golden hair, and the large cross that hung around his neck.

"I think that perhaps Lord Perceval lacks the experience needed for such a perilous journey," said Merlin.

"We bow to your wisdom," said Arthur, "but surely, there is none among us as pious as this man? We say he shall go."

Perceval bowed slightly, and allowed a small smile to escape his lips as he glanced briefly at Merlin. He then turned his head towards Launcelot, who nodded, his face stern but accepting.

"What say you, Lord Perceval?" asked Arthur.

"I work to the glory of my heavenly and earthly lords," he replied shortly.

Silence fell upon the company; no one dared draw breath without fear of drawing attention to himself. The king looked to Merlin once more, but his advisor shook his head.

"Fellow kings, lords, warriors," said Arthur, rising from his seat, "we have spent this night uncovering the greatest quest of this fellowship. Now, it is time to retire and meet tomorrow, to finish the business of this realm before we depart, each to his lands and the destiny of the new year. I bid a good night to all."

He held his hand out, and Guenevere stood gracefully, placing her own upon it. They stepped down from the dais and walked around the table. Guenevere had always wondered why her father had kept it; she had been even more mystified that Arthur had insisted that it be part of her dowry. Equality in Christian fellowship was supposed to be symbolized by this unwieldy round table; no one, she supposed, held that dream except her husband.

As Arthur and Guenevere left the hall, flanked by half a dozen servants, the remaining men turned to scrutinize the young stranger in the chair. He leaned back, stretching out his legs, and returned the stares defiantly.

Chapter Two

As a courtesy to a new guest, and a kinsman of King Pelles, Galahad was invited to refresh himself before retiring in the quarters reserved for distinguished travellers to the court at Cataviae. A young woman led the way across the courtyard to a small, timber building, constructed in the square style of the old Roman way. As Galahad left the hall, a large dog roused itself and snuffled eagerly at his hand. Galahad scratched its head. The girl looked down inquiringly; she had not far to gaze, for she was small, and the dog almost the size of a pony.

"This is Samson," said Galahad by way of explanation. He offered no more, and she did not press.

Galahad studied her from the back as they walked through the environs of the keep. She was indeed petite, but not squat as so many short women he knew, who made up for their height with their girth. Her hair was the Collor of jet, and hung, loosely tied, almost to her knees. The hands that held her skirts delicately above the earthen courtyard were white, and her fingers long, elongated by the nails that extended far beyond them. She must be the daughter of a chieftain, serving as a courtier, he thought, for she displayed no physical appearance of lowly stock. He followed her obediently into the quarters, where a wooden tub was being filled with steaming kettles of water by a male servant.

The room was well lit with candles, and Galahad now examined the girl's face as she turned to him. She was aware of his scrutiny, and held his gaze for a few moments longer, as if challenging him to find fault. There were none that he could see. Her face was unblemished, as white as her hands. Her eyes were green and almond-shaped, framed by dark lashes. Her lips were reddened slightly, he thought, calling attention to a mouth that was just wide enough to be striking, yet not enough to be ugly. He realized that he had said nothing since they left the hall.

"What is your name?" he asked lamely.

"Nivene," she answered. Her voice was sweet and low. He could not think of anything more to say. She smiled at his awkwardness and turned to the tub.

"You are acquainted with this type of bathing?" she asked.

In truth, Galahad's only baths had been in the river, or under buckets of cold water that the young men threw at each other in Pelles' courtyard. But he was not perturbed, for Conlaed had warned him of the likelihood of such occurrences.

"We are not ignorant of old Roman ways in our northern lands," he said, as loftily as he could manage. He was not sure that she believed him, but she turned and picked up some linens.

"These are to dry yourself with," she said.

"Of course," he replied.

She same close, and looked up into his face.

"Let me assist you," she said smoothly, and she put her hands to his neck, to unfasten the clip that held his cloak. She laid it over a stool, then turned back to him and slipped her hands under his tunic, pushing it up his body. He was suddenly embarrassed, although it was common even at Pelles' court for the women to aid the men. He knew that most young men would relish being undressed by a beautiful girl, that she might even expect him to make advances, but her presence only discomforted him. He was glad that she could not see him blush as she pulled the tunic over his head. She stood back and regarded him for a few moments, her eyes travelling slowly down his torso.

"Do not worry, I will leave you to strip yourself. May I bring you anything? Clean clothing?"

"These will do well enough to sleep in," said Galahad offhandedly.

Nivene bowed her head, and, pulling her skirts around her, left the small chamber. Outside, he heard Samson shuffle to his feet, and Nivene's voice, low yet sharp, as she said something to him. When he was sure that she had gone, Galahad opened the door to let the hound inside. He rubbed him roughly along the length of his back.

"Guard the door for me, Samson," he said. The dog settled down once more, at the threshold. Now Galahad felt safe enough to divest himself of his leggings and climb into the small tub. He had to bend his knees to fit in, but he had to admit that the scalding water felt good to his aching muscles after several days spent on the back of a horse.

Galahad was almost drifting into a doze when he was disturbed by a movement from Samson. The dog's ears lifted as he heard footsteps, and his limbs stiffened in anticipation. Galahad motioned him to stay quiet, and he hunched down. A knock sounded.

"Sir, I have come to help you to bed." It was a man's voice, the rough accents of a servant. Galahad relaxed slightly. He called out for him to enter. The man did so, eyeing Samson rather nervously.

"That's a rare size of dog you have there," he said.

"Yes," replied Galahad. He was always proud of the reaction Samson provoked in people. "He is a faithful hound, too, and obedient."

"Did you bring a tent? Many of the lords are encamping on the plains outside the keep - it's more comfortable at these big gatherings." Galahad shook his head.

"Then I'm to say that you can sleep at the head of the hall. There's pallets for the lords."

Any space on the floor in a sheltered room would have been welcome to Galahad after his rough journey; a pallet sounded like luxury. He rose up from the tub, feeling the cold air hit his steaming skin. The servant helped him to dry and dress again. Then Galahad followed him back across the courtyard towards the hall.

"Is the woman who aided me - Nivene - is she the daughter or wife of one of the lords gathered here?" he asked guardedly. The servant cautiously surveyed the courtyard.

"She is with Merlin," he said quietly and quickly, and hurried on.

Once at the hall, Galahad picked his way across the sleeping men. He was well-practised at this, and disturbed few. In the far regions of the building, where the men of higher rank lay, he espied a pallet that did not have a dark hump upon to signify a sleeping body. He negotiated a path towards it and lay down quietly, pulling his cloak about him. Although his eyes were closed, he could hear men stirring, raising themselves to look at him, perhaps wondering if he would be living in the morning. He smiled in the darkness. He liked his chances now, he thought.

There were not many men still lying abed when Galahad awoke the next day. The caution of the night before had given way to exhaustion, and he had slept heavily. He cursed inwardly at his lack of alertness, but still, he was a little relieved to see that he had made it safely through the night, despite his bravado. He sat up, running his fingers through his thick hair by way of a preliminary neatening. As his vision sharpened, he saw a boy hovering nearby. The lad approached hesitantly when he saw Galahad sit up.

"Lord Galahad? My Lord Perceval sent me to attend you."

Galahad looked across at the boy, remembering the events of the night before. The youth stood, not quite patiently, awaiting an answer. He had a visage which indicated that he, too, was not tied to Arthur's land and keep, but a nobleman's son in service. There seemed to be an elaborate hierarchy at the court, Galahad thought. It would take some time to understand who was who, and who might be trusted the least. The boy, though, he decided, did not look well-trained in subterfuge, so he tried a direct assault.

"Where are the Lords Perceval and Launcelot?" he asked.

"They are meeting together, in Lord Launcelot's quarters, out on the plain," said the boy.

"Well, boy, you may help me get ready, and then you can show me the way. What is your name?" he added, softening a little.

"Oswald, my lord."

"Then come here, Oswald, and carry my saddlebag for me."

Once outside, Galahad dipped his face into a barrel of rainwater and shook his head back. Samson wandered over from his leisurely examination of the courtyard, and bent his own head to take a drink. By the smell of his breath, he had been charming or intimidating the cooks into handing over scraps, as he usually did back home.

"There's a comb in there somewhere," Galahad said to Oswald, indicating the bag. The boy rummaged in it, and produced a small bone comb. Galahad ran it through his hair, and then rubbed his hand along his chin. No need to shave. He needed a clean tunic, though, for, even in the fresh, cold air which was blowing in the new year, he could detect the odours of a week of adventure. He pulled it over his head, undoing the good work of the combing, and handed it to the boy.

"Take this to whomever washes the visitor's clothes."

He shook his other tunic out of his bag: a sturdy, but well-made travelling piece, embroidered at the neck and cuffs by his mother. Appropriate for facing Lord Launcelot, he thought. This sudden thought jolted him back into the resolve that had held him in the hall the night before. He tugged it on determinedly and threw his cloak around it. Then he took the bag from Oswald and slung it over his own shoulder.

"Come, then," he said abruptly, making off for the plain in long strides. Samson trotted effortlessly beside him, but Oswald had to speed his steps. They left the main gate, walking along the wide rampart that ran beneath the wooden watch tower, and stood at the top of the hill, looking down onto the vast encampment that represented the great yearly meeting of the warriors of Arthur's realm. Galahad had passed through it in the dark the night before, and had not been able to appreciate the enormity of the gathering. A town of canvas met his eyes, perhaps as crowded as Eboracum, the stronghold of the North, which he had visited once with Conlaed. There were small, serviceable tents for servants and slaves, long shelters that stabled precious horses, and many fine tents, coloured and hung with pennants, that signified the dwellings of under-kings and other men of rank. Here and there, smoke rose from a small fire, showing grey against the thin, white fog that hung among the canvases. Galahad turned back to Oswald, who had caught up with him and stood, panting, the tunic still clutched to his chest.

"Show me the way, then."

Oswald started off down the slope, glad to be able to set the pace. As they came into the environs of the camp, several guards stiffened, looking intently at Galahad and cautiously at Samson, but they let him pass upon seeing Oswald. Perceval's servant was clearly known, then, thought Galahad. They wound their way through several smaller tents until they were suddenly facing a large one, whose canvas was overlaid with cloths of deep blue and green. A pennant flew from the top, depicting a golden dragon with outstretched claws. Galahad steeled himself.

"Let me announce you, sir," said Oswald hastily, fearing a breach of his duty, but Galahad walked past the boy and pushed open the canvas flaps to enter the tent.

Inside, the tent was sparse, resembling that of a general on campaign, but its few furnishings were sumptuous. A pallet lay in one corner, spread with a thick, fine wolf fur. Beside it stood a small, carved chest, upon which balanced a painted pitcher and a set of wooden, etched goblets. At the foot of the bed was a stand, with a tall sword resting in place. Its leather scabbard was studded with glass beads, and the hilt that showed at the top was worked with fine glass in the shape of a dragon's head. Its blue eyes winked at Galahad. He instinctively put his hand to his side and rested it upon his own dagger, concealed beneath his cloak.

The two men sat on cushioned stools at a large table, strewn with a few maps. To an uninitiated onlooker, it would appear that they were engaged in casual conversation: Launcelot sat with his leg sprawled over the arm of the stool, leaning upon the table as he idly worked patterns upon it with his finger; Perceval was inclining forward, a goblet in one hand and a game piece in the other, which he was engaged in placing upon a board as he talked. Even in the shade of the tent, Galahad could see the men much more clearly than the night before. Perceval's true age was difficult to judge; he was obviously not a youth, but his blond curls lent him a look of a younger man. This morning, they were tied back with a leather lace, and Galahad could see his face. He had a high forehead and prominent cheekbones, and his chin was square and cleft slightly. It was a striking, handsome combination of features, but it clashed disconcertingly with the marks of piety he carried: a plain, dark tunic and a large, silver cross of knotwork which hung on jet beads. His hands also were bare save for a single gold ring that he wore upon the little finger of his left hand.

Launcelot was definitely past the days of his youth, but he was far from unhandsome. His hair was thick, a golden brown intermingled with grey, which was beginning to have the upper hand. He wore a moustache that hung down past his lips; it was neatly trimmed, unlike that of most of the men with whom Galahad was used to living. As he talked, his eyes creased deeply, but his skin did not have the slackness of old age. His frame bespoke muscles hardened by years of warfare, and, unlike Perceval, he indicated his position with a handful of rings and torques, glinting gold, red and blue in the light of a small charcoal burner that was near the table, giving some heat on the chilly morning.

The men exchanged a look as Galahad stood in the doorway, but they continued with their conversation. He took a stool that was in the corner at the tent's entrance and carried it with one hand to the table. He set it down firmly and sat at the end, between both men.

"My lords," he said, keeping his voice steady, "I see that you are already making preparations for our quest."

Perceval was the first to reply. He looked pleasantly at Galahad.

"Did my young ward, Oswald, attend you as I requested? I saw no evidence of your own manservant, so I thought it right to extend the courtesy of my personal retinue."

"Yes - I thank you. My own servant travelled as far as Camulodunum, but I sent him back to King Pelles with news of my safe arrival. I knew I would have no need of him on my journey."

"Indeed?" It was Launcelot's turn to reply. His voice was deep, and slightly amused. "You seem to have great confidence in your mission. Perhaps it is justified, seeing that you have survived your first night here. As you asked, we are indeed discussing the possible courses of action for the king's quest. There are many routes through the old Western Empire, but not necessarily many allies upon the way. It is a long road."

"There are secrets in Rome," said Galahad. "About the Grail. The knowledge passed there, but not to those in power." The two men raised their eyebrows.

"My kinsman, King Pelles, holds descent from Joseph of Arimathea. He has the holy stories committed to his memory. He says that a written record is concealed there." He did not particularly believe his grandfather's ramblings, but the information gave him confidence.

"We would rest at Rome come what may," said Launcelot. "We might indeed pursue this idea, if we judge this boy's words to be true." Galahad smarted. He could feel the heat rising in his face, and hoped that the dimness of the tent would conceal it.

"Well, he has not died, which suggests some favour with the Lord, or others less holy," said Perceval. "Do you worship the true God, young man?" he added, looking him straight in the eye. His own were a cold blue; they made Galahad uncomfortable.

"I have ever been brought up in Christian worship. We are not all stuck to the old gods in our northern kingdoms," he said, a little more defensively than he had intended. Perceval smiled suddenly, and turned back to Launcelot.

"So, there is the question of the route from Gaul to Rome. How stands the sway of Clovis in the mountain regions? I think we might travel as a small band through Gaul on Arthur's reputation, but it would be wiser to enlist a troupe of men familiar with the Empire."

"Should we need such aid?" asked Galahad. Launcelot turned his head sharply.

"You may have travelled though Britannia on the name of your devil-spawn kinsman, but you'll find that Pelles' title has no protection for you in foreign lands. This is not some ceremonious rite of passage, boy; it is a dangerous task for seasoned soldiers."

Galahad was enraged. He gripped the edge of the table, his fingers turning white. Yet he dare not speak unless he were sure of his words. Perceval pushed another disc across the gameboard and looked up.

"If you have been chosen by fate and the king, we shall help mold you to this venture. Do you hunt the stag?"

Surprised by the turn of the question, Galahad was truthful.

"Occasionally. There is more call to keep the wolves from our keep of a winter."

"There is to be a hunt this morning; the younger of our fellowship are permitted the foremost places to prove themselves. Perhaps you should join them."

"Perceval, you are right," said Launcelot, his calm regained. "And forgive me - I promised to help Bors ready his son for the chase. I desire that my nephew should distinguish himself. Please, stay as long as you will." He stood to leave, placing a hand upon Perceval's shoulder as he passed. He nodded briefly to Galahad. They watched him stride through the doorway.

Perceval rose from his seat, tapping the gameboard contemplatively with his finger.

"How closely are you related to King Pelles?" he asked suddenly.

"On the female side, near enough," said Galahad.

"I give you this advice: do not act until you are sure of your destiny." Then he, too, was gone.

Galahad decided that if he were to be rejected by the men with whom he was thrown in fellowship, then he had better explore alliances elsewhere. Nivene was clearly a dangerous friend, but Oswald might make a good start, especially if he were the son of one of Arthur's men. He found the boy back at the keep, hovering by the washerwomen, who were boiling great cauldrons of water to accommodate the needs of the gathering.

"Mind you harm not my Lord Perceval's things!" he was saying anxiously. "He must look his best for the king."

"Boy," laughed an old, virtually toothless woman, "he needs nought but a monk's habit."

"I'd go be shriven by such a man of God!" said a young girl. Several others sighed in agreement. Oswald blushed.

"You should not be talking in such a way of a lord!" he said, but the girls just laughed and kissed him "for his master". He struggled from their grip and had turned about to retreat when he saw Galahad smiling at him.

"Oswald," he said, "I see you have great loyalties. You must be a worthy ally." He put out his hand. The boy grasped it formally, but smiled in return, grateful for the rescue.

"It is not easy to do your duty among gossiping women," he said, with all the archness a young boy could muster. Galahad kept a straight face.

"You are assigned to my aid," he said. "I have need of help to ready me for the hunt. Have you witnessed it before?"

"Oh yes, my lord," said the boy eagerly. "Last winter, my grandfather - Earl Kay," he added, proudly, "took me behind him to watch the chase. The older men go only to judge and protect the younger, you know."

"I had gathered that much," said Galahad. Inwardly, he was thinking: Earl Kay's kin; Perceval must be of repute to have the wardship of the grandson of Arthur's senechal. He was glad that Conlaed had schooled him so well in the politics of Arthur's court, and, suddenly, he wished the old monk were with him to lend wisdom as the occasion arose.

"Do they take their dogs?" he asked.

"Yes - but I think none could match yours. Does he hunt?"

"He has saved me from wolves and boars; he still bears the scar on one shoulder to prove it," said Galahad impressively. Oswald's eyes widened.

"I wish I had a hound like that," he said, "then the maidservants would not tease me because I am young, and I venture I could escape chapel services sometimes and go hunting with him!" Galahad was inwardly amused. He guessed which part of wardship under Perceval chafed the most.

"Maybe one day you will," he said, "but for now, I need your help. Where is the weapons store? I have sword and dagger, but no spear."

"This way, my lord. I know the weapons master," said Oswald importantly.

Galahad followed the boy away from the washerwomen towards another corner of the keep, where two buildings sat side by side. From one, smoke billowed through a large opening in the roof, and the ringing sounds of foundry work echoed forth. The one next to it, Oswald informed Galahad, was the weapons store. The door was open, and they entered. In the dim light, Galahad could see two or three other young men engaged in the act of choosing their hunting equipment. They were turning over various pieces and discussing their merits. Behind them hovered a stooped, middle-aged man, quite bald, but with burly arms that bulged out from a sleeveless leather tunic. He muttered advice now and then, and returned the weapons to their original positions, scowling, as the youths moved on. Oswald walked over and touched the man on the arm. He turned round, and changed his expression to a smile as he saw who it was.

"Master Oswald - on an errand for Lord Perceval?" His voice was low and rather slurred.

Oswald shook his head and pointed to Galahad.

"The hunt," he said, slowly, and imitated the action of throwing a spear. The man nodded and beckoned Galahad over.

"You're with Lord Perceval?" he asked. Galahad nodded.

"You can speak, lad, if you say things clearly to my face. I'm not completely deaf. The wars did for my ears, then the foundry for my back, but I'm no imbecile yet," he laughed, slapping one of his hunched shoulders. "How heavy can you carry a spear?"

Galahad looked at the spears lined up against the wall behind the weapons master. He selected one whose shaft was about the width of two fingers.

"About this," he said, touching it. The older man pulled it out of its rest and handed it to him. Galahad held it horizontally, weighing it. He nodded.

"This is fine," he enunciated to his face.

"A good spear - you're welcome to it, but take care, or you'll answer to me," he said, laughing in a deep, disjointed fashion.

Oswald tugged on the man's apron, and he looked down kindly. "How is my sword, Master Adean?" asked Oswald eagerly, making signs which evidently formed a language between them.

"It's well, Master Oswald. I oiled it just the other day. It'll be yours sooner than you know."

"It was my father's," said Oswald to Galahad, by way of explanation, "and it will be mine as soon as I am old enough. My father served King Arthur well, and so his special sword is kept here, to be ready for me, as soon as Lord Perceval permits."

"And Lord Perceval will see to it that you become a worthy man before it's placed in your hands," said Adean sternly and approvingly. Oswald rolled his eyes. "And you know it well," he added, catching the reaction. Oswald found his boyish grin again, and bowed to Adean.

"But now I must go to aid my lord's guest," he said solemnly. With a last, wistful glance towards the shelf where his father's weapon lay, he led Galahad outside.

"Master Adean is very strict," he said, "but he likes me. The other boys daren't enter by themselves."

"Indeed?" said Galahad. "Well, you had better tell me what I need to do next. Is that the gathering for the hunt?" and he indicated the gates of the fortress, where men on horse and foot were beginning to mill.

"Yes, we need to hurry. Is your own horse here?"

"In the stables. At least I know where that is." Galahad had left his horse, one of Pelles' finest, in the personal hands of one of the senior stable lads, with dire warnings to take good care of it. The lad had taken one awed look at the fine mare and the dog that came up to her flanks, and sworn an oath that she would be as fresh as a foal in the morning.

When the two got to the stables, they found that he had not lied. The horse and Samson smelled each other and began to whinny and whine respectively. Samson bounded into the stables, his arrival accompanied by startled curses from the stable boys who had not yet encountered him. Galahad strode in after him, and found his horse, ready to be loose. He patted her neck, and felt her over. She was indeed rested - and had been groomed until her chestnut flanks shone. His saddle was cleaned, too and hung over the edge of her stall. He fitted it on her back, but she scarcely noticed, for Drystan had ordered it to be crafted to fit each contour of her body. Galahad ran a hand over it in satisfaction, resting lightly on the front pommel. Then he took her reins and led her outside. Oswald was standing waiting, holding the spear. He looked up.

"Is that a good horse?" he asked. Galahad nodded.

"She's a purebred, an old Roman line, brought from Araby, it is said. King Arthur will not have many better."

"Sir, if you have no more need of me, may I go to my grandfather? I am permitted to ride with him again."

Galahad looked at the lad. He himself had not experienced the common anxieties of wardship, being sheltered within Pelles' keep for his whole life, yet, now and again, a ward had made a brief appearance at his grandfather's court, usually as an unproclaimed hostage for the good behaviour of some under lord. Most had displayed an outward indifference to their plight, but he had known that many were lonely and scared. Oswald must be happy to be in his grandfather's presence for a few precious days or weeks, however well he was treated at Perceval's hands. He smiled and nodded.

"Yes, you have served me well. Enjoy the hunt."

"I will be sure to watch out for you," said Oswald, and he ran off happily.

Now that he was armed once more, and in possession of his horsc and dog, Galahad felt a little less apprehensive about facing the hunt. His grandfather had been careful to send him away fitted as well as he knew for Arthur's court, and his grandson certainly considered that he would not disgrace himself. He patted Samson on the head and then mounted, nudging the mare towards the gathering at the edge of the castle grounds. As he neared, he saw Perceval in the rear. The warrior nodded to him.

"Do you wish me to introduce you to some of the others with whom you will be hunting?"

"Thank you," replied Galahad, "but I shall let them judge me for who I am." Perceval gave a brief inclination of his head and moved his horse to give him passage forward. Launcelot was busy at the side of the gathering, giving last minute advice to a youth ornamented with rather more jewellery than one would expect for a hunt, and he did not turn to acknowledge Galahad. Others took notice of his presence, though. Several young men whispered among themselves as he rode forward;

others stared in silence. Galahad returned the stares. At last a youth rode up to him.

"So, all are asking, are you a mortal or a ghost?"

Galahad grinned in spite of his resolution to be dignified.

"I am flesh and blood," he returned.

"Then we are also wondering by what sorcery you survived placing yourself in the seat of peril."

"It was no sorcery, but destiny. I am Galahad, kinsman of King Pelles," he said formally. The young man bowed.

"And I am Eldol, son of Lord Bediver."

"I am glad to be acknowledged by the son of one of King Arthur's most trusted men."

"We are all equal in the hunt. I wish you as well as anyone else. And now we are about to begin, for the queen rides out."

Galahad looked beyond him to where Eldol had turned and saw a group of women riding towards them. Guenevere was in their midst, a green cloak shimmering about her in the frosty, morning sun. Her face was framed by a hood of the same material.

"Some ride for the honour of ladies in this hunt," said Eldol. "Many account it an honour to ride for the queen."

"Aye, well, they can only ride *for* her, unlike Launcelot," came a low comment from somewhere among the crowd, followed by stifled sniggers. Eldol glared.

"It is a privilege to venture in the name of Queen Guenevere," he said to those around him.

"Eldol wants to take Launcelot's place," said a rather heavy-set young man, the one with whom Galahad had seen Launcelot talking.

"Aye, well you'll not win today; I will wager that personally," said Eldol, hotly. Galahad turned away. He had no wish to be embroiled in youthful quarrels his first day at court. He looked at Guenevere, who was wearing that same, serene smile he had seen last night. She looked perfect, like something out of a bard's story, far from the pained flesh and blood that clad his mother. She was seated lightly on her grey palfrey, her long, gloved fingers holding the reins against the pommel, her back straight, the outline of her thighs showing gently beneath the rich cloth that covered her and her horse. He did not wonder that she inspired devotion; she reminded him of Elayne as she had seemed in his childhood. He felt a stab of hatred towards Guenevere. She, unknowing of his emotions, cast a look in his direction; not inviting, or even questioning, but designed, he knew, to let him know that she was aware of his presence. He returned the look for a moment, and then turned his horse around, moving it back with the others as Arthur came into the courtyard.

The king looked to be in a spirit of revelry. He raised his hand, smiling as he acknowledged his men, and rode over to Guenevere to take her hand and kiss it. She bowed her head and permitted the smallest curve to grace her lips in reply. Then Arthur turned to face the crowd of warriors, ladies and common folk who had assembled to follow the chase.

"This is the day of our traditional Yuletide hunt, when we allow our youth to lead the way and show their readiness to aspire to our fellowship. We look for deeds, not words today; therefore I shall restrain you no longer. Our huntsmen have found a stag and are even now awaiting your presence beyond the gates. On the sound of the horns, the gates will be opened. May victory come to he who is most worthy!"

At once, there was the sonorous wail of a thin horn, and several men pulled open the large timber gates, hiding behind them quickly as the riders surged forward to reach the lands beyond the keep. Galahad kicked his horse in the flanks, and she bolted forward with Samson at her side, who was adept at dodging hooves.

They rode down the plains outside the keep, past the encampment to the wooded land beyond. Arthur's huntsmen were waiting to indicate the trail of the stag that they had flushed out that morning. The dogs at the fore of the crowd quickly picked up the scent and plunged through the undergrowth into a small coppice, as the riders parted to go around each side. Galahad looked about him swiftly; he saw Eldol move to the left, and decided to follow him. Samson had gone with his own kind. The riders waited eagerly to see if the stag would race forth, but the dogs emerged alone, and milled about for a while, until they picked up the scent again and moved to the west. All ran down a small hill to a stream, where muddied hoof prints had torn the bank. The dogs ran across, and again stopped, not finding the scent straightaway.

The stag was clearly a seasoned runner, thought Galahad. He must had travelled along through the stream to avoid leaving a clear trail. He glanced at the countryside; downstream was another wooded area.

"At left, Samson!" he called, pointing as he drove his horse that way. Samson pricked up his ears and followed his master. Soon, he rediscovered the trail and set off. The others had been quick to spot Galahad's reasoning, and were thick about him before he could take a lead.

"Good work," called Eldol breathlessly as he plunged past.

Galahad looked about him as he let his horse follow the crowd. Behind were the older warriors; he thought he could spot Oswald riding with his grandfather on a large warhorse. Most of the ladies were following sedately at the rear, but Guenevere was neck and neck with one of the young men, her hood back and her hair streaming behind her. A shout made him turn back suddenly: the form of a stag could be seen in the distance, at the edge of the trees. A horn sounded, and a baying arose among the hunting dogs, who knew the meaning of the signal. The stag froze for a moment, then bolted back into the wood. The hunt surged across the meadow after it. There would be little room amongst the trees for a crowd of horsemen, Galahad reckoned; he needed to make sure that he was one of those who made headway. He lowered himself over his horse's back and pressed hard with his heels. She felt his command and lunged forward against her reins, eager to be free from the unfamiliar herd that surrounded her. They reached the wood with Eldol and three other youths; Launcelot's nephew was behind them. Galahad saw Eldol's look of satisfaction as he blocked his rival's way.

Going into the woods was dangerous, but Galahad was used to the forests that encompassed his grandfather's estates. His mare, too, was sure-footed among the roots. Galahad kept his head low, avoiding branches. Other youths were not so careful, and he heard startled yells and curses as they received wounds at the hands of the trees. One horse stumbled to a halt over a root, and the rider let out a yell of rage and disappointment, but Galahad kept on. Ahead, he could see Samson, pursuing an audible trail of crashing undergrowth as the stag leaped on ahead of its pursuers.

Then, all at once, they were free of the wood again, and charging across a heath. Now, the stag was within clear view, and tiring of the chase. Galahad could see the steam from its breath rising before it as it made its last bid for life. The young warriors were heading for the kill. Galahad put his hand to his back, pulling up the spear that had been fastened behind him. Samson was at the stag's heels. Galahad called him back and raised his spear. He leant back in the saddle and threw it, but as he did, another spear arched through the air in front of his, hitting the stag square in the flank. It fell to the ground, quivering. Galahad looked round: Eldol was smiling broadly as he rode forward and leaped from his horse to slit the stag's throat. The body heaved and fell still. Galahad rode up and dismounted.

"You are a worthy huntsman," said Eldol, "and your dog must take part of the credit for this kill." He was panting as he spoke, and his forehead glistened with sweat, although it was a cold morning.

"I could not have done better than you," said Galahad truthfully.

The rest of the court was rapidly gaining on the two. Launcelot's nephew rode up slowly, his face unable to conceal his irritation. Eldol could not resist another smile, though Galahad kept his emotions under control. The older warriors were soon upon them. Perceval rode through the crowd and looked down at the stag, then questioningly at Galahad. Galahad shook his head.

"He was scarcely a breath behind me, my lord," said Eldol.

"Is that so?" said Perceval. "Then you have done well, for Eldol is perhaps our most accomplished young hunter."

People moved aside as Queen Guenevere rode through, Launcelot by her side. Even after the rigours of her ride, she seemed as poised as ever. Her hair was tucked smoothly into her hood once more, and her face showed no flush, though her eyes were sparkling. Eldol bowed low.

"The kill was for you, my queen. May it be to your honour."

Guenevere held out her hand to Eldol, who took it as if it were made of glass, and brushed his lips against it.

"It was a noble chase, Eldol, and I am pleased in your accomplishment." She looked at Galahad. "You, too, rode well, Lord Galahad. We saw you constantly at the fore of the chase. We shall, I think, miss other acts of your prowess in your untimely departure." Launcelot glowered behind her. Galahad bowed stiffly.

"I strive always to do my best."

Launcelot rode close to Guenevere, but before he could whisper his opinion, Arthur came to the fore of the celebration, and Launcelot pulled away to let the king through. The Regissimus looked as satisfied as if he himself had felled the hind.

"Aha, Eldol, so a prize for our queen! Well, the beast gave a worthy chase. You shall have the first cut of meat when it is roasted for the meal tonight, and a place of honour to eat it. Friends," he continued, turning to the riders closing in on the scene, "this hunt is over, but the day is not. You are free to seek other quarry on our lands, or enjoy the revelry of the day as you see fit. My business is the realm; Yuletide is yours, and we shall meet at sundown to feast together."

He raised a hand in farewell, but was immediately lost in the crowd of men who surged around him, hoping for impromptu audiences on the ride back.

Several huntsmen moved forward, knives at the ready. They slit the stag's belly there on the grass, and pulled out its entrails, chopping them roughly as they cast them to the waiting dogs. When they had done this, one of them sewed up the abdomen with a thin strip of leather, and then they tied the legs together and slung it onto a wooden frame that was pulled by one of the larger horses. Thc triumphant hunting party began to disperse in the direction of the keep and camp, behind their king and queen.

Galahad waited for Samson to trot over, his muzzle dark with blood, wagging his tail. His master leaned down to scratch his head.

"You have two noble animals there," said a voice beside him. It was Perceval again.

"I thank you, my lord. You grace me with your company once more."

"If we are to undertake the perilous crossing of several empires in fellowship, I wish to know the man with whom my lot is thrown."

"And I, too. But perhaps not all men might think on this."

Perceval leaned towards Galahad from his saddle, looking him squarely in the face.

"Lord Launcelot is the best warrior of any empire you might care to name. His calling is his passion, his passion his calling. It may be that on rare occasions his emotions obscure his reasoning, but that is when comrades such as myself are by his side to see what he cannot. And I do see," he said, reaching out with his dagger to flip Galahad's cloak aside and reveal the dragon's head gleaming from his own scabbard. Galahad looked up at him.

"Have you told him?"

"That is between the two of you. But I warn you, do not let the telling jeopardize our quest. I intend that the Grail shall be found to the glory of God."

"As do I," replied Galahad firmly. "I shall not deceive your lordship in this matter."

"You shall not deceive it in any matter," said Perceval, as he swung around and rode off. He looked back over his shoulder.

"You may sit with me at the feast tonight." Galahad nodded his head. Samson pushed at his foot, and he glanced down.

"Foe or ally, Samson?" he said. "Maybe neither." And he, too, made for the keep.

Chapter Three

Guenevere stood silently in her rooms as her maidservants prepared the small bath. She watched as the steaming water was poured in and rose oil dribbled across the surface, its scent rising in the mist that evaporated into the cool air. She let the maids disrobe her, and waved them away as she stepped into the tub. She felt the heat tighten the skin on her thighs and sank down slowly, relishing the slightly uncomfortable feeling of hot water on her cold body. Then, she leaned her head against the edge, and reached for a cloth. She let it float in the water for a few seconds before smoothing it down her neck and along her arms, which she stretched out languidly, admiring her white skin. She circled the cloth idly around the bath, and leaned back again. She knew that she had a beauty beyond that of all other women her age; it was one of her weapons. Her body had not sagged with the battering of incessant pregnancies, and her skin was still virtually unlined. She knew not whether these blessings were due to the God of Arthur, or the Old Ones, so she continued to pray to both, though she did not let Arthur know this.

But now her mind was not on Arthur, but the new arrival, the young Galahad. She did not usually exert herself to win the adoration of the younger generation; she had enough sense to see that a middle-aged woman chasing young men was an easy object of ridicule. Still, some did become enamoured of her, and she permitted their worship, though she gave them but the merest hint of encouragement. But she had felt no attraction for them - until now. Galahad stirred desires within her that she thought were reserved for one man alone, though she did not understand why.

Launcelot had not been much older than Galahad when they had first met. She smiled to herself as she remembered that day, when she was waiting in trepidation for the convoy that was to take her to a new home and a husband she had met but once, and barely remembered at that. Her father, Leodegran, was triumphant, having secured an alliance with the man who was the acknowledged High King of Britannia. He had always openly hoped great things for his beautiful daughter, but this was an undreamed-of destiny. And her dowry had been so little, hardly more than her face and the huge, ancient round table that had stood in his hall for generations. He saw great days ahead for himself, with Arthur as his son-in-law.

As for Guenevere herself, she had been groomed from childhood to know that her value was in her body, and now, at fifteen, she was poised to take her place in history. Still, she was afraid. She had captured the love of a young warrior-king, but his face was a blur in her memory and nothing upon her own heart. She was leaving the world in which she had been cocooned for the dangerous realm of high politics, and she was clever enough to know she would be a vulnerable novice at court.

She stood with her father at the gate of his keep, watching as the procession of Arthur's court came into view. She knew that Arthur himself would not be there, and she was glad of the chance to compose herself as she journeyed from Luguvalium to his court. Now she was nervous, trembling imperceptibly as the cavalcade came into sharper focus, the shimmering metals and gaily-coloured cloths gradually metamorphosing into people and carriages. At last the royal train came to a halt before the gates. One man broke away from the ranks and rode ahead, to where they were standing. He alighted from his horse and came close, falling to one knee before Guenevere, his head bowed.

"My queen," he had said. Then, he raised his head and looked up into her face, and in that moment she wished with all her soul that he was Arthur and she need go no further. The women at court laughed and sighed over the tales of love at first sight told by the bards; when she met Launcelot, she knew that she loved him, not from that moment, but from eternity, that there had never been a time when her soul had not been yearning for him. She could not remember what she had said, but he had arisen to stand tall over her. Then, her father had interjected, and taken Launcelot's gaze away from her. There were further formalities as he gave his over-rehearsed speech to the king's proxy. Leodegran was proud, but Guenevere could tell he was a little afraid of Launcelot. At last, they turned and began to supervise the loading of carts.

When it came time for her final farewells, she embraced her weeping mother and sisters, but they had already seemed almost strangers. Launcelot helped her into a litter, lined with furs and silks to keep out the cold, and curtained for privacy. He rode along beside her for the first part of the journey, and she kept the curtain pulled back to talk. He informed her of the country where Arthur's court was situated, and described her new home in meticulous detail. It would take them a week to travel, he explained, but camps had been set up along the way, and her own quarters had been built at each stage, by Arthur's command. She was not to lack for anything.

While they travelled, he talked in generalities. Yet that night, as they made their first camp on a plain filled with tents and her lone building, he came to sit with her, to keep her company he said. He brought a gaming board, and they began to play. Guenevere was already a skilled player, and he had to concentrate, furrowing his brows so that his golden-brown hair fell across his forehead. Smilingly, he admitted his first defeat.

"You are a good strategist," he said. "But have you been adequately trained to be Arthur's queen?"

"I know the duties of running a household of great size," she had replied, proudly. "I can direct servants, serve honoured guests, -"

"But you will need more than household skills to survive at Arthur's court," said Launcelot. "You will need more than even your beauty. You must look as innocent as the dove and yet be as wise as the serpent, and know how to evade those who would seek your downfall." He leaned over the board and laid his fingertips upon her own, stroking her nails lightly.

"You are a beautiful girl. Yet I will teach you to be a beautiful queen, and I will be your champion." He looked straight into her eyes for the second time since they had met, and she understood that he, too, loved.

Yet he did not touch her as a lover. Throughout that long week, they remained side-by-side, sharing idle conversation within the hearing of others, though each word was charged with a thousand meanings they could not utter. At night, they played at games of strategy, while he taught her how to manouevre through the treacheries of the court; each move symbolized a step in a courtship they could not admit, and each defeat was a glad surrender of the one to the other. Then, gradually, safe from the ears of attendants, they began to whisper tentative words of love.

It was only on that final night before they reached Arthur's court, that the enormity of their passion became too much to bear. As Launcelot leaned over the board to point out an alternative move, he touched her fingers, then her cheek, and suddenly his lips were upon hers. She had never been touched by a man in that way; she had never felt that urgency of desire that can pervade every part of the body. He rose and pulled her across the table into his arms, scattering the game pieces across the floor. He seemed rough and gentle at the same time: his hands sought her thighs; pressed her to him, and she pushed back against him without knowing why she did it.

"I cannot take your body yet," he whispered hoarsely. "It is Arthur's. But after - we shall find a way."

"Must I go to him?" she said, and began to weep. He kissed her tears away fiercely.

"I vowed to my king to deliver you to him, and I will keep that vow. We must both be loyal to Arthur, no matter what comes."

She had felt then the first pang of sorrow and anger that punctuated their relationship; she had not understood how he could relinquish her, did not comprehend the man of passion and loyalty before her. She hardly knew when he left her quarters, his presence remained with her so powerfully. She took the touch of his hands to bed with her that last, lonely, sleepless night.

She rode beside him for the approach to the castle the next day. Neither one spoke. The weight of her ceremonial dress and jewellery bore down on her, but she held her back straight. She would not show weakness any more, for she was to bear a silent burden for the rest of her life. She saw Arthur awaiting them, surrounded by the pomp that Launcelot had described to her so vividly on their journey, and for the first time, she composed her face into the expression of serenity that was to be her public demeanor from then on. Launcelot dismounted from his horse, and held his arms out to her. She leaned forward into them, but he kept her at a distance. Holding out his hand for her to place hers upon it, he led her before Arthur. Then he knelt, and, echoing the scene of the week before, he looked at Arthur and said,

"Your queen."

Guenevere felt herself trembling as she remembered, and she steeled herself, for crying was so detrimental to one's looks. Instead, she set a leg upon the edge of the bath, and washed it slowly. They had been loyal to Arthur, both of them. They saw that in him lay the security of the realm, and they had both worked over the years to preserve the fragile alliance of Britannia's rulers. They would die for him, even as they would die for each other. But Launcelot had been her champion, too, and a childless queen needs more than her comeliness to preserve her throne. Their trinity upheld the kingdom, but Arthur did not know - not even after all these years - that his crown was bought with their lovemaking.

But why was she reminiscing? Was it because she was afraid for Launcelot on his perilous quest, or was it because of that boy, with his honey-brown hair, his soft hazel eyes and his strangely determined air? She thought of his face, dwelling upon its details, and suddenly her hand froze in the act of bathing herself. Her eyes narrowed. She understood. Abruptly, she stood up in her bath, and a maid hurried into the room at the sound, to throw a robe about her.

"Fetch Lord Launcelot," she hissed.

"But, my lady, this is not a safe time - "

"Now!"

Launcelot was talking with Bors and Perceval when the summons came. Perceval's lands were adjacent to Bors', and they were arranging the care of the former's demesne.

"Perhaps you would take Kay's grandchild, too, if the Lord Seneschal agrees. Oswald is a good lad, though he has a way to go to reach the spiritual disciplines that make a man. He needs a stern hand."

"Come, now, Perceval, you are quite fond of him. I saw the knife you gave him at Christmas."

"Well, he will make a good warrior, but I am not blind to his sins." Still, Perceval smiled as he spoke.

"We hope not to be away above a year," said Launcelot. "I think we may travel swiftly, if the seas are good, and the boy is not a hindrance - yes?" He spun round at the voice of Guenevere's maid, whispering tentatively at the door.

"Sir, the queen demands an audience. She says it is about the quest."

The other two looked quizzically at Launcelot. He shook his head in answer, but still, he rose, and bowed.

"We shall talk later. See if you can get more out of that boy, Perceval."

He followed the maid to Guenevere's rooms. He entered to find her waiting for him, dressed in a loose-fitting white robe that still managed to fall gently around her curves. Her face was pale, and her hands were clutched against her skirts.

"Leave," she snapped at the maid, who was glad to scurry out of earshot.

"What is it?" asked Launcelot. He was accustomed to finding he had offended her over some slight, but he could think of nothing he had done wrong this Yuletide, when they were able to snatch extra, precious moments under the cover of court revelry.

"What do you mean, bringing your spawn here, flaunting him under my nose?"

"Beloved, I have no child. I am not like Bors, bedding any servant girl who flashes her eyes at him. You know I am yours alone." Some fit of jealousy, he thought, or perhaps a malicious rumour.

She stared at him, seeing the truth in his words.

"Do you not see?" she demanded. "The hair, the expression, the lineage itself? Galahad is your son - yours and that whore daughter of Pelles."

She had never uttered Elayne's name, though she knew what had taken place. His guilt had driven him to confess, to weep and beg before her, was it nigh on seventeen years ago now? She had hit him, she saw. His face blanched to a hue that resembled hers. He sat down and put his head in his hands.

"I told you," he muttered, "I was bewitched. I never knew it was she."

"How many times?" Guenevere almost spat. "Are you going to tell me that you sired that child in a single night?"

He shook his head, keeping it still buried in his hands. Guenevere came over to where he was sitting. She kneeled down before him, pulling his hands from his face, forcing him to look at her.

"Why is he here, why has he not declared himself? Does he mean harm or good? God's life, Launcelot, you are about to journey across the world with a saint and a bastard, and you do not even know if you will be safe in your own company, let alone that of any barbarians you meet!"

"I will be safe with Perceval," he muttered, almost absentmindedly.

"Will you? Do you think he cannot know, after all the time he has spent with the boy? Why has he not revealed the truth to you?"

Launcelot shook his head. "No, he would have his reasons, but they would not be treacherous. But my - Galahad, why did he not tell me? I have been nothing but harsh with him since he arrived." He stood up.

"Where are you going?"

"To find him, of course. I will have the truth, or I will not set a foot out of this kingdom."

"Yes," said Guenevere bitterly, "go to him, what do you care for my pain? Go, go to your son."

Launcelot looked her in the eye. "He was meant to be our son," he said. He turned and left. Guenevere stood, watching the blank door, her hands clenched. Her breathing came in gasps, but still she did not let a tear fall. When she uncurled her fists, she looked down at her smarting palms, to see the reddened marks where her nails had pierced her skin.

Launcelot barely saw the way before him as he stormed across the courtyard. Several men turned to greet him, but their salutations died upon their lips as they beheld his visage. He came upon Oswald, playing with Samson. The two were wrestling on the ground, and Samson's wide canine grin was matched only by Oswald's delighted laughter.

"Boy!" he shouted. "Where is Galahad?"

Oswald stopped and sat up, making a futile attempt to push Samson away.

"Practising arms with the other young men, my lord. Shall I fetch him?" But Launcelot had walked on past the startled boy, not bothering with an answer. He bore towards the armoury where the practice ground was situated. Sure enough, he could hear the dull clashing of metal on wood, or the sharper clang of metal on metal, interspersed with good-natured oaths and grunts of determination. He rounded the corner and the group of young warriors came into view. He scanned the scene rapidly for Galahad, and saw him with Eldol, practising sword parries. Most of the combatants stopped as he made his way through them to the two youths. Eldol was facing him; he put his sword down and stood, panting. Galahad turned to follow his comrade's gaze. He stared defiantly at Launcelot, though he knew in a moment why he had come.

"A word with you," said Launcelot, shortly. Galahad stooped and slowly wiped the blade of his sword on the grass. Launcelot's colour heightened, but he said nothing. The others stood hushed, afraid of the consequences of this insolence. After a pause, Galahad stood, his weapon still clutched firmly in his hand.

"I am ready," he replied. Launcelot swung round and walked off without a word. Galahad followed him to the Great Hall, eventually sheathing his weapon. The hall was empty in the middle of the morning, and it seemed vast, even in the dim light which was all that could penetrate through the tiny slits that functioned as windows. Launcelot led the way to the table of Arthur's fellowship. He placed a hand on it, and turned round. His face was a combination of anger and sorrow. For a moment, Galahad felt compassion.

"Why did you not reveal yourself to me - to your king?" Launcelot's voice was controlled; he enunciated every word distinctly.

"I had not yet reason to do so. Besides, how can I perceive what the court itself knows of your conduct at Pelles' court seventeen years ago? Would you rather I had sullied your reputation," Galahad put a sarcastic tone into the word, "when your secret could have remained hidden?"

"What reason were you waiting for? A tactful moment? An opportunity of vengeance? Christ in heaven, I am your father!"

"You have not been so for these sixteen years, and I did not travel here to request that you acknowledge me."

"I did not know of your existence."

"It would not have been hard to seek news of Pelles' daughter. Half the countryside in the north knows of her derangement." Galahad spoke calmly, but he let a bitterness tinge his words.

"You could not understand what transpired," said Launcelot quietly. "I do not even comprehend whether she had a knowing part in it all, but there was a great deception. I have never harbored anything but regret and penitence for the episode. Until -"

" - now?" said Galahad, challengingly.

"Until," said Launcelot deliberately, "you are a man of some experience, you will not be able to understand yourself. But I shall take responsibility for you here, and your position shall be recognized."

"I do not seek favours; I have been accepted on my merits thus far."

A servant cracked open the door to the hall, but, seeing the two in discussion, hastily withdrew. However the interruption was a welcome break to the flow of the conversation. Launcelot took a breath and began again.

"We have not had an auspicious first meeting, but I will not shirk my duty. I want you to sit with me at the meal tonight, as my acknowledged son. It is better thus than to wait until everyone is whispering about this secret. And whether or not you respect me as a father, if you wish to return alive from our quest, I suggest you learn to work closely with Perceval and myself."

Galahad could not deny this without appearing weak or spiteful in his reasoning, and he had no wish to present himself thus before his father.

"I intend to return alive," he said shortly.

Launcelot took this as agreement.

"We must ask an audience with the king. It would be impolitic to act without his knowledge."

"And I suppose I am to act the dutiful son?"

"The Regissimus wills a kingdom of order, and his will is to be ours. This is our united strength, a lesson you must learn. Will you meet me on this?" He did not offer a hand; he was not prepared to meet with an insult.

Galahad nodded shortly. They stood for a few moments, facing one another in silence. Then they turned and left side by side.

The meal that night was both a triumph and a trial for Galahad. It seemed that no sooner had he and Launcelot emerged from their audience with King Arthur than the whole gathering had gotten wind of his parentage. Some offered friendly salutations, others made subtly derisory comments. He could not tell who ultimately meant him well.

He sat next to Launcelot at the end of the head table; it would have been unthinkable to do otherwise, though he would just as rather have sat beside Perceval, or with Eldol and the other young men. However, Eldol himself had a place of honour for the season, as the victor of the stag hunt. He sat at the opposite end of the head table, occasionally grinning across at Galahad in recognition of their mutual notoriety. As Galahad glanced down the table past Arthur, but the king caught the turn of his head and raised a glass in his direction.

"We salute you, Lord Galahad, as our youngest questor, and as the son of our closest ally and comrade, Lord Launcelot."

"Indeed," said Guenevere smoothly, "we are astounded that we did not sooner see your noble lineage in your features and bearing. But we are curious that Lord Launcelot was not informed of the existence of his son by King Pelles."

"You are right, lady, but still, we are mindful that Pelles has been always a good ally, and has helped us hold our own against the Dux Britanniarum," replied Arthur.

"We live in times of constant strife, my queen," replied Galahad, deferential but cold. "My grandfather may have felt that it was safer to conduct matters thus. I myself have not always been cognizant of my full heritage. It was sufficient to be the heir of a king."

Guenevere inclined her head and smiled, raising her own glass to Galahad.

Nivene appeared at her shoulder, a flagon in hand, to renew Guenevere's cup. She glided down the table, refilling cups as necessary. At last she came to Galahad's place and leant over to serve him, brushing her breast lightly against his shoulder as she did so. He pretended not to notice, though his colour deepened slightly. Perceval, sitting across the table, witnessed the scene. He inclined himself towards Galahad.

"It is always better to seek the truth and to give it, and then you can remain pure in heart - and body." Nivene, who was approaching him, gave no visible reaction as she poured the wine into his goblet.

"How fares your sister, my lord?" she said, in a voice ostensibly low, but designed to carry.

"She does her duty, as do we all," he replied, without looking round at her. She let the merest smile flit across her lips as she moved on.

Some warriors, at least, were enjoying the merriment of the season, and appeared to be happily in their cups. Bors was good-naturedly teasing Merlin, who seemed to Galahad to be surprisingly tolerant of the old soldier.

"Did you not see these events under your nose, my seer?" he asked.

"On the contrary," replied Merlin, "if you had followed my story of the Grail, you would have noted that I revealed the presence of the descendants of Joseph of Arimathea."

"He speaks true," answered a grinning Lord Kay, punching his comrade's shoulder. "You were not listening, or you were too busy thinking of your wine or women." There was general laughter, and Bors raised his goblet to all.

"While I have life, I shall live it!" he declared, and tossed back his drink.

From across the hall came the strains of a harp being played softly for tuning.

"Ah yes, a song for the winter's evening!" declared Arthur, beckoning the player forward. Galahad sat back a little, relieved that the attention was to be focussed away from him. The bard came towards the table, playing his harp in a lingering manner. He was a man of middle age, thin, his face deeply lined, but his fingers were long and his hands moved lightly across the strings.

"What do you have for us tonight, Siawn?" asked Arthur.

"A tale of Britannia, my lord. A tale of Gerontius, the Vortigern, ruler of this realm in our great-grandfathers' time." He waited for Arthur's nod of approval, before striking a chord, and beginning his recitation.

He began with a long genealogy of kings, heroes and semi-divine rulers who had governed Britannia of old. The names were familiar to all present, yet they listened attentively, nodding at the remembrance of the stories brought to light by the passing mention of a hero whose praises they had heard sung many a time. Gradually, when he had transported his audience to the time of legend, Siawn came to his chosen subject, and began to relate the numerous victories of Vortigern, as the leader came to be hailed. Then he came at last to the story of Vortigern's attempt to construct a tower in the mountains of the western provinces. He told how, each time the foundations were laid, they would crumble away, to the confoundment of the ruler and his council.

"Many a wise man was sought, but none could tell the mystery of the cursed stronghold. At long last, one man, more ancient than the rest, declared that the tower could be built only on the blood of a child who had no parents. At this saying, Vortigern was perplexed - what child could be found who came forth into the world without parents? As he and his court contemplated the meaning of this revelation, a young boy was brought before him, the son of his rival. His mother and father were dead, killed in an uprising against Vortigern himself, fighting for the Roman Emperor Constantine against the new ruler of Britannia. Here, Vortigern realized, was the answer to the riddling words of the soothsayer: an orphan whose blood could be shed that the tower might be raised."

Galahad smiled and looked to the king, as did others present, for all knew who this mysterious child was, though the bard did not yet reveal his name.

This boy, Siawn declared, was brought before Vortigern to hear the declaration of his fate. Yet he did not quiver or beg for his life; rather he stood boldly before the throne and proclaimed that he knew the truth of the king's problem. He disclosed that beneath the foundations were two warring dragons, whose battles shook the tower to the ground each time men attempted to raise it. Vortigern ordered the excavation of the site, and, sure enough, when his men had dug deep, to the rock beneath the foundations, two dragons, one red and one white, burst up through the earth and flew into the air.

"Their battle was fearful to behold," chanted Siawn, striking a discordant theme upon his harp. "The two beasts of hell clashed together in the skies above Snowden; their wings were as thunder, and the fire that issued from their cavernous mouths burned the trees around them. Their talons, which were as long as swords, rent each others' skin, and the blood that fell to the ground hissed and bubbled, searing the earth beneath. For five hours they fought, till at last the bloodshed ended as the white dragon crashed to the ground dead, and its conqueror let out a screech of victory before flying out of sight.

"As the awed witnesses gazed upon the receding dragon, the boy spoke up again.

"'Behold, the victory of the red dragon: so shall the warriors of the white beast be defeated by those of the red!'

"Those who were with Vortigern's court were astounded at the prophecy and boldness of the boy: with one voice they declared that it would be an act of shame if he were to be slain. Vortigern, in his wisdom and beneficence, conceded, and declared that the boy's life should be spared. Yet, he decreed that he should be shut up a prisoner in the very fort which was to have been built over his bones. And so, the boy remained and grew to manhood, awaiting the time when the Almighty should bring him forth to fulfill his destiny. And that, my lords, is a tale for another night."

The bard smiled as he finished, and bowed to the applause from the hall. Siawn had chosen well: a tale of the miraculous child who grew up to command Britannia - and to adopt Arthur as his son and successor.

Galahad looked up from his cup to see Nivene still standing at the corner of the table. She let her eyes catch his for a brief second, but she did not acknowledge this glance. Instead, she slipped away, leaving him the one puzzling on her meaning. He turned his attention back to the feast, where the mood swung towards celebration and nostalgia, as the men reminisced on Britannia's glories. Galahad was pleased that they were lauding the past, for at this point he did not care to speculate upon his role in the future.

The next morning was cold and wet, and the wind showed signs that it was the harbinger of the deep winter months that came so soon in the new year. The court was making its way from Castellum Cataviae to Glastonbury, where a service was to be held to bless the year's upcoming campaigns. Two monks led the procession on foot, trudging across the stony way, their heads bowed and covered with thick cloaks against the dampness that seeped into everyone's clothes. Behind them, Arthur rode slowly on his horse, one jewelled glove upon the reins and the other bearing his pennant, the red dragon flying upon the white cloth. The horse, a tall, grey stallion bedecked in rich cloths of red, snorted and pulled, eager to pick up the pace, but the king held him firmly. About the horse and rider, the other warriors jostled, their own steeds impatient with the enforced slow pace. Galahad had chosen to ride towards the back, with Eldol and other young men, and Launcelot had not gainsaid him, for his own place was one of honour near the king, one that he could not demand that Galahad share. Behind the horses, a few litters bore the noblewomen and one or two revered, ancient men, no longer able to seat themselves upon a horse.

Eldol was in high spirits, and pleased with the revelation of Galahad's birth.

"I knew that I had met a noble and worthy companion," he said, as they came side by side for a few minutes. "It has been a time of good auguring for me. I trust that the year will bear out my ambitions."

"You have hopes of advancement, then?" said Galahad, neutrally.

"I wish for a worthy commission, perhaps a good place in the summer's campaigning. But I am not the only one who lives in perpetual hope: a king without an heir must make a choice someday. Perhaps one of us here may rise to greatness as he did."

"Well, you may count me as a safe ally, then," replied Galahad, "for I have no such ambition."

"Not even as the son of Lord Launcelot?" said Eldol quizzically.

"I did not choose my parentage, and I do not need its honours thrust upon me. I have my own path, and I will travel it."

"Then you must watch for the snakes that others will place in your way." Eldol smiled, and pulled in his horse a little, so that it fell back towards the litters, and the presence of the queen. He bowed at the gilded litter, and a slight rustling of the curtains indicated that Guenevere had acknowledged his presence. Galahad set his face towards the front of the line, and rode on.

As they traipsed along the wide way, Glastonbury arose before them, nestling below the higher hill, Glastonbury Tor, that shared its name. Though it lay not within a prosperous town, Galahad had not seen a religious community of its like since that sole journey to Eboracum. The cluster of buildings surrounding the larger church might have constituted a small village; he found it difficult to believe that such a number of monks might really exist in one place, being used only to the missionaries that came in ones or twos to the northern regions.

The cavalcade mounted the slope and drew to a halt before the entrance to the monastery. Servants came forward to take charge of horses as the noblemen dismounted. As Guenevere's litter was brought to the entrance, the throng of men parted. She alighted to take the hand of her husband and stand before the waiting abbot.

"Welcome, Regissimus of Britannia," he said. He was a small man under the gaze of Arthur, grey and gnarled, but the king bowed reverently, and Guenevere followed her husband's lead with her own obeisance.

"Father Abbot, we are privileged to come here and ask blessing upon the year's work. We ask that we may enter within your walls and worship."

"The High King and loyal son of the Church is always welcome within the abbey. Come." He turned and led the way through the gate. Arthur and Guenevere walked behind, with other monks taking up position as escorts.

As the court made its way into the small enclave, Galahad saw something of what he knew Conlaed must have left behind on Aran. Small, modest huts were huddled together to form the groups of individual cells for the monks. To one side lay a burial ground for the brethren, and for nobles who expressed a wish to lie amongst the prayers of the faithful. A low mausoleum punctuated the simply marked graves; it was said, Galahad knew, to house the bones of some of the old Scots saints, the converters of Conlaed's isle.

The church itself was not a building to inspire awe, but Galahad could clearly discern that its plain wattle and daub walls had outlived generations of worshippers. “It is said,” whispered Eldol at his side, “that disciples of our Lord travelled with Joseph of Arimathea to Britannia and built this church with their own hands.”

Galahad was not accustomed to worship within such an edifice. His grandfather had, under the influence of Conlaed, allowed the construction of a small, wooden room that formed the church for their community, but Galahad had never been inside such on object of permanence - almost of eternity, it seemed to him. As he entered, he stretched out a hand and touched the wall, trying to imagine a connection to Christ through placing his hands where perhaps one who had embraced the Lord had paused as he rubbed earth into the cracks; he marvelled at the thought of it. Once inside, he watched from the rear as the king and queen took their places upon two carved chairs, laid with embroidered cushions. The rest of the court gathered in the central space, watching the monks standing before them. The large band of warriors, some scarred and battle-hardened, some young and filled with dreams of military glory, made a deep contrast with the smaller gathering of religious men, clothed simply in long, undyed tunics, their hands and faces showing signs of battle done only with the toil of a life that sought to find a meaning between servitude of body and soul.

At an undetected signal, the monks began to sing, unaccompanied, their voices echoing back from the thick walls to fill the hall with an unearthly refrain. Galahad shivered involuntarily; though the words were known to him, he had never before heard them intoned in this manner.

As the service progressed, the abbot faced the congregation.

"It is the will of the Regissimus and that of the Church that the endeavours of his realm for this year of our Lord, be blessed as holy undertakings. We pray, therefore, to thee, Lord Almighty, that the works of these thy servants' hands may be used to implement thy will for this kingdom."

He looked around. "We ask, also, that those who are to embark upon the quest to see the Grail of our Lord Jesus Christ, come forward for the blessing and protection that his name gives."

Galahad started, and was nudged forward by one of the young men. Launcelot and Perceval had already made their way through the shorter distance to the front of the congregation. He followed slowly, trying not to look at the eyes turned upon him. Soon, Galahad stood with them, hoping that his feelings of awkwardness did not show. Perceval was as resolute as ever, his eyes burning with a steeled fervour; Launcelot appeared grim. The abbot raised his hand and made the sign of the cross in front of them.

"Lord, who held the cup on the eve of thy death, and blessed it, and by whose wisdom it has been hidden these many years, watch over these thy warriors as they seek to bring this, the most holy of objects, into thy Church. Guard them as they enter the realms of thy enemies and the enemies of thy sovereign. Let them not be assailed by those earthly and spiritual powers that would seek to bar their way. Sanctify their hearts and minds that they may be worthy to bring thy holy Grail into this land for thy glory. Amen."

Perceval crossed himself; the others stood, their heads bowed. Galahad had absorbed enough of Conlaed's teachings to feel slightly uncomfortable, though he assuaged himself by wondering at Launcelot's adulterous hypocrisy.

All at once, by some signal, the service was completed, and the court turned and drew to the sides of the hall to make way for the royal entourage, led again by the abbot. Galahad was glad to merge with the crowds once more as he made his way out into the cool, damp air of the abbey courtyard. The world outside seemed vast and bright, yet slightly unreal after his immersion within the dark, echoing, ethereal walls of the abbey. Most of the court were eager to get back to the end of their secular festivities, but Arthur lingered, talking with the abbot. Guenevere stood by, a look of piety fixed upon her alabaster face. At last, the abbot bowed, the king took his leave, and all were free to depart.

Several of the horses were pulling impatiently at their reins, whinnying for their freedom and their riders. Galahad found his mare swiftly, and rubbed her neck affectionately. He mounted and waited for the cavalcade to begin filing out of the abbey grounds. Eventually, the ranks began to end, and he joined the younger men who were bringing up the rear of the party.

As he rode, Bors' son fell in with him. Galahad looked over suspiciously, though he bowed his head graciously.

"It seems that you will be marked out for great things this year," he said levelly. Galahad shrugged his shoulders and made a polite but noncommittal noise.

"And is it true that you grew up not knowing that Lord Launcelot was indeed your father?" His voice was a little louder, and he began to look about him to be certain that he was gaining an audience. And indeed, several of the youths were paying attention to the exchange.

"Politics is a complicated game," said Galahad quietly.

"But did you not ask? Or is it natural that northern boys know not who sired them? Barbarian ways are, I confess, unknown to me."

Galahad gripped his reins. He knew that Launcelot's nephew wanted a confrontation, yet he dare not expose himself to the disapprobation of the fellowship, especially on the return from a holy service. He kicked his horse's flanks gently, and she pushed forward.

"Does your silence denote agreement?" said the youth, more loudly. Galahad gritted his teeth, though his countenance did not change. The youth laughed deeply. Galahad pulled up his reins and swung around, though he knew not what he might do to save his face. But at that moment, Eldol came, walking his horse back through the crowd. The group of interested onlookers grew more animated.

"Are you attempting to spoil the holy day with your sinning tongue?" he asked pointedly. The youth reddened.

"I only asked if northerners habitually do not know their sires," he said, repeating his words for the benefit of the crowd.

"Well," said Eldol, "perhaps we might say that southern boys only believe they know who their fathers are."

A large guffaw spread through the young men surrounding them. Eldol turned to Galahad.

"Ride with me, I pray you. There is conversation of worth in the company ahead." He turned, and, after a moment's hesitation, Galahad followed. He began to think that perhaps he was not so alone, after all.

Chapter Four

Galahad was glad when the world began to thaw and give way to the first cold, muddy days of a spring, which, although now tentative and grey, promised to warm into more pleasant weather and an end to the weeks of waiting.

He had been at Arthur's court for over a month now, long after the winter festivities had ended. The kings and magistrates had been eager, in the end, to return to their towns and estates before the snows of winter threatened to hamper their way and leave their lands vulnerable to raids and famine in the absence of leadership. They were glad, too, to know their fate for the year, bar the unknown but expected attacks of the Angles or the Irish in various parts of the realm.

Eldol was particularly happy. Riding upon the success of his prowess at the Yuletide competitions, and the promise of his skills attested to by others of the fellowship, he had, he told Galahad almost gleefully, secured a prominent place in the summer's planned northern campaign.

"And it is thanks to you," he said, "for King Arthur wishes to subdue the lands around the Dux Britanniarum's realm, in order to warn him against taking action upon kings such as your grandfather." He did not have to elaborate. Galahad knew that an old, possibly heirless ruler was a tempting target for the power-hungry. Eldol saw his recognition.

"You have been a friend, and the opportunity for my advancement," he said generously. "I will do my utmost to show loyalty to your family in repayment. Only, remember me in your future triumphs."

"We know not what Fate intends for me on this quest," said Galahad soberly. "But I will not forget you."

He had, indeed, been sorry to see Eldol go. He had found a few tentative companions among the young men whose early political leanings inclined them to Eldol's camp, but he had not wholly trusted any others; it seemed both pointless and dangerous. With his departure, he was alone indeed, for Perceval, the only other person he trusted, had already returned to his lands in order to ready them for his absence, taking the reluctant Oswald in tow. He did not mind too deeply though, for the remoteness of Pelles' court had meant that he was often without suitable companionship of his own age, and there was time aplenty to muse on his situation.

One uncomfortable consequence, however, was that he no longer had reason to decline so many of Launcelot's requests to accompany him in the king's business. His father had remained behind at court to assist in the planning of the year's campaigns and lend a final authority as magister militum before setting off across the lands of the old empire. He had invited Galahad, albeit stiffly, to observe his work, and, even more tentatively, Galahad had accepted. He knew that a thorough knowledge of his father's character was necessary, but he could never forget for a moment the other - the true - parent he had left in the northern lands.

Thus, much of his time was taken with this uneasy alliance. If he were truthful to himself, he had to admit that it was by no means a wholly painful duty. He and his horse enjoyed drilling; he had been introduced to such combat practice by

Drystan, but the opportunity to follow the best cavalry unit in the kingdom could not be turned down. And he did not think he was boasting to himself when he thought that he made a good showing. He had even seen Launcelot nod approvingly at him once or twice. He did not mind, either, the occasional council meeting which he was permitted to attend. Pelles had spent little time preparing him for government, and consequently his interest in matters politic had not been quashed by hours of enforced instruction. He noted, of course, that he was granted entrance to meetings whose agenda consisted of only the most mundane items, but nevertheless he listened with a keen ear, lest he miss any information that would prove pertinent.

Then a period of deep winter settled in, and men were keen to find excuses to stay within the walls of the Great Hall. Military exercises were shortened, for not even the added warmth of woolen leggings beneath the customary leather could keep the chill from muscles. Galahad, accustomed to the more bitter and prolonged northern winters, minded it less than others, yet even he was glad to retreat to the fire that now burned permanently in Arthur's hall. The evenings brought good cheer, even to the shrunken host within the walls, and ale and stories abounded. The bard, Siawn, was worth his keep, though Galahad had heard renderings as good from the wandering bards of his country. Siawn also tended to focus on sycophantic histories of Arthur's adopted ancestry, and gave less time to the heroic tales of gods now declared dead, or men whose real fame still rose to the stars.

It was one such evening when, as the applause for Siawn was dying away, Launcelot came and sat next to Galahad. The younger man nodded stiffly in greeting.

“Did you enjoy the tale of Londinium?” Launcelot asked. The bard had been telling of its legendary founding by Brutus. Galahad nodded again.

“Would you find pleasure in visiting the city itself?”

Galahad started, then composed himself.

“It would of course be of interest,” he said noncommittally, “but I understand that the Regissimus does not hold a court there.”

“Indeed, no, it is not a strategic post at this moment, but it is important enough in its own way. The queen wishes to spend time there as soon as the roads are passable, to meet with members of her family and select gifts. There will of course be a substantial guard. Would you join us?”

Galahad was torn: he had no wish to be a party to whatever adulterous relations would proceed from this journey, yet he yearned to see the city of which he had heard so much. He also saw little profit, and possible danger, in remaining alone at Cataviae. It did not take long for curiosity and prudence to win out.

“I should like to come,” he said, cautiously. Launcelot appeared satisfied.

“Then you should prepare at once,” he said.

That was his longest conversation with his son for the next few days; in that period Galahad only caught glimpses of him striding from council to armoury or stable to the king’s chambers, arranging the expedition with the same precision he had in military exercises. Galahad himself had few possessions to pack: a change of clothing, some coinage; gifts from Pelles. All the jewellery he owned could be worn on his person. It took him less time than polishing his saddle, a task which sheer boredom had made him wrench from the stable lad who had quite taken to it. Yet, though packing his belongings was an easy task, it made his mind restless. Each time he tried to walk away from his saddle bags, he felt compelled to return, to brush his fingertips nervously across the place where, tucked safely inside his tunic was a small, iridescent vial, set carefully in his hands by his grandfather. "You will know when to use it," he had smiled coldly at his grandson. Would he? Galahad wondered. When the moment came, would he?

Yet for now, as soon as the snow was no more than isolated patches on hard-frozen roads, though it filled the ditches and fields still, the queen's court packed wagons for the journey, and prepared to leave. Galahad watched as the king bid farewell to his wife and entrusted her to Launcelot's safekeeping. Launcelot was solemn, Guenevere dignified and chaste, as befitted a queen commencing a journey of state. Galahad noticed Nivene amongst the queen's women, laughing and chattering as she helped to pile furs into litters. She did not turn to look at him.

Guenevere did not accompany her lover on horseback for most of the journey. Instead she lay cocooned in the relative warmth of her litter, sheltered from the elements by thick curtains, sometimes accompanied by one of her women. Her attendants alternated between riding aloof and solemn, taking the dignity of their queen, and urging their pretty horses forward amongst the men, making eyes at the guards from the depths of their hoods. Galahad suspected that the journey was an opportune time for more than its chief participants. Launcelot rode just before thc queen's litter, with Galahad at his side, imparting information concerning Londinium, which saved them both from the compulsion to speak of more personal topics.

"It is not what is was in the zenith of the days of Rome's rule," he said, "but it has still retained a culture to be envied. The great palace is now crumbling away, but the fort, where we are to stay, is for the most part almost as magnificent as it was in the days of the empire." He commenced a long history of the city that had Galahad lost about half way through.

In truth, the conversation whiled away the time for both of them as the entourage made its slow procession along the great Fosse way, a track known for generations, but widened and levelled by the Roman invaders to provide as much ease of travel as was possible across the southern lands. Galahad himself had picked up part of it as he had made his way down to Arthur's winter court, and he recognized the old mile markers, now mossy and weatherbeaten, ignored by the generations who were already forgetting their Roman origin.

On one occasion, when the sun shone weakly but invitingly, and the terrain had been particularly tedious, Guenevere emerged, clad in a fur cloak whose hood virtually obscured her face, to take a place beside Launcelot on horseback. Galahad fell back and allowed them to speak privately. As he rode on, lost in his own thoughts, a small figure cantered up behind him.

"Are you contemplating the wonders of our first city?" The voice was low, yet honeyed: Nivene. Galahad turned as she came up beside him. She was riding a slim chestnut-brown mare, which somehow suited her own small frame. Like her queen, she, too, was wrapped almost to obscurity in a cloak of fox furs. Only her nose and eyes were visible, but Galahad could see the intention in her face.

"I suppose you have been there before," he said. It was not worth pretending superiority with Nivene; he knew that she would see through it - and let him know as much.

"Indeed - the queen aids the Regissimus in fulfilling the royal obligations to the city, and it has been my pleasure to accompany her on several occasions. The surroundings are not as inviting as at Cataviae, I think, but the river is a sight to behold. The city is considered by some to be the heart of Britannia; it is quite fitting that its pace and atmosphere lends itself to intrigues, especially those of the heart."

She let her foot brush against Galahad's, and he moved his horse slightly ahead. He felt her eyes boring into his back, and knew she was staring at him in amusement. He turned back to face her, but she had already swung her horse around and was engaging a young guard in conversation.

Although he was determined not to appear overawed at the sight of the old city, Galahad could not help drawing breath as they came towards the walls one morning, two days later. They rose, tall and impenetrable, a bulwark of stone; they must be as thick as a man's reach, he thought. What would Pelles not give to be able to fortify his own keep in such a fashion? Around him, by the side of the road that led to the gate, the land was scattered with monuments and stones, most slipping at an angle, many worn away, but a few still standing. Galahad stared at the images: a man in some type of military dress; a relief of a hunt; the head of a youth.

"This is the old graveyard," said Launcelot, beside him. "It is an impressive tribute to our forebears, is it not? They remembered their own ancestors in stone; we choose only songs and memories."

"It seems that songs may last longer than monuments in people's hearts," replied Galahad drily, looking back at the memorials. He reflected on the usual funeral pyres set outside Pelles' gates, always in defiance of Conlaed's plea for burial against the day of Resurrection, and always carrying, in the slightly drunken behaviour of the mourners, a hint of barely suppressed pagan beliefs. Those ways would be a long time dying, he thought.

The party narrowed itself as it came towards the gates, allowing Launcelot and his chief soldiers to form the vanguard. A few men were waiting in battle garb at the entrance. They bowed low to Launcelot, recognizing the standard of the Regissimus at once, and led the way into the city. Galahad felt a pang of trepidation as he passed though the gates, as if he were about to enter another realm. However, what he saw was not in essence foreign from his own world, although its setting was architecturally different and on a scale several times that of his grandfather's kingdom. He observed the same mix of poverty and riches in the streets, whose paving was beginning to crumble under neglect. Many shops and dwellings were of solid brickwork, but others, abandoned or not, were decaying from neglect, and here and there he spied a wooden shelter built among the ruins of a stone house. The people, too, mingled, rich and poor, stopping to stare at the royal cavalcade as it made its way in enforced slowness over the road.

They travelled by the broader straight streets to the fort at the north of Londinium. Enclosed in its own little town within the larger municipality, it stood defiantly at the head of the city it had once ruled, and whose slow apostasy from Roman ways it now witnessed. Galahad followed his father through a narrower but better guarded gate to find himself in a courtyard that was as green as the land outside the grimy city. It was surrounded by a colonnade whose tall pillars were punctuated by neatly pruned trees and which were fronted with neat strips of cultivated earth. Conlaed had told Galahad of the gardens coaxed from the uninviting soil of Aran, and of the ancient, wondrous gardens of past kings, but he had never actually seen earth tilled for anything other than a utilitarian purpose. He wondered who might have the time and skill to perform such a task - were there monks there?

His question was answered in the actions of Guenevere and Launcelot, who now stood side by side, smiling at the approach of two old men who appeared in almost every way a reflection of each other. Each had the same, balding, grey hair, trimmed short against his head, and a reddened and roughened nose and ears which seemed to have grown even as the rest of his face had shrunk. They even walked together in a slightly humped, shuffling manner, and grinned in unison as they bowed before their visitors.

"We are pleased to find you well this winter, and attendant to our needs," said Guenevere, in a manner that was so genuinely pleasant that Galahad was taken aback for a moment.

One of the men replied in a dialect that was a confusing mixture of Latin and British. Galahad followed as best he could.

"Our queen, it is honourable always to have you dwell in our villa. We are caused to live only to its service." The other elderly man nodded vigorously and smiled widely to reveal a mouth almost devoid of teeth.

"Your quarterings are ready, and await your pleasure," he added, and it was the turn of his image to nod in a similar fashion.

They stepped to one side, sweeping their arms ceremoniously in the direction of the buildings. Guenevere and her women moved forward to the right hand side of the courtyard, where they soon disappeared through the colonnades. Launcelot was giving a few cursory orders to his second in command, a burly Welshman, who in turn dispersed the troops and supplies with oath-strewn edicts. Galahad hovered, uncertain of his place now in this new world. His father finally turned back to him and smiled apologetically.

"You must pardon me. We take only our trusted troops and servants with us to Londinium each year, and they are, for the most part, familiar with these environs. Come, Romulus and Remus will show you to some quarters that are a sight more comfortable than those you had on the road, and even in the Regissimus' Great Hall."

"Romulus and Remus?" Galahad repeated awkwardly.

Launcelot laughed. "The old brothers. I do not even think that those are their real names, but they have been answering to them for as long as I can remember. I gather it is some long-forgotten jest. They are the only survivors of the old Roman legions who used to be stationed here, and they have taken it upon themselves to maintain the fort in its past glory, as least as much as their aging bones will allow. There are many acres, yet they tend them all as if they were a troop rather than two elderly men."

One of the brothers returned to hover about Galahad now, smilingly indicating the way he should go. He passed with him through the columns and into a doorway. A small hall was in front of him, neatly paved with red, tessellated tiles. Smaller doorways led off from it, and one of the men pointed forward.

"For the son of the Lord Launcelot," he said, making a small obeisance, and almost being knocked sideways as Samson bounded in, fresh from his lightening inspection of the courtyard. Galahad scowled. Was his own parentage so obvious? He hurried on into the room. It was small but clean, and tiled in a similar manner to that of the hall. In one corner stood a small brazier, and opposite it was a raised pallet decked with blankets and furs. A narrow shelf was balanced above it, upon which sat a lamp and a statuette whose image Galahad did not recognize. He began to thank the man, but he had already hurried on to his next task. Galahad stretched and sat down, and Samson stuck his nose in his master's face, an irritating yet comfortably familiar gesture that settled him again.

In her own room, far more spacious than that of Galahad, the queen was pacing as her women set out the accoutrements that she carried with her: her chest of clothing, a smaller one of jewellery, the cosmetics and lotions with which she staved off time. She was both exercising limbs long-confined to her litter and contemplating her objectives. She always felt a certain relief to be free from Arthur for a period, when he went on his yearly campaigns or she was permitted to make a progress of her own. It was a freedom from an overruling authority, and, though she might not admit it, from a tinge of guilt and resentment that she could not be the queen he had envisaged when he chose her a score of summers ago. She paused in front of the icons placed upon her table: the triple mother goddesses who formed her secret, feminine counterpart to the Trinity of Arthur; Isis, beloved still of many in Londinium and whom she chose to favour while in the city as a guardian of her sojourn; then an image of the Virgin, who, according to the accounts of the monks, retained a perpetual virginity and youth despite being a mortal mother. Guenevere considered each in turn; who would be her best help in her new endeavour?

"My queen." It was the voice of Nivene. Guenevere turned to discover that the other women had left. She relaxed a little, although she did not let her visage change.

"My queen, you wanted to explain my task."

“Yes. I have work of import for you here. How do you judge Galahad?”

Nivene was not surprised by the question, for she had followed her queen’s thoughts for many years, since she was old enough to carry a serving tray steadily before her.

“He is untried, yet he holds some secret desires and horrors which lend him strength.”

“Delve into his innocence, Nivene. You are to seduce him, to make him beholden to you.”

“That may not be the simplest of tasks. He is afraid.”

“Of you?”

“Of women.”

Guenevere allowed the smallest smile to escape from her lips. “That may be true, since he was raised among the wild, northern she-demons.” She mentioned no names, but the hatred was there.

“However,” she continued levelly, “he is about to face a quest that may result in his death, and warriors who are to go into battle are held by a far stronger instinct than that their swords may conquer.” She breathed deeply, feeling again the bruises and pleasure she experienced in meeting this male need.

Nivene nodded. “I shall strive to be successful,” she said. “His defences may be weak in this strange city.”

“Find the breach, Nivene. I need to have him conquered.”

Galahad strode about the courtyard in the early morning light. Romulus and Remus were once again shuffling in and out of sight, tending to matters that he could not fathom, but which seemed to be important to them. Samson was bounding through the colonnades after some cat; Galahad heard his howl as the irate feline turned and, no doubt, sliced his nose with one, vicious swipe. Samson never did learn to avoid cats, for he could not comprehend how so small a creature could be so deadly.

Galahad turned his attention back to his own situation. He had been interested in coming to Londinium, for he had avoided this post on his way to Arthur's court, even though it had added some miles and a more uncomfortable road to his journey. He had not been ready to face the city, and he had not wanted advance warning of his arrival to be conveyed to the king through the messengers he felt sure would be stationed at such a metropolis. And now that he had finally arrived, he was unsure of his role in the city. He had - and desired - no function in the queen's formal meeting with her family, and no position within the small army that was providing the defence of the walls. He must, he decided, find or make his own opportunities here.

Launcelot, also of habit an early riser, even when removing himself from Guenevere's arms, came through into the courtyard.

"Galahad, there is food in the dining room. Come, eat with me." It was not a request, so Galahad followed him to a room which he had not entered yesterday.

"Romulus said that he and his brother have only just been able to coax the furnace into working this morning," said Launcelot casually. Galahad was just beginning to wonder what he meant, when he was struck by the sudden warmth of the room on this cold winter morning, when there was not a brazier in sight. His senses whirled for a moment, then he looked down: the heat was emanating from the floor itself.

Launcelot saw his discomfiture, but acted graciously. "It is the underfloor heating," he explained as if Galahad could immediately understand this reference. "The hot air from the furnace is carried in pipes under the floor. Unfortunately, it no longer works in many rooms, but we have the comfort here, at least."

"I have seen some of the existing Roman accomplishments at Eboracum," said Galahad. "A system for piping water, for instance."

"I think that unless the land is subdued and kept in peace, the skills of the Romans will soon pass from memory. Already, I know that the fort will most likely die with its faithful guardians. Only Arthur," Launcelot added, looking hard at Galahad, "can offer any hope of accomplishing this, and the possession of the Grail would be a great talisman for the Regissimus and for the whole of Britannia."

Galahad inclined his head. He did not feel ready for a debate at this early hour. He directed his gaze instead to the table, which was set simply with baskets of bread and a jug of beer. The warm aroma of the newly-baked loaves made his stomach stir, and he sat down to eat, suddenly hungry. If he were to face this new world, he might as well be fortified.

"...and her family are to arrive in a few days, we think," Launcelot was saying. Galahad had ceased to pay attention, and pulled his concentration back hastily. "I shall be supervising the selection of gifts for them, as well as supplies for the court, and you may come with me. It will be an opportune time to learn a little of the ways of the city."

Galahad's induction into city life was not half as traumatic as he had feared. He had been raised on the edge of civilization, and was accustomed to feeling his way along a route when he knew little more than his destination and the general direction of travel. He had traversed the countryside down to Cataviae with little need to ask for assistance. The city, once he overcame his initial disorientation at an unfamiliar terrain, was in truth little different. As he ran errands with Launcelot and the ubiquitous bodyguards, common, it seemed, to many men of worth in this supposedly neutral town, he soon found a pattern to the city. The purveyors of the more luxurious goods dwelled in the safer areas, the food vendors traded near the roads which passed on through to other towns, and the custodians of crumbling amenities still provided baths and leisure activities near the areas which were home to aristocratic, but no longer affluent, families.

Launcelot suggested that he might take time to choose gifts for his family. "They can be sent up north in the summer campaigns," he said. "Your grandfather's court will be one of the most important stations. I will pay for your purchases, if you wish." Galahad had brought money with him, but had had little occasion to spend it. He decided that he was not averse to using Launcelot's wealth for his own ends.

They were visiting a jeweller's near the ruins of an old basilica. The shop was constructed in the manner that characterized many of the buildings of Londinium: a small, rectangular room whose long side stretched back beyond the street which it faced. Its only light came from the large opening in the shop front, from which a table shelf was suspended. The jeweller was a dark-skinned man with a halting accent, an immigrant from across the seas. He was evidently familiar with Launcelot, though, and greeted him warmly.

"You have more needs, my lord? I have a new consignment from Gaul, one to please the ladies, and gain favours from the men who give them. Come, look." He laid out a handful of pieces before them, and Galahad almost gasped as he looked down at the bracelets and torques, fashioned from beaten gold and inlaid with gleaming ceramic pieces and glass. He picked up a bracelet decorated with green and white ceramics in the shape of an elongated dragon that encircled the band. He thought of his mother, whose hands and slim arms were the one outstanding beauty which remained to her.

"I will take this," he said. The jeweller opened his eyes wide.

"An excellent choice, but it is one of my finer pieces, and the price is not perhaps one that every young man would care to pay, unless it were for his lady-love."

"Or to honour his mother," said Galahad, a little offended, but taking the opportunity to remind his father of Elayne.

"I will pay," said Launcelot shortly. The vendor sensed an argument lying beneath the words of the two men, and chose, in the interests of a sale, to divert a confrontation at his shop.

"There must be other women for whom either of you desire to purchase a gift. Only for those so discerning as to choose such an armlet can I offer these fineries." He brought out two thin, gold head bands, wound with silver wire. Launcelot indicated his interest and one was soon set down next to the bracelet.

"Do you possess any adornments suitable for a northern king?" enquired Launcelot. "The quality of these pieces is worthy of your grandfather," he added quietly to Galahad. Galahad was hesitant; he knew that he had to choose a gift that would indicate to Pelles he was in control of his destiny in this southern kingdom, but one which would not suggest arrogance or independence from the distant king. He gazed, perplexed, at the array of torques and rings laid out before him, and only half-listened to the discussion between Launcelot and the jeweller. A ring would be suitable, he thought. Not too large, yet ornate enough to convey his message. He chose a thick, gold band etched with knotwork and set with smaller bands of turquoise around the outside edges. He tossed it into the pile even as Launcelot and the jeweller were arguing over the merits of another ring. Launcelot stopped and perused it, and after a few further negotiations, the jewellery was carefully wrapped and placed into the hands of a guard.

"Now, who else deserves gifts from your hands?" asked Launcelot. He seemed to be in a jovial mood - perhaps the atmosphere of the city enlivened him, Galahad thought. He decided to risk his next request.

"I have - I had - a tutor from my infancy, a monk from Aran. He is very learned, and I know it would please him more than any earthly thing to possess another manuscript. I understand that these are costly, but I am willing to defray the expense."

"Londinium is not the centre of writing," said Launcelot. "For that, we would have to look to Rome, or your tutor's native Hibernia. But I do believe that there are some manuscripts extant at the fort. Why do you not peruse them - you can read, I infer? - and make a selection. We can send along materials for copying instead."

"Thank you." For a moment, he genuinely felt his words. He wanted to delight - and impress - Conlaed whenever he saw him again.

"Now, is there any other business that you wish to conduct?"

"No," replied Galahad, lying again. He needed to purchase a gift for Drystan, but he knew implicitly that he dare not purchase it with Launcelot's money; it would be as gall to the Pict. He decided to come out alone later.

In fact, he had plenty of chances to slip out virtually unnoticed over the next few days, for the queen's kinsmen arrived at the city, and Launcelot was occupied in overseeing their stay and keeping the various troops from the drink-sodden revelries which would begin in camaraderie, but sink into petty quarrels and fights before returning to a bruised and bleeding friendship, if one were lucky. Galahad took Samson for a better bodyguard than any Arthur's army could provide, and searched the city until he found a dagger he thought the horse-master would appreciate: stout and heavy, the handle set with bone and carved into the shape of a double-headed man. By the time he returned on the day of his purchase, pleased with the gift and with his success in negotiating Londinium's streets and shops, the fort was bustling and smells of a substantial meal were wafting through the courtyard. Samson made for the kitchen; he had already made sufficient acquaintance with the old brothers to merit a dish set permanently outside the door. Galahad saw Nivene approach. She had not met with him since their arrival, and he could not tell whether she was genuinely busy or avoiding him. Her manner, however, revealed nothing of her opinion.

"There is a celebratory meal tonight. You are bidden to dress as the grandson of a king and sit with the family of the queen." She waited for his affirmation, then sauntered away, her hips swaying slightly as she walked.

Launcelot had purchased new clothes for Galahad, so he felt no embarrassment at this command. Back in his room, he selected a blue tunic - a colour which his mother always favoured on him - and wore two modest gold rings as adornment. His eye fell upon a wide, bronze armlet. It was etched around with angular birds, whose eyes were set with red and blue stones, a treasure from Pelles' coffers. He pondered it for a few minutes, placing it around his wrist, taking it off, holding it up to the lamplight, and then finally deciding that he should make a greater show, and leaving it in place He combed his hair and felt to see if his earlier shave had been sufficient. He nodded to himself; he was not given to ostentation, as were many of the elite of Britannia's small kingdoms, but he did not want to suggest that Pelles' splendour was waning. He snuffed his lamp and went out.

The meal was in the small refectory. Some ancient couches had been cleaned and polished, and were placed around the room in a circular fashion. Small tables were set at each place.

"Are those two ancient soldiers ever going to accept the ways of the Britons?" asked a middle-aged warrior in exasperation. "I am wearying of eating like a eunuch rather than a man." He flexed his ring-laden fists in show of his manliness.

"We are to eat as the great generals did," said Launcelot. "Perhaps it will inspire us."

"But where is Rome now? Did she heed our forefathers' pleas for aid against the men from the northern isles?"

"Uncle, do not say anything in their presence," urged Guenevere. "It does not befit us to offend the aged. And see what they have chosen for you." She smiled as she lifted a red bowl, decorated with a once white, now yellowed, relief, which depicted several women in acts of copulation. The older man laughed in a conciliatory tone.

"There is life in them yet! Very well, I agree to be pleasant, though I prefer my hall."

Galahad was seated in a corner of the room, beside some minor cousin who had come for the excitement of the old city, just as he had. He was not over-inclined to make conversation, but he strove for politeness' sake to engage his companion, and they had at least their comparisons of Londinium to share. On hearing Guenevere's uncle complain, he looked down at his own dish. It was similar in hue, though not quite in style; the brothers had evidently gathered together as much of the old tableware as lay uncracked. It showed a soldier, who was facing combat, his arms locked around his weapon, which was an enormous phallus protruding from his loins; the tableware was indisputably gathered for the tastes of army men. Galahad's companion laughed at it in a somewhat adolescent manner, but Galahad placed the dish down in distaste. He had little appetite for his meal. Instead he observed those around him. Launcelot and Guenevere were reclining side by side, sharing a table. Although their attention was ostensibly turned to those on either side of them, their movements indicated that they were acting as couple. Nivene was serving Guenevere's uncle, and deftly avoiding the hand that was raised just a little too high towards her breast as she bent to fill his glass. She glanced in Galahad's direction and offered a brief smile of resignation and friendship. He was taken by surprise, and returned the look without thinking.

The evening passed slowly for Galahad. He had scant interest in the occasion, and his dinner companion, although from a good, fighting family on the Welsh border, had evidently not experienced sufficient combat to harden him into manhood. Galahad found him rather immature, though not lacking in the arts of conversation. They soon lapsed into mutual drinking, which made them more kindly disposed to one another. As the dinner progressed, Galahad noticed in a remote fashion that he was becoming rather inebriated for the first time in months. He seldom dared become drunk in his grandfather's presence, and he had been carefully keeping a level head at Arthur's court. He thought briefly that he should curb his drinking, but then Nivene was at his side, refilling his cup and whispering that he was one of the only trustworthy men in the room. He raised his wine to her and drank deeply in respect.

The served part of the meal drew to an end, and Romulus and Remus, Nivene and a few other women set up the drinking vessels and left the company in private. They sat or reclined, talking comfortably by the light of the oil lamps. Guenevere's young relative slipped out after a serving girl who had been making eyes at him, or at the copious number of rings he wore, and Galahad took his own opportunity to escape. He rose quietly and stepped out into the courtyard. The cold air hit his face and he reeled slightly. He could see Samson's dark shape across the way, by a brazier guarded by a few soldiers who were sharing warmth and scraps. He smiled; that dog was anybody's companion, until they threatened his master, when he would turn like a Judas and rip a limb without thinking.

He turned and walked through the colonnade to the hall where his sleeping quarters were. As he entered, he saw a crack of light coming from his door. He felt for his dagger and, creeping forward, pushed the door quietly. It was Nivene, trimming his lamp.

"I am no assassin," she smiled, seeing his weapon clutched in his hand. He noticed, though, that the outline of a similar weapon was clear under her tunic, resting against her thigh.

"I was not expecting you," he said lamely, concentrating to pull together his befuddled senses. He glanced towards his saddle bag; it lay undisturbed in the corner of the room.

"I assumed that many would find it a little difficult to ready their own rooms tonight. I hope mine is not an unwelcome intrusion. If truth be told, it seemed preferable to do such service than to remain in the presence of certain guests." She sat down on the bed, still smiling innocently. Galahad sat beside her; he could not fathom what he should rather do.

"Soon, you will leave us, for foreign lands and foreign dangers," she sighed. "You have the heart of a true warrior, boldly staring death in the face."

Galahad shifted, but found that he had slid nearer to her. A musky, heady perfume came to his nostrils; he saw the oil gleaming between Nivene's breasts. It mingled with the alcohol and started his head spinning again.

"You need to rest," she said. She leant over and gently placed her hands upon his chest, letting them slide down his tunic as she guided him down to the bed. Her face was close to his, and her black hair was falling over her shoulders, embracing them both in a dark veil. Her fingers found their way under his tunic and lightly stroked his flesh.

"You should not go into danger without knowing the sweet blessing only a woman can bestow," she whispered.

Somewhere at the back of his mind, Galahad knew that he should bid her leave, but the singing in his head and the stirrings in his body urged him to let her continue. She put her mouth softly against his, and he tasted her sweet breath as he returned the pressure. Her kisses slowly grew more insistent, and she paused only to pull his tunic over his body. He put his hands on her sides, letting them migrate to her breasts, which he stroked timidly through her dress. She gave a tiny moan, making him shiver with the excitement of this new power.

Nivene raised herself above him, and guided his hand to lose the laces at the front of her dress. He fumbled, but she laughed quietly, showing her perfect teeth - Lord, why had he not seen before how desirable she was? - and aided him, grasping his fingers and slipping them into her bodice. He felt her secret flesh, traced his fingertips around her swelling breasts; she cupped his hands in hers, pushing them against her. He bent his head to kiss her neck, followed the pulsing vein down to her shoulder while her hands sought his loins and pressed upon them, making him leap to her command. He began to pull up her dress, and she lifted her arms to help him.

He dared not face her body at once, but pulled her to him, burying his head in her hair. He started to kiss her again, on her neck, on her shoulder, looking down at her bare, curved back. He caught sight of a tattoo on her shoulder blade, a mark he had seen before, that he recognized. Galahad started back, his head clearing in an instant. Nivene knelt looking at him, her hair cascading down over her breasts. She smiled, acknowledging his shyness, and leant towards him, but he put out his hand.

"I cannot," he whispered. He closed his eyes and turned his head away, his momentary passion replaced by a revulsion and fear. He remained that way for some time, leaning his head against the cold wall of his room, hoping that when he opened his eyes again the hallucination would have vanished.

"You need not fear, *I* shall tell no one," said Nivene smoothly. Galahad glanced round to see that she was dressed once more, and giving him the ironic smile he more closely associated with her. He watched miserably as she glided from the room; she would blame his impotence, perhaps whisper it abroad, though she claimed otherwise. But - and he shivered, realizing how cold he was devoid of his tunic - he could not couple with her, not with anyone. He closed his eyes again, and wrapped his arms around himself as he murmured a prayer for protection taught him by Conlaed. No, not ever - and least of all with a druidess.

Galahad found his excitement with the city to be tainted those last few days. He derived but a small comfort in examining the remains of the library; it was mostly scraps of writing he knew were not Christian, but he found, tucked away, an epistle. He thought it was part of that of Saint Paul to the Romans, but he had not been as good a student of Scripture memorization as Conlaed had wanted him to be. Still, he knew that the monk would be pleased with his gift, and he rolled it carefully around the wooden dowel which had held another manuscript, and then wrapped it in some rough homespun. Launcelot had been true to his word and purchased some writing materials; Galahad was grudgingly impressed that his father had found time amongst his duties to remember a once-mentioned wish. He had imagined that any spare moments would be filled in the presence of the queen, but the lovers appeared to conjure time itself, for they always looked perfectly fulfilled, yet they were never seen in compromising circumstances.

Nivene had not made any effort to avoid Galahad, though he certainly had attempted to evade her. He had to suffer her presence at mealtimes, as she continued to serve. Her visage never changed as she leaned down to pour his wine of an evening, but he saw laughter in her eyes, and he would redden. Launcelot noticed and thought that Galahad had conceived a liking for her.

"I have advice for you," he said casually one day as they were beginning to supervise the loading of the carts which would take them home. "There are in the world many soft, compliant women in whose arms you could lay your life, and to find one is a prize beyond measure. But, I tell you in confidence, do not trust a certain small, dark-haired beauty. She has knowledge beyond that you could fathom for one of her youth or her sex."

Galahad glowered, though he knew the justness of the counsel.

"I do not have aspirations in that direction, no matter what it may seem. If I appear a little discomposed, it is the result of a small misunderstanding. A *private* matter," he stressed. Launcelot put his hand upon his shoulder. "Do not take offence. But wait. Wait for the moment when you cannot do otherwise than love. Then will you begin to live."

Galahad was relieved finally to leave Londinium. He rode near the head of the entourage, far away from the women, rarely acknowledging others of the party. As he guided his horse slowly across the great Thames bridge, he wondered at the skills which had spanned it and left a monument that still held strong. The river was a mile wide in places, though shallow, and it teamed with life: fish jumping in nets; strange foreign boats bearing merchandise to the great port of Britannia; sea-going vessels of the Saxons whom the citizens warily watched go on their way to other territory. He speculated as to what the city had truly been like in her apex under Roman rule, and whether Arthur could bring sufficient peace to restore her prosperity, as he had to other towns deeper inside his strategic territory. He was still contemplating this question, enjoying a moment of distracting thought, when the company approached a band of travellers along the way.

"Move aside for Queen Guenevere, consort of the Regissimus!" a soldier began to cry. The motley band of riders turned, some looking in amazement, and prepared to pull their steeds to the edges of the way. Galahad stared at them, and started. He kicked his heels and galloped forward to a man on a small horse. They both dismounted, and Galahad clutched him in a tight embrace.

"I am glad to see you," he blurted, sophistication lost in relief.

Conlaed held him at elbow's length, smiling back, though with a searching look in his eye.

"I gather that my arrival has come none too soon," he said.

Chapter Five

Galahad informed Conlaed as best he could of the fortunes that had befallen him since he had last seen the old monk. They rode side by side for much of the progress back to Cataviae; after Galahad had made formal introductions on his tutor's behalf, they were generally left to themselves. No one was overly surprised that King Pelles would have sent a retainer to check upon the condition of his grandson.

"And I did not need much persuasion," explained Conlaed. "Your grandsire sees a connection between our lives, having, in his mind, dedicated me to you since your birth, and, for my part, I was curious to come south. It is almost a generation, I declare, since I have visited the southern realms of the Britons. The wandering Brothers can minister to the king's household as well as I, and the infrequency of enforced services will, no doubt, please many."

Galahad laughed quietly. He was often irritated at the monk's propensity to hold forth with an air of practicality and assurance on any topic, but for the moment, at least, his familiar tones were comforting. He wished he could find words to tell Conlaed of his encounter with Nivene, but he still shied away from voicing the incident and giving it life once more.

Their progress back to Cataviae was slower than their initial journey. Wagons were laden with purchases intended to feed and clothe the household, and luxuries to be given as largesse or enhance the splendor of the court. The guards were increasingly alert as they moved into the territory between Londinium and Cataviae, where towns under the active law-enforcement of a local lord were scarce indeed. On several nights, the safest lodgings were to be found upon a wooded heath where the queen's pavilion could be erected and the men spend the night alternately on duty and snatching sleep around the fires. One such night, Galahad and his tutor were sitting by the campfire after the women were safely ensconced in their tent. They were momentarily alone: the other men were on watch or milling around the camp, checking on horses and supplies, and cleaning equipment before settling in for the evening.

"You have been so full of tales of Londinium," began Conlaed, "that you haven't yet told me of Cataviae. Has it met your expectations - and my description? I have been absent from that world for many years, and much must have changed."

"In general, it is as you guessed, though I could not have imagined the myriad of details - the routines, the alliances, the protocol. Sometimes it is difficult to keep abreast of all the day-to-day realities, let alone anticipate what the next day will bring."

"Has the experience been a good one, though?" The monk was gently probing, offering an opportunity where he saw a need.

Galahad lowered his voice. "It is not always easy to tell friends from enemies, and many forces are at play. Even at this court there are adherents to druidic belief, many of whom have influence, men and women."

"Indeed?" said Conlaed, resisting a backward glance at the entourage. "It is well then to watch your steps. A man who looks to that end for power," (he did not mention Pelles by name), "is, at the last, only as strong as that which finds him, yet a woman can employ other talents of -persuasion - to widen the net of her demonic masters."

Galahad heard the words behind his utterances: I guess something of your troubles, and you need not tell me aloud. He felt somewhat comforted, but still perplexed.

"Yet why does the Regissimus not put an end to it? Is he really unseeing?" he whispered.

Conlaed shook his head, but reassuringly. "Old habits are not easily given over, even in a king's court and among the most illustrious of the land, and a ruler cannot command the wills of his subjects. Yet the great Regissimus is known as the champion of Christ among the Britons. Before you were born, he rode into battle at Badon Hill with the image of our Blessed Virgin on his shield, and many say that they saw her hands raised in benediction as he smote the heathen and drove them from his kingdom."

Galahad nodded; he had heard the songs oft enough: how dragons had flown above Arthur's forces, raining fire down upon their enemies; how Saint Michael himself had been sighted in the heavens, urging the king's men to greater acts of valor.

Launcelot strode up behind them, a quiet smile flickering across his lips as he heard the topic of discussion.

"You were there, my lord, of course," remarked Conlaed, with the deferent forwardness that only one of holy orders might use in front of a nobleman.

"I was, and it was a hard battle. Though I saw not the Virgin give her blessing, we were surely favored of God to have won.

We fought for two days, against the most fearsome alliance of barbarians you could care to name: the Icelingas, Baldulf and Colgrin; King Aesc of Kent; King Aelle of Sussex, and countless other minor kings and rulers. On the first day, we made no inroads upon the barbarian Angles; their pagan shield wall held fast against us. That night, they encamped to a hill, and, though we knew that it was not in our favor to fight uphill, nevertheless we decided to assay an attack.

"We moved before the sun could whisper of our coming, in hopes of finding the Angles unready, but they had anticipated us and were waiting, armed and in formation. We fought on, pushing our way to the level mount of the hill through the blood of our people. Even though we had cheated fortune and won the ascent, the Angles were not to be deterred, and they rallied, standing shoulder to shoulder, ready to grind Arthur's ambitions into the dust with his bones. We had one final hope - the king's own cavalry. He called his horsemen to him under his own banner, and, crying out in the name of the Lord, charged forward into the line of our enemies. They broke as a dam when pushed too far, and the torrent of our troops spilled forward to meet them, man to man.

"Many kings died that day; many kings and many lords died in the days that followed as we hunted them across the land. The price of their defeat was grievous heavy for them, and perhaps those who died were the only fortunate ones. Elsewhere there were exiles, forced migrations, whole settlements razed to the earth. 'It must be made known,' said Arthur to his men, 'that -"

"- 'that judgement has come to the barbarians, that those who do not accept a peace under me will find bloody warfare with me'," finished Conlaed quietly. He looked up to see Launcelot and Galahad staring at him. He smiled ruefully.

"Yes, I was there."

"But the Scots from the Western Isle did not ally with us."

"I am only half Scots, Hibernian, Irish, whatever you may wish to call my people. My father was of that isle, but he traveled to Wales in the company of the son of a defeated nobleman, brought there to live as a hostage for his clan's compliance. My mother was the daughter of a local elder, who fell in love with his dark eyes and wild hair. She gave him her passion and her jewels, and they fled back to his home to marry in defiance of her father, though his prowess as a warrior eventually brought his father-in-law's approbation. So I, too, was a warrior. But this is a digression from our tale. My adventures, though of import to me, are of little interest to this company. Suffice it to say that I swore to the Lord, that if I lived through Badon, I would lay down my sword for him, and I kept my word. But you have not furnished us with the conclusion to your history," he said to Launcelot, "for you have not related how the Regissimus purchased a peace sealed with the blood of the pagan, which has reigned to this day. Mysterious and mighty are the works of the Lord; who can comprehend his ways?"

"Who indeed?" said Launcelot quietly. "When I remember the battles of my youth I wonder why I was destined to wear a badge of honor when so many others now wear a shroud."

The tale had gathered a small crowd of wakeful men to the fire. The watchmen had forgotten their place and were looking with a soldier's respect at this monk, who had fought in the battles that sealed Arthur's early ascendence in Britannia. Even Galahad could not hide the curiosity and awe in his expression when he looked at his old tutor. But the monk would talk no further of his past, neither on the entreaties of his friend nor those of the assembled men.

"I vowed that I would be born again into the service of God," he said. "Had I not been overcome by a weakness in recalling the battle that turned my life to him, I would not have mentioned my history. *Only*," he stressed, "if there is dire need would I recount my past or use those skills I acquired as a soldier. The greatest gift man has to give is to lay down his life for another, not lay another's life down."

With that, Galahad had to be content, though, as he sat looking into the animated pictures sent up by the flames his imagination saw Conlaed in them, traversing land and sea, and fighting with all the famous kings he could recall from the bards' songs.

They made their approach to Cataviae on a winter's afternoon. The sun was showing signs of strengthening, and the occasional bud on a tree, a tiny speck of green against the dark silhouette of branches, signified that winter's reign was drawing to a close. The light, though not full, lay low on the horizon and dazzled the eyes of horses and horsemen alike; man and beast shifted and moved their heads from side to side trying to see the way ahead clearly. Eventually, the fortress grew sufficiently large against the horizon to block out much of the blinding sun, and they were able to relax for a moment before assuming the final poise of a royal cavalcade.

As they reached the slopes of Cataviae, the procession halted that Guenevere might emerge from her litter and take her place on her horse at the head of the company. She was clothed in the finest dress that Londinium had been able to offer: a slim, green-blue tunic embroidered with heavy silver thread at hem and neck. About her forehead she wore a gold and silver band which Galahad recognized from his expeditions with Launcelot; he wondered if it had been a commission or a personal gift. Yet if it was a subtle message for her lover, Guenevere revealed no self-consciousness in her demeanour. She was regal and impassive, like a queen in a tapestry. Her hair, flowing down her back, even resembled silken skeins of thread. Though she had travelled with the company for many days, no man could take his eyes from her. Even Conlaed was unable to disguise his admiration, though he restrained from comment out of respect for Galahad.

They rode on towards the fortress, the spirits of the men lightening or stirring in turmoil as they returned to their beloved women or faced the truth of a new love they had conceived for one of the queen's retinue. Yet all were glad to shake off the dangers of the road and be within the walls of Castellum Cataviae.

Arthur himself stood at the gates ready to receive his queen home. He could not restrain a look of joy as he watched her approach. His battles were his mark in the annals of the bards and monks, but Guenevere was the jewel in his crown of victory. He recalled that day, nigh a score of years ago, when he had waited, as he did now, for her arrival, her first arrival as his queen elect. He had felt almost sick in his stomach as he watched her ride to the gateway, a slim, shining figure as beautiful and composed as a statue, more radiant than the girl he had last seen almost two years before, but whom even then he had claimed as his own. As soon as he took her hand from that of Launcelot, he knew that he was king indeed. Arthur shook himself suddenly; the past was not for kings, and his present was as glorious as he had been able to imagine in those days of youth and promise. He had a blood heir in his sister's infant son, and many worthy men he might adopt. His work would endure.

The company paused as they reached the gate of the keep. Arthur walked forward and held out his hand to Guenevere, which she clasped, bending down to kiss a large ring upon his knuckle. Then, he stretched up both arms, and caught her as she slid deftly from the saddle to the ground. Placing a hand upon his, she turned with him towards the waiting entourage.

"Your servants have performed their duties in exemplary fashion, my lord. We have much for your pleasure, and sought to exalt your name in your demesne."

"We shall hear presently from Lord Launcelot," said Arthur. "Let him see to his men and then show himself in our chambers to give his report." Launcelot bowed.

The keep swelled to a hubbub as people flocked around the returning company, to greet friends, relatives and lovers, to aid in the unloading of the carts, or simply to gain news of Londinium, an unimaginable distance from home for many enslaved to Arthur's service in this place. A young boy wove in and out of the small crowds, making his way to the men on horseback. He grinned as he caught sight of Galahad, and waved enthusiastically. Galahad steered his horse towards him, and, leaning over, caught him up into the saddle.

"It is good to see you back at Cataviae, Oswald. How have you been faring?" he smiled, watching as the boy fingered the new, stamped leather reins that Galahad had been given, another gift from Launcelot.

"Oh, as well as I might, under such rule as I am subjected to," said Oswald in such a martyred tone that the older youth had to keep himself from laughing.

"You do not appear to have receive overly harsh treatment," he said diplomatically, "though I am sure that your trials were hard enough."

"I am only thankful that the Lord Perceval is at present in contemplation at Glastonbury, or I might be in trouble for leaving weapons practice."

Galahad jumped down from the horse, leaving Oswald to ride alone as he walked beside him. The boy sat up straight, glancing around to see if any of his contemporaries could see him riding the horse of Launcelot's son, the Grail questor. To his satisfaction, one or two did. He rode on at a leisurely pace beside Galahad, chatting unselfconsciously about the minutiae of his life.

Galahad had momentarily forgotten Nivene, and was unaware that she was riding close behind them. She was ostensibly facing ahead, but her eyes were darting around the courtyard. In the entrance of the Great Hall, she espied the shadow she had been seeking. Suppressing a shudder, she fixed her face into a smile reminiscent of that of Guenevere, and lightly kicked her heels into her horse's flank, moving forward to the stables.

Although Cataviae was only slightly less foreign a place to Galahad than Londinium, he found himself relieved to be back at the fortress. Londinium was a city where intrigue and diplomacy could not be avoided; at least here he could choose to be a plain soldier and find a routine of discipline in the daily exercises exacted from him by Launcelot or one of the cavalry leaders. He felt an added comfort in the presence of Conlaed, whose measured judgement he valued. The monk treated him more as a peer than a pupil now, and even though Galahad knew that he was in truth the old man's social superior, he was nevertheless aware of his own intellectual and moral inferiority, and of his need for him. It was a great regret to him that he could not persuade Conlaed to stay at Cataviae with him; the monk preferred to move on to Glastonbury within a few days.

"I spent much time there at Glastonbury during my days as a novice," he said by way of explanation, "and I have a desire to see if any of my fellow monastics from that era still dwell there. This is a soldier's world; there is no obvious place here for another monk, and, as soon as I have the lie of the court, I will leave. My presence at Glastonbury will also give you an opportunity to retreat," he added, though he did not say from what.

Still, for the time being, at least, Conlaed was with him, watching and discerning, and keeping a fatherly eye upon the servant who had travelled with him, a stocky, swarthy Pict by name of Talorc. Although Talorc had Drystan's colouring, he had none of the horsemaster's tersely reticent nature, and was wandering the keep cheerfully, insinuating himself with all the groups that made up the underclass of Arthur's court: foot soldiers, house slaves and even the washerwomen. Of the latter, one young Saxon girl in particular was taken with him, and would be ready with some teasing remark whenever he appeared. When this was pointed out to him by Conlaed, Galahad realized, to his amusement, that it was one of the very girls who had affected to swoon over the blond, slim Perceval.

But she would not have sighed so readily had she seen Lord Perceval on his return to the keep. He arrived back two days after the Londinium party, slipping quietly through the gate with a few men. Galahad's first knowledge of his reappearance came by chance. He and Conlaed were making a visit to the small chapel in the hopes of finding a writing desk of some description, that the monk might begin the transcription of the text he had very gratefully received. He had already made extensive tours of the keep, apart from the area which contained the armoury and training grounds, and he wished, he said, to do something useful.

As they entered the chamber from the brighter light outside, it took a minute or two for their eyesight to adjust to the room, with its small windows and lamplight. Blinking, Galahad realized that two other men, not monks, were already there, sitting on a narrow bench which lined one wall. When he finally focussed, it was difficult to hold his expression. It was Launcelot and Perceval, but Perceval had shorn his blond curls, and his skull was nearly visible under the short stubble that remained. He had clearly been fasting, too, for he was no longer merely slim, but sinewy as a willow tree; lack of food had evidently not interfered with intense physical training.

"You need not wonder at what you behold." Perceval struck first, disarming Galahad. "It is only fitting that preparation be made for such a task as lies ahead of us. I would advise that you, too, arm yourself for both the spiritual and physical rigours of the journey."

"He has at least been excelling in the latter; had he been remaining here, he would be assured of a place in the cavalry." Perceval raised his eyebrows at this hint of praise from Launcelot, but made no comment.

"And that is what we shall need. We were in fact," Perceval explained to Galahad, "discussing who shall travel with us. We have decided that trained cavalry is our best option."

Galahad was in truth relieved to find them, for, since meeting with Conlaed, he had formed a mission in his mind and had been awaiting the moment to reveal it. Despite that, he could not quite chose to ignore the slight of his exclusion from the discussion.

"I did not expect to find you designing strategy in the chapel," he said levelly.

"There are few private places at a king's court. Given our business, it does not seem irreligious to choose such a place," replied Launcelot. He looked behind Galahad to the figure of Conlaed.

"Perceval, this is my son's companion, Brother Conlaed, from King Pelles' court."

Perceval nodded at him. Galahad took his opportunity.

"He has experience as a soldier, and he is schooled in the customs and languages of many kingdoms. He would be an aid to our party, and I believe he should journey with us - if he so wishes." He spoke quickly, afraid he might not be able to finish if he hesitated. He glanced back at Conlaed, whom he trusted had read his mind; the monk did not look surprised.

"Only those who have proved themselves worthy can be our companions," replied Perceval. "Yet if Lord Launcelot is satisfied, then I am certain I will be also."

Galahad flushed on Conlaed's behalf. "He will give you satisfaction."

"My lord," said Conlaed gently, "I have fought and prayed all my life. I choose now the latter, but I am still able to perform the former, though my soldiering days took place during your boyhood. Simon the Zealot was adjudged worthy to be an apostle; so might I venture with you."

"If you fight with the sword as you fight with words, you will outstrip us all," observed Perceval drily.

"We would welcome your experience," added Launcelot.

Perceval had changed subtly, Galahad thought. There was an edge to his character, sharper than before; whether of fanaticism, battle-readiness or a combination of both, he could not measure. Yet Galahad also understood even now that he would rather travel with such a man than two score boon companions.

However, his satisfaction at gaining the companionship of his tutor was short-lived. As they reemerged from the chapel, their quest for the desk momentarily abandoned, Conlaed put a hand upon his arm.

"I think that the time has come for me to prepare myself within the walls of a religious community once more. I intend to move to Glastonbury until the day of the quest draws close. I thought that you might be amenable to accompanying me; it never does the soul of a secular man harm to seek time with monastics."

Galahad was disappointed, but he heard more than suggestion in the voice of his tutor. This, coupled with gratitude at Conlaed's unarguing acceptance of his request, forced him to acquiesce.

"I am always glad to journey with you, however near or far, though I suppose that you know the way of old."

"Very much of old," replied Conlaed, "and the landscape has changed somewhat with prolonged settlement, but, yes, I have recollections of the road. It is a simple enough journey, but always more pleasant with a companion."

"Are you going to leave Talorc behind? I do not think he has shown any inkling for the monastic life." The Pict was now openly courting the favours of the little Saxon laundress.

"I agree; it will do you no harm to have a man of your own here, and he is a competent guard, however lax he may appear."

"I did not think I had created enough enemies to warrant watching my back."

"You do not have to create enemies to gain them," replied the monk.

They set out the next morning for the Glastonbury community. Although the harshness of winter was waning, it had been replaced by a persistent cold dampness, and the two were chilled, despite their thick cloaks. Steam rose from their horses' nostrils to merge into the light mist that moved across the road from the surrounding marshlands. Both men sat a little uneasily, wary of the fact that their vision was limited, though they expected the way to be safe. Samson trotted in and out of view, his ears pricked, his nose ready for each new scent.

Galahad and Conlaed spoke sparingly and quietly on the way. The monk was preoccupied, remembering, as he admitted to his former pupil, his previous sojourn at the monastery.

"A generation of monks has passed through its walls since I was a young novice at Glastonbury, and I suppose that many of my Brothers have moved on, or been translated to Paradise. Yet I cannot but hope that one or two remain, to affirm for me my link with such a holy place."

"But why did you go to Glastonbury, Brother Conlaed?" asked Galahad curiously. "It is so far from Aran and your home."

"I told you that I gave vows at the end of my service as a warrior. In the zeal of a new convert, I sought the nearest community that would accept me, that I might arrive in my homeland a soldier of the faith rather than the sword. As I was completing my duties after Badon, I met with a Brother on the road, who was returning south to Glastonbury, and I took my place beside him. So, it was the site of my novitiate, and of the few years I passed in preparation before I was judged fit to be sent on the longer journey to the land of my fathers. It was only there at Glastonbury that I learned to read and write, and found an aptitude for the stillness of study that I would not have believed possible in one who had been a man of such action. That was my personal miracle, my transformation, and I owe it to the Brothers whose mutual prayers made it manifest."

It was difficult for Galahad to imagine a conversion from a life of activity such as he loved, to one of willing passivity. Although he had learned to wait when absolutely necessary, it was only in order to judge the correct time to strike, be it at the hunt or in battle. 'Be still and know that I am God' was an aphorism Conlaed had often directed at him by way of admonition. His tutor had known him all his life, he thought, and yet he himself had seen only a fraction of that man who was his spiritual and, often, practical father.

Their mutual reveries took them most of the way to the hills that, surrounded by the marshes that rose and fell with the seasons, made a virtual island of Glastonbury and the surrounding lands. A few wisps of smoke shaded the mist as they rose above the rough earthen bank which served as a boundary for the monastery. Conlaed's visage was a blend of happiness and trepidation as they began to climb. Galahad, mindful of where he was approaching, called Samson softly to his side, and the dog, weary from the long walk, fell quite willingly into step beside his horse. They stopped at the entrance, though it was not guarded, and waited patiently for a monk to become aware of their presence. A young man was nearby, feeding some chickens. He looked up and smiled at them, then finished emptying his basket of scraps before placing it carefully upon the floor and walking towards the travellers. He bowed low.

"What may our community offer you?" he asked. His voice was even, indicating politeness but no curiosity; the monks were accustomed to all types of people coming to their door: nuns, warriors, royalty, even a few repentant brigands.

"I am Brother Conlaed, of the court of King Pelles, formerly of Aran - and first of this community," said the older monk. "I am on business at the court of the Regissimus, and desire to spend some time in contemplation here. My companion is the grandson of King Pelles, and has accompanied me on my journey."

The younger monk's smile broadened.

"A Brother is always particularly welcome in the Lord's name, and I remember the young prince from the king's service at Yuletide. I am Brother Coroticus. Our Father Abbot will be pleased to meet with you."

He pushed open the small gate and stood aside to let the two men in. Once inside the community, they dismounted. Coroticus directed them to where their horses could be refreshed and tied, and waited while they briefly rubbed them down and led them to the trough. Then, he indicated that they follow him across the modest courtyard, flanked by chicken coops and a pig sty, a humble entrance to the church Galahad had attended some months earlier. He had hardly noticed these details back then, he thought, when the scene was filled with the foreign splendour of the court. Coroticus led them to one of the larger building interspersed among the huts. He stood respectfully by the door for a few moments before knocking. A voice indicated that they should enter, and he led the way inside. He briefly introduced them, and then left about his business.

Galahad ducked slightly as he came through the small entrance. Inside, thc single room was sparsely furnished, but was, as far as he could see in the dim light that came from a small chimney opening and various candles scattered about, clean and solid. The earthen floor had been covered with boards, and a small dais along the north edge served as a sleeping area. A sturdy, unembellished table and three chairs took up much of the room, and a single book lay neatly on a small shelf. The abbot stood ready to greet them.

"It is good to meet one who is of our fellowship of old. I confess that I have been father of this community but ten years, come from Tintagel, but we have Brothers who may have been your contemporaries. We shall meet with them anon, but first you must tell me the intention of your visit."

Briefly, Conlaed repeated his mission.

"Indeed, a time of preparation is warranted for such a task," said the abbot. "This young man has already received our blessing, and is welcome to stay and receive instruction also. The Lord Perceval," he smiled, "has as you know just left us, but he is almost as much a tutor to us as we are to him."

"He will, I expect, spend some time among us," said Conlaed, answering to save Galahad awkwardness, "but his chief practical duties will lie at the court of the Regissimus. However, he is my pupil of recent years and I know that he will see the necessity for spiritual as well as bodily readiness."

"Well, as pleased as I am to meet with you, and eager, also, as I am to learn of Aran and your experiences, I know that you yourself must desire to search out any companions of your days here. Follow me, and we shall see where our older Brothers are at work."

They followed him out of the dwelling, to discover that the world around them was at last illumined by a thin band of daylight pervading the thinning mist.

"The scriptorium first, I think," said the abbot. He walked the small distance across the path worn in the grass to another of the larger buildings. As they entered, Galahad saw that this one was better served by natural and artificial light, and had a table that took up its length, set with small sloping desks at which a few monks were engaged in the painstakingly slow business of copying texts set out before them. A bent old man was moving from place to place, nodding, encouraging and correcting. Conlaed hesitated, not wanting to supercede the abbot, but the old man turned to them first. He stared hard at Conlaed for a moment.

"Brother Conlaed? Or have my years clouded my perception of your face?"

"No, indeed." They came forward to meet in an embrace.

"Brother David, I am glad to see you still at the task which you taught me so well."

"The Lord has blessed me; my back is bowed, but my hands suffer none of the pain we are to expect in old age. I am past three score years and ten, and I am still permitted to serve him as best befits my talent. And do you still practice what I taught you?"

Hearing the tone Conlaed so often used with him, Galahad was amused - and enlightened. He realized that he was staring at the old man and checked himself, but no one had noticed, absorbed as they were in their reunion.

"I cannot write as often as I would," Conlaed was saying, "though I rose to be an assistant in the scriptorium at Aran. Life at Pelles' court gives me periodic cause to write, and I copy when I can. I have brought some materials with me, discovered at Londinium by my former pupil." He indicated Galahad, who bowed slightly, hoping he would not be called to answer for himself.

"Well, it is a good thing that you will be able to copy under my eye. I have no doubt that lack of practice has marred your hand, which was quite remarkable by the time you left my tuition." Galahad could not help smirking, but even Conlaed was enjoying the admonition.

"Now Brother David," said the abbot. "You perhaps can tell us. Who else if anyone remains from this Brother's days with our community?"

The old man scowled and scratched his head.

"Well now, let me see. We were a small people back then, and a migrant one, too. Brother Finton?" Conlaed shook his head. "I think - Brother Lucius and Brother Owein?"

"Owein of Gwynedd?"

Brother David nodded.

"Then we shall lead you to meet with them," said the abbot. "Brother Lucius is in charge of our cooking, but Brother Owein, alas, is unable to do much by way of physical work. However, he still serves us with prayer, and he supervises the kitchen gardens; you may see him there at this time of day."

"Do you wish me to remain behind?" Galahad said in a low voice. "A first reunion should be private; I would not want to stand between you and your friends."

"I want my old companions to see the young man who has been my life's work for these sixteen years, but I understand - it is awkward to stand and watch old men dragging up a past you cannot share. No, no," he added, stopping Galahad's protest, "there is no offense. Why do you not apply yourself to lodging for us? There will be time enough to make these introductions."

So it was arranged, and Galahad was sent with another monk, Brother Gildas from the scriptorium, to ready a room while Conlaed went in search of his past.

"There is a vacant dwelling suitable for a Brother of our rule," said the young monk anxiously as he trotted across the courtyard. He must be my age, thought Galahad, but no one could mistake us for companions. The monk was thin and somewhat pale, and looked as if he had already spent some years being bent under the monastic rule. Galahad could not resist a circumspect inquiry.

"About seven years now, as I reckon it," Gildas said in reply to his question. "My parents thought it best, and it has been so for me."

Galahad rather considered that the boy's parents had thought him useless for all else, or an expendable part of a burgeoning family, but he attempted to check his thoughts - he was after all on sacred ground, and who knows what divine curse might strike a sacrilegious man in such a place? He pulled his attention back to the young monk, who was addressing him again.

"Are you in need of a dwelling such as we reserve for noble visitors?"

"I will be here but a few days. I can share the floor of Brother Conlaed's cell if he does not object."

The monk looked relieved to be spared the trouble. He led Galahad past the church again towards the small group of huts that served as the individual homes of the monks. They varied in age, though not essentially in style: small, rounded, wattle and daub structures, simple, but sturdy in construction.

"It is modest, but if you are accustomed to bearing some privations, you will be dry enough," and he ducked under a small doorway into a hut. Galahad followed. He was correct: there would not be much room for the two of them, but the tiny home looked to be soundly waterproof and almost sweetly clean. He thanked the Brother, who appeared glad to abdicate his task and scurry back to the safety and relative grandeur of the scriptorium.

Galahad put down the saddlebag he had been carrying over his shoulder, and emptied the contents onto the single low pallet. The scent of beeswax pervaded the hut; Conlaed had packed his own candles, it seemed. An odd gesture, thought Galahad, yet undoubtedly preferable to the faintly rancid stumps of tallow that sat stolidly on the ledge that served as a shelf. The bag also yielded quills, a tightly rolled sheet, a few bags of dried herbs, and a knife. Galahad arranged and rearranged these few objects several times by way of marking the minutes until he might seek his tutor again. He had just given up playing with them when Samson bounded in and almost crashed into the opposite wall, sending the contents of the hut flying with the impact. He whirled around, his large paws tripping over the bag, and leapt up excitedly at Galahad.

"There is definitely not room for you in here," said his master, pushing him fondly to the ground. "Let us see where Conlaed is."

The dog pricked up his ears at the recognizable word, and trotted out again. Galahad followed, and took a quick survey of his surroundings. The settlement was small, though one could see the minute sprawl of its growth that infringed on the basic orderliness of its pattern. The huts were clustered together in this western portion, and the church and courtyard lay to the east. To the south, some small gardens and a kitchen were being tended by monks bent assiduously over their task. Galahad caught up with Conlaed as he was exiting the refectory.

"Did you meet with the others?"

"Yes, and a goodly sight it was to behold their faces. I shall find true rest here until it is time to go across the seas. Perhaps I shall return for my final years. I apologize," he smiled. "Meeting with old friends and learning of the deaths of so many others pushes my thoughts beyond this life. I have many years and many blessings to anticipate, and you have more. Let us live in the present. Did you arrange our quarters?"

"Well, I arranged them," began Galahad, and they moved on, sharing their stories.

The few days Galahad spent at the monastery passed in the blinking of an eye, he thought, as he and Conlaed stood at the gate that morning, saying their farewells. He had found himself slipping into the monastic routine with surprising ease, for there were always men happy to take an extra pair of hands and put them to use repairing a building or turning over the earth. There was the scriptorium, too, a fascinating place, not least because Galahad had still not stopped delighting in the discovery of his tutor's own master. The monks were busy copying out the gospel of John "to send to the brothers at Tintagel" as Gildas had explained, not overly pleased at being interrupted. Still, Galahad knew that he could not have stood the rule for his whole life; he even wondered at Conlaed, autonomous for so long at his grandfather's court, who now rejoiced in humbling himself before his brothers.

"You must remember the discipline you have experienced here, and carry it with you through your next few weeks at Arthur's court," said Conlaed in his tutorial tone. Galahad embraced him, grinning.

"Like Brother David, will you never stop teaching me?" he asked.

"Never," smiled Conlaed. "You may have a tutor no longer, but you are still capable of learning from an old friend. Take care," he added.

Galahad mounted his own horse, and kicked its flanks lightly. It set off, leading Conlaed's horse which was tied behind it. Samson trotted alongside as they left the monastery. It was a clear day in contrast to his arrival, and he could see almost to Arthur's keep. This spurred him on, and he covered the miles swiftly. When he entered the gates of Cataviae, Galahad discovered that the court had taken on a peripatetic air once more, as small groups prepared to make their progresses around the kingdom, or bands of warriors from neighbouring lands stopped to pay homage before the season for missions further afield, and ask protection or renew alliances. Some faces he recognized from the Yuletide gathering, others were new, but all took on a different context now that he felt a familiarity with the workings of Arthur's court.

Launcelot affected pleasure at his return, though he remained more absorbed in the business of organizing the ranks of cavalry and aiding government than in his newly found son. Galahad did not seek his company much outside of military drills, whose enjoyment had not yet faded for him. Both Launcelot and Perceval remained infuriatingly calm and silent on the question of their journey. Launcelot informed him that conditions were not yet right; Perceval told him to pray for patience and let himself grow as he waited.

He was seated next to Perceval one evening at the meal, his favoured place now that Eldol had moved on. He found the man's fanaticism oddly reassuring in a court where little - words, deeds, or gestures - had but a single meaning. Perceval's hair had begun to grow out again, but his face still had the gaunt appearance of one who perpetually fasted. The court, save for a few close companions, treated him with respectful reticence, which he seemed to prefer. Bors, one of the former, felt no imperative to cease his jovial baiting.

"Lord Perceval, you should not give locks of hair to every woman who desires to cast a love spell over you!" He rubbed Perceval's scalped and grinned.

"I think, my lord, that you have worn yours out in the same endeavour," he replied, with but the hint of a smile. Bors, whose head was almost as smooth as an egg, guffawed appreciatively.

"They pull it out by the fistful," he boasted, "is that not so?" He turned to Nivene who was serving wine and beer at the head table, and his eyes lingered a few moments on her breasts, rising provocatively from her tightly-laced dress.

"My lord, I never get through the throng to try," she said as she moved deftly out of reach of his hands. She moved along to Galahad's place, and leant over him as she poured the wine.

"Meet me tonight," she whispered, without catching his eye. "Forgive me, and aid me."

Galahad made no reply. She slowed her pouring. "Merlin wants the Grail for his own. I can stop him if you will be my ally. I need you, my lord."

Only for a moment did Galahad feel the pull of her smooth entreaty; then the truth of what she was filled his senses, and he stared down at his trencher. He did not believe for a minute that aiding the Grail quest was her purpose, and he did not wish to know what was. "No," he muttered firmly. Nivene made no reply, but drew herself upright and continued down the table.

Galahad watched from the corner of his eye as she paused by the seat of Bor's son, Aeneas (Galahad had finally discovered his name, and its irony was not lost on him). The youth was already showing the signs of favouring his father, physically at least, and developing a lecherousness and corpulence checked only by hard fighting. Nivene's hair fell over his shoulder as she poured his ale, her head turned close to his face. He did not think to hide his look of lust, though Nivene retained an aura of innocence.

Galahad was not alone in watching Nivene's progress. Merlin was following her with his eyes as he sat, slowly rotating his cup upon the table. When she approached, he indicated that he wanted a drink. As she bent down by him, he caught her arm with his hand. Galahad divined no outward pressure from Merlin's gnarled fingers, but he saw Nivene's face grow pale and her body stiffen against pain.

"She has chosen her game," said Perceval low in his ear. Galahad pulled himself up; he had not realized that his thoughts had been manifested.

"It matters not to me," he replied, also low. Perceval nodded approvingly. Aeneas was smirking in anticipation, making little effort to conceal his ambitions for later that night. If it had been another, Galahad might have thought to warn him, but instead he allowed himself a small smile of satisfaction. "Vengeance is mine, sayeth the Lord" - this was what Conlaed would say when Galahad wanted to act the angry young prince and punish a servant for some slight. There was a particular pleasure in knowing that the weapon of divine retribution would be that which had sought to wound him.

The feasting was heavier than usual that night, for the leader of Viroconium Cornoviorum, an important power in West Britannia, was being entertained. Many warriors, including Bors, had slumped across the table before Arthur and Guenevere had retired to their quarters. Perceval left as soon as the Regissimus had gone, rising soberly from his seat. Launcelot rose too, though less steadily than his friend. He was still handsome, even when in his cups, not suffering from the flushed skin and slack features that beset so many others.

The two older men strode across the hall, letting others hasten to make a way for them. They left in the direction of their quarters, preoccupied with a reflective conversation. Galahad looked up from his own discussion with another youth, but he no longer felt continual resentment at his exclusion from their comradeship; he knew it posed no threat to him. Across from him, Aeneas also looked up, and hauled himself groggily to his feet. From the grin upon his face, Galahad knew whom he had spied. He could not help glancing over his shoulder in the direction of the door. A slim shadow stood in a corner of the threshold, holding a small flagon. Aeneas stumbled towards it, falling over a sleeping soldier on the way. He reached the door, his shadow obscuring that of the woman, and in a minute, both were gone into the night.

Galahad slowly drained his cup before quietly slipping from the head table. Only a few men around the hall were still awake, engaged in drinking challenges or deep in earnest, drink-sodden conversation. Others had found a space along the sides of the hall, wrapped their cloaks around themselves, and fallen into an exhausted sleep. A few were in dark corners, and the surreptitious noises that emanated from there indicated furtive copulation with some serving woman or paramour. But Galahad was used to such scenes from his own grandfather's hall, and he picked his way across the crowd, barely registering the acts unfolding before him.

Outside the hall, he gave a low whistle. Soon, a muzzle was thrust into his side from behind him, and Samson's reassuring face was staring up at him. The cooler air and the late hour had jolted Galahad beyond tiredness, and he suddenly felt the need for some space after the confines of Londinium and the monastery. He made his way to the gatehouse, his dog trotting at his side, sensing some new excitement. They greeted the guard and slipped through the gate which he cracked open for them.

Samson immediately began bounding down the side of the slope in the direction they had taken for the stag hunt. Galahad followed on, his strides gaining momentum as he went down the incline. The moon was a pearl in the sky, full and luminous, and Galahad had no trouble in marking his course.

Freed from the urgency that had accompanied the hunt, Galahad was able to absorb his surroundings. He passed lightly over the plain which had held the winter encampment, and made his way towards the wooded lands. They bore only a poor resemblance to the great forests of his home, but they still offered concealment and stillness. To Samson, the woods offered a rabbit, or perhaps a badger; the dog delighted in the perilous combat offered by this long-clawed, sharp-toothed woodsman. More than once, he had been the bloodied victor of such a battle.

At this hour, the woodland was at its quietest. The predating owls and foxes had found their meals, or retreated, hungry, for rest, and the smaller creatures of the night had followed suit. Dawn had not yet enticed most of the day's animals from their nests and dens. Still, Samson snuffled through the rotting leaves hopefully, trying to find a trail that held promise. Galahad picked his way along a small path worn through the undergrowth, outwardly alert for disturbances, but inwardly contemplative.

He was, though he would not have admitted it, even to Conlaed, weary of this slow game of diplomacy and conspiracy. That Launcelot and Perceval, two such seasoned warriors, could wait so patiently upon circumstances they never seemed to wholly explain to him, was the cause of much frustration. He had been schooled by the tormented years of his childhood to appear impassive to events, but the multitudinous intrigues of a large court were a strain upon his resources. Perhaps, he thought, his old tutor had been wise to establish a haven outside Arthur's domain.

In front of him, Samson pounced upon a grass snake, but it wriggled from between his great paws and darted into the undergrowth. The dog barked after it a few times, then turned his attention to other scents. Galahad glanced up; the trees were not as tall as those of his beloved retreat of the north, but their bare branches were sufficiently tangled to form a screen through which the dying night broke intermittently upon the woods. This at least was a was a place which held no mysteries, thought Galahad, looking ahead through the tessellation of light and darkness. He continued on until he found a large, felled oak blocking the narrow pathway. Samson had leapt upon it and was balancing unsteadily, his toes splayed out over the curve of the trunk. Galahad reached up and gave the dog's head a rough scratch. Then, sitting down, he placed his back against the wood, feeling its rough firmness through his thick cloak. He closed his eyes to think, but in a few minutes he had drifted into a light but dreamless slumber.

Galahad was roused from his brief sleep by Samson, who had jumped back to his side of the wood, and begun turning over the leaves with his muzzle, flicking damp fragments up into Galahad's face. It was not yet dawn, but the deep blue of the night sky had begun to pale. Galahad was in a buoyant mood now; as always, the forest lent him a momentary freedom. He stretched up a little as he stood, and adjusted his cloak about him before heading back towards Cataviae.

It was as they neared the slope that they saw two other figures emerge from the far end of the keep, obviously cognizant of some exit with which Galahad was not familiar. Instinctively, he fell down upon his stomach, and Samson, accustomed to his master's ways, followed suit. As he peered through the grass, Galahad spied the same slim figure that had enticed Bor's son the night before. However, the person who accompanied her could not be her new lover, or whatever had become of him. It was taller, yet slightly stooped, and lacked the bulk of the young warrior: Merlin, Galahad decided. The old man carried a rod with him, while a small sack was slung over Nivene's shoulder. They were travelling in the opposite direction from Galahad, and soon slipped out of sight.

Cautiously, Galahad raised his head and shoulders, then stood once more. He did not need to wonder about the business of druids in the full spring moon. He understood Merlin's ways, more so than many other members of the court. He believed with Nivene that Merlin wanted the Grail, that he had allowed Galahad to live because he thought the young man was a means to gain it, and, fearful though this knowledge was, it still perturbed him less than the personal evil he had left behind. He re-entered the gates and circled towards the rear of the settlement, where Launcelot, Perceval and a few others had chosen to raise their tents and avoid the noisomeness of the Great Hall. An old Roman custom, Galahad thought, but one which had not survived long in the bitter north. As he reached the tent he shared with Launcelot, he could hear the murmurings of Perceval's predawn prayers. Suddenly, he felt tired again. He made a short answer to Launcelot's sleepy query, and fell down upon his pallet, finding a sounder sleep than before.

He awoke for a second time, almost shamefully late, to find the keep buzzing around him. He put his head from the tent, and caught sight of his Pictish servant chatting nearby. He called out to him.

"What goes on?"

"My lord," said Talorc, relishing his role as informant, "news of wonder: Merlin has disappeared."

Chapter Six

In all his time at Cataviae, Galahad had never seen the keep in disorder, even when it had been host to hundreds of warriors. Now, it seemed that work had been suspended, as all, from the washerwomen to the earls, stood in groups debating the disappearance of Arthur's adviser. As Galahad walked towards the weapons store and training ground, he caught snatches of theories, from murder to faery abduction, from assignations with Satan to betrayal of the Regissimus. But he knew, and his head was pounding, not from drink, but from the knowledge of the choice he had to make.

Neither Launcelot nor Perceval were to be found near the training ground. Instead, Galahad was waylaid by his peers, who were holding their own council. Some displayed the level judgement of their elders; others betrayed an immaturity that Galahad found irritating. Aeneas was one of the latter. Looking decidedly dishevelled, he was nevertheless attempting to claim a voice in the fray.

"Merlin was taken by the demons he calls gods; many saw the fire flash from the mount this morning - they took him into their hell."

"Sunlight is not hellfire," said another, more soberly, "but he may have mortal abductors. Now, son of Launcelot," he said, turning to Galahad, "what say you?"

Galahad was startled for a moment at this deference to a position he had not assumed. He drew a breath: speak, but say nothing, he thought.

"Do any report seeing his departure? Were there no mysterious circumstances of the night?" He hoped that another would have seen what he did and the burden might pass from him.

"None that we can glean, but there are ways out from this keep known to none but the king, and perhaps Merlin. It is said that secret tunnels were constructed when it was raised, and the builders afterward put to death to hide their knowledge."

"And why would Merlin venture out from them if not to make a pact with the devil or his minions?" asked Aeneas, angry at being dismissed.

"Did not you make a pact with a demoness last night?" said another youth tauntingly. "Did you not take Merlin's mistress? Why might we not think that you killed him over it?"

Aeneas flushed deeply.

"She's more a bitch than a demoness, not worth spitting on a man for, let alone killing."

Several youths jeered maliciously.

"Gave you a hard night, did she? Perhaps she thought your father would be a better ride."

"A few more jibes and there will be a real body for the lawmen to find," said Aeneas, pulling his dagger from its sheath. The taunts died down amid a few grudging remarks, and returned to the matter at hand. Galahad, glad of the diversion, slipped away and made for the Great Hall. Most of the older warriors were in informal council, but his father was nowhere to be seen. He did catch sight of Oswald, though, lurking in the shadows of the doorway. He beckoned, and the boy came readily into the light.

"Lords Perceval and Launcelot are in private session with the king," he answered to Galahad's question. "I think a few others are with them."

"What truth is known?" Oswald listened well to his elders' business, and was too much in awe of his friendship with the older youth to conceal his discoveries.

"My lords were talking briefly as they left for Arthur's quarters. No one can be found who saw Lord Merlin last night, but they think it has to do with his following of the Old Ones, though the king," he paused and continued in a lower voice, "he does not acknowledge these practices to exist in his court. And they were talking of those associated with him, especially the dark-haired one, the Lady - the Lady - "

"- Nivene?"

"Yes, that's her, but then someone said that she had been..." Oswald trailed off again, shy of making reference to the act.

"She was in the company of another?" asked Galahad helpfully.

"Yes, yes, and then they were gone from my hearing. Is it true, my lord? Is he murdered?"

"We do not yet know that. Perhaps he will return and make fools of all the gossips," said Galahad, though he did not believe his words. He was relieved, though, to find that Launcelot was not accessible, for he could justify delaying his decision.

"What should I do?" Oswald was still at his elbow, eager to be of assistance.

"Keep watch, and keep quiet; that is the way to learn." And perhaps, he thought, that should be his own maxim until he knew the certainty of his suppositions. He smacked Oswald lightly on the back, and walked back across the hubbub of the courtyard.

Arthur rarely quarrelled with his wife; she did not care to exhibit extremes of emotion, and she held an air of superiority in her beauty that was able to awe even the man who had united Britannia. However, he was barely able to contain his agitation as he paced her quarters. She stood by her bed, watching him.

"My king, you are walking many miles for this matter. You valued Merlin, but you are Regissimus still, and your judgement has always been final. Your strength may increase from this, not be lessened."

"Men do not disappear unaided," said Arthur shortly. "There may be a conspiracy that aims higher than my counsellors, and I am about to send forth two of my most trusted generals far beyond the limits of my realm. The way is open - "

" - for us to consolidate power, to show that any leader is only as strong as you permit him to be."

"Or that anyone can successfully launch a plot against my government."

"You know well that Merlin kept secret counsel with many. In all likelihood, this disappearance is a result of a personal conflict. There has been no information to suggest otherwise."

"Then let us turn to that. There is one who is attracting the attention of some of those whom he held in his own court - your young woman, Nivene. Why do they flock to a woman barely out of childhood?"

"Many think her privy to his secrets; that does not make her guilty."

"Was she his paramour?"

"My lord, if your people cannot discern the truth of that rumour, why think you that mine can? The old man lusted after her, but I do not believe she succumbed."

"Perhaps - " Arthur paused, knowing the import of his next words - "if she were questioned..."

Guenevere's eyes narrowed. "We both know of what nature that interrogation would be. A few hours with your torturers, and she would confess to numberless witchcrafts and murders - and what would be said of me? Do you wish to reign devoid of your elder counsellor, in the absence of your senior generals - and with a compromised consort?"

"You are held above suspicion."

"Then hold my court above suspicion!" Though she stood well below Arthur's shoulders, the queen now seemed to tower over him.

"There has to be an answer, or we will be seen as helpless."

"Then find some other scapegoat. There are a myriad of men whose deaths would serve us. This young woman is nothing to you, and loyal to me. Create a reason and a culprit, and still your shaking throne."

Arthur knew that he would sacrifice anyone to his goals, and indeed had done so often, but, with the Grail quest looming, he was loath to commit such a sin so nonchalantly. He hesitated. Guenevere read his face and smiled darkly.

"So, this is a season of repentance? You think that God will be convinced of your change of heart? He made you Regissimus, Arthur, and he set you above the petty lives of others; if you need to make a pageant of justice, so be it. But you shall not make a mockery of me." She was ice, cold and unmoving, defying her husband to find a place where she would melt.

Arthur was defeated, even as he had known he would be; he was subject to no one but God and his wife. Now he came forward, slowly, his hands outstretched in a plea.

"We must find a resolution - together. I need you to rule with me."

Guenevere took his proffered hands without emotion. He knelt before her, pressing his head against her skirts. He would trade half his kingdom, he thought, for one fleeting moment of assurance that she loved him as he loved her, that she was truly his. The queen looked down, both exultant in her power and mildly contemptuous that her husband - the Regissimus - should abase himself before her. She slipped a hand from his and placed it upon his head.

"We shall win through," she said. "But there are sacrifices."

"I am willing," he whispered. Guenevere knelt down, pulling his head to her shoulder.

"You are God's fool, Arthur," she said quietly, "but you are my king."

In the midst of this chaos, it was decided that the Grail company should proceed with preparations for their departure, as they waited for word that the seas were becoming favourable. Galahad gladly seized the opportunity to make the journey back to Glastonbury to fetch Conlaed. As he reentered the gates, he found his old tutor at work in the gardens, sleeves rolled up despite the cool air, cheerfully hoeing as he talked to his friend, Brother Owein, an ancient man who appeared to be twisted, rather than seated, on a small chair. Conlaed laid down his hoe and strode forward to embrace the youth.

"It is good to see you here among us once more," he beamed. Brother Owein raised himself slowly from his chair and tottered off discreetly, "to stop the young men from gossiping when they should be muck-spreading," he muttered.

"You look uncommonly well," said Galahad, truthfully, for he had never seen the monk radiate such health.

"Ah, you never saw me perform manual work at your grandfather's court," he said. "If the truth be told, I missed it."

"But I thought you were a part of the scriptorium," said Galahad.

"All must take time from other allotted tasks to feed the community. It is good to stretch one's limbs after hours at the desks. But as for you, now, my son, you do not look to have found rest for soul and body."

Galahad took no offence.

"Great matters are being debated at court, and there are lesser ones which concern us. But they can wait until we have time to discuss them at length. Most importantly, we are readying ourselves to go, and we need to collect any letters the abbot might wish to send to Rome."

If Conlaed felt disappointment at being taken from his Brothers so soon, he did not show it. Instead, he turned towards the low stone wall near the garden and took another hoe which was lying against it. He handed it to Galahad.

"Then here," he said. "You must aid me in finishing this bed before I may take another task."

Galahad took the hoe and followed his tutor's lead in methodically walking backwards in a line, breaking the clumps of earth before his feet. Conlaed did not ask for news; instead he let a silence lapse as they worked the ground. After the uproar of Arthur's court, Galahad was grateful for the dumb companionship.

It was not until the evening, after they had met with the abbot and made a formal request for his missives, and after Galahad

had supped with the monks in the kitchen that served also as a refectory, that Conlaed took him for a walk around the perimeters of the community. As they strolled, Galahad related the events concerning Merlin. Conlaed expressed surprise - news had not yet reached the monastery - and he was curious to understand the details.

"But there is one thing that concerns me personally," Galahad added. "I believe that I may have been the last person, or the second to last, to see Merlin alive, in the company of another, although I cannot swear without all doubt that this is so."

"Indeed?" said Conlaed. Galahad explained the incident, without referring to Nivene by name.

"Then why did you choose not to reveal such information? Because you cannot be certain? Because you do not wish to be embroiled in the intrigues of court? Or personal misgivings?" He looked hard, but kindly at Galahad, who blushed, glad of the dimming light.

"All these, and perhaps others," he admitted. "The person involved has, I believe, created an alibi - perhaps it is a true one - but I am suspicious because this person attempted to lure me into performing such a role." He was aware of how awkward his explanation sounded in its concealment. "Then, there is a connection with the queen's court."

"You have a dilemma indeed," said Conlaed. "It is a grave thing to implicate any man, more so a woman - for it is a woman, is it not? - in a murder, but it is also a personal sin and earthly crime to conceal one."

"But if she was wrongly accused and suffered tortures..." Galahad was not overly sensitized to the cruel punishments he had seen meted out in Pelles' court, but the thought of the beautiful, tiny Nivene suffering was distasteful to him.

"Then you should clear your conscience. Relate what you think you saw to someone of importance that you can trust. Perhaps the Lord Launcelot."

But if they do nothing, am I truly cleared of blame?"

Conlaed sighed. "As much as we can ever be, my son."

"Well," said Galahad hesitantly, "then there is another matter, of importance to us both." He explained other events of those days, which had almost passed unnoticed. He was partially aware of his Pictish servant's involvement with the Saxon girl. It was only before his departure that he had noticed she was wearing a blushing smile and a thickening waistline; he was not interested in women's lives, but he had seen those symptoms too often in his life to mistake them.

"So," he finished, "as the representative of my grandfather, I must dictate the reparations or consequences."

"Have you spoken to Talorc? You need to discern his intentions."

"I confess that I have not had the leisure, but he has not cast her off, that much is certain; I think there is an attachment."

"Then that, at least, we may deal with openly upon our return. It will take us a few days to get the abbot's letters ready - maybe we shall find some resolutions in that time."

They walked on quietly, through the courtyard and toward Conlaed's small hut. It was still almost bare, save for the pallet that served as bed, chair and table; only the narrow shelf showed any ornament, a spare tunic, folded neatly but hanging over the edge, and an enamelled cross, a gift from Pelles which Conlaed had been wearing before he took his place at the monastery. Even in its simplicity, the hut had taken upon it the character of its occupant, sketched lightly against the grey-brown walls. It spoke of a studied and intelligent humility, just as the functional opulence of Launcelot's tent proclaimed the character of an assured warrior prince.

"I shall find another pallet for you," said Conlaed.

"There is no need. I managed before, and can do so again. Besides, I brought some furs, a gift from Cataviae. I shall use those myself, then leave them for the monastery. I dare say I shall sleep soundly after my journey and forced labour."

"Then you shall make me regret I did not make it part of your education, for you were always a terribly wakeful child, as I recall."

Galahad was correct: he rested well, and was ready to be reabsorbed into the life of the Brothers the next morning. They in turn were always willing to include others in their salvation of faith and works, and accepted Galahad back as naturally as if he had never departed, just as they accepted all strangers who came to work alongside them. He passed two measured days waiting for the painstaking task of composing and dictating letters to the pontificate to be completed. As Galahad was sharpening quills for Brother David the second afternoon, the only task he was allowed to handle in the scriptorium, despite Conlaed's assurances of his skills, a respectful knock came at the door. A middle-aged monk peered into the room.

"The abbot has called a general meeting after the end of assigned tasks. Brother Gildas has had a vision concerning the Lord's Grail." There were astonished murmurings, silenced by a look from Brother David, then all bent assiduously to their work until a small bell tolled their release, and they scurried from the scriptorium and across the courtyard.

Galahad squeezed nervously into the small church alongside the Brothers; other visitors had been forbidden entrance. The monks lined the walls leading up to the abbot's seat at the front, and Galahad and Conlaed took places near the top of one line.

The customary silence was observed as they waited, and it was difficult to judge how curious the monastics were. Brother Gildas stood at the head of the other line, looking steadfastly down at the floor, his arms folded in his sleeves. At last, after minutes that seemed to stretch out endlessly in the eternity of thc sacred space, the abbot walked through the line and took his seat before the altar. He laid his hands across the arms of the chair and looked down the line of monks.

"Brothers, as you have heard, I have called a meeting to discuss the vision of Brother Gildas, which was related to me this morning. I requested that the Brother not reveal his vision until he stood before the community, that our collected wisdom and inspiration may be brought to bear upon it, rather than idle gossip and speculation. Brother Gildas, let your fellows know what was given to you."

Gildas raised his head, and without stepping forward, began to speak quietly.

"As I lay on my pallet last night, I fell asleep quickly, as usual after a day of blessed work. As I dreamed, I began to see a picture of the Grail and a group of questors. One was clutching his heart, ripped from his own chest, and another was touching the stem of the holy vessel, although it was burning the flesh from his fingers. At this point I woke shuddering, or seemed to wake, for my hut was not as it appears to normal eyes. It was somehow more spacious, even in the dark. I saw a figure, quietly radiant in golden hues, not like a man or a woman; I discerned it to be an angel. As I lay still, and crossed myself, the angel gazed down upon me, and though it did not speak, it leaned forward and touched my forehead. In that moment it vanished, and I came to my full senses. I found that I now knew the import of my Grail dream.

"Of those who quest, there will be men who will have their hearts laid bare before our Lord. One or more will not return; the Grail will be their deaths. That, simply, is the message." He concluded and recommenced his scrutiny of the earthen floor.

"You have heard what our brother says. Our task is twofold: to decide whether it is a divine vision or a deceit played upon him, and, if the former, to make sure that we have understood its full meaning."

There was silence for a few moments. Then Brother David spoke.

"Did you test your vision yourself by any means, to determine its origin?"

"As I said, I crossed myself in the presence of the angel, and it did not recoil. After, I prayed for the remainder of the night, and received no indication that I had been played false by a demonic spirit."

"You are not given to visions, Brother," said another. "Why do you think this should come to you, who have nothing to do with the quest or the questors?"

"I do not know, and do not presume to judge. That is your privilege."

A few more questions of this nature passed back and forth, until the abbot spoke once more.

"I hear that the general opinion is that this vision or dream is truthful - do the Brothers agree?"

All nodded.

"Very well, then we are open to discern further into what Brother Gildas saw."

"Did you see any particular signs and tokens about any of the questors; any detail that might mark out or symbolize a certain person?" Galahad looked up; it was Conlaed's voice.

"None that I recognised, Brother. I saw no clear physical features to distinguish any man whom I have seen."

"What were they wearing?"

Gildas related briefly what he had seen.

"I see no signs," said Conlaed hesitantly, "but I ask my Brothers to make discernment in this point."

Again, the young monk was questioned closely, but, much as Galahad wished or dreaded, neither he nor the company could assign a face to the figures in Gildas's dream.

"We must assume," declared the abbot, "that the vision was general, perhaps a warning of the serious nature of this journey."

"It would seem," said another, "that those undertaking it should be shriven and prepared for death."

"As is my Lord Perceval," said the abbot, nodding approvingly. "Brother Conlaed, Prince Galahad, I would recommend such a course before you leave." Both bowed. "Then is there further business on this matter? No? Then I thank you, Brothers, that you have shown us once more capable of coming together to reach a consensus in our lives. Such was the nature of the first Christian communities in the days when the memory of our Lord was fresh in the minds of those who had walked the shores of Galilee with him; so do we tread those steps when we are faithful to their ways."

He stood and walked from the church, and the others filed out slowly behind him. Gildas glanced up to catch Galahad in his gaze, then dropped his eyes once more and strode quietly away. For a moment, Galahad felt an affinity with the young man, bearing as each of them did a shared burden of unwanted knowledge. But then he considered the thin, bowed figure moving through the gloom, and shivered. Gildas seemed already half in his grave; at least he, Galahad, still had a chance at life.

When he emerged into the sunlight, Galahad stood squinting, looking for Conlaed, who had somehow slipped past him. He did not see him in the courtyard; nor was he in the scriptorium or the gardens, where Galahad searched next. He wandered the small confines of the monastery, Samson bounding at his side. He knew that many of the Brothers were looking surreptitiously at him as he made his way past them, but he could stand the concern of the monks better than the gossip of Arthur's court, and he took no offence.

He eventually found Conlaed in the graveyard beyond the church. The monk was looking up at a small mausoleum, half sunk in the ground. At its head stood a tall stone cross, perhaps the height of four or five average men. The intricate knotwork carved in panels up its sides indicated the work of a Celtic craftsman.

"The burial place of Saint Indract," said Conlaed softly, hearing footsteps behind him. "It is good to be among Hibernian saints, and to see where the bones of old comrades lie. I seem to spend much time here, feeling the blessing of Brothers gone to Paradise. It would be good to make my final rest among my Brothers," he added quietly, "but I know that God's will may be otherwise in this quest."

Like most youths, Galahad did not care to be reminded of mortality. He turned Conlaed's attention back to the present.

"Gildas' vision is an unknown quantity in our task," he replied shortly. "We know that we are not undertaking a simple errand. And come what may," he added, with a new note of earnestness, "I swear that you will rest where you desire, be it twenty days from now or twenty years."

Conlaed smiled at his young companion.

"So be it," he said. "I accept the words of a man."

They rode silently through the gates of the monastery for the last time. Galahad was subdued from the shriving he had received at the hands of the abbot. He felt as though he had touched the realms of the dead, and he was eager to escape to those of the living. Conlaed, too, was quiet. Galahad had not chosen to be present for the farewells his tutor had made with old friends, so briefly found before another parting. He, who had never had a lifelong companion, unless of course he counted Conlaed or Drystan, could barely fathom what it meant to have a friendship that stretched back a score or more years. What would it mean to feel rooted in another's history, to have the loyalty that made Launcelot and Perceval so formidable?

"What is capturing your thoughts so?" smiled Conlaed, breaking the stillness which had been marked only by the sound of horses' hooves and Samson's great paws.

"Many ideas," said Galahad, carelessly but truthfully. "What is the difference, Conlaed, between a man you know, perhaps for many years, and a friend?"

"A shared life; being able to bare your soul; having shown your worst yet knowing you will go uncondemned; being willing to risk your life with this person at your side; long hours at the ale table - many facets make the precious gem that is friendship. And then, as a young man grows, those he knew as superiors may become friends. I believe, for example - "

But the example was lost by a shout from in front of them. They pulled up their horses, and Galahad put his hand to his sword, but he relaxed after a moment, as the figure came into clearer view, bouncing unevenly upon a pony.

"Talorc!" said Conlaed. "I would recognize that reluctant horseman from many a mile away. He must be jolting well in rhythm to his curses. I remember my first long journeys on horseback; I thought the abuse to my nether regions was a divine warning of hell's tortures."

Galahad drove his own horse a little forward, tactfully removing himself from another reminiscence. Sure enough, he could catch snatches of Pictish maledictions adding saltiness to the marsh winds. He urged his horse forward, but Samson beat him to Talorc. There was a flurry of shouts as the dog put its paws up the pony's flanks, nearly reaching its back. It made as much of a show of bolting as a fat little mountain pony was able, cantering towards the other horses with Talorc clinging to its neck.

"Is aught wrong?" called out Galahad as he came into close earshot.

"I bruise my arse traipsing across the devil's roads, and then your demon of a dog tries to bite my pony's head off, and you want to know if there's anything wrong?"

"I was referring to matters at the keep," said Galahad, trying to sound severe as he choked back laughter.

"Oh, nothing wrong with those southern weasels. Lord Launcelot was only wanting to make sure that you were leaving, because they're getting ready for the expedition. Something about good sailing tides. They put a man to death for Lord Merlin's vanishing, too," he added casually.

"They discovered a guilty party?"

"Well, I suppose they did. It was one of the slaves, a troublemaker anyway, and he confessed to handing Merlin over to some people he didn't know. But you know, his family got a fine young pig just after."

"Compensation?"

Talorc shrugged. Conlaed and Galahad glanced at one another. Then Conlaed shook off the question and turned to another.

"Talorc, I hear that you are forming a family. I presume a wedding is planned and you were just waiting to ask your lord's permission?"

Talorc grinned broadly, unabashed.

"Well, I have a bonny woman - and who would think you'd find one here among the Southerners? But as for wedding, I reckon we're handfast, and she's a bondwoman, so she can't leave here."

"A matter for you, I believe," said Conlaed, turning back to Galahad.

"You'll speak for me?"

"If you let Conlaed marry you and your woman." Talorc pulled a face of reluctance.

"Only then," said Galahad sternly.

"Well, so be it, but I don't know why the old ways don't suit. Handfasting is good enough for most. What they'll think about us having some ceremony with a monk, I don't know."

"But God will think well, Talorc," said Conlaed mildly.

"If it'll bring us good luck, then I suppose..." Talorc trailed off, uninterested in the theology of his nuptials.

Conlaed opened his mouth to correct him, but thought better of it. He clucked amusedly to his horse and walked on.

They reached the keep before the afternoon sun had begun to climb down, though not as fast as they might had they not been obliged to go at the pace of Talorc's stout pony. Galahad sent his servant off to the stables with the horses, glad of a rest from the Pict's tongue. Talorc had taken upon himself the position of a manservant, and felt it his privilege to talk freely with his masters, regardless of their view on the matter.

"Well," said Conlaed quietly as they strode through the keep, "are you going to let justice stand as it does?"

"Would you? How do I know if the truth has been discovered?"

"The time for truth may be past," admitted the monk, "it would not restore an innocent man - if innocent he be - to life."

"That is no answer, Brother."

"You must find your own."

Galahad stared miserably into the distance. What could he do? To give a confidence to Launcelot was anathema to him, and he was afraid that Lord Perceval's zeal might push them into destruction, for who knew how high the murder really went? And then, who was he in Arthur's court? A bastard, the child of a princess and a lord, to be sure, but still, when it came down to it, a bastard. How could his accusations stand after judgement and sentence had already been enacted? If he found a way, he vowed to himself, he would speak. If he could. The promise was cold comfort.

Part of the final preparations was to choose weaponry and make practice. Conlaed agreed to select a sword, but he refused to do the latter.

"If I am constrained to protect someone, I will do so," he said, "but I am not going to rehearse a killing. I have committed enough in war."

He went on alone to the weapons store while Galahad was attempting to perfect a new style of turning with his mare. The younger man was so preoccupied in his manoeuvres that he forgot his surroundings, and did not notice Oswald running across the courtyard waving at him. The boy had put a hand on the horse's flank before Galahad registered his presence. Oswald was flushed and full of his news.

"I saw a strange thing just now, my lord, betwixt your tutor and Master Adean."

"And what might that be?"

"Well," said Oswald, eagerly, too full of his important discovery to be circumspect, "I was in the armoury just now, looking at my father's sword, and cleaning my own, when your Brother entered, asking for a weapon for the journey. Master Adean didn't hear him, of course, so the Brother had to tap him on the shoulder. When he turned round, both of them started as if they'd clashed shields, then they threw their arms round one another and laughed, like the old men do at feasts, you know." Galahad nodded. "Well, then they began talking loudly, and smiling - I think they are old friends," he concluded triumphantly.

"What were they talking of?"

"Oh, I don't know really, times of yore, battles and so on, like the old men, as I told you."

"You recall no specifics?" Galahad was mildly aggrieved; Oswald might at least have gleaned a crumb of gossip.

"Why do you not ask him yourself? He is still there."

Galahad jumped down off his horse and handed the reins to Oswald, striding off across the keep. The boy in turn shouted for a servant so that he might run after the older youth and not miss a rare opportunity for excitement. He caught up, panting, just as Galahad ducked under the door to find the two men talking animatedly, as Oswald had described. Conlaed turned to look at his observers and smiled.

"I see that a reconnaissance party has reported my recent movements." Oswald and Galahad both blushed. "I do not deny old friendships; their renewal is sweet, and if anyone must assist me in the choice of weapon, I had rather it be an old comrade-in-arms. He turned back as Adean tapped him on the arm.

"I've some swords from the last great wars," he said, "and they need to feel the hands of good warriors again, though I'll reckon that you're not used to carrying that great sword you used to have. That dagger there must be the biggest weapon you've had for years."

"You may be right; I am not worthy of a great weapon." Conlaed gestured as he spoke loudly into Adean's ear.

"Ah, a good swordsman never loses his instinct. Come here," and he took him to a corner, where some swords lay on a shelf, carefully wrapped in leather.

"I keep them polished; they're near as good as the day they were hammered. Not for youths," he said, glowering at Galahad and Oswald, who were lingering behind.

Adean picked up several swords, one at a time, weighing them through their wrappings. Finally, he settled on one.

"This feels as if it should be yours. Go try it."

He followed Conlaed out into the weapons practice area. There, he watched carefully as the monk unwrapped the weapon. It was a long sword, a spartha. Its wrought metal hilt glinted, reflecting the sunlight in Conlaed's face. It was unadorned with jewels, but decorated with snarling, intertwined lions. The blade was perfect but for two tiny spots of tarnish. Adean took the leather from him and slowly Conlaed clasped both hands about the hilt.

"Go on," urged Adean as his old comrade hesitated. Conlaed glanced round at his small audience.

"You will see this but once," he warned. He bent forward for a few moments, curved over the downward-pointing sword. Then, with a low, muffled cry that they could not interpret, he swung himself up and back, and swept the sword in a mighty circle about his head. Adean grinned in satisfaction, but Conlaed had beads of sweat upon his brow, though there had been little effort involved in the manoeuvre.

"The spirit is never lost," said the weapons master gruffly.

"That is what I feared," said the monk shortly. "I pray this is returned to you unused."

"Well, whatever you do with it, keep it ready for its work. Come, I'll give you a scabbard. They're no good for long storage, but you'll need one now." They turned together towards the darkness of the store, and Adean gave his friend a rough shake on his shoulder as they entered. Oswald skipped after them, but he was waved away by the weapons master. He began to slink off, a little petulant at not being privy to further secrets. Conlaed turned to look back at him.

"Adean tells me that you are like to resemble your father and grandfather in soldiery," he said. Oswald straightened up and walked on jauntily. Galahad grinned and followed after the boy. He would let them talk, like old men.

Galahad did not have enough leisure to meddle in Conlaed's past at that time, though, or to think of Merlin, for he still had Talorc's affair to tend to. He had approached Lord Kay earlier to offer a price for the woman's release. The seneschal, on hearing that she was no more than a young washerwoman, laughed and told him that she was of no importance; he declared that she could be presented to King Pelles as a slave so that Galahad might do what he wanted.

"These Saxons breed well," he had said, "and you might want to take her away from a dark little Pict."

There had been Galahad's dilemma. He had no desire to enslave this woman, though he was used to seeing the odd slave at Pelles' court. Talorc was a freedman, and he considered it unfair to gain him a slavegirl. He had broached the matter with Conlaed, who cautioned his altruism.

"It is not wise for you to be seen as overly involved with the affairs of a lowly manservant, nor to argue with Arthur's seneschal. Take her as she is offered."

"But the Church eschews slavery; you taught me that."

"Yes, but I also taught you common sense, or I trust that I did. Take the woman as a slave and do what you will with her status."

"Yes, but then her family is entitled to no legal compensation, other than largesse."

"Give a marriage feast."

"Yes!" Galahad was relieved to have worked through this tortuous path. "I shall pay for a pig to be slaughtered for them."

"You had better select a pair of sucklings; a pig is an ill-considered generosity."

Galahad was abashed. "How does a man govern without an advisor?" he asked ruefully.

So, he had taken the monk's guidance, thankful and guiltily resentful, and accepted Talorc's woman. He had ordered the requisite sucklings, also, and was reassured and gratified by the satisfaction the girl's family expressed as to this arrangement. Or at least, this was what Talorc informed him. Now, he was going to meander over to the servant's quarters and put in an appearance at the wedding feast. Conlaed had already married the couple that morning at the threshold of the small chapel; "resigned and uncomprehending" he had described them wryly, "but we may only hope that exposure to the Lord may eventually make some impression upon them."

Galahad came to from his musings as he neared the corner of the keep where the servants and slaves lived, coupled and died.

The smell of roasting pig wafted over to him, and the sounds of merriment indicated that ale was forthcoming, too. He slipped quietly among the throng, who were gossipping and dancing with abandon, glad of any excuse to lift their heads from the ruts of their lives. Talorc was sitting on a bench, his arm around his new bride, who was bulging rather than blushing. He waved his mug in Galahad's direction.

"My lord, we give you thanks for the feast, don't we Enid?"

Enid, whose name Galahad had heard spoken for the first time, grinned, showing rather good teeth for a peasant, and nudged Talorc before giggling.

"Oh, she's shy, not used to talking with men of power, as I am," Talorc boasted loudly, so that others could hear him. Galahad humoured him and sat on the bench, taking a proffered mug; the ale was rather rough, but he swallowed it. Enid slipped away to talk to some of her women friends, and Galahad took the opportunity to discuss the impending journey.

"I gather you'll not want to be going with us across the Western lands?" he asked tentatively.

"Well, I've no calling to leave dry land, and I'm a family man now. But, since you ask, I've been told that there's room for more men in the king's army that's headed north soon. If you'd see fit to be asking Lord Bors, I thought I'd go along. It'd get me north, and there'd be room for my woman to go along with the supplies." He did not mention the whores. Galahad sighed; if the beer had not gone to his head so quickly, he would have been irritated. He had a feeling that Talorc was leading him gently into snare after snare. He needed not have worried about his own enemies in the keep.

"I will consider the situation," he said haughtily, "but I give you no word. The interests of King Pelles must be served."

"Aye, aye," said Talorc routinely. His wife returned to him at that moment, and he pulled her down onto his lap, forgetting his conversation. She put her arms around his neck, and Galahad, smelling the onion-saturated sweat that exuded from her, left quietly. He made his way around a circle of couples, dancing to a surprisingly tuneful singer who was beating time with a drum fashioned roughly from a hollowed log and animal skin. A hole was being knocked into a second barrel of ale, and men and women were jostling each other good-naturedly as they waited for a mugful. A steward had appeared and was herding those late for their tasks, ignoring the bawdy jokes and abuse that were ringing about his ears.

Galahad met Conlaed as he was going towards his tent. The monk was discretely carrying his new weapon, wrapped in the leather that had kept it in good condition over the years.

"All is well?" asked his tutor.

"Nearly all, though Talorc now wants a part in the northern army. What shall I do with him?"

"Ah, the perils of benevolent leadership," smiled Conlaed, and walked on.

Galahad cornered Bors in the Great Hall that night, making sure that he was out of his cups, and Bors was firmly in his.

"What's that?" said Bors, looking up from his wine. "A Pict wants to fight with my Britons? Well, I like their maniacal spirit in battle, but he'd have to not pick fights in camp, or he'd be flayed."

"He already has the comradeship of several of your men," soothed Galahad, "and he would want to restrain himself, as he is bringing a new woman home with him."

"Well, there'd be room with the other whores, no doubt. We cannot keep them from the camps."

"She is his wife, though I do not presume she would be overly particular about her company," Galahad checked himself from sounding too concerned, but Bors was interested in his slip.

"Better than a whore, you say? Then she might do well. There is a lady travelling with us who could use a serving maid willing to go north." Galahad remained silent, but Bors could not find a similar discretion. He put a hand on Galahad's shoulder and pulled him closer, grinning.

"I've a concubine. A good morsel; I'd perhaps have married her if my wife wasn't still taking up room on this earth. Not that she does not manage my lands well, and is pious to the point of near chastity. But if she were not the mother of that addle-headed son of mine, Aeneas, I'd be looking to a religious community to take her." Bors' son glowered from lower down the table, as if he divined that his father was using his name. Bors grimaced.

"The idiot could not even seduce such a woman, let alone make her his own, but he is my flesh and blood, so I am honour bound to attempt to refine his boorish life." Galahad barely listened to Bors' final words; his stomach was turning in fear or disgust - he could not even himself fathom which. He knew what had taken place, and why.

At the end of the bench, Nivene looked up. The hand that was visible as it clasped a jug of ale was newly adorned with two enamelled rings whose polished stones glinted in the flames that lit the hall. She gazed pointedly in the direction of Galahad and Bors, and smiled.

Galahad was not altogether surprised to meet her that night. He was walking back to the tent when he heard her low voice from the shadows.

"Ah, Galahad," she said in a quietly mocking voice, "it would have been so sweet."

"A sweet victory for you," he replied shortly. Nivene laughed.

"Perhaps. But I could have helped you also."

"You are only interested in the Grail for yourself."

"The Grail?" she said. "That is for the old men with their old tales. I need no mythical talisman for my power; your Grail has no interest for me." She took a step closer to Galahad. He leaned back slightly.

"Not all were asleep that dawn," he ventured. "Not all were safely inside the keep."

She was silent for a moment. "But you did not tell," she said. "Why? You do not want anything of me - no aid, no favours. Ah, a sense of honour, then? Well, Prince Galahad, I hope it serves you one day."

"Did you kill him?" He did not know what made him ask - he did not want an answer. Nivene reached out and put a hand over his heart. It felt cold inside him.

"Be safe, Prince Galahad," she murmured. "Perhaps we shall meet again, though I do not see your face in my future." She kissed her fingers and put them to his lips, slipping away into the night. He stood awhile, feeling the pressure of her fingers fade away. No, he could not imagine himself in her future, but he fancied he saw the coffin of Bors' wife.

At times, Cataviae exhibited an organic life of its own, working smoothly and seamlessly with the king at its head; it had been so at the Yuletide celebrations, when hundreds of people had been welcomed and absorbed into its body with nary a hint of disturbance. It did so now, as preparations for the year's campaigns began and the keep readied its soldiers for the long marches and prepared itself for the absence of its king. The main army would march north to harry the Dux Britannica, and would plunder the land for food as it went, but basic supplies were still needed. The smithy billowed smoke all day as wagons and weapons were mended; the washerwomen recruited to repair tents cursed almost as loudly as the men as they stabbed their fingers in attempting to rectify the damage inflicted by last year's army; the soldiers themselves grumbled quietly as they drilled in the rain and were lectured by Launcelot and Bors on military strategy and obedience.

From the larger cavalry, a small contingent was hand-picked by Launcelot for the quest. Most were not young men, and all had seen service under him or Perceval. It was almost a bodyguard, thought Galahad when he observed their choice, and it had no loyalty to him. It was the day before their departure, and he was seated with Launcelot and Perceval in their tent. They were gathered around a long campaign table that came apart for easy travelling. Launcelot pushed down on it to ensure it was in a stable position before laying a map upon its surface. He ran his finger along a line which stretched through what stood for Gaul.

"Our couriers tell us that King Clovis is currently moving residence to Orleans; I suggest that we take the road to there and find an escort if possible to take us through southern Gaul; the Regissimus will furnish gifts, and an offering not to interfere with any campaign that might intrude upon the borders of Britannia Minor."

"I agree; the risk is minimal," Perceval nodded. Both turned to Galahad.

"What is your opinion?" asked Launcelot. Galahad wondered whether he was being scorned or deferred to.

"A wise counsellor seeks the knowledge of others where his own is lacking," he said in a dignified manner. "I am a good warrior: I can manage war dogs; I ride well; I am experienced in campaigning in the wilds; I have the Grail knowledge of my forefathers," he stressed the last, "and I will learn, quickly, as needed."

The two older men did not smile condescendingly, but looked at him in approval.

"A well-considered attitude," said Launcelot, "and one which you will need with our company, who must accustom themselves to your rule."

"Why have all been chosen from your older cavalry? Surely a range of ability would be useful?"

"All must be able to be general, soldier and servant as need arises: that includes us. We want no hot-headed youths in a mission which will take us so far from aid."

"Not all youths are hot-headed; nor are all older men sober. And surely we should consider carefully whom we take on a sacred quest?"

"They are our instruments; we are God's," said Perceval shortly.

Galahad refrained from observing that he alone had been granted a divine commission, according to the lore of the Grail, but Launcelot caught his thoughts.

"You have been chosen," he said, "for whatever reason. You are also my son; it is your decision alone whether you need to prove yourself to our men."

"My mother is the daughter of a king - I know how to govern men."

Launcelot flushed deeply.

"There are to be no personal disagreements between us upon this journey," interjected Perceval levelly. "We must swear a holy oath, here and now, that we will be united, and will do whatever necessary to aid one another in our quest." He placed a hand upon the table, over the marks that indicated Rome. Launcelot hesitated a moment, and then placed his own on top. Galahad swallowed and laid his own smooth hand upon the weapon-worn ones of the older men.

"I swear," they said together. Perceval crossed himself and allowed a short smile.

"Then we are truly prepared," he said, "and all other business is subject to this rule. Now, Launcelot, let us trace the Roman roads on this map again. At least all roads do still lead to Rome, even in the days of a dying empire."

Since he was a stranger in these southern lands, Galahad had but few farewells - two, to be precise. He formally gave Talorc leave to march with the army of the Regissimus, though with orders that he was bound to return to Pelles' service when they reached his lands.

"Aye, I'm sure I'll have had enough of southerners by then. But my woman is taking on all sorts of airs at being a maid to Lord Bors' lady; I doubt she'll want to return to washing clothes."

"Oh, I expect she will find that being under such a mistress is not that easy," said Galahad wryly. Even though he tried to nonchalantly avoid Nivene, her increasingly sumptuous appearance was difficult to let go by without mental remark; it contrasted so strikingly with the black face of Bors' son.

The other good bye was one of genuine affection. He searched out Oswald, and found him at Adean's storehouse, looking rather red-faced as he assisted the weapons master in packing armour for the campaigns. Adean was offering little, rough kindnesses in a sporadic manner, but Oswald's head remained resolutely bowed.

"Oswald, what ails you?" asked Galahad, knowing that an open question was ever the best with his guileless young friend.

"I am staying here with my grandfather to aid his work at the keep, while all others are going to seek glory!" he said through teary eyes and clenched teeth.

"But I thought that you wanted to be with Lord Kay, that you were pleased Lord Perceval did not give you over to Bors' wardship," said Galahad quietly.

"Well, I do, but I want to be a man, like my father, too. Lord Perceval could make use of me - I know he could. Why do you not ask him?" he blurted out accusingly.

Galahad put an arm across his shoulders. "It is true that you will always be of infinite use to Lord Perceval. But if you want to be a man, I have a job for you here. You know that Samson has got the king's best hunting bitch in whelp?" Oswald managed a smile - he remembered the cursing of the hunting master, until the man had discovered the sire. "Well, I promise that one of the puppies will be yours, to train as I trained Samson. A warrior needs a good battle dog. It increases his strength five fold. I will expect to see a dog worthy of its sire when we return."

Oswald's face lit up. "You will really arrange that?"

"Of course - I have a claim to the whelps anyway. You will keep this as a solemn promise?"

"I promise!"

Adean smiled, though he had not understood but half of the conversation.

“So, you will be a man here? Good - now get back to your work, boy.” He cuffed him affectionately round the ear and nodded to Galahad in thanks.

Life seemed to be nothing but a series of departures at this juncture, thought Galahad as they finally took a formal leave of the king and queen. All the questors were stiff and reserved, turned inward to the strengths which would take them through the journey. There was little reality in the valedictions, but they understood their function as symbols of the divine favour that reflected upon Arthur. The king’s standard bearer was holding the banner of the Virgin, which had taken the Regissimus to his first great victory almost a generation ago, and Arthur himself sported a large golden cross inlaid with pearl, and an attitude of regal piety.

Guenevere held her serene gaze over the small band of men. She had prayed fervently to God - Launcelot’s only god - that he would protect his warrior. But she would not reveal this, even to her lover. She must believe that he was still invincible; he must believe it, too. Soon, Arthur would go north with his summer campaigns, and she would be left to rule with Lord Kay. He was pliable; her plans would run smoothly. No, she should allow no room for outward weakness. But still, she would pray on.

Was it worth it? Galahad wondered for a split second as they turned and set their horses towards the gates. Life here seemed so remote now from Pelles’ tales and commands. He felt his saddlebag hard against his calves. Could he achieve his task, surrounded by so many who had no personal loyalty to him? Would this journey be as inconclusive as all others he had undertaken since leaving his grandfather’s home? He glanced ahead at his father. I am Elayne's son, he thought, and spurred on his horse.

Chapter Seven

Perceval might have stated that all roads led to Rome, thought Galahad, but he had omitted to add that not all former citizens of the empire actually cared that they should still be accessible. True, the Regissimus had ensured the perfunctory maintenance of the routes he used to march his army about the country, and others, laid upon ancient highways, were still well-travelled and passable, but the Roman road as a display of power and ingenuity was fast disappearing among the weeds that forced their way between cracks in the stones. In some places, the roads lay half-finished, abandoned as the isle of Britannia itself was deserted by Rome, and the travellers had to pick their way unevenly over the layers of stone and gravel which had not been paved over. The party was making their way west to the port of Clausentum, through lands generally loyal to Arthur's regime. Still, they travelled warily, for, as Launcelot observed, "Many a rebellion is hatched over ale in the months spent at winter's hearth," and ports were always the first to suffer in Angle or Saxon invasions.

The company planned to move from host to host across the countryside, and although all were comfortable sleeping under the heavens with nothing but their thick cloaks for protection, a roof of some sorts and a fire and supper someone else had prepared enabled them to conserve a little more physical and mental strength for the long journey. Their receptions were varied: some were pleased with the favour of entertaining the men of the Regissimus; others gave grudgingly of the supplies left at the end of a long winter, and at such places the soldiers slept with their swords unsheathed, wrapped in their cloaks. They were joking now, as they rode behind Launcelot and Perceval, of their previous night's rest.

"I think he would have given us pig swill if he had been able. He's so tight, I bet he grudges sparing a fart!"

"Oh, but the women, though, they were loose enough!" grinned a fair-haired man, Caius by name, kissing his fingers to his lips. "And they were wild for you, Paulus - you could have had any one of a dozen."

The man whom he was addressing turned and smiled. He was the most striking of the company, with unblemished, creamy brown skin and hair that curled tightly, in a manner that Galahad had never before seen. He was slightly taller than average, and gracefully muscled, and bore his physique with a good natured humour, often exhibited in the full, deep laugh that he was displaying now.

"They would have been pretty playthings, but when I love, I shall know."

"Who said anything about love?" replied Caius, and the others joined in the laughter.

Galahad, riding just in front of this banter, shifted uncomfortably. It was not that such talk was new to him, or that he objected to it; he had been hearing much worse since before he understood what the words meant. But he wondered if they expected him to join in, or whether they supposed him to have taken the same vows of chastity as Launcelot and Perceval. He turned to Conlaed, but his tutor, for the moment, was the subject of their conversation.

"Tell us, warrior monk, for you have lived as soldier and religious. You know the burning that goes through a man who faces death. Is it not unnatural that Paulus here could hold himself back?"

Conlaed smiled politely, though he disliked attempts to draw out his past. He was respected for having been a fighting man, and for the sword that Adean had given him, and this caused the men to approach him with a reverent ease.

"There are many urges that drive a man's battle lust; I think that chastity may give as effective a spirit as licentiousness. Your lords have no trouble."

"Well, we know one is a saint, and the other is held by the charms of his lover - if he betrays her, his insides will turn black and boil." The last was spoken low, by Marcellus, a squat, determined soldier who lacked most of his front teeth. If those concerned heard his remarks, they made no comment from the head of the column.

"So," drawled Paulus, "there seem to be two rival ways within this company. Let us see who has the strength to kill more infidels. I already know who will come home richer!" He was referring to the habit the others had of giving trinkets to the women who bestowed their favours upon them; each soldier had his portable wealth in an array of adornments for bartering purposes.

"Which side are you on, young lord?" asked Marcellus in a friendly, yet challenging tone.

"Yours," replied Galahad, looking back at all the men. They nodded approvingly at thc ambiguity of his manner.

"You will make it yet," said Paulus.

In a few days, they had reached Sorviodunum. The garrison was housed in a hilltop fort which towered over the small but bustling settlement nestled in the river valley below. The top of the fort's buildings, however, were scarcely visible above the massive bank which surrounded it, a construction that spoke of origins beyond that of the Romans who had inhabited it for so many centuries. They followed around to the east side of the fort, where an entrance was marked by a pair of large wooden gates and the presence of several sentries.

Marcellus reached into his pack and pulled out a small flag upon which, as he unfurled it, Arthur's insignia, the red dragon, could be seen. He attached it to the hilt of his sword and held it aloft until a sentry waved a similar banner in acknowledgment. The party dismounted, for the slope of the hill was too arduous to force their horses to climb after a day's hard riding. By the time they had made their slow way to the top, the gates had been opened, and the Comes, Honoratus, was waiting to greet them. Galahad vaguely recognised him from the great Yuletide gathering.

"My lords," he said, reaching out his hands to Launcelot and Perceval, "it is good to see you in these lands." The men grasped his arms in greeting.

"Does it go well with you and the domain of the Regissimus?" asked Launcelot. Honoratus looked more serious.

"I have no ill reports," he replied, "but there is the scent of trouble arising from Clausentum. Cerdic, a Saxon who governs as tribune under us, has fallen out with the Magistratus Belgarum, and no agreement has been reached."

"Is it still Nathanus who governs Belgarum?" asked Perceval. Honoratus nodded.

"He is a determined man; he will be sure to act swiftly, though perhaps without full consideration," said Launcelot.

"Indeed. I am hoping that a small action will settle the dispute. But this is all secondary to the hospitality you are owed. I will have your men escorted to the barracks to rest awhile, and have one of my own rub down your horses."

"This shall be a welcome rest for all," said Launcelot. "A night or two among people whom one can trust implicitly will be a novelty to our journey thus far."

"Then we must extend the hospitality to the rest of your company. Whom do I have the pleasure of greeting?"

Launcelot presented Conlaed and Galahad formally. Galahad no longer cringed at the description "son", though he still did not wholly own it. Honoratus raised his eyebrows slightly at the introduction, but said nothing. He led the way to the west side of the fort and the small headquarters, which had a modest meeting hall, roughly tiled with local brick, and a few small rooms leading off from it.

"We cannot offer the luxuries of a fort such as Londinium, but I have a room that the four of you may comfortably share, if this is acceptable." Launcelot indicated his satisfaction, and Conlaed and Galahad were sent ahead, while the Comes discussed politics with the others.

"This city is near the family lands of the Regissimus, is it not?" asked Galahad as they stretched out on their pallets for a brief rest. The spaciousness of the room indicated that it had not originally been utilised as sleeping quarters, but now a simple bed lined each wall and a small table sat in the centre affording ease of movement around one another.

"Ah, you are retaining my information at last," replied Conlaed with a sigh of satisfaction at the rest from riding. "Yes, the domain of the Ambrosii is close by. This city was governed by Arthur's kinsman, Caradocus, until his rebellion of recent years. The new Comes is indisputably a man of Arthur."

"And this tribune? Ceric?"

"Cerdic. I know little of him, though he has been in his position for some years. But, if my memory serves me, he has some sort of link with the abbess in these parts. He has power in a key town, an ideal port for the king's fleet, and neither his nor Arthur's side must truly want to make an open enemy of the other."

"How did you come to be so versed in statecraft, Conlaed? Surely you could not have learned all this in my grandfather's court. I know that I did not."

"I wanted to know why I was fighting," said the monk. "And that is why I then stopped."

They remained at Sorviodunum for two nights instead of their customary one. Launcelot, in his capacity as general for the Regissimus, was interpreting royal policy for Honoratus, and, with him, he and Perceval were occupied in the formulation of a plan that might contain the uneven tempers of the magistratus and tribune. Implicit in this discussion was also an assessment of the risks in marching a small military party to the port of Clausentum. For their part, the cavalry members slipped unobtrusively among the ranks of Honoratus' soldiers, which contained many of their comrades, and participated in the drills and duties of the defending force. As they worked and joked, they listened well, and reported back that Honoratus' words, at least, were truth in this part of the country.

Galahad, for his part, hovered at the garrison attending to the debates of his elders. He did not assuage his curiosity by travelling down to the settlement at the foot of the hill. From his vantage point, he watched the town below; it was obviously a thriving trade post, for carts hustled to and fro continuously through the tiny streets to a market area from which the faint sounds of commerce floated up to the fort that seemed oblivious of the world it supported. He still chafed at these exercises in waiting, being used to raids and punitive attacks rather than anything resembling a campaign. Yet he began to see their sense. It was like the games of strategy that Perceval was so fond of playing; one thought before the move, of where one might go, what might await, how this would affect the move thereafter. And sacrifices were sometimes necessary in order to ultimately win.

His reverie at the wall was interrupted by the approach of the three leaders, who were talking earnestly as they surveyed Honoratus' accomplishments. They nodded at him, and continued, implying that he was welcome to their discussion.

"If I may speak freely," the commander said, "I like it not that such distinguished soldiers as yourselves are leaving the country. I would be grateful if, as you near the coast, you would remain silent on the matter of your journey's duration. We are a prime target for any invasion advancing from the ports."

"We would not put your garrison in danger," Launcelot assured him.

"But what of the Regissimus? How stands he? You say that Merlin is probably dead. Who lends strength to the king's word?"

"Merlin's ways were dying before he did," said Perceval. "It does not weaken the throne."

"I live far from court and near the Saxon heathens," said Honoratus, "and I am not so sure that old beliefs are vanquished."

"They may be so at court," replied Launcelot. "The woman to whom Merlin's faction turned, his paramour, we think, has chosen the safety of the north and the bed of a lord. The power of the old demons is scattered, hopefully for ever, but at least for longer than we shall be gone."

"Then you believe that we are safe - at least, as much as we ever are?"

"I advise that you be wary, but do not show it. Arthur is destined to die in his bed: none could be so foolish as to risk losing the united power of Britannia in a premature lust for personal sovereignty." Launcelot waved his hand over the land before them as he spoke. "Arthur has named no heir yet; they all have a chance to succeed bloodlessly."

"Not all who rule are wise," remarked Honoratus, "but this fort has outlived them all. We shall hold out for the king, if it comes to it." He began to move on, and they followed him around the wall. After a last glance at the slopes that defended the keep, Galahad turned and joined them.

It was on the road to Clausentum that the fellowship was enlightened as to the plans of its leaders. Perceval announced that they were intending to make a circuitous route that took them to the port via the church lands ruled over by the local abbess.

"It will enable us to come upon Clausentum with the advantage of better knowledge," he said, "and of course, to make plans with my sister."

"You sister is the abbess?" Galahad was surprised.

"No," said Perceval shortly. "She has not yet been called to that degree of service, but she is nonetheless the chief assistant to the abbess herself."

Galahad looked to Launcelot, who made no comment; he must, as usual, be wholly privy to Perceval's thoughts, he mused, irritated.

"You will be glad of the opportunity to see her, my lord," said Conlaed pleasantly, breaking the barrier. Perceval nodded, and a smile played about his lips.

"Thank you, indeed, but I make the journey once a year to visit her."

"That is indeed a rare dedication to a sibling, and to be recommended. Is this a pilgrimage of a few years' standing?"

"It has been ten years since she took vows, since we decided that she should be Christ's bride and no other's." Perceval began to look ahead, but whether to think or control his emotions could not be discerned. He fell silent, and would speak no more on the matter, but as they began to approach the nunnery, he lost a little of his iron composure, and began to reveal a slight agitation, alternately nudging his horse forward, and reining it back. Launcelot and the rest of the men made no reaction, and so Galahad and Conlaed followed suit.

The boundaries of the land were marked by the beginning of farmsteads, quite large for that area of the country. As the company rode along the way that bisected the fields, they saw groups of people, mostly families, methodically tilling the soil. One or two had oxen which pulled simple ploughshares, but most trudged through the stiff, ankle-deep mud and manure, bent double as they hacked the ground into furrows. They raised their heads as the soldiers moved past them, but, recognizing at one experienced glance that these were travellers and not invaders, they returned to their task. Only the odd small child remained standing, transfixed by the sight of such magnificent horses and men, until a rough tug on its tunic from a sibling or parent returned it to its task.

"These people look as well as those that work my grandfather's farm," whispered Galahad to Conlaed. The monk nodded in acknowledgment.

"The abbess must be a good manager. It is fortunate that the Church finds it possible to give able women their true vocation."

Within an hour they reached the small hill upon which the community had settled. A low fence snaked unevenly around its circumference, and a male servant was peering over the entrance nervously watching their approach. When he discerned Lord Perceval, he smiled and pushed open the gate, which was barely wide enough to accommodate a single horseman. The others reined in their horses that Perceval might enter first. He glanced down at the servant as he entered.

"Is your venerable abbess free to accept visitors and allow me to seek the company of the Lady Helena?"

But before the man could reply, there was a cry from across the courtyard, and a figure came, not quite running, around the corner of a hut. Perceval slid from his horse and paced forward. Their arms became outstretched as they reached touching distance of one another, and they fell into an embrace. Galahad watched, transfixed. If this woman had had her hair cropped as her brother's, he realised, they might be one and the same person. She bore his features exactly, with just enough of a hint of femininity in her dimpled chin and high cheeks to give her an ethereal, almost androgynous, beauty. Galahad was struck by thoughts of the descriptions Conlaed had given him of angels, neither male nor female, who bore God's glory in their own splendour. He watched her move back and touch her brother's face tenderly. When at last she began to look behind her brother to his party, Launcelot dismounted and came forward. He bent his knee briefly and kissed her hand.

"Lady Helena," he said as he arose, "it is a pleasure to meet with you again. I have not seen you since you were a child. You are a jewel to your family."

"I remember you well, Lord Launcelot," she replied, in a rich, low voice that made the other warriors start and stare. "It was the first winter when we were allowed to travel to the festivities at the court of the Regissimus. You danced with me, although my head scarcely came up to your ribcage. It was a kindness a small child does not forget."

"You honour me in its remembrance."

"But this is the present, and it is a pleasure to have your company in our community. Mother Abbess will be pleased to greet you. But what brings you this way - business in the Ambrosii lands?"

"I will explain at length when we have the leisure," said Perceval, "it is a mission to holy lands, to seek a prized relic."

"It must be precious indeed to demand such a distinguished cohort." The Lady Helena hung on her brother's arm as she looked around at the men. Even Caius, who had been so loose in his description of other women, blushed and bowed his head.

"Your twin is right; it needs long elucidation," said Launcelot. "But we also come seeking help from you and your abbess concerning the political situation."

"Ah yes, her brother is fermenting unrest again. Come, come, I was forgetting myself. She will be glad to see you and to arrange accommodation."

The other soldiers, so sure of themselves on campaign, were nervous within the walls of a nunnery. However, the male servant came to their rescue by leading them off with the horses to a guest area screened with a light wall woven of rushes. Launcelot exchanged brief orders with them before following on with Perceval. As he and Conlaed walked respectfully behind Helena and her brother, Galahad was still trying to put these two pieces of information together. He had seen twin calves or lambs, but never people; he had not known that it was possible to have a twin brother and sister. He had, of course, heard tales of women who lay with two men in one night and conceived a child of each. But if that were true, how could they look so alike, and how could a woman such as Perceval's mother have had two lovers - surely an unlikely event considering the piety of her children? He was also assimilating Helena's own offering of information, that the abbess was the sister of the rebel - and presumably pagan - Cerdic.

The home of the abbess, like that of the abbot at Glastonbury, was roomier than the huts of ordinary religious, but not more decorated. A small table was crowded round with several simple stools, and a small, stout woman was seated at one, studying several tally sticks set out before her.

"Mother," said Helena softly, "my Lord Perceval is here, with Lord Launcelot, and a company on a mission abroad from the Regissimus."

The woman turned around. She was middle aged, her face lined with small creases that deepened as she smiled. Her features were small and rounded, from her hazel eyes to her small, dimpled chin. Her hair was a blend of brown and grey, and coiled neatly at the base of her neck. She reached out her hands to Perceval and Launcelot, showing roughened fingers that clearly participated in the work they organized.

"You are welcome in the Lord's name, and that of our community. It appears from our Sister's introduction that we have weighty matters to elucidate. Please, sit down. I am afraid that I have not fine furniture, but it serves its purpose, as should we all."

Helena and Conlaed immediately stood back to let the other men take the three stools opposite the abbess, then sat respectfully behind them. As Perceval sat down, Helena moved her stool back closer to her brother again, and placed her hand upon his shoulder. Almost absentmindedly, she began to massage it lightly as he talked. The abbess, if she noticed, made no comment, apparently used to the visits of Perceval.

Launcelot briefly and unemotionally outlined the events which had led to their arrival. As he described the commission, the abbess began to look very interested, and Helena, wide-eyed, began to grip her brother's shoulder.

"And you say that this young man, King Pelles' grandson, is a reputed descendant of Joseph of Arimathea, and the chosen seeker of the Lord's chalice?" Galahad held himself in composure, not willing to affect holiness or show any indignation at not being directly addressed.

"This was the decree of Merlin, proved by his survival after taking the Grail chair in the hall of the Regissimus."

The abbess looked hard into Galahad's face.

"Well, well. A young instrument of the Lord. It is a hard task for one of such youth, but still, I hope that your age at least presages purity, does it?" She turned her musing into a question directed at Galahad.

"There need be no questions on that account," he said, desperately wanting to squirm under the penetrating gaze of the abbess.

"Has the abbot at Glastonbury affirmed the validity of this quest?" She had turned back to Launcelot and Perceval.

"He has," said Perceval shortly, "and we have been shriven for a journey so perilous to our souls and bodies."

"You, my lord, are always in a state ready to die, though I cannot say that I know the same of the rest of your company." That same challenging look, this time directed at Launcelot and the others. Launcelot was neither embarrassed nor angry, having been forewarned of the forthright probing to come.

"Our lives may not be as exemplary before God as that of Lord Perceval, but we are faithful in this undertaking, and we are prepared for its risks."

The abbess nodded. She looked them over again, trying, Galahad thought, to find a weak link, a source of confession.

"Then if this is your commission, what is the purpose of your visit here? A farewell to our Sister, Helena, or spiritual aid? Or is it simply that you wish to avail yourselves of our plentiful stores?"

"A courtesy visit to kin and to a notable religious leader would naturally be reasons of importance," said Launcelot smoothly. "However, it will be of no surprise to yourself that we are bound for Clausentum, and desire knowledge of the unrest there from one intimately acquainted with Cerdic."

The abbess smiled ruefully. "He may indeed be my brother, but I could not say that we think alike."

"You might, however, venture to perceive *how* he thinks?" suggested Perceval calmly. She assented, appreciating the direct assault.

"He thinks like an unbeliever interested only in those gods that offer hopes of power. I have not had personal contact with him since this dispute began, but I have my servants who treat with the town for trading purposes, and they always bring word, direct, or indirect, of my brother. From what I understand, he has made one argument too many with his superiors in the government of the Civitas Belgarum. Clausentum is prosperous, and heavily - one might well say unfairly - taxed; on the other hand, my brother seeks more autonomy than he can be expected to wield. He and the Magistratus Nathanus have never been compatible, and I fear that their official and personal differences may soon come to a head."

"Do you anticipate military action?" Launcelot was interested in the abbess's easy discussion of politics.

"One would like to deny the possibility, but I would not be surprised if this were to occur. Cerdic must hope for disgruntled allies to appear from these environs should he launch a rebellion, though he may not," she added, "expect me to lend my farmers. I would not act against my brother, and I would give him sanctuary, but I will not be joined in a godless uprising."

"Your candour is illuminating," remarked Launcelot, "and, as we thought, it opens the question of whether we might have safe passage from the port. Do merchants and political messengers still have free traffic to and from Clausentum?"

"At the present, yes. It would also be my pleasure to send you with a known servant as a token of my responsibility for your presence."

"We may well accept your courteous offer."

"But now, the day draws to a close, and we have devotions to make in our community. You are welcome to stay the night here in our simple guest quarters, or we may find alternative accommodation for you at a farmstead. Either, I think, will be as good as many you have encountered on your way. Do you intend to stay for any length of time?"

"We will allow you private worship; we take prayers with our own brother." Perceval indicated Conlaed, who had been sitting quietly and very attentively toward the back of the hut. "After, we will inform you of our decisions as to our sojourn. We intend to press on with our mission as swiftly as we may, but your information certainly urges us to caution."

He and Launcelot rose and bowed, and Galahad hastily followed suit. After a nod of dismissal from the abbess, they filed from the hut. Helena, after a brief kiss of farewell, left her brother, to remain inside. They walked quietly to the corner of the enclosure where their men waited, lounging outside the tiny guest quarters and talking, hardened to the cold evening air. Samson and the other hounds were curled up against the wall of a hut, but their ears were pricked for danger in an unfamiliar setting. The men began to come to attention as they saw the others approach, but Launcelot waved them down. He himself came over and sat upon the edge of a rough bench shared by two of the men.

"What think you of staying here the night?" he asked.

"If truth be told, we agree that we would rather not be in the company of so many religious women," said Paulus carefully. Launcelot smiled.

"I thought indeed that it might unnerve you - or disappoint some." He glanced at Caius. "We can sleep on a nearby farm."

"Will she send a message to her brother?" asked Caius.

"I believe not," replied Perceval. "I have known her for many years; she would never betray her own flesh, but she has never actively aided him, least of all now when her community could suffer from complicity in any uprising." The men seemed satisfied with this conjecture.

"Good," said Launcelot. "Then we stay one night, and discuss our next move."

After brief devotions, led by Conlaed, who had a care for the shallow capacity of soldiers to withstand the piety of their superiors, the party made known their intentions and were led out by the same male servant who had greeted them at their arrival. It was a short journey to the main abbey farm, and they walked their horses down the slope and west, to a sheltered area of land whose fertility was proclaimed by the dark green growth that covered the fields, and the substantial orchard beyond, and whose trees were just beginning to show glimpses of pale, new leaves.

"The abbess is a woman of rare ability," remarked Conlaed, surveying the scene.

"She would have conducted herself well as a tribune," replied Perceval. "She has overseen the physical and spiritual salvation of this land almost singlehandedly."

"Do you know her well?" Conlaed was curious.

"Not intimately, but I have long been a witness to her deeds. Her rule has always been firm and of vision."

"And Helena is happy there?" asked Launcelot quietly.

"We both chose to give our lives to serving God. She is content to be called to this place."

The conversation was halted by their arrival at the small farmhouse at the centre of the homestead. The farmer, a stout, bald man with little hair and fewer teeth, came ambling out of the house to see what the arrival presaged. He frowned when he saw the servant at the head of the party, obviously aware of the imposition about to be placed upon him. After a few minutes' consultation, he turned back and called into the house. A much thinner woman, with long, graying hair and a tired face, came out, suckling a child and pushing away one that clung persistently to her skirts.

"Do they want feeding?" she said to her husband, ignoring the men themselves.

"Aye. Throw some more meat and such into the pot. You'll be sharing our stew, if that's not too lowly for you," he said challengingly to the company.

"Our lady abbess has warned you to mind your tongue and your duty before, man," said the servant haughtily, glad of an opportunity to exercise some superiority.

"Don't bring us trouble," pleaded his wife quietly. "I'll make more food, but it'll have to be from the stores meant for the ladies in the big house."

"That's acceptable," said the servant. "They'll sleep in the barn?" The man nodded sullenly. "Well, I'll be back to the nunnery before it gets too dark. But mind yourself, they're soldiers all, and you'll have no one to blame but yourself if you get your throat slit."

He left the group with a bow to Launcelot and Perceval. The farmer stood still for a moment, and then snapped an order to his wife, who trudged indoors again. He beckoned to the party with his head, and they followed him a short way from the house where a large barn stood.

"There's room among the hay now it's near Spring. There's a board round the back where you can tie your horses, and water there, too. I'll set a torch outside the barn, but you can't take one in."

"We are not stupid, man," said Paulus. The farmer stared at him, struck silent by his appearance.

"Aye, I'll see that your food is getting ready then," he said hurriedly, and was off at a rapid pace towards the farmhouse.

"You should have said you were a demon, Paulus; then we'd get no more trouble!" laughed Caius.

Meanwhile, two of the other men had taken the horses to be watered, and Galahad had disappeared into the barn. He emerged in a minute.

"Well, it's fairly made, water-tight as far as I can see. There are rats, though, so we'd better send in the dogs first." He whistled, and Samson came running from across the farmyard, the others, who had acknowledged him as their pack leader, following close on his heels.

"Rats, Samson," said Galahad quietly as he stood aside from the door. Samson pricked up his ears at the familiar word which usually signalled a diversion. He dove in among the hay with his companions. As the soldiers settled down outside, they began to hear scuffles and the occasional squeal, canine and rodent, as the cull began.

Soon, the farmer returned with a torch and some rough bread. A little girl with a runny nose followed behind, staggering under the weight of two jugs of ale, and a smaller child stumbled in her tow with an armful of wooden cups, making a rather dismal procession. He set the flame in a stand away from the barn door, and told them that there would soon be stew to follow. The children came forward reluctantly and held out their burdens. The soldiers took them, nodding thanks, but they had already scurried back behind their father, not lovingly, but fearfully, as though they had already been cuffed and warned how to behave. The family traipsed off again, leaving the men with their partial meal.

It had been a long day, and hours since their last sustenance, and so the bread was half gone by the time the wife came haltingly along, slowly carrying a small cauldron of steaming stew at arm's length. Bent back with the weight of the pot, the shape of her body revealed yet another pregnancy in progression. Paulus came forward and took it from her. She was too grateful and exhausted to bother to be startled at his complexion. He flashed his wide grin, and she managed a thin half-smile of her own before returning to the house from which the screams of small children could be heard across the courtyard. By the time Paulus had set the pot down, Conlaed had fetched the simple wooden bowls they carried with them. He began to ladle it out quickly and offer it round.

"You'd think that fat old man was past getting anyone with child," said Caius through a mouthful of stew-laden bread.

"My mother died with her sixteenth," said Marcellus, sucking on his hunk.

"How many of you lived?"

"Three." The others grunted sympathetically.

The smell of extra food brought the dogs from the barn. Samson stuck his bloodied muzzle in Galahad's face, and he brushed him away, throwing bread onto the floor for him. One of the other hounds had a deep bite on his lip, but the dogs were otherwise only slightly wounded, and elated at the chase.

When the meal was over, Conlaed collected the dishes and went to the small pond to rinse them out. Marcellus rose and went into the barn, and began throwing out the carcasses the dogs had left. There were sounds of muffled cursing as he found himself bound to dispatch a few which had not quite been killed, and more warm bodies flew out of the door. Paulus kicked them into a pile away from the barn. Two farm dogs trotted over, interested in the smell, and Samson's pack began to growl until called off by Galahad. In a short time, the soldiers had settled their environs and retired to the barn. It was difficult to see inside until their eyes became accustomed to the dimmer light, for the barn was windowless apart from one high opening, and the light that came through the door. As Galahad had noted earlier, it provided a good shelter from the elements, and comfortable beds in the form of the piles of hay each man was fashioning for himself.

After the confusion of the day, most of the company readily fell asleep. Galahad stayed awake past the time when he could hear deep breathing coming from the others. Unless exhausted, he could never rest until he had mentally sorted the events of each day, weighing information and judging his conduct; he dared not be less alert to the events in which he was enmeshed. He was distracted from his thoughts, however, by the sight of Perceval's dim shape, leaning up against a crude bale of hay. He thought at first he was in prayer, but as he watched, he perceived that Perceval's attitude was one of deliberation rather than supplication. He lay quietly, watching him, but Perceval sensed that another was wakeful, and turned in Galahad's direction.

"I am sorry," said Galahad in a low voice, "I did not mean to disturb your reverie."

"It is no matter," replied Perceval. "I was only ruminating on our possible actions."

"Are you afraid for your sister here if a rebellion were to arise?" Galahad risked the probe, knowing that darkness could often help cover the inhibitions of daylight.

"I think of her, yes, though I am not afraid for any of the community here. She has a place in the events which are unfolding; I know not yet what it is." With that, he slid back down against the hay, signalling his withdrawal from the conversation. Galahad, too, turned his head into the folds of his cloak and found at last a welcome sleep.

The business of the farm woke the party early. Animals were clamouring for their feed, and the cold air was pierced with the cursing of the farmer, punctuated by orders barked to children and other slaves.

"You would think that being given a farm such as this to run, he might find a more cheerful attitude towards his lot in life," yawned Paulus as he sat up and shook the hay from his hair.

"Aye, well some can make honey bitter to themselves," replied Marcellus. "Me, I think my day will be the same whether I bless it or curse it, so I bless it in case it is my appointed day to die."

"Now that's a cheerful thought for the morning," quipped Caius, ducking as an opportunely discovered rat carcass flew at his head. The door of the barn was unceremoniously flung open and the farmer poked his head around it.

"There's bread and cheese at the house. Do we need to bring it down to you?"

"We shall fetch our own food," said Launcelot, very calmly, Galahad thought, for one who could have the man killed with a word. But then no one cared to lose the good will of the abbess, not to mention her insightful advice. Two of the men left to fetch the meal. The voice of the farmer could be held shouting after them.

"Hey! There's a cess pit down the way - you've no need to piss against my walls!"

"Well then, I know where that old man's likely to end up before we leave," muttered one. Neither Launcelot nor Perceval made any remonstrance to this. They were in a corner of the barn, conferring quietly. Launcelot turned and beckoned Galahad and Conlaed.

"We have no desire to delay the next stage of our journey," he said, "but we think that another day spent here would allow us to send some of the men to scout the area for information and for ourselves to conclude business with the abbess. At the least, we need supplies for the sea crossing; we can take the extra weight now we are so close to Clausentum. What say you?"

“I am in agreement,” replied Conlaed. “Our Mother Abbess has offered us a servant, but we should still take independent knowledge with us to the port.” Galahad nodded.

“I have no objections,” he said.

As the men gathered to break their fast, Launcelot outlined their tasks for the day.

“Paulus and Marcellus: you can scout the road ahead and see if any of Cerdic’s men are wandering the countryside yet.”

Galahad smothered a smirk at the thought of the most conspicuous pair creeping about the countryside. Perceval caught him out of the corner of his eye.

“Do not doubt,” he murmured, “that these two can make themselves more invisible than the beetles that creep in the grass.” Galahad bent his head and swallowed.

“...and that leaves you,” Launcelot was saying to the last pair, “to spend the morning getting information from the remaining homesteads, and to check at the abbey by midday for instructions on where we can requisition supplies. Any questions?”

The men shook their heads. “Then we shall regroup here after the middle of the afternoon.”

The farmer did not disguise his gladness at seeing their departure, not his displeasure at being informed they would return.

“Mind you bring out your better ale tonight!” warned Marcellus, fingering the hilt of his sword.

The largest party rode on towards the nunnery as the others dispersed around them. It was raining a fine mist, and the moisture collected slowly on them and their horses as they made their way upwards out of the farmland. Galahad wrapped his woollen cloak more closely about him, glad of its imperviousness, but his mare twitched her ears and shook her head each time the dew shower collected too heavily upon her.

The abbess was engaged with a merchant when they arrived, but Helena was ready to greet them. She took the reins of her brother's horse while he dismounted, laying her head against the horse's neck as she patted it firmly.

"I miss a good horse," she sighed, smiling. "Do you remember Lady, my mare?"

"She was the tallest mare we had ever seen, but you insisted that you could ride her, and you made me stoop so you could step on my shoulders and climb up to her. We both got beaten for your riding her without permission."

"Yes, but they let me keep her until I came here."

"I never let anyone else ride her," said Perceval quietly.

"But we must not bore you." Helena turned back to the others. "Mother Abbess should be finished shortly. May I help you in anything? I have a man who can pasture the horses competently while you are here," and she turned to call to a young nun, who scurried away on her errand.

The abbess was soon with them, looking very satisfied.

"Thank you for your wait. We had some seasoned wood that I have been trying to sell at a good price, and I was loath to dismiss a potential buyer. Have you thought on my offer? Here, let us come into my quarters and not be rained upon." She continued to talk as she led them inside. "Now, I too have been considering, and it would, I think, be advantageous to me if I could prevail upon you to carry a missive to Rome. Renewed contact with the Roman Church could bring authority and perhaps a missionary to our coast. In return, I am willing to make a gift of supplies."

"It would be an easy task to bear letters for you," said Perceval. Helena caught his sleeve. "I might, however, venture to ask that you send them with a verbal messenger to make your case. My sister could be under no safer escort, and she could reside at Rome until we returned there on our way home, and perhaps learn much of import for your abbey."

Both the abbess and Launcelot looked startled; the latter flushed a little.

"Helena," said the abbess, " you have conceived a passion to be gone from here?"

"Oh no, Mother; it came to me, as you were speaking, that we might make representation better in person?"

"You have been here for ten years, and you now doubt your call? Is your devotion in question?"

Helena's eyes brimmed over. "No, no, Mother," she said anxiously, "it only seemed that circumstances had arisen where I might help this Order further its cause."

"The thought was mine too," interjected Perceval firmly. "We both of us have sworn to serve God alone. We could do much for you, especially considering the uncertain actions of your own brother."

"This needs to be plumbed to its true depths," said the abbess, suddenly severe. "Will you others excuse us for a short while?" Launcelot, Galahad and Conlaed ducked out of the hut, leaving the brother and sister to face the abbess alone.

Outside, Launcelot began to pace, red-faced, about the courtyard.

"He told me not of any plans he had to bring her," he was muttering.

"I think they truly spoke from the inspiration of the moment," said Conlaed quietly, "though the rumination of many years may have been its source."

"It is not a heavy burden," replied Launcelot, looking round at him, and glaring at some nuns who were watching curiously.

They scattered under his gaze. "I do not, however, like surprises," and he switched his glare to Galahad by way of illustration.

"Nor do I," retorted Galahad hotly, holding his own. Conlaed stepped in.

"Lord Perceval does not act irrationally - am I correct?"

"He is fanatically rational," replied Launcelot grimly, "but where his sister is concerned, I am not sure."

After a short while, three figures emerged from the hut. The abbess did not bear the look of satisfaction she had worn when they had met her that morning, but she was collected. Helena was happy, and Perceval was inscrutably composed.

"It has been decided, bar any final insights that I may have," she added, looking severely at the twins. "Now it remains to us to discuss what you may need for your journey. I must attend to the work of the Sisters for a short while, so I will leave you to negotiate among yourselves." With a short nod, she was striding towards the garden where the nuns were busily turning over the sod for the spring planting.

"We must talk," said Launcelot shortly to Perceval. He swung round and walked off a little way; Perceval followed with no show of taking offence. Helena made her apologies to the others and set off for her own morning duties. The two men talked in low voices, but without any tones of animosity that Galahad could discern.

"Surely bringing a woman is an added risk," he said to Conlaed.

"Perhaps it is calculated to pay off in Rome," replied the monk. "The abbess is not without power in this part of the country, and bringing her assistant under the influence of Rome would be welcomed."

"You think that Perceval is trading his own sister for our advantage in the Grail quest?"

"I think he wants her companionship, but I believe he would - as he has done - sacrifice that for his idea of religious duty."

Perceval and Launcelot returned to the others, the latter looking very much assuaged.

"It is agreed," said Launcelot, "if you, Conlaed, will act as her religious superior, and co-protector with Lord Perceval."

"I would be pleased to offer such guidance," said Conlaed.

"Very well. We intend to conclude our business today and be off as soon as the light permits tomorrow morning. Can you assist the lady abbess in drawing up her epistles?" Conlaed bowed his head. "Then we shall leave you here to manage affairs, and join our party tomorrow. Look for us shortly after it is light enough to travel. We are agreed?" he said, turning back to Perceval.

"We are agreed," he echoed.

"Then let us find the abbess once more, and secure our journey as best we can."

If the men were weary of tracking the countryside, they did not acknowledge it, but silently regrouped and set off that afternoon on their new tasks, gathering supplies and choosing a suitable horse for Helena, the latter charge falling to Caius' expertise. Galahad would have opted to go with him - his appreciation of horses having been honed by the fine instinct of Drystan - but he was instead compelled to plot route and strategy with Perceval and his father. The soldiers had not had any disturbing news to report; a feeling of unrest had been permeating these environs, but none of Cerdic's men had been that way testing the water for possible recruits. A merchant on his way to Aquae Sulis had grumbled about a more stringent inspection of his goods, but the port was still doing business as usual, and the king's fleet was safely moored and guarded.

"Then we press on," announced Perceval, as the reports were finished.

Supper was perfunctory that night, with little conversation, perhaps because none could discuss the question uppermost on his mind, that of their new female companion. They were also silently readying themselves for possible combat as they neared Clausentum. In the stillness, they could hear raised voices from the house, and the sudden cry of a woman. Paulus lifted the dagger he had been using to fish out his meat, and flung it into the earth.

"Tomorrow," he muttered.

They took it in turns to watch that night, in order that they would be ready for the first hint of daybreak. When the time came for them to arise, they had to kindle another torch from the embers of the one which remained so that they could saddle their horses quickly. They did not attempt stealth, for they knew that the animals which wandered the boundaries of the farmyard would announce their movements, and, sure enough, the farm dogs were quick to jump up and offer a tentative bark at Samson and the other hounds before being silenced by their growls. The chickens followed, clucking in alarm, and a moment later the door of the house was flung open with the accompanying sounds of sleepy profanities.

Launcelot led the men as they walked their horses across the yard. He stopped at the beginning of the road to mount. As he looked round, he asked, "Where are Paulus and Marcellus?"

"Thanking the host as he deserves," said Caius, and though it was dark, they could sense his grin. From back in the farmyard, there was a yell, proceeded by a dull splash, and more shouts. Launcelot kicked on his horse and began a slow procession across the countryside. In a few minutes, they were joined by the missing soldiers.

"Well?" inquired Caius in a low voice.

"The man liked a filthy mouth, so we gave him a filthy place to put it. He regretted not keeping it shut," replied Marcellus. Paulus' deep laugh confirmed the story, and the others joined in. Launcelot began a perfunctory remonstrance, but it dissolved into a snort, and even Perceval was shaking as he pushed on ahead.

When they reached the gates of the nunnery, Conlaed and Helena were waiting with the servant. The two men were holding the reins of their horses, the servant's being a docile-looking mare which was used to conduct the nunnery's business afield. Helena was looking down the file of men for her own horse. She walked swiftly towards it, pausing to kiss Perceval's hand in greeting.

"It will be a pleasure," she breathed, stroking the flanks of the chestnut-hued stallion. She put her hands upon the edge of the saddle and, with little effort, pulled herself up. She was wearing breeches under her skirt, and slung across her shoulder was a bow and quiver. Kicking the horse gently with her heels, she moved it forward towards her brother.

"Shall we go?" she said. "We do not want to delay upon account of this diversion."

"You have all the papers?" Launcelot addressed Conlaed. The monk gave assent. "Then we follow you," he said to the servant.

The group reconfigured itself behind the abbess's servant. Launcelot and Perceval took the head, with Helena behind, under the aegis of Conlaed, and Galahad bridged the divide between the lead party and the cavalry. For the first part of the journey, he focussed upon Helena's back, staring at the long golden braid that fell to her waist over her cloak. It was doubly conspicuous next to her twin's slowly growing stubble. Like her brother, her age seemed indeterminate, and in accepting celibacy she had further defied the chief ravager of women, childbirth. He wondered what the bond must be between two who so resembled one another that to see them together was to imagine a soul and body greeting one another at the Resurrection.

When he grew tired of speculating, he turned his attention to the route. It was a well-travelled road, an ancient way paved by the Romans, but now slowly returning to its natural state. In some places, the stones barely showed through the mossy grass that was creeping across them, but the ease of journeying a wide road had ensured that sojourners had at least kept its width trampled down. They stopped to rest their horses at noon and allow the dogs to hunt in a wooded area near a stream. Helena put down her quiver to kneel and scoop some water into her bottle. Launcelot picked out an arrow and turned it over admiringly.

"This is well-made," he remarked. "Is it the work of a local craftsman?" Helena nodded.

"There is a man near Sorviodunum who supplies the army."

"And is there call to arm the nunnery?" asked Conlaed, curious.

"It never hurts to be prepared, but no, we really stock them for the benefit of visitors who want to hunt."

"My sister is omitting to mention that she was - is, I trust? - a supreme markswoman," interjected Perceval. All turned to look at her, and she blushed.

"It is the blessings of an infirmity," she confessed. "I am troubled with the far sight; I have difficulty clearly discerning what is close to me, but I can see an arrow's path far into the distance."

"Can you see that oak sapling between the broken sycamore and larger oak?" asked Launcelot.

"It is possible," murmured Helena, picking up her bow. Taking an arrow in her hand, she carefully fitted the notch into the string and raised the bow. She held the arrow straight, looking down it with one eye half-closed, then pulled back her elbow, bending the bow. In a second, she had let the arrow fly, and before she had lowered the bow, it had struck home halfway up the thin trunk of the little oak. She smiled quietly to herself. Behind her, the group of men let out a spontaneous round of applause.

"Welcome to our ranks, lady soldier," said Paulus, with a small flourishing obeisance.

After that, the atmosphere of suppressed questioning at Helena's presence was broken. If the soldiers were still wary of travelling with a female for practical reasons, they no longer carried a sense of her helplessness. She, for her part, was perhaps even quieter than she had been, as if desiring to negate her momentary display, only talking softly with her brother who occasionally dropped back to share a thought.

Toward the end of the afternoon, the road took on an incline, leading them up to a small crest. The landscape around them was subtly changing; the grass was becoming harder and needle-like, and the flowers sparing but tenacious shrubs that bent stubbornly with the increasing breeze. At the top, the servant paused, bringing the party to a halt behind him. As they looked down the other side of the slope, they saw the coast, and the small, dense settlement that crowded against one area. Squinting through the haze, they could see the movement of one or two boats, and a gathering of larger ships a little way out to sea.

"There is Clausentum," said the servant rather unnecessarily.

"The Regissimus' ships are waiting for us," said Launcelot in a determined manner. "Let us see whether they are still under his control." Pushing his horse past that of the serving man, he began his way briskly down the path. With a desultory check of their weapons, the rest of the group, too, lurched forward and made for the port.

Chapter Eight

At first glance, Clausentum did not appear to be readying itself for trouble. The town had not been fortified; indeed, parts of its wall were in disrepair, and the townspeople who greeted them with stares at the beginnings of the settlement did not exhibit the strained suspicion of citizens fearing conflict. It was a market day when they arrived, and they had been overtaking carts on their route into the town. Nevertheless, there was the presence of more warriors than might have been expected.

"Shall I lead you to the tribune's quarters?" inquired the servant as they passed through the gate.

"We should check with the ships at dock," replied Launcelot, "but it would not be wise to cause unnecessary offence, even to such an inferior."

"I will take some of the men to the ships, if you would care to take a small delegation to the tribune," said Perceval. It was swiftly agreed upon that Perceval should make for the water with his sister, Conlaed, and two of the men, while the remainder would follow Launcelot.

Within the town itself, the streets were becoming crowded as people made their way towards the centre to barter goods and exchange gossip. The servant pushed ahead with his horse, gaining more than a few curses as he forced people aside for the party to follow on. However, the curses fell to mutterings as they saw the armed soldiers behind him.

The tribune's quarters lay just to the east of the marketplace, barely cut off from the town outside by a tiny courtyard. But, if the breathing space was tight, it was nonetheless welcome to the riders.

"I swear the people themselves stink of fish in this sea town!" grumbled Marcellus as he dismounted.

Paulus was about to answer derisively, when he was stopped by the appearance of one who bore himself with the air of authority. The abbess's servant went forward and made obeisance.

"Your honour," he said, "I have escorted under your sister's goodwill this party travelling from the court of the Regissimus, led by the Lord Launcelot."

"So, you are here," he said, glancing over the party. "I have been awaiting your arrival since the king's ships began outfitting themselves at the port." He made a perfunctory bow to Launcelot. He was not a brother to the abbess in the same way that Perceval was to Helena: there was a superficial resemblance about the mouth and eyes, but where the abbess was firm bodied and lively, he showed a stout, barrelled chest and a body which tended to corpulence. His dress was also a contrast to his sister's modest habit. He wore an embroidered shirt over his gleaming leather leggings, and gold threads were woven into the bindings that cris-crossed up his legs. His hands were adorned with heavy rings. And yet, though he affected the signs of indolent wealth, there was still a hint of the warrior within, a warning in his eyes that he was not to be provoked.

"Tribune Cerdic," began Launcelot, "since you have been appraised of our coming, I shall not waste time reiterating our intentions here. We intend as brief a sojourn as possible; if our ship is ready, we shall sleep aboard it, but we will of course require your cooperation."

"You mean supplies, I suppose. We are a prosperous town, but burdened by the tributes demanded by the Magister Belgarum. Nevertheless, we can offer you a welcome fitting for courtiers of the Regissimus. You will dine with us tonight? Then, if you would send one of your men to talk with my steward, we can make suitable arrangements."

Launcelot indicated Paulus to take this task.

"I have work to do. The Regissimus expects much from our small port," said Cerdic. His attitude made it clear that he was unwilling to offer anything else by way of help or pleasantries. After a moment, Launcelot gave him a formal dismissal, and the men mounted once more to make for the port.

"Our tribune is a man of few words but much intent," remarked Launcelot to Galahad as they rode out of the quarters.

"He reminds me of some of the under kings that owed tribute to my grandfather," replied Galahad. "They see only the shared title 'king' and resent having to submit to authority before their own followers. Cerdic wants this petty kingdom."

"And more. The environs are no more than inhospitable marshland, but I dare say that he has ambitions to have it nominally under his sway. We should not underestimate him - he is a seasoned warrior."

They skirted the market, making their way down gradually inclining streets to the port, following the circling gulls. Soon, the masts of ships could be seen above the rooftops, and then the heads of horses. As they reached the dock, they saw Caius and another soldier holding the horses near two broad ships.

"The others are on board," he said in answer to their query, and, as they looked up, they spied Helena at the prow of one of the boats, waving to them. Launcelot and Galahad embarked and came over to join her as Perceval was turning from his inspection of supplies already gathered. The sun glinted upon his golden hair as he faced into the light. He squinted slightly as he lifted his head to face Launcelot, and he put his hand up to shield his eyes.

"Did it augur well?" he asked.

"His claws are not yet out, but neither are they blunt. I see no wish in him to carry his quarrel as high as the court. Has there been any impediment in the outfitting of the king's ships?"

"There has been all necessary cooperation, although no offers above and beyond what was requested. However, we need not infer anything from that."

"Those are Cerdic's ships along the coast?" Launcelot was pointing towards two narrow, mastless, Saxon-style ships in the distance.

Perceval nodded. "Our captain tells me that they are in the pay of the Regissimus, commissioned to watch the coast. However, I warrant they are observing us more closely than the sea at present."

"Perhaps a night in Cerdic's company will yield information. Are we ready to sail?"

"As long as the winds remain favourable, I am informed that we may launch as early as dawn tomorrow. They have just finished loading the hay."

"We take the horses too?" interrupted Galahad incredulously.

"Did you think we would abandon them to Cerdic?" asked Launcelot, amused.

"No, but I have never seen a ship that carried horses. Will they not be terrified?"

"If they are tied well and given to the charge of a good horseman, they will survive as well as those men who lack sea legs," smiled Helena, strolling leisurely but surely across the gently rolling deck.

"I know not what stuff my legs are made of," said Galahad apprehensively, "but I would not volunteer myself as stableboy for such an expedition."

"I sailed from Ireland, but we left our horses on either side of the emerald sea," offered Conlaed. "Still, I have heard that the Norsemen take their favourite horses on long journeys, and that the emperors would bring theirs from Rome to the shores of Britannia itself."

"A good horse is an extension of one's body," said Helena. "One would as little think of leaving behind a trusted companion as cutting off one's sword arm."

"We have an Amazon in our midst," quipped Launcelot, kissing Helena's hand. She blushed. "No, my lord, just a woman who loves horses too much. I wrestle with Scripture, not weapons."

"The word of God is as a two-edged sword," Perceval commented. "Are we prepared for tonight's verbal parley?"

The feast was rather duller than the London banquet that Galahad had been forced to attend. He found himself seated next to Helena, a companionship for which he was thankful, though he was a little shy of this beautiful, sclf-assured woman. Still, he did not wish for proximity to Cerdic, who was flanked by Launcelot and Perceval. The tribune wore all the adornments they had seen earlier, and had supplemented them with a wide, beaten gold torque, set with blue and green glass, which glinted from between the edges of a fur collar. He constantly drummed his fingers on the table, but whether to indicate his thoughts or to display his rings was uncertain. Launcelot was initiating a discussion of the landscape surrounding Clausentum; Galahad turned his ear away as Cerdic began a description of the marshes. Helena was more ready with conversation than her brother, and had steered Galahad gently round to a discussion of his family before he had realised the confidences he was imparting. She listened sympathetically as he described his mother.

"Does she know or understand of your acquaintance with your father?" she asked.

"I am not sure what reports she has received, or whether my servant has yet arrived back at my grandfather's court. Communication is nigh impossible, and I would not want to disturb her peace, if she has any at present."

"Lord Launcelot feels that he caused an unwitting wound," she said quietly, "and you have seen that he is not a man to deny the responsibilities placed before him. Perhaps he believes that a direct attempt at reparation or reconciliation would cause more harm. All our actions are flawed; even when we act from love, we can strike one another cruelly."

Galahad could not help flashing a glance at Perceval, but if Helena discerned his gaze, she said nothing.

Suddenly, the guests were disturbed from their various conversations by a commotion in the courtyard. At the sound of metal clashing against metal, all leaped to their feet, their hands on their own swords.

"A soldier's quarrel, no doubt," began Cerdic, "and nothing to worry yourselves about. Please, be seated, I will send my steward - " but he was interrupted by a shout that clearly came from Paulus. With no regard to their host, the guest party pushed its way past the servants trailing in with dishes, and sprang into the courtyard, spacing themselves out cautiously. Cerdic and others of his men followed behind at an oddly sauntering pace.

In a corner of the quad, Paulus was restraining one of their men, while two of Cerdic's soldiers were similarly grasping the arms of one of their own. Both soldiers were bloody, though it was impossible to say whether one had wounds and the other only his blood, or whether both had struck home. Launcelot and Perceval strode forward, and at the sight of them, Paulus let go the man, who ceased struggling to stand stiffly. He had a gash above his eyebrow, which was dripping blood down into his eye, and he kept blinking to brush it away as he stared defiantly at his superiors.

"What has caused you to offend the hospitality of this town?" snapped Launcelot. The soldier shook his head.

"It was a quarrel, sir, as senseless as these two dolts here," offered Paulus, obviously irritated with his companion.

"On what grounds?" No one replied. Cerdic caught up with the fray and struck his man around the head.

"Was your tongue ripped out? What did you say?"

"It was on the matters of the realm," he muttered. Cerdic's lowered his eyebrows. He leaned forward into the man's face. "If you have been spreading false rumours..." he threatened in a low voice.

"It was concerning the Regissimus." Launcelot's man finally spoke up.

"His honour," said Paulus grimly. Cerdic looked hard at his own man, and then glanced back at Launcelot whose face had grown heated. The corners of his mouth twitched.

"A foolish disagreement on politics, no doubt," he said, "and not one that we need probe further than to mete out punishment, or do you think otherwise, my lord?"

"I do not approve of ill-considered actions," said Launcelot through his teeth, "even if they spring from a truly-placed loyalty. I will speak with you shortly," he continued, turning back to the man. "For now, wash yourself and settle with your fellow soldiers."

"Give him five lashes and let him clean himself up," ordered Cerdic, indicating his own man, who looked sullenly down at the ground as he was roughly hauled away. "Now, perhaps if we could put this unfortunate incident behind us, we could continue our meal?"

With a meaningful glance back at Paulus, Launcelot followed his host back to the hall. Cerdic called for more wine, and insisted that everyone's glass be filled.

"To the honour of rulers," he declared. He set down his glass and wiped his lips. "Such as it is," he added. The heads of the fellowship turned towards him.

"Ah, but have you not heard? I think not - you learn but of the Magister Belgarum's stories. It is sad, a disgrace," he shook his head dramatically. "His wife - she who should most guard her honour, for it is her husband's, has, I am reliably told, taken a lover." He paused and turned to Launcelot, who was sitting stiffly.

"You are silent, my lord, and perhaps with good reason, for words must fail. A man close to the Magister, they say, his right hand, has been cuckolding him. A treachery worse than rebellion in my opinion, for it dishonours both the adulterers and their ruler."

Helena clutched Galahad's arm, but he needed no hint. Even from their distance, they could see that Launcelot was white around the mouth, that his every muscle was tensed with the effort not to succumb to Cerdic's goading. If he defended his own sense of honour, he admitted the worst and gave Cerdic a reason to rebel, and if he questioned the tribune's own loyalty, he gave an insult that again, could justify the answer of insurrection.

"But my lord tribune," interjected Perceval, seeing that Launcelot could not trust himself to answer, "surely you do not place faith in rumours? I am certain that even news of yourself is distorted by the time it reaches the ears of your own sister."

The counter attack worked for a few moments. Cerdic clearly wanted to know what reports of himself circulated abroad; he averted his gaze from Launcelot for the time it took him to master himself. But it was enough for his victim; Launcelot regained his own resolve, and when Cerdic returned to the baiting, he found his trap empty.

They made their base aboard ship that night. Helena was afforded a canvas curtain at the stern, but refused offers to search out a more suitable cot, declaring that a camp bed was more than adequate for her needs. The others spread out mats across the deck; the horses were stabled with the tribune's. The remainder of the meal had been conducted in a stiff atmosphere. Cerdic, not willing to admit defeat, had continued his hints, though his smug joviality was strained, while Perceval and Conlaed worked in tandem to cover Launcelot's silences. There had been little information forthcoming after the incident in the courtyard. The offending soldier was being sent back to Cataviae, ostensibly with news of Cerdic's fermenting rebellion, but also, as he knew, in punishment for his lack of restraint.

“We cannot risk a man who might rise to a fight at slight provocation,” Launcelot had said dismissively to Conlaed when he had suggested clemency. “All here should know the bounds and rules of their allegiance.”

Surprisingly, there were no expressions or murmurs of dissent from the others, even when out of earshot of their leaders. As they came close to leaving the shores of their home, they began to feel the reality of their mission and the singular duty to which they were called. They settled silently on the boat that night, save for Caius who was guarding the horses, in fear that one of the quality steeds might mysteriously go missing. Galahad had been a little afraid that he would discover a weakness on the water such as he had heard Drystan complain of, but, after a mild discomfort, he grew accustomed to the slight sway of the boat accompanied by the splash of water against the sides.

Out in the open, they awoke with the rising sun, and readied themselves for the crossing. Their captain, a legionnaire named Quintus, confirmed the winds.

“When we get beyond the bay we can use the sails fully,” he said, “and we’ll be across within a day or two.”

“And if we cannot?” Galahad could not help asking.

“Then we row - very hard,” said the captain sternly.

The sound of neighing brought men forward to help lay the broad gangplank from the ship’s side to the dock below.

“I’ll need aid,” called Caius, “and something to blindfold them with.” Paulus came down the gangplank with some spare cloaks. Caius gently draped one over the head of a horse, and led it towards the plank. When it felt the slope and heard the hollow ring of its hooves against the wood, it shied back. Caius held its reins firmly.

"We'll need a leader," he continued. "Lord Galahad, you've got a way with your horse. Can you lead it behind me? Bring that hellhound, too. It may steady them." Galahad came down, followed by Samson at his heels, reeking of the fish entrails he had begged from the fishermen who had sat gutting their catch by the port that morning. He took Caius's lead in blindfolding his own horse, talking gently to it as he led it forward. When the first horse sensed another behind it, it calmed down.

"Now, follow my pace," said Caius, and he began once more to pull the horse up the slope. This time, after a moment's hesitation, it began to move upwards unsteadily. Galahad pulled his horse close behind, and Samson trotted up the side. In a minute, they had hauled the horses over the edge and down into the ship. On the fore side, there was a rail to which the reins were fastened. Helena stood by the horses, stroking their muzzles and whispering to them as the others were reluctantly loaded. The ship's captain watched to make sure that all were securely tied.

"Are you ready to set sail?" he asked Launcelot. Launcelot nodded. Quintus barked some orders at the other sailors, who leaned over the ship's side to free it from its dock. They took their places at the rowing stations, alongside Launcelot's men. At the command of the captain, they leaned forward and began to pull the boat through the water. It seemed to Galahad to take ages before he felt the boat begin to move against the tide, but slowly it began to inch its way from the dock and through the shallow waters. He listened to the synchronicity of the oars, as the sailors worked as one to create a quiet rhythm that signalled the boat's propulsion. When they were out of the shelter of the bay, the captain called upon two of his men, who set aside their oars and began to pull up the mast which had been lying in the centre of the ship. The sail, which to Galahad had been wrapped around it in a seemingly haphazard fashion, unfurled elegantly as the mast was hoisted into position. It soon caught a stiff wind, and the rest of the oarsmen slowed their task to a halt. Quintus crossed his arms and nodded.

"If this wind keeps with us, we'll have a good crossing."

Now that the ship was wind-driven, she needed only her assigned crew to manage her, and the others were left to what little leisure they could find in such a tiny space. Paulus and Marcellus had found some fishing lines and now they were angling over the side of the ship, laughing and talking.

"In all the times we've fought together," Marcellus was saying to his friend, "I've never asked you where your people came from. You didn't get that dark under this sun!"

"My mother was brought all the way from Carthage, the great granary of the Roman Empire," said Paulus, jerking up his line, only to find it empty. "She was of a noble line, enslaved to a Roman general, who brought her to Britannia to serve in a villa he built. But my father, a Briton warrior who had risen through the ranks to win his own wealth, caught sight of her at a feast one night, and fell in love. He bought her - not for half as much as she was worth, my mother used to say, though it was a fortune - and then freed her and wooed her until she gave in. Even after they were wed, she made him and his household convert to her Christianity before she would let him touch her. She is a rare woman, and not to be crossed."

"She lives still?"

"Aye, though my father is dead. She is still a woman of beauty, and there are always several suitors hanging about the place when I go home. But, for all her pride, I think she loved my father beyond all others, and cares not to marry again."

"What a perfect love story," smiled Helena who had wandered across the deck, curious at the rendition of Paulus' history. "It should be told to a bard and committed to his songs."

"You, too, my lady, have the beauty of one who should be celebrated in verse."

Helena shook her head. "But I have no romances or adventures to make me worthy of such treatment. It is you who are going on a quest that will be heralded."

"Perhaps you will find your own place in it."

"To seek fame, and rise among the stars," murmured Helena, leaning dreamily over the edge of the ship. "Oh, Marcellus, you have a bite!" Marcellus turned his attention back to his line and gave it a swift jerk. Sure enough, it pulled taut and he lifted a writhing fish out of the water and slapped it onto the deck.

"A cod," said one of the sailors, coming over to see the catch, "and not a bad size, either." Marcellus held it up.

"The length of my forearm," he said proudly. "Caius! Caius! Leave those horses and come see!"

Caius was sitting with his back to the side of the ship, among the horses' legs. His eyes were closed, but he opened them slowly to look in the direction of Marcellus' shout.

"I think I'll stay with the horses, if you don't mind," he said, closing his eyes again.

"He's green!" laughed Paulus. "Why, the horses have better sea legs than he does! Come, friend, a sea jig will do you good!" and he danced around by way of illustration. Caius did not open his eyes again, but raised an eloquent gesture by way of answer. Conlaed approached him, and leaned down sympathetically. He produced a small, gnarled, creamy object from a wrapping.

"Here, try chewing on this. It is ginger, and is supposed to aid nausea. I bought it in town yesterday from the doctor." Caius held out his hand, and took the offered medicine. He bit off a small lump and chewed it for a second before spitting it out in disgust.

"I'd rather be sick, thank you," he said.

Despite Caius' infirmity, the voyage was not rough, at least, not by the captain's declaration. Galahad, who kept quiet about his own slight returning queasiness, found interest in watching the shore recede from sight and the vast grey-green ocean opening up before him, moving like an enchanted plain that possessed a life of its own. Occasionally, some great white sea bird swooped down to grasp at a fish which had ventured too close to the surface, and soared back up, sometimes only momentarily successful as the prey, too large and vigorous for its talons, would twist itself free to plunge beneath the waves, leaving its captor shrieking angrily as it circled the site of its loss. Galahad knew that the sea they were now traversing was but a tiny part of the ocean, but it still seemed limitless to him, who had never before been beyond the shores of his homeland, let alone seen the beaches or cliffs that comprised them. The time during which they were out of sight of land, though in reality but a few hours, were a disquieting age, even more so as daylight began to fail and the ship sailed into unbounded darkness. He watched as the sun slipped into the darkening water. Could it really come out again? he thought for a second, before reason took hold of him and he remembered that Conlaed had said that the sun travelled around the world; it did not die and find rebirth each day as his nurse, Morgain, had sworn when he was at her knee.

Most of the party, untroubled by such problems of astronomy, were asleep as they approached the shore under the light of the stars. Only Perceval and Helena were in the stern talking softly, and Galahad and Conlaed were nearby, surveying the heavens, when the captain gave the order to anchor the ship just outside the mouth of the estuary.

"We'll wait until dawn to move into Quentovic, if that pleases you," he said to Perceval.

"You have the preeminence in nautical matters," he replied, "and we could do no more in Quentovic by night than we could do on this ship." Helena bade them goodnight and retired, leaving Perceval and the others to contemplate the night.

"You have been into Gaul, my lord?" asked Conlaed.

"Yes, though not for several years. I was part of the campaigns in Britannia Minor, and I travelled with the party that treated with King Clovis. But I was only young myself - I will have no claim upon the king's memory."

"What was he like?" said Galahad.

"He was a Frank among the Franks. He followed the hallowed custom of Frankish royalty of never cutting their hair, and I remember that it fell to his thighs, a formidable sight among the clean-shaven and shorn Romans. He is a man of some intelligence, but also of great ruthlessness. You have heard the tale of the Soisson's vessel?" Galahad shook his head, though Conlaed nodded.

"Well, after his early conquest of Soissons, his soldiers plundered the land, and, pagans that they were then, this included the desecration of churches. Among the treasures they stole so irreverently was a vessel of great worth, which was claimed by the Bishop of Soissons as his own possession. Clovis, who had always sought to be on good terms with the Church, requested it over and above what was owed him by the rules of division of bounty, intending to return it to the bishop and continue in his goodwill. However, a soldier, angered at his master exceeding the bounds of his authority, clove the vase in two, declaring that even the king himself should only claim what was allotted him by fate and tradition. Clovis took no revenge at that time, but, many months later, he came face to face with that same soldier while reviewing his forces. He rebuked him for the poor state of his axe, and, as the soldier looked down, the king swung his own weapon, and split his skull in two, declaring, 'Thus did you treat the Soissons vessel.' Now, though, he is a true son of the Church, and perhaps in that capacity we should fear him even more."

"You think he will be too interested in our quest?"

"I think we shall have to tread carefully when upon his soil," replied Perceval enigmatically, as he bid him a good night.

If the party would have to walk with care, the horses, at least, were grateful to walk at all, and, once they had been pulled, sliding, down the plank onto solid ground, stood, stamping in relief as their riders unloaded the boat. The dogs bounded around furiously, stopping every few seconds to mark some new territory.

"We thank you for hazarding the journey with us," said Conlaed to the captain. He shrugged.

"Those were my orders. Now, we turn merchant and buy supplies for the court before we return."

"Tell the Regissimus that we will send word ahead as quickly as we can when we again return to these parts," said Launcelot.

The group mounted and turned itself to face inland. They skirted past Quentovic, having no need yet for provisions, or to advertise their presence in a town teeming with itinerants, to pick up the road that led in a southerly direction to Orleans. Here, the landscape did not differ much from that of Britannia; they might have been moving inland from any coastal town as they made their way past gorse bushes and wiry grasses not yet ready to put out blooms but clinging tenaciously to the sandy soil though buffeted by the chill, salty gusts. Finding shelter in a foreign land, however, was less easy than traversing the countryside. Marcellus had a good grasp of the Frankish tongue, and many of the people also still spoke a Roman dialect that provided a useful, if stilted, means of conversation, and, if all oral communications were futile, the sight of a party of soldiers arriving at a settlement was comprehensible enough. Even so, they spent several nights under the stars.

"We are approaching the lands where the Frankish rulers patrol more closely," said Launcelot one night as they sat around the fire, eating rabbits caught by the dogs. "We may well expect to be confronted by the king's men, especially if any of the villagers have thought to attempt to send word."

Perceval stared into the flames. "We need to learn our stories," he said. "What we will tell Clovis, and what we will allow to be discovered as the 'real' truth."

"Will he believe falsehoods?" asked Conlaed. "You said he was a man of intelligence."

"Not one lie, but we must convince him that the second, the one he ferrets out beneath our words, is the truth."

"That is where our Lady Helena must come in," remarked Launcelot. "It is a pity that she and you so resemble one another, Perceval, for we cannot conceal that connection at least, but we may use her beauty to our advantage."

"You intend to place lie upon lie on a holy quest, and you expect me to be complicit in your plots?" asked Helena incredulously.

"Helena," said Perceval, in a tone that Galahad had never heard him use towards his sister before, "you know that service to the Most High requires sacrifice. Do you think that such a sacred mission will not be beset with such demands? We know that Queen Clotilda is a woman devoted to the Church to the point of fanaticism. What would be her temptation to sin upon learning that we are to seek the Grail? Would not she covet it for the Frankish kingdom? We know the Franks embrace the murdering of their relations as a way of life - what would they care for us in the face of such a prize?"

"If she is as pious as it is said, surely she will not stand in the way of the one whose right it is to seek it?" Helena indicated Galahad, who flushed, thankful for the reddening firelight.

"We have the abbot's letters," he said, unsure of what was intended for Helena but loath to let her be a victim of stronger wills.

"Letters written to the Pope and sealed by the abbot. What good would open missives be? If we are murdered and they burned, what will stop Clovis from seeking the prize?" Launcelot threw a rabbit bone into the fire.

"Remember also who is his Holiness's nearer neighbour," added Perceval. "If he did learn of Arthur's loss, whom would he ultimately back? When is the Regissimus to march on Rome?"

Helena looked aghast at her brother.

"You speak thus of the Pope?"

"We are a free Church. Our ways are not wholly Roman. He is to be revered, but he is human."

He held out a hand to his sister, who was biting her lip and staring fixedly at her feet. As she clasped it, she looked up into his face. He continued in a softer tone. "We need you, Helena. We will bear your sins of lying, if you are thus constrained, in the protection of the Grail, but we cannot succeed without you." She nodded.

"I will do what you will," she whispered.

"We are grateful, lady," said Launcelot formally.

"The first tale must be simple, but not opaque," said Perceval. "We are travelling to acquire certain holy relics, and to treat with kings upon the way."

"Arthur is securing his shores against further Saxon invasion," suggested Galahad. Launcelot nodded.

"Yes, that will seem to fit with the offer we have for Clovis."

"And the second?" said Conlaed, clearly resigned to expediency. "Should it not appeal to the queen?"

"Yes," replied Perceval, "and that is where Helena will aid us, for she will be sure to gain the queen's ear as a nun. We must let Clotilda persuade Clovis to let us proceed towards Rome without impediment."

"Then it should be an especial treaty with Rome, but one of internal affairs only. The Pelagians still abound - let it be an offer of welcoming missionaries to root out heresy and return Britannia once and for all to Rome." Galahad stared at Conlaed; he knew that the Celtic traditions were engraved upon the monk's heart, and that interference from Rome was the least of his desires.

"And if the king were, it might be suggested, willing to sacrifice certain of his men who held such heresies..." continued Launcelot. He turned to Helena. "My lady, could you do this for us?"

"She can," said Perceval, interjecting upon Helena's silence. She closed her eyes and nodded slightly, still holding her brother's hand. "Be strong," he said softly, "for you will do great deeds for us." Galahad looked away uncomfortably; the smooth words reminded him too painfully of what he had left behind, a coercion as strong, though loveless.

There was no more to be said in conference. They pulled their cloaks about them and huddled down to keep the night air at bay. Their shapes were only visible against the flickering firelight which played against their stillness and made light of their determination.

It was Samson who first alerted Galahad to the fact that they were being trailed. His forays off the path, usually aimless, became patterned and insistent, as if he were checking a particular scent. He started to dart back and forth at his master, giving short, low barks, and his behaviour began to disturb the other dogs. Galahad kicked his horse forward to Launcelot's side and informed him quietly of his suspicions. Launcelot scanned the lands around them; they were in a slight valley, dotted with woods, not an optimal position for defence.

"Tell the others to pull closer together, and send Marcellus to the rear," he said in a low voice. "And unsheath swords."

Galahad passed down the line quietly relaying the orders. There were soft scraping noises as weapons were pulled from leather scabbards and concealed within cloaks. Helena twisted her quiver from her back round to her side, looking determined, although her fingers trembled slightly as she held the reins. No one betrayed awareness, yet all were watching their surroundings, casting a glance around as they casually looked back to joke to a man behind them, or observing the land to the side as they called a dog to heel. Much as Galahad would have liked to allow Samson to confirm the whereabouts of their uninvited company, he did not want the dog to raise the alarm with them, and, reluctantly, he kept him by his side.

Samson's ears remained pricked, and soon he commenced a small, whining growl, holding himself back to his master's will, but ready to rush forth at command. The other dogs raised their hackles. The men stiffened at his warning; soon they did not need to pay heed to Samson, for the sound of hoofbeats came near enough to fall within the human range of hearing. Launcelot and Perceval led the way onward, pushing towards a distant incline, hoping to gain ground in case the encounter were to be hostile. They moved swiftly, in tight formation, listening to the approach of the riders through the trees. Finally, when Galahad thought he could bear the suspense no longer, he heard a shout and the sound of the final approach. At a word from Launcelot, they moved into a circle, holding their weapons at the ready.

A horseman burst through the undergrowth, leaping across a small ditch to land a few feet from them. He pulled his horse back tightly, and it reared up. The rider's long hair streamed out against the wind. His face was masked by a helmet whose nosepiece came down over his face. It appeared almost too ornate to be used in battle - it was adorned with copper plates etched with interwoven circular patterns and fixed with gleaming rivets. A net of chainmail hung down behind to protect his neck. He sat tall upon his horse, and the arms that held the reins were thick as tree limbs, and decorated with winding bracelets.

"Who comes into the territory of King Clovis?" he demanded in the Roman tongue. Launcelot bowed on his horse.

"A delegation from Arthur, Regissimus of Britannia. Whom of the king's family do I have the honour of addressing?"

The rider took off his helmet. He had glass-blue eyes, surrounded by fine creases, and an aquiline nose. Though he was evidently not above twenty, a long moustache framed his lower face, falling down each side of a grim-set mouth. He scanned the party, pausing at the faces of Perceval and Helena. He licked his lips briefly.

"I am Prince Clodomir, son of King Clovis. We are well met, for I and my men are riding to Orleans to meet with my father.

You will be able to travel under safe escort," he said, and they did not miss his slight emphasis upon the last word.

The rest of his men had ridden up behind him, about twenty in number. Galahad tried to hide his relief that such a band had not been hostile. The men were mostly younger than the Briton warriors, though what they gained in youth they seemed to lack in discipline, for they jostled and milled around on their horses, throwing comments in the Frankish language, and laughing. Several stared unashamedly at Helena, who pulled back behind Perceval. He said nothing, but moved his cloak so that his sword hilt was visible.

"Indeed, we thank our good fortune," said Launcelot smoothly, "it will lessen our danger and add to our profit."

"You have an interesting company," said Clodomir. "Explain them to me." Launcelot did so briefly.

"A man and woman of the church, eh? Well, my mother will be pleased to meet with you; she is ever zealous in her devotions to such matters. I concern myself with the real business of managing the realm for my father. Your men can ride with mine; I dare say they can find ways to communicate. My Lords Launcelot and Perceval, you shall ride with me. I have escorts for the others, who can manage in the Roman or Briton tongues." He turned back to his men, and called out a couple of names. Two warriors came though the ranks, better dressed than the others. Clodomir assigned them to Galahad, Conlaed and Helena. Then he raised his hand, and the rabble began to form into something resembling a column, and to move along the road.

Clodomir was clearly pleased to have intercepted the messengers for his father, and maintained a casual but pointed questioning of his companions. Launcelot and Perceval answered with as contrived an air of disingenuousness as they could manage. Nor were the others exempt from interrogation. Galahad listened for the trap in every question, whether it be a query concerning his homeland or a complimentary comment on his war animals. He made answer, though he was careful to say nothing of importance.

If the party was under a new pressure, at least they had the convenience of travelling in the party of a prince, with its attendant comforts, when they stopped at the estates of wealthy or noble men, both Franks and Gallic Romans, who had found prosperity in the union of the old and new kingdoms. At each stop they were met with a feast which was claimed to have been hastily prepared at the sight of their arrival, but which in fact bore the marks of foreplanning provided by a scout. Such nights offered a little respite from the conversational dances of the day's ride.

"We hear that your king, Arthur, upholds the Roman ways," one of the older Franks was commenting to Perceval as they rode together on the last leg of their journey. "My mother's family is of the Roman line."

"It would be truer to say that we are Roman Britons," replied Perceval, "but yes, he holds the fabric of the empire intact."

"He must be the last in the western empire."

"Think yourself fortunate," interjected another of Clodomir's noblemen from behind, "you have the privileges of your old ways with the protection of the greatest warriors of the west."

The man cringed and glanced nervously ahead to where Clodomir was riding, but the prince had not noticed his suggestion of discontent, for he was deep in conversation with Helena. At least, the conversation was deep on his side; she was answering as politely and briefly as she could.

"I grant you," he was saying, "that women can find power within the Church. But that is for the ugly and dowerless; one of your looks and pedigree could do just as well for herself - and the Church, of course - at the side of a great man. Take my own mother. There is not a more pious woman in the whole kingdom, not even counting the holiest abbess, but she has more power for her own ends than any who have sworn to abjure the embrace of a man and shrivel in a nunnery."

"It is a call, my lord," she replied cautiously, "and one that has, if you will forgive my opinion, little regard to face or fortune."

"Our nunneries are full of unmarriagable daughters and repudiated wives," laughed Clodomir. "Were they called or were they pushed into their retirement?"

"Perhaps the Lord was in charge of those plans which seemed to be of man."

"Perhaps," he grinned, as he ducked under a branch. Helena took advantage of the momentary pause to fall back a little closer to Galahad and ask a trivial question about his horse, which he endeavoured to turn into a conversation. There was more warmth than substance in their words, and it did not keep Clodomir at bay over long. He pulled back his horse until she caught up with him.

"You give much attention to striplings, Lady Helena. You are, I suppose, not used to the company of men?"

"The worth of a person's conversation is oftimes not dictated by his age," replied Helena archly. Galahad bit his lip. The insolence of great princes had to be suffered by lesser men; only a woman, who rarely had power to lose, dare hint at her opinion. However, Clodomir, it seemed, was too sure of himself to understand the direction of the remark.

"True, and you will know how true when you meet with my brothers. Even this youth will seem a sage!" He pulled up his water bottle and threw its contents down his throat, wiping his mouth ostentatiously from elbow to sleeve to indicate how pleased he was at his cleverness. Helena brushed her foot surreptitiously against Galahad's, smiling.

Later, as they stopped to water their horses, Perceval came over to check on Helena's comfort. His sister was seething with vexation.

"I can hardly bear him," she whispered. "He has been paying attention to me since our parties converged. Must I endure him?"

Perceval embraced her. "We need to keep the mission safe, my dearest," he murmured into her ear, "but if he touches you, I will run him through, be he prince or the Holy Father himself."

In a few more days, they reached Orleans, one of the huge estates of the Frankish kings. Clovis was, as Clodomir explained, progressing to Paris, by now his favoured seat, but Orleans would still be a sight to impress them.

"My brothers also will be converging upon Orleans for the final royal progression to Paris," he explained.

"You have several brothers, do you not, my lord?" asked Perceval. Clodomir's brow darkened. "Yes, two younger than myself, Childebert and Clotar, and another, elder, but not of the Christian union between the king and my mother."

"Theuderic, yes? But he is still a legal heir?"

"Co-heir. His stakes are high, I would not recommend that your party throw themselves into his camp," replied Clodomir, looking pointedly at Launcelot and Perceval.

"We do not come with the intention of aligning ourselves with factions," replied Launcelot. "We are but bearers of missives from the Regissimus."

"Your king reserves high titles for himself."

They made no reply to this, for the gates of the royal residence were thrown open ahead of them, and people were milling out to form a welcome for the prince. He pulled ahead of Launcelot and Perceval and dug his heels into his horse, which set off at a dangerous run towards the crowd. There were shrieks as women tried to push out of the way, and a few shouts from young men who attempted to run alongside the prince. Laughing, he shook off a bracelet into his hand and raised it high for them to see. Then, whirling it around his head, he flung it before him, that anyone who might try to grab the prize would have to risk his horse's hooves. Most drew back, but a couple ventured to speed forward as the bracelet fell, flashing, in the sunlight. The horse was galloping down upon them, and, at the last moment, one of the youths stopped, but the other continued, bending down to grasp the bracelet as it hit the ground. It slipped out of his fingers, and he fumbled for a second to catch it again. As he looked up, he saw Clodomir bearing down upon him, and, even from a distance, the fear upon his face could be seen. A scream was heard from the crowd, and then a mighty shout as the prince pulled his horse into a jump and it soared over the head of the youth. After a momentary pause he stood up, and waved the prize with a shout, grinning and trembling at the same time. His friends flocked to him, and he was lost in a small crowd of congratulators.

Meanwhile, Clodomir had wheeled back to where his men stood. He came to a halt in front of Helena, breathless and triumphant.

"I'll wager that you do not see such horsemanship from your men of Briton!" he boasted.

"No, my lord," said Helena, at a loss for other words. Satisfied with her confusion, he laughed and sped towards the palace once more.

"Is that how one lives when one is constantly in danger of fratricides?" she said quietly.

"He may yet die before his brothers get to him," muttered Perceval.

Chapter Nine

The party was not even permitted to rest or refresh themselves before being ushered into the Great Hall by Clodomir to await the presence of the king; he clearly feared that to let them out of his sight was to allow another to snatch the advantage of acting as their sponsor. Having led them in, though, he left them to their own devices in a corner while he went to join a group of young men near the dais, who were exchanging remarks casually, though holding themselves as though they were alert to any whisper which might concern them.

It took no thought for the Britons to realise that they were seeing the royal brothers together. Clodomir stood nearly a span above his young siblings, as Galahad reckoned it. The younger brothers looked to be close in age to Galahad himself; the youngest barely had the beginnings of a moustache, though his hair fell in waves down the length of his back. Another man stood just to one side, half paying attention, but gazing around the room sullenly. His colouring was darker than the others, and he stood taller than Clodomir, yet there was enough of a resemblance to mark him as Theuderic.

"See where brotherliness and ambition meet," whispered Conlaed. "I would not like to be part of such a family."

"But did not our own Regissimus pursue the grandson of Aurelius, his own adoptive son, to death?"

"The young man committed an act of treason in time of war; the king, I am sure, did not act lightly. Yet, you are blessed to be a single heir."

"Do you observe the lion cubs?" murmured Launcelot over Galahad's shoulder.

"I think they are rather observing us," replied Galahad. The brothers had perhaps been mentioning a name of one of the party, for they glanced in their direction almost simultaneously. Clodomir made the motions of finishing his conversation, but Theuderic had broken off before he ended, and strode across the hall to meet them. They bowed formally.

"Lord Launcelot, I am pleased to greet you. Lord Perceval - I think I recall a visit to my father's court some years back. You were with your father."

"I am gratified that you recollect my presence. I of course remember you and your father well, but I did not expect mutual recognition."

"We are of an age, I think; I was eager then always to make comparisons with young warriors of my generation."

"I am sure from what I have heard that you seem like to make a better comparison with your father," said Launcelot.

"As your son does with you." Galahad bowed stiffly.

"I trust that my brother made a fitting escort?" asked Theuderic, changing the topic. From across the room, Clodomir was glowering at the apparent proselytizing of his prize.

"He acted impeccably as a Frankish prince," said Perceval. Theuderic laughed.

"He has already blundered into offence, then, I see. He is not accustomed to restrain his thoughts."

He was interrupted by the sounds of the king's and queen's arrival. He bowed slightly once more.

"I bear no design against neutral parties," he said in a low voice, as he went to take his place before the throne.

King Clovis would have been unmistakably the father of Clodomir and the others, even had their long hair not identified them as the ruling family. They combined the colouring of their mother with the bulky physique of the king. Clovis's hair still reached down to his thighs, as Perceval had described it, though it was grey. His moustache revealed the original deep brown of his hair, though it, too, paled to grey as it blended down into the hair that fell across his shoulders. Although his face was creased, this did not detract from a vibrant authority which emanated from him as he sat upon his throne. He wore a long yellow tunic, edged with gold thread, over which was an ermine jerkin. His hose were of fine wool, and his leather shoes were jewelled at the eyelets. Next to him sat the queen. She was slightly younger than her husband, and her light brown hair was only faintly streaked with white. She, too, wore it long and flowing, and it almost reached the ground as she sat. Her dress and over tunic were of dark red silk, similarly embroidered at the hems and sleeves with disc patterns. A necklace of enamelled gold discs hung low down on her tunic, and she wore earrings with red and blue cloisonne stones set about a gold cross, which swayed as she leaned forward slightly to examine the new guests who were announced suddenly by Clodomir in a booming voice that sent them hastening forward to the thrones, straightening their cloaks and adjusting their belts as they went.

Clovis raised his eyebrows upon hearing the introduction, and looked keenly at Launcelot.

"We have heard of your prowess, my lord, and will be pleased to discuss whatever your king has seen fit to offer, as well as your mission. But first, we will make available our resources for your refreshment. My man here" - he indicated a servant to his left - "will be your escort during your stay, and will offer all assistance."

"Your majesty," Launcelot bowed, "may I call to the attention of your gracious queen that our Lady Helena, sister of Lord Perceval, is a nun? If we might beg appropriate shelter for her..."

"She may go to my quarters," said Clotilda, in a heavily-accented Roman tongue. An older maidservant came forward and curtsied first to the queen and then to Helena. She and her brother exchanged a long look, and then she followed the maid from the hall.

Other introductions followed, and the newcomers from various lands and regions were invited to share in a welcoming drink, but all formal business of the mission was delayed until the next day. The night was given to the ceremonies of hospitality, though it did not escape most of the party that Clovis could be deliberately biding his time to weaken the guard of his guests. They remained in the Great Hall only as long as courtesy might dictate before withdrawing to seek their beds. The guest quarters proved to be no more than a small separate hall, already occupied with the belongings - and guards - of others. But there were pallets aplenty, and it would at least be less noisome than the Great Hall after an evening of eating and drinking. They commandeered an unclaimed corner and set up a guard of their own.

If they had expected Clovis' words to promise an early meeting, they were disappointed. The fellowship was as free to congregate as any other group at a court; that was, free to be held in suspicion and spied upon by any other interested party. They chose their first meeting after their arrival to be in the open, among the horses and dogs being groomed and exercised by Caius who had retained control of their care. He had little of the Frankish tongue, but enough of an ardour for his horses to make his authority over them obvious to the most obtuse Frankish stableman. There was not much to report thus far.

"The web of loyalties at this court is not as tangled as it seems. All want to be seen as supporting the regime; some look more towards the new kings, but plain factions are sparse." Perceval stroked his horse's neck as he spoke.

"Who knows what will erupt with the death of Clovis?" mused Launcelot. "Theuderic and Clodomir appear the strongest, but the smallest adder may be as deadly as the largest. Yet that is not of import to us, though it may be useful to report to Arthur. We know we shall be watched; it matters not by whom, as long as we remain unshakeable in our story. Clovis will not let us pass through his kingdom until he believes he knows our very thoughts."

"Our task, apart from care of our belongings is, I presume, making contacts among the Frankish servants and soldiers?" asked Paulus.

"Yes, but be careful of the tongue you speak in when conversing together," warned Perceval. "We know not what spies might be put in your path. Marcellus, you speak much of Paulus' African tongue, do you not?"

"Yes. It's a useful tool for secrecy."

"Then you can coordinate efforts, but be on the watch for veterans of the Roman army who might recognize your speech. I doubt that Clovis has many interpreters here, but we should not underestimate him."

"The youngest son is of your age, I believe," said Launcelot to Galahad. "It may well fall to you to make an alliance there. Watch him carefully."

Galahad nodded. He wanted to ask after the Lady Helena, but he dare not. Something in Perceval's eyes told him that it would not be a welcome question. She was out of their sight, and they would just have to trust that they were still acting the same pageant.

Until the day he left his grandfather's court, Galahad had led a life structured by others or the demands of being an heir. Now, he was a minor, base-born son, and expected to create his own role, except that there was no public one he cared for. His unspoken intention remained, he told himself: he would find a way to make Launcelot pay for what he had done to his mother - and himself. Yet, he found that as he travelled further from his past in the company of his father he had to remind himself of his resolve lest it be lost in the demands of the fellowship. And while he waited, what could he do? The mundane activities of a prolonged stay at court - repairing and honing equipment, laundering, exercising the horses - were overseen by the soldiers, and he was once again left chafing at the inactivity that Launcelot and Perceval took so calmly. He understood now why older men had been chosen for the expedition; they had the patience of experience. He had nonchalantly mentioned his frustration to Conlaed.

"But there is an activity in stillness, both for the monk and the warrior," his tutor had said. "Think of the snake or fox. It will be quiet and still for an impossibly long time contemplating the prey until the time is right to strike. In stillness you can learn and profit."

So Galahad tried to learn. He took up his assigned task of cultivating a relationship with Chlotar, who was judged the least wily of Clovis's pack. He decided not to be the one to make the first approach. Instead he watched the prince surreptitiously as he went about his daily business. He noticed that the young Frank spent much time overseeing the training of the royal dogs, a duty surely not thrust upon him by his father. Therefore he made sure that Chlotar was about one morning when he put a fortunately obliging Samson through his paces with his horse, practising weaving under and around the mare's legs as he rode. The bait was easily accepted. Chlotar came forward to scratch Samson's head and hold his muzzle as he looked appreciatively at him.

"A fine dog," he remarked in a voice that revealed only a recent deepening. "Is he a war hound?"

"He was not specifically bred for war, but I would not do without him in battle," replied Galahad. "He has been at my side since he was old enough to cease suckling his dam. He and I are attuned to one another, and I can trust him better than any man."

"That would not be too hard in a court," said Chlotar, giving a small laugh. So you, too, are uncertain, thought Galahad.

Thus in a quiet way a tentative alliance was made, though its terms were those of two young men working to fathom one another. Chlotar's attempts to glean information were, however, more transparent than those of Galahad, as he hesitatingly explored diplomacy. His probings were not difficult to evade without giving offence. Still, he was a Frankish prince and not to be taken lightly, nor given the impression that he was seen as such.

They began to work together in training some of the dogs which Galahad and Chlotar judged most likely to make something of themselves other than pack hunters. They patiently bribed them with tidbits and praise to learn some of the finer tricks of battle dogs; Galahad was pleased to learn that his new companion shared his convictions on training without harshness. A dog trained for war had to kill for love of its master. Fear did not make it single-minded - only slavish devotion could do that.

"I see you have to train a dog not to understand men but horses," remarked Chlotar as they were riding along, and persuading the animals to perform the trick Samson had executed so very well.

"A cavalryman may be aware of the presence of a dog, but he sits higher than a horse, and his vision is not the same. Neither does he have to worry about his footing; he expects his mount to do that."

"And how does your horse know not to kick the dogs?"

"She does not. Her only instinct is for Samson. They are allies, almost family, perhaps better," he laughed casually. Chlotar smiled in acknowledgment.

"The temptation of inheritance breaks blood allegiances."

"I come from a sparse line. I have not that fear," replied Galahad.

"My father had no brothers to compete with, yet he established his kingdom on the deaths of his relatives, who met with violent ends." Chlotar casually related the fates of his father's cousins whose kingdoms and lives fell to their ruthless relative. "Some say that he had his cousin, King Chararic, and his son shorn and ordained priests to exclude them from the succession," he said contemptuously, with a shake of his own mane, "and even that did not spare them, for a chance remark caused them to lose their heads. My father does not take words lightly."

That was only the first of Chlotar's tales. Over the next few days, he imparted many stories of the assassinations and treacherous alliances that expanded and consolidated the Frankish throne. At first, Galahad had wondered whether to see in them a warning, but he decided at last that the theme was merely coincidental to their situation, and that Chlotar sought only to boast and vaguely intimidate. He saw these histories, thought Galahad, in the same context in which he himself viewed the intrigues of his grandfather. These were deeds beyond the ordinary happenings which governed the lives and deaths of men, and they required a certain detachment if one were not to fall prey to their horrors. He gazed across at the young man telling his tales as he petted his favourite bitch. He had believed that he himself had only created such a barrier because he was so alone, but here was a prince with two parents, joined, if the tales were true, as the result of quite a romance, and with siblings if these should fail, and yet he felt just as persecuted. Galahad frowned. He did not like his new world; it did not make sense.

It was not Galahad but Chlotar's brothers whose actions finally extracted a confidence useful to the party of Britons. Though Chlotar knew he was set to inherit equally with his siblings, a sense of being dismissed as 'safe' obviously rankled and he was determined to prove himself as a man though he had scarcely a hair on his lip. In particular, the practice of rival drinking was popular here among the warriors. Galahad had never cared for it when it had occasion to take hold at Pelles' hall, and had cultivated the art of appearing to drink liberally while retaining his senses. Chlotar, however, had not fathomed this trick and was regularly found slumped over the table after an evening of following his brothers' lead.

This night, Clovis and his queen made their usual progression through the hall to the dais. Behind them swelled a retinue of man- and maid-servants, and nobility who served in court positions. A group of soberly clad women were close behind the queen. Among them, Galahad espied Helena. She had been kept from their company since her arrival, and they could not yet ascertain how deliberate this was. Some of the fellowship, though they dared not say this aloud to Perceval, speculated that she had withdrawn herself to avoid fulfilling the deed she so despised. She did not appear guilty, though, and she had at least found favour with the queen, for she had evidently been given gifts: her travelling dress had been exchanged for a blue tunic and an overdress of slightly deeper hue, upon which her golden cross stood out starkly. Although her clothes were plain, they fitted smoothly over her body and caressed her as she walked. Even Launcelot smiled as he gazed upon her. Clodomir, scanning the crowd, caught sight of her at the same moment. He drained the wine cup he was holding and leered. Galahad suddenly felt that he knew what a brother must feel towards a sister. He shuddered.

However, though he wanted to find a place by Helena and share their stories, he had other business. He watched and waited until he could find the moment to slip into a seat beside Chlotar while the young prince was still coherent. He was gazing at Helena, who was sitting quietly with the queen's women.

"The woman is of rare looks, is she not?" he said slyly, nudging Galahad in the ribs.

Not you also, thought Galahad. "She is as noble in spirit as in body," he replied guardedly.

"She has already been the subject of an almighty argument betwixt my father and my brother Clodomir. We could hear them outside his chamber."

"Is there aught to relate?" asked Galahad casually, relieved that the interest was not so personal. Chlotar swallowed the bait, and told his tale. Clodomir had revealed his liking for

Perceval's sister, and declared that he would have her as his wife or concubine - he cared not which as long as he was in possession of her before they left for Paris. Clovis had berated him for his stupidity. What single man, he had said, could think that he could take a woman from under the dual protection of her brother and the Church which was her spouse, and expect no dire consequences? Clodomir had argued that that was his father's concern, that he wanted a word from him and a price to give Perceval and Launcelot for their inconvenience. There had been a roar, and Chlotar had had to duck as a goblet came flying out of the window, a usual sign of the king's enragement.

"He called him names that stained my mother's honour beyond redemption!" grinned Chlotar. "My father declared that no exchange would take place under his acknowledgment of the union."

"So what will your brother do now?"

"He usually finds a way to get what he wants. Any man would sell his sister to a prince for the right price, would he not?"

"What of your mother's wishes?" asked Galahad cautiously. Chlotar took another draught of wine.

"She thinks she can stop him," he boasted in a low voice, looking round for any of her retinue, "but he is headstrong. He will find a way around her. We all can, you know."

Galahad was not sure that the wine was talking rather than the youth, but he did not feel easier at this information. He lingered on, steering the conversation towards more innocuous themes of the merits of British and Frankish women, until he saw that Chlotar's eyes were beginning to swim and that his concentration was waning, then he moved back to his seat amongst his own party. Not without trepidation, he leaned over to Launcelot and Perceval and hesitantly imparted his information, keeping his tone low and casual lest suspicion should be aroused in those nearby. By the time he had finished, in a few minutes which seemed an hour, Perceval looked as though he might commit murder. He sprung up from the table where he was seated, as if to strike down Clodomir that instant. Several heads turned.

"Patience, patience," soothed Launcelot. "It is a private desire, and not a public shame to us."

"Not public? I see him - the court sees him - he is like a rutting stag. If it were not for the queen, our mission would be in tatters by now, and we might be food for the crows." His voice was low and controlled, but venomous.

"You set the stakes," Launcelot reminded him gently, "and the Lady Helena agreed. It is not a major battle, and it is nearly won. She shall not be scathed."

"We did not agree to place her in the path of a sacrilegious whelp."

"There are limits in place. This is a Catholic court, governed by a Catholic king."

"A man but one step removed from paganism. Who is to say that the king is a real convert, or a Catholic from convenience? He favours the son of an unholy union."

"Clovis would never agree to such a match."

"That is what I am afraid of," said Perceval more quietly, taking his seat once more.

"You think the king would look away when a nun was forcibly taken as his son's concubine? Clovis could not allow the insult to his guests or his Church."

"What would it matter to him if she were taken to some obscure estate far from the influence of the Church?" Perceval smashed his fist against the table helplessly. Launcelot put a hand upon his arm.

"She is a sister to us all. Her honour is ours, and we will not allow any compromise."

"You cannot know," said Perceval, speaking slowly to control his wavering voice. "You cannot possibly know."

This incident decided one matter at least: personal contact with Helena was a priority, even if it caused them to come close to self-betrayal. Therefore, Perceval seized an opportunity to claim her from the queen on the way back from the chapel the next morning, brazenly demanding a brother's privilege to take his sister for a walk. He could make use of his handsomeness when he chose, and he had no difficulty in persuading Clotilda to grant his desire. Brother and sister ventured away from the queen's retinue out into the royal orchard, which was deeper in blossom than those they had left behind in the cooler realms of Britannia. Apple and peach trees intertwined their boughs, while a few curly-haired sheep, evidently of a rare breed, grazed the grass beneath, quite unconscious of the petals which were settling softly on their coats and dappling their ivory wool with white and pink. Helena and Perceval strolled arm in arm until they met, by orchestrated chance, with Galahad and Launcelot, as they came to a pair of seats fashioned with turf, in an area which offered seclusion yet a good vantage of their environs.

"How goes it, lady?" asked Launcelot, when he had kissed her hand.

"The queen is a noble and pious lady. Her company is pleasant and I am shielded from many disagreeable aspects of court life." She left Clodomir's name unsaid. "It is an existence almost as ordered as the one I left: we weave or sew, and hear the divine offices read throughout the day. There are rarely any visitors."

"Has she inquired as to our mission?"

"Yes. Her dialect and accent are strong - and I emphasize mine also. We have to concentrate to understand one another, so this helps the ambiguity of my message. She asked me about the missives of the abbess, which I had no cause to conceal, and then enquired as to Arthur's intentions regarding his treaties with rulers in these lands. I - I told her that I hated to lie, but that I believed, though I was not wholly privy to your deeds, that a greater plan was afoot for Britannia and her relationship with the Church at Rome."

"Did you outline the story for her?"

"I made it more obscure; she is no fool, despite our difficulties in communication. I thought it better to permit her to draw the conclusions begged by my evidence." She flushed, and Perceval put an arm about her waist in comfort.

"You are doing well, and your continuation is vital." Launcelot nodded in agreement.

"But what of your part?" she asked. "My brother has said that the king has spent but little time in audience with you."

"Clovis has said virtually nothing to us concerning our declared objective; he fills the space with diplomatic niceties. We presume that he has decided to gain the truth from those around Lord Perceval and myself."

"And in our belongings," said Perceval. "Our quarters have been searched."

"The abbess's letters? Were they read?"

"They are unopened. We gave our missives to Paulus' safekeeping. Clovis' men have been one step behind us. Galahad has just been to talk with our men, and their story tells us of spies among the common soldiers."

"Their poor grasp of the Frankish tongue, at least, as Clovis's men think it to be, has been an opportunity for carelessness around them," said Galahad, picking up the report from Launcelot. "For example, they plied Metellus and Paulus with ale and quizzed them on their journey, getting a web of confused detail for their trouble. Then, thinking they had them in their cups, they began talking with one another right in front of them about who should report this to their superior."

"We are fortunate that our men keep clear heads," remarked Helena.

"We are more fortunate that Frankish beer is so weak," replied Galahad, smiling. It was a small joke, but it momentarily broke the tension of the discussion, and it was appreciated by the others.

"Is our time here at an end? Have we accomplished as much as we can?" asked Helena.

"Clovis is satisfied with the ostensible terms of allowing us safe passage in return for Arthur's word that he shall not interfere with his ambitions, at least this side of the water. What he thinks of our supposed mission to Rome, I am not sure, but we shall test him, and seek to depart as soon as we may," said Launcelot. "I think not but the king must be convinced that he can get no more information from us."

But Clovis would not hear of his guests' departure as yet.

"We have one last expedition in which I insist you participate," he smiled as they made their formal request for dismissal. "Your men can make ready for your journey while you come with us. We are to have a service at the cathedral here, and then a deer hunt for both men and women. I look to see at least one of you distinguish himself, providing, of course, that God is on your side tomorrow."

Launcelot had no choice but to acquiesce, and the party became part of the king's entourage that made its way to the cathedral of Orleans the next day. Helena broke away from the company of women to ride beside her brother. She seemed relieved that her commission was nearly over, and laughingly complained of being forced by propriety to ride side-saddle once again.

Galahad had been impressed by the age of Glastonbury, and the simple edifice which seemed to link to the stories of the humble disciples, yet when he saw Orleans, he had to stop and draw breath. The building was made almost entirely of stone bricks and towered up as high as the tallest trees Galahad had seen, maybe as high as nine or ten men. Near to the ground, arched windows ran the length of the main building, while above them circular and semicircular windows sat in between the arcs. All were glassed; Galahad was not sure that he had ever known it possible for so much glass to exist in one place. At the top of the walls, patterns were marked out in contrasting red stone: diamonds along the roof line, and circular decorations below.

The entrance was so large that the whole of the king's party could have ridden in comfortably; however, they dismounted and filed in. Galahad glanced around at his companions. Only Conlaed and Helena visibly expressed their impressions. Helena leaned a little towards Galahad and whispered in his ear, "Only think, if this is but a shadow of Rome!"

Indeed, he could hardly conceive such a possibility, for he had scarcely begun to comprehend this cathedral itself. As they entered the central aisle, they were walking between a colonnade whose carved columns reached to the vaulted, wood-lined ceiling. The church was spacious and light, much more so than the timbered buildings he had experienced in

Britannia. Between the columns, he caught glimpses of the mosaics that lined the walls. Constructed from coloured marble, they depicted scenes which he recognised from Conlaed's teaching, and cruder church paintings: Christ in majesty; the evangelists; the Flood. The pictures merged one into another as Galahad made his way down the aisle.

The Mass was conducted in Latin by the Bishop of Orleans, a stout man whose geniality was evident even through the solemn words of the Eucharist. If he was master of all this, thought Galahad, he must have reason to be content; neither Clovis nor Arthur would ever likely attain such a dwelling as their own. But then, they displayed earthly majesty; the Church articulated the eternal. Clovis tried to merge the two, supplicating himself in the presence of the body of Christ before demonstrating his power over mortal creatures in the hunt.

The religious stood in the apse of the cathedral, ostentatiously ignoring the finery and position of the courtiers. They were far more regimented than the monks and nuns whom Galahad was used to seeing, gathered but loosely under the ideals of the Celtic Church. Conlaed, it was true, was noticeable among them, with his sombre garb and tonsure, but he was shaved in the old manner, from ear to ear, rather than bearing the crown of the Frankish monks. Helena, though, might not be singled out as anything other than a pious noblewoman in her plain but finely-spun clothes. Galahad realised suddenly that he was no longer paying attention to the service, and he guiltily forced his concentration back to observance of the Host being elevated before the court.

The service over at last, the court streamed out, intent on its entertainment. Some, such as Queen Clotilda, were quietly fulfilled with their religious experience; most were eager to escape to the challenge of the day. They spilled out onto the open plain, where a stag and doe had been flushed out for the men and women respectively. The men and dogs went off in one direction, while the women were led on by huntsmen in another.

Chlotar rode past Galahad on his way to join the king. He reined in his horse for a moment.

"Make sure you all ride well," he said in a low voice. "My father sets you a trial; I hope you pass."

So their mission was to be put before God, thought Galahad. He did not feel the compulsion to prove himself that he had in the hunt at Arthur's court, which seemed so long ago now, but he was not averse to at least outdoing Clodomir. As he looked across at Launcelot and Perceval, he could read the same emotions in their faces. The prince in question was at the head of the hunt, close by Theuderic. Perhaps, thought Galahad, he would be too preoccupied with his own scores to watch for avengers at his back.

The dogs, who had been running back and forth in front of the horsemen, finally picked up the scent of the stag, and began to bark furiously, waiting for the signal to give chase. Clovis gave a shout in the Frankish tongue, and they leapt forward. Samson may not have understood the language of the king, but he knew the universal language of the hunt, and sprang out from under Galahad's mare to join the fray, affrighting several horses and earning curses from their riders as he fearlessly wove his way among their legs. As the riders picked up speed across the plain, Launcelot rode up beside Galahad.

"Ride to help Theuderic," he hissed. "We will take on Clodomir."

Galahad fleetingly imparted his information.

“Well, Lord Perceval would like to be the avenging hand against Clodomir. Perhaps more than we are on trial,” Launcelot replied grimly.

Galahad scanned the party ahead to see the eldest brother riding neck and neck with Clodomir, but he recognised some of those coming up behind as members of the younger prince’s party. He manoeuvred his horse to the edge of the hunting group, and pressed hard upon her flanks to bring her fast up the side. As he came to the men following close behind Theuderic, he pulled his reins sharply, cutting in front of them. He did not look behind him, but he could hear the rate of their horses’ hoof beats increase as they strove to gain the lead on him. He wove slightly from side to side as he galloped, impeding their progress. Theuderic was moving ahead of his brother, who was being flanked by Launcelot and Perceval.

There was a howl in front as one of the dogs was kicked by the stag. The wounded animal leaped back among the pack, momentarily putting them into confusion. The stag took its chance to abruptly change direction, moving at an angle which was taking him across Clodomir’s path. As Galahad looked sideways, he saw one of Clodomir’s men take advantage of the hesitation of the hunters and push his horse past Perceval, forcing him back and letting his prince break free. Perceval’s face was set grimly as he reluctantly reined in his horse and looked for an angle to make another attack, but it was difficult, as the stag was attempting to double back around a wooded area, and the hunt was breaking up, with some pursuing the animal’s heels while others tried to double guess its path and arced round the other side of the trees.

As the men pushed on, pursuing personal rivalries along with the stag, the women’s hunt had been conducted according to a more sedate code. A few were determined huntresses, and were riding their horses hard behind the huntsmen who were leading the chase for them. Many were simply glad of the opportunity to gather together in a relatively free setting, or were waiting to rejoin the men and snatch some unchaperoned conversation. Helena was not overly interested in the hunt itself, but she enjoyed the ride, and kept close to the leaders. The queen rode at the back with her young daughter, merely observing the game. As Helena glanced back, Clotilda indicated to her, and she dropped back beside her.

"You ride with skill, lady," she remarked.

"I was fortunate to possess a good teacher at my home, and an advocate in my brother."

"The Lord Perceval is an exemplary brother." Helena bowed her head in reply. The queen leaned over towards her.

"You have protectors, but you must be on the alert. My son will obey me by force when he is in my presence, but I cannot say what he will do when away from my influence. Always use the utmost caution."

"I will, your majesty." Helena knew not to elaborate her reply.

"Well, ride on. You deserve to show your talents today." Helena bowed once more and kicked her heels into the horse's flank, pushing it easily to the fore again.

The young doe was not that hard a prey, as Helena saw it, but the huntsmen were driving her on, keeping just out of her reach, in order to delay her inevitable death and create entertainment for the women. The dogs snapped at her hocks but kept at bay. Gradually, a small wooded area came into sight, and the huntsmen called to the dogs, who hung back reluctantly to run with their masters. Most of the horsewomen fanned out to encompass the trees, while a few kept their pursuit of the doe, pushing her forward into the coppice. She sprung, panting, into the undergrowth, looking for one last, agonized bid to elude the hunt; she soon realised that she was trapped. She began rushing back and forth maniacally between the small trees, desperately looking for a way out, but all sides were barred that the ladies might have a target for their fine arrows. Helena looked on in distaste.

"What fair chase is that?" she murmured, watching as the women, laughing, fitted their bows. Suddenly, there was a baying sound from behind them, and the stag emerged around the side of the coppice, closely pursued by Clodomir, who was raising his spear to strike home. Helena wheeled her horse around, snatching an arrow from her quiver and pulling her bow back against it. As Clodomir let go his weapon, she fired an arrow. It shot swiftly through the air, passing the spear to land in the throat of the stag, which fell to the ground leaving the spear to glance its side.

Clodomir began to look around, rage darkening his brow. Then he caught sight of Helena. He looked at her incredulously for a moment, then, seeing her empty bow and flushed face, he knew that the truth was inescapable. A curious mix of annoyance and lust passed over his visage, but Helena was not looking at him. She was smiling at her brother as he came forward at the forefront of the hunt. He caught her message immediately and raised his spear in salute.

Helena rode to the stag, which was being circled by the dogs, and dismounted, kneeling over it to pull out her arrow. Her eyes filled with soft tears.

"As the hart panteth after the water brooks, so panteth my heart after thee O God," she whispered.

"Why weep for a necessary deed, lady?" said a low voice within her ear. It was Clodomir, breathing onto her shoulder. She froze, but he did not remove himself. She could feel him gazing upon her neck. "You have won more than the stag this day; rejoice in the success ordained for you."

"What manner of woman have you nurtured?" Clovis was booming at Perceval, but in a jovial tone. "I had heard that the Briton women would follow their men to battle, but I did not know that they were members of your armies!"

"My sister receives the blessings of a life dedicated to God."

"Then I shall turn monk and look for such success on the battlefield!"

Perceval rode on to where his sister was attempting to rise slowly, impeded by Clodomir who leaned over her still, shadowing her body movements. When she saw that her brother was near, she twisted away more boldly and ran to him, leaving the prince to take the jests of his brothers. Perceval dismounted and embraced her.

"You have revenge," he smiled. She glanced back at Clodomir.

"I hope so," she said.

Chapter Ten

Clovis could offer no more objections to their immediate departure. They had fulfilled their duties as guests, and Clotilda was an advocate of their mission to Rome. Moreover, the Frankish court itself was preparing to progress to Paris, and a delegation led by Theuderic and Chlotar had already travelled ahead to ready the royal residence. Before going, Theuderic had sent a manservant to meet quietly with Launcelot and Perceval, and had offered a small scouting party to see them to the borders of the Frankish lands, a token, he said of future friendships between the two kingdoms. Unspoken was the chance to humiliate his brother should Clodomir attempt any violence. Lancelot accepted.

"They will meet us a day's journey from here," he explained to the others. "We shall thus minimize appearances of an alliance."

"Can we wholly trust him?" asked Galahad.

"I do not trust him as an ally, but as the eldest son whose chance to be sole heir is endangered by his stepmother's insistence on the old tradition of equal inheritance."

"You think he hopes for Clodomir's head?"

"He would certainly not pass up the opportunity."

"Then we are his bait," said Conlaed.

"It is a good enough trade," said Perceval bluntly. "We need friends on any terms."

They slipped out quietly the morning before the court itself was due to move, having paid their respects to the king and queen the night before. In spite of the uncertainty, the party was restored from their stay, and replenished with fresh clothing and provisions. Galahad was not displeased with his new cloak, more ample than even the tough homespun of his northern home. It was fur-lined and fitted with a deep hood that could be drawn down over his face to provide protection and concealment. He glanced around at the rest of the party. He caught Helena's eye, and she winked at him as she pulled her own cloak over her dress and breeches, ostentatiously smoothing down the folds of the fine, pleated wool. He was glad at her show of lightheartedness, for he had observed that her moods subtly affected that of the group as a whole. If she was anxious, they were protective; if she was angry, they were vengeful; and if she was blithe, they were somehow more relaxed.

It was therefore in a positive mood that they left the Orleans court on the route that would eventually take them out of the Frankish demesne and across the mountains into the Ostrogoth kingdom. The air was cold and damp, but they scarcely noticed under the shelter of their mantles. A light drizzle intermittently dappled their clothes and horses, turning to a fine steam as it evaporated around the horses' mouths and nostrils.

Following the lead of the hidden day, talk was muted, relegated among the leaders to sporadic discussion of their journey. Behind them, though, Paulus and Marcellus were passing the time by debating the merits and demerits of Frankish soldiers.

“They’re warriors who fulfill their reputations,” said Marcellus. “They have the spirit of the battle in them.”

“Yet they lack discipline,” replied Paulus. “They risk falling into the classic rabble of the barbarians in the heat of the fight.”

“I think their current leaders hold them together. Theuderic has a level head, but Clodomir...” Brows darkened at the mention of the queen’s eldest son.

“He lacks judgement, though he’s not a fool. I’d lay a wager that he’ll be the first brother to kill another.”

“Unless Theuderic strikes lucky among us,” ventured another.

“You can trust these Franks less that we used to trust the foederati we hired,” grumbled Marcellus.

“Trust or not,” interceded Conlaed, “they will be watching our backs before the end of the day, so you will need to find a way to make a truce with them.”

Theuderic was true to his word. As the afternoon began to wane, a group of horsemen came into sight, moving gently but purposefully down the road towards them. The leader raised his hand in greeting as they approached, and they thankfully recognised the prince’s men. He had sent six warriors; they were mostly a little younger than Launcelot’s cavalrymen, though the leaders obviously had some years upon Theuderic himself. One sported a battle scar running across his right eye and down his cheek, which puckered his skin and shone against his wind-tanned face.

The two parties slowed as they came together. The Frank’s leader, the scarred man, bowed before Launcelot and Perceval.

“I am Isembard, general and advisor to Prince Theuderic,” he said brusquely. “Have you perceived anyone following you as yet?”

"None," said Launcelot, "though this is a strange country to us."

"Aye. Well, if we press on we may put enough distance between us and any who might wish to - meet with you. Will you permit me to lead the way? There is a safe villa some miles ahead, and we can reach it shortly after nightfall."

Launcelot gave assent, and the two groups reassembled themselves into one, with the two older Franks at the head of the party and the others mingling with the soldiers at the rear. They quickly made it clear that the escort was no social courtesy, for they pushed on grimly, taking the party at a brisk pace that forced the dogs to cease running back and forth and instead trot swiftly alongside the horses.

As the sun dipped below the treetops, they led the group abruptly off the old Roman road and onto a narrower track which led down a slope to a fairly level plain and a view of a modest estate. Isembard sent a man ahead to announce their arrival. He returned to inform them that none of the family were present, but the slaves and servants left to run the place were welcoming enough.

"The family must seek royal favours," said Isembard cynically, kicking his horse forward.

By the time they had ridden the few minutes into the courtyard, it had become ablaze with torches as the household hurried out to greet its guests. Slaves were waiting with cups of wine; others stood ready to take the horses to the stables. There was a squawking in the background as several fowl were plucked from their roosts and taken to slaughter for the benefit of the guests. The glowing fires that burned continually outside the kitchen were hastily rekindled to a blaze and cauldrons set upon them. The horses, at least, were glad that rest had come to them, and tossed their heads and stamped when their riders dismounted, as if to shake the memory of the men from off themselves.

The steward bowed low to the party. He began to speak in a Frankish dialect that was translated for the Britons as he proceeded.

"Welcome, you who come from the glorious court of King Clovis, in the name of his willing servant, my master, Lucius Iucundus, who is at this moment travelling from his estates in Fleurs to pay homage to the king at Paris. I understand that I entertain men from the court of the renowned King Arthur also. Welcome, lords."

Isembard stood, looking impatient, as the formalities dragged on and the slaves scurried back and forth behind the steward. At last the man finished and waved his hand towards the hall. All trooped forward gladly, saddlebags slung over their shoulders. Inside, fresh straw had been laid against the walls for bedding, and jugs of wine were being placed upon the long table. The air was smokey, for the central fire, too, had been stoked up hastily for the guests.

Dishes of eggs were brought in, to bide time while the meat was being prepared. The Franks sat down without any ceremony and began to eat hurriedly, like men accustomed to being on the march. Galahad noticed Conlaed and Helena pausing to silently bless their food before beginning. He waited awkwardly, a swift grace running though his head before he took up a spoon. The eggs were coddled with herbs and wine, and were warm and creamy to the taste. He lent half an ear to the conversation between Launcelot, Perceval and the leading Franks, who were discussing the next part of their journey.

"We should leave before dawn," Isembard was saying as he helped himself to the meat which had been carried in so quickly from the cauldron that it was almost still bubbling.

"And we should order the steward to erase all traces of our visit," said Perceval. "Then at least anyone would have to threaten our progress out of him."

"True, though the route itself is easily followed - we have no alternatives. But if we hide the pace of our travel, it will lend uncertainty."

Galahad was not sure that he liked the assumption behind the words. He had formed no faith in Clodomir during his time at court, but he was not sure that Theuderic's men were to be trusted much more. The feeling that he might be part of a trap was more than somewhat disquieting, even if he were surrounded by comrades-in-arms. Those around him were not betraying similar thoughts in their faces, but they held themselves more upright than usual as they ate. He noticed suddenly that two of the men - one Frank, one Briton - had not sat down to the meal with them. They must have been left to guard the estate, and probably each other. The Franks, at least, seemed unconcerned at the thought of potential combat, and readied themselves only by drinking as much wine as they could extract from the steward, who was eager to please but still obviously taking stock of the estate's provisions as he watched the hungry band.

Even though he felt uncertain of his safety, Galahad slept more soundly than he intended after the final hard ride of that day. The straw provided for bedding was thick and fresh, and his cloak made a comfortable barrier between it and his body. Perceval placed Helena behind the screen that separated the main part of the hall from the serving area, and slept with his back to the other side; there had been no question as to whether they should entrust her to a strange women's quarters. With the extra members in the party, it was not necessary for the leaders to take a part in a simple watch, and thus, in the morning, Galahad was as rested and ready to leave as the servants were to see him and the strange alliance depart the villa.

This routine continued for the next few days. The Franks drove the group on as fast as they could, given that there was no change of horses. The system of estates established by Roman rule had not deteriorated under Frankish dominance, but had continued to flourish, and had been adopted by many considering themselves more Frankish than Gallo-Roman; consequently there was usually a comfortable rest within reach of the travellers at the end of each day. Many were masterless, with owners away at other residences or making the journey to Paris to pay homage to Clovis as part of the maintenance of their wealth.

However, by the fourth day the smoothness of the journey began to abate. The estate they arrived at that night did not have the atmosphere of a household surprised but willing to entertain guests with such close royal connections. Moreover, as Perceval noted, their food was not overlong in appearing, "As if, perchance, they expected us," he muttered to Launcelot. Paulus was sent to patrol the immediate environs of the estate but returned with no definite news.

"They've been herding swine out to pasture today," he said. "Any hoof prints that might have existed have been obliterated."

"We can extract the truth," said Isembard bluntly. "It won't take long with country servants - or their masters."

"It may be more advantageous to ascertain the truth for ourselves," replied Launcelot. "Then perhaps, if there are any in communication with our hypothetical companions, they shall think they are undetected."

Isembard grunted assent rather grudgingly.

"What route do you think they are taking?" asked Conlaed in a placating manner. Isembard accepted the conciliatory offer and began to outline the possible byways that would allow a party to loop around the Roman road.

"Do you think they left ahead of us, or are they riding beyond our pace?"

"If they left from Orleans, then no one made report, which means that they are not Clodomir's men, or not his best men. If they began after us, then they must be changing horses to ride this fast, and that is not in their favour if it comes to conflict." Having demonstrated his superior reasoning, he quaffed his wine and nodded in a gruffly smug manner at the others.

They left the next morning with no concrete information, but a sense of ill ease at the atmosphere. Isembard was once more muttering remarks about interrogation to himself in a disgruntled manner as they made their way back onto the highway, but once there he remained silent and alert for the rest of the day, riding aloof from the party. The Britons let him be; they themselves spent the journey preoccupied with their own thoughts of the battle ahead. The soldiers caught the mood of their leaders, and much of that day's march passed in almost unnatural silence.

The next estate told the same tale - a wary steward, a courtyard that had been overrun with herds, a house just a little too prepared for unexpected guests. Before Launcelot could raise the subject, two of the Franks had taken the steward behind the stables and extracted information from him. A group of young Frankish warriors, he said, noble youths among them, but not one of royal blood, had arrived the night before, coming down from the eastern byway with threats of their own.

After consultation, it was decided to send scouts to ascertain the route of what all assumed to be Clodomir's men. Marcellus and Paulus went in one direction and two of the Franks took the other. No one who remained slept hard that night. The servants and slaves were put under guard against treason in their quarters, with threats that their building would be put to the torch with them inside if any were found to have escaped. A flaming brand was set in the ground outside their doors as a token of the Franks' intentions.

Paulus returned when the night was past its darkest hour, moving quietly across the hall to Launcelot, but still waking all the warriors, who were alert to any sound. He reported that he and Marcellus had found the tracks of a mounted party; they had followed at least some of the tracks to the next village, but there were signs of doubling back, of scouts splitting off from the main party to check on the progress of the Britons. The return of Theuderic's men confirmed these suppositions. By now all the travellers were fully awake and had slipped mutually into a conference from which none were excluded.

"Do you know what they are waiting for?" Perceval asked the Franks bluntly.

"If they are biding a suitable time, I would only suggest that they want distance from Paris; if a place, there are a couple of areas along this road that would be more vulnerable to an ambush, but not many. The Romans built this for their armies, and they were no fools - at least those who were not their emperors." Isembard paused, considering.

"There is a slight valley about two days' ride from here, and then, maybe three or four days on, we have to cross a river. Those would be ideal places for an attack."

"Then we should move off the road," said Marcellus. "I don't want to be an easy prey for young thugs."

Galahad spoke up. "But we would lose speed if we took to the byways at once. I agree that we need to avoid placing ourselves in a weak position, but we should perhaps move off the path only periodically."

Launcelot nodded approvingly. "We should at least camp away from roads and dwellings."

"Perhaps," said Helena haltingly from the shadows, "perhaps you should make a compromise, a truce of some sort. I have endangered you - I would be willing to help." She did not elucidate, but they knew what she was offering.

"We accepted you into the party, and your abbess has provided us with valuable credentials for Rome. There is no going back on our word - you stay with us." The others murmured agreement at Launcelot's words.

"There is also no guarantee that Clodomir, or someone else, would not have pursued you anyway," said Isembard. "If you were thought to be conducting a mission dangerous to the empire of Clovis, any number of groups might have been dispatched to impede your progress."

"Have you?" said Marcellus hotly. Isembard laughed.

"My prince has only one aim in this expedition - to further his interests at the expense of his brother's. We will not break faith with you on this occasion."

"We are losing sight of the imperative," said Conlaed. "How do we place ourselves in the advantage now?"

"We should camp off road," replied one of thc Franks. "These servants are too easy to frighten, and they care not who they give their information to, if it will save their hides."

"So we agree on limited evasive action?" said Isembard. He looked around at the heads nodding in the semi-darkness. "Good. Then, let me trace our paths for you."

Isembard's explanation and its discussion took up the central hours of the night. Then, since all were awake and disinclined to seek further rest, they packed up before dawn, sending two men to raid the storehouses before they let the servants out of their quarters. They were saddling their horses as the steward emerged looking nervously affronted. Isembard tossed him a coin which he caught reluctantly.

"Give our thanks to your master," he said, grinning.

Galahad remembered well the tension he would experience before a punitive action upon one of his grandfather's transgressing underlords. He would begin to feel an increasing tightness about his torso as he approached the village or estate where they were to fight. As they waited for the signal to attack, his body would coil itself, ready for the release of battle, so much so that he would wonder if he would lose all self-control when he sprang into action. Once he urged his horse forward to the conflict, though, all his fears were forgotten as he laid about him, separating friend from foe in moments he barely registered before his sword struck.

This situation, however, was distinctly uncomfortable rather than merely tense. Not knowing whether they were trailing or being trailed gave no focus for his mind. He also found it difficult to push from his consciousness the fact that he would be facing warriors better than most he had yet encountered as his enemies, and he was angry with himself for losing the advantage of confidence. Beside him, Conlaed was drawing his fingers across the hilt of his sword and muttering prayers at the same time. Launcelot and Perceval were ahead, pushing forward quietly, but exchanging the occasional word without turning their heads towards one another. Brothers-in-arms, they understood one another's instincts; Galahad wished fleetingly for such a battle partner.

The party drove forward as quickly as they could, mindful that they would have nowhere to adequately rest themselves and their animals that night. One of the dogs was limping slightly by the end of the day, but it kept up with the party without trouble. They made camp that night away from the road, eschewing the paths to pick their way carefully through the wooded land that lay down below. They were forced to dismount and lead their horses between the trees, careful not to leave too many clues as to their route. They ate a cold supper, consisting of the food they had gleaned from the last estate; Launcelot and Isembard had agreed that a fire would be nothing but a beacon to their presence.

When they had found water for their horses, and the dogs had returned from their own hunt, dragging back the body of a young fawn to gnaw at their leisure, the group settled in for the night. The weather was not cold, and their clothes afforded more than sufficient cover. Helena nestled down against her horse, a little way from the men. Galahad would have liked to talk to her, to occupy his mind with calmer thoughts, but he felt awkward about approaching her. Instead, he settled down with his back to Conlaed, to snatch some rest until it was his turn to act as scout and watch.

Near dawn, the men were awoken from a fitful sleep by Marcellus.

"They are circling around from the bridle road to the west," he hissed as he went from one man to another.

"All of them?" asked Launcelot, instantly awake. Marcellus looked back and nodded as he moved round the camp, picking up his horse's saddle.

"It's good to fight on an empty stomach," growled Paulus as he checked over his sword. "It gives an edge to your work."

"Can we make it to a vantage point?" asked Perceval of Isembard.

The Frank looked stern. "If we move swiftly, we could set ourselves on that clear incline where we left the road. But we would have to risk them splitting off and coming at our backs across the highway itself. If they think we're moving ahead, though, they might decide they have no time for such strategies."

By the time he had finished his comments, the group was ready to leave. Launcelot sent the column off in strict order, placing Galahad with Helena and Conlaed in the centre.

"You do not need to give thought to my protection," she said gravely.

"I was not; I expected you to fight with us," said Launcelot. His voice was strong, but those who heard him thought that he spoke only to create confidence rather than belief.

"You do not need to fear, lady," said Galahad. "My sword is ready."

"And so are my arrows," she replied. "I will look to your back."

Galahad marvelled silently at this solemn, graceful woman. As she readied herself, she seemed little different from her brother: their strong, chiselled faces were both set in determination; they carried their reins lightly, their hands ready to move to their weapons. Yet she also had just a slight aura of hesitation, and a glance towards her sibling indicated a lack of total self-assurance, perhaps a dependence, that made her seem more humane, more approachable than the flawless Perceval.

Conversation stopped as they hurried back through the undergrowth. The dogs, sensing a fight, were on edge, and growled low at any sign of other life: a stick cracking, a mouse scurrying across their path. They did not bark, for they were trained to stay silent until the moment of conflict. Some way to their left, a flock of birds rose into the air, crying indignantly. Galahad jumped involuntarily and all glanced round. No one spoke, but they knew the disturbance was caused by another group of travellers. They picked up their pace.

The route was short, but every step seemed to have been stretched threefold since they had first paced it the night before. Their own footfalls seemed heavier, and even their breath was audible as they moved up the slope. Gradually the trees and undergrowth petered out and they found themselves in a clearing at the edge of the road.

Isembard spoke quietly to Launcelot and Perceval, then they turned and began to move their men swiftly into a formation for battle, small as the company was. They spread out slightly in an ellipsis, ensuring that there were warriors to detect and begin to repel any plan of Clodomir's men to ride up from the side and surround them. Helena and Conlaed stood back within the group; Helena loosened her cloak from her shoulders and took an arrow from her quiver, resting it lightly against her bow. Galahad set himself before her on his horse, his sword drawn. Samson and the other dogs stood at his side ready to worry the legs of the soldiers.

"Make sure they know which Franks are the enemy," quipped a soldier, looking down at the hounds. A few men smiled.

Then, hoofbeats gradually became audible, signalling the quickening approach of their adversaries.

"They are losing their restraint already," remarked Isembard.

"Father, pray now," said Perceval shortly. Conlaed lowered his head.

"To God, the Lord of Hosts we commit our souls and the battle," he said briefly. The others crossed themselves, and a few uttered an audible "Amen". Then, they waited.

At last, when Galahad felt he could hold himself still no longer, the riders came up through the undergrowth. They had not expected the Franco-Briton party to be taking a stand, and the leaders hesitated for a second as they saw them waiting on the path. Then one let out a long cry, and they plunged forward. The others waited until the first horses had almost crested the hill, then Isembard raised his sword and kicked his horse, and the men in front threw themselves towards Clodomir's men.

Galahad shouted down at Samson, who by now was trembling with suppressed ferocity. He leaped among the horses, followed by the other dogs, jumping at legs and whipping themselves out of the way of the swords. Samson sunk his teeth into the hind leg of a stallion, which reared up in pain and tried to kick out. As its rider spent a precious second trying to bring it down, Galahad rode in and brought his sword up through the man's stomach below his leather chestpiece. As he pulled his arm back, the man slumped forward, blood running down his thighs and his saddle as he slipped to the ground.

Though Galahad did not look to his side, he heard Paulus and Marcellus fighting hard, shoulder to shoulder, with two men who had dismounted. Perceval had ridden in front of him and met with a leader of Clodomir's band. Their horses jerked backwards and forwards, attempting not to clash as their riders thrust at each other. In a moment, Perceval managed to catch the other's arm, and, coming in close, kicked him off his horse, which trampled him as it desperately tried to leave the fray. Perceval leaned down and stabbed the man down through his shoulder into his chest as he struggled to his feet.

As Galahad turned to find another target, a friendly Frank beside him was struck to one side, and a warrior pushed on towards Helena and Conlaed, grinning at the easy prey before him. He was almost upon them, protected by his comrades who turned their struggle to preventing the protection of the two, when Conlaed raised his own sword and let out a cry, as he had done that afternoon so many lifetimes ago, it seemed. As the man thundered on, unable to stop, the monk threw himself from his own horse onto that of the Frank, taking them both to the ground. They rolled over, and leaped to their feet in the same instant. The Frank yelled something in his own tongue, enraged and contemptuous. They clashed swords, meeting close until Conlaed pushed back. He was older, but had his weight on his side, and he unbalanced the Frank again, though not enough to make him fall. The warrior swung his sword around; Conlaed met it and tried to cut up towards the man's arm, but he brought his sword arm back and slashed towards the monk's stomach. Conlaed jumped back, but his cross, swinging out low on his chest, was cut off. As the Frank smirked, Conlaed flew forward with more agility than Galahad ever knew his tutor to have possessed. He held his sword high and level and brought it into the Frank's neck. His head fell back, half-severed from his body, his eyes still wide with surprise, and his lips quivering.

Galahad pushed forward towards Helena, forcing one of Clodomir's men to turn and engage him. He was young, Galahad thought in the split second of recognition as the fight began, younger than himself, perhaps, on a first raid. The boy was a good swordsman, but unsteady on his horse; it only took a minute or two for Galahad to severely wound his right arm. One of Theuderic's men rode up and grabbed his reins, snapping something that Galahad presumed was an order that the boy was a prisoner.

Helena had been sitting back from the fray as the men fought those coming towards her. Once or twice she had raised her bow, only to lower it to her thigh again, waiting for a time when she would have no choice. Suddenly, she stiffened; she set her arrow to its bow, and sat up tall. Pulling back the string, she aimed in what seemed to Galahad, making for her defence, to be his direction. He stared as the arrow flew towards him, then past his ear. He heard a gurgle, and looked round to see a man behind him desperately clutching at the arrow as it stuck deep in his throat. Helena had saved him from an attacker. He looked back up at her fleetingly as he wheeled around - she was flushed and open-mouthed, but she was already fitting another arrow and looking for a target.

In a few more minutes Clodomir's men had been all but slaughtered. Two made for the forest, but they were on foot, and their fellow Franks swiftly caught up with them and cut them down, whooping in triumph at the final kill. The only one who remained was the young prisoner, who watched his comrades die, his staring eyes revealing the fear that his fixed features were trying to hide.

Panting, Galahad let his sword hang by his side. He looked around at the party, taking a mental count. One of Theuderic's men was missing, presumably lying among the dead, and one of their own men was sitting down, holding a blood-stained cloth against his collar bone, while his arm dangled limp. One of the dogs, too, the one with the injured foot, was lying dead, but Galahad saw to his relief that Samson was bounding, unhurt, towards him. He slid from his sweating horse and put his arms around the dog's neck as it reached him.

"You gave a good fight," said Launcelot. Galahad looked up to see his father standing over him. Taken off guard, he smiled.

"Do we only have the one death?" he asked.

"Aye, we matched them in numbers, but outclassed them in experience. And there are none so fierce as countrymen who fight one another - the Franks made most of the kills."

"Helena killed, too," said Galahad, looking over at where she had been seated upon her horse. She was now in the embrace of her brother; the intimacy of their faces made him turn back quickly.

"I was not merely raising morale when I said she would fight," replied Launcelot. "She has her brother's steel, and she is a rare archer." With a slap on Galahad's shoulder, he went back among the soldiers, organizing the clear-up. The unwounded men began to drag the bodies away from the edge of the road, making a pile in the woods beyond. They returned with the valuables and useful armour.

"You can share that later," said Launcelot. "For now, clean your weapons and make ready to meet."

Conlaed had turned his attention to the badly wounded soldier and had left his own bloodied weapon on the grass. He was gently feeling the man's collar bone.

"It is not broken," he was saying. "I think the sword merely caught it. The muscle is cut, but it will heal if we bind it well and keep it clean. I shall get some water boiling." The man winced at the monk's probings, but he looked relieved to hear the verdict.

The young Frank and lone survivor had been pulled before Launcelot and Perceval by Isembard. He was pallid from loss of blood and his wound was continuing to seep through the half-clotted scab, but he set his lips and looked pathetically defiant.

"What do you need to know of him?" asked Isembard.

Launcelot looked at the youth, then at the older soldier. "He is your man," he said, "ask him what you will." He turned back to his own warriors.

"I am Prince Clodomir's man," the boy said bravely.

"You will wish you were no man's unless you answer my questions," said Isembard. He pushed the tip of his dagger into the boy's wound, and a cry escaped his gritted teeth.

"That is a gentle demonstration of my seriousness," he said. Galahad, too, turned away at this point. He had never had a stomach for the torture of prisoners, and used to flee into the forest near his home whenever Pelles was extracting information from unfortunate men. He had not thought that Launcelot would abandon the boy so readily to the revenge of his countrymen. Feeling uncomfortable and at a loss, he wandered across the small battle site. The ground was clear, but stained and rutted where hooves and boots had dug into the soil. The pile of armour and weapons stood at one side. As he idly looked over, he saw one of Helena's arrows upon the top. He pulled it out and searched for others, finding two more. He wiped them on the grass as best he could, but the blood had already dried and stained their shafts. He carried them across to where she was rubbing down her horse. He held them out silently. She took them and contemplated them.

"Thank you, Prince Galahad," she said quietly. "I do not know when we shall find fresh supplies."

"Are you - I mean to say - do you, are you comforted?" he stammered. Helena put out her hand and enclosed his lightly. She smiled sadly at him.

"It is not a deed I have committed before, and I shall not pretend to be wholly at ease with myself, but it was in defence. He -" she stumbled as she spoke his name " - Clodomir - he cared not if all were to be killed for his lust, even my brother." Her eyes glistened. "You, Launcelot, Perceval - all of you put to the sword. I do not regret doing my part in your defence."

"Your arrow saved me from attack. I am grateful."

"You are more than a man to offer such thanks to a woman, but I accept them, and, I hope, your true friendship."

"You have my pledge," he said, "and my aid whenever you may need it."

The young prisoner did not take long to confess all he knew, Isembard reported to the gathered men. Clodomir had sent the company to abduct Helena and take her to his estates near Orleans. They had been told to leave no one alive. They had not at first anticipated Theuderic sending a contingent to aid the Britons and had only discovered that fact when they arrived at an estate after them.

"There is no more use for him," Isembard concluded. "Shall I kill him now?"

"Make it clean," said Launcelot shortly. Galahad looked to Conlaed for an objection, but the monk said nothing. He was sitting apart, staring down at his sword, rubbing it slowly and methodically with a rag. His broken cross, recovered from the battle ground, lay in his lap. Isembard sent a man back to where the youth was tethered to a horse. He loosed the bond and led him towards the wood. The boy knew; he said nothing, but he looked wildly around at the group of men, searching for a face that might take pity on him. His eyes alighted upon Galahad, his captor. Galahad held his gaze for a moment, then lowered his head. He saw the logic of delaying Clodomir's realization of the defeat, yet he saw also the magnanimity in allowing a boy warrior to return honourably from his first conflict. But he dared not show a weakness by pleading such a cause, and so he let the boy walk, pale and faltering, to his death. No sound came from the wood but for a thump as his body hit the ground. Helena and Perceval crossed themselves.

Galahad wandered over to Conlaed and sat down. His old tutor glanced up at him and then returned to his business of cleaning an already spotless weapon.

"You had no choice," said Galahad hesitantly. "You fought with us."

"I know. I took that burden upon myself when I agreed to come on this quest. It does not mean that I have to condone my deeds."

"The Lady Helena has accepted her actions as defence."

"It is her first kill," said Conlaed bluntly. "She will be shocked, afraid, perhaps a little elated at her power, but she will not be sickened. That comes when you have spent year after year hacking men to pieces and wandering battle fields putting the wounded - friend and foe alike - to the mercy of your sword point."

Galahad sat silently. He had been raised considering war as business, and much as he respected and loved Conlaed, he could not afford to consider the monk's view.

"But the Lord sent armies to defeat his enemies. You taught me of such," he said at last.

"Yes, but I came to know that I was not led by divine inspiration. Sometimes I feel that I must spend my life atoning for that."

Perceval approached them, and they raised their heads.

"Brother, will you come and shrive the company? Then we may go on with forgiveness."

Conlaed put his sword aside and picked up his cross. He knotted the broken thong together and slipped it over his head once more. Then he rose to face his companions.

Chapter Eleven

Theuderic's men left the party at the foot of the path that would lead them into the mountain pass. They had guided the Britons on a south-winding route that took them around the shores of a vast lake that was itself the reflection of the unimaginable heights of the mountains beyond it. The leave-taking was formal, but there was genuine respect in the words exchanged, for they had fought side by side and forged the bond of the sword. They handed over their food supplies and filled the Briton's bottles from their own.

"We shall take supplies enough at those homesteads we passed a mile back. The land here is fat; they'll not even miss it, though they'll grumble and hope for compensation." Isembard gave his grim smile.

"What are these peaks?" asked Conlaed.

"The Alpes? None have Frankish names I know of, but I've come this far only once before. The largest one, over there, that's Alpis Graia by the old Roman name." All turned to contemplate the grey and white mass. "The road you'll be taking should be fairly passable. The Romans worked on it. It was their main road into Gaul. Stories say that it was the one that a great African conqueror took when he invaded the heart of the empire, and he walked monstrous beasts across it."

"Elephants," put in another Frank.

"What are they?" asked Galahad.

"They're as big as a hall, with tusks like boars, only the length of a man, and they can stamp on you like you'd stamp on an ant," the Frank said. "Some say, too, that elephants are still there in the pass," he added, pausing triumphantly to regard the paling faces of a few of the Britons.

"And if there were, how would so many others have made this journey?" asked Isembard scornfully. His companion shrugged.

"We will emerge in Ostrogoth territory when we get through?" asked Launcelot, pointedly ignoring the flow of the conversation.

"This is a no-man's land," replied Isembard. "Who can rightly say where the influence of Clovis ends and that of Theoderic begins? Watch closely for the sympathies of the people you first encounter - they may be Frank, Goth or Roman."

"We will use your name with discretion, but your service will be fast in our memories. Return in safety." Launcelot reached out his hand, and Isembard clasped it firmly.

"One more thing, though," said Isembard as he made to leave, "and I would have forgotten had I not heard that idiotic tale. There is a beast of sorts you must look out for - the warm mountain winds. If one should come, take care to find safe shelter. It can cause a great fall of snow and ice, I am told."

His duty over, he turned his horse abruptly and left, his men trailing behind him. The Britons watched as the Franks began to retrace their steps through the pastures.

"Do you think they'll face a revenge party before they get to Paris?" asked Galahad.

"One of their own men lies dead. They will probably welcome a chance for further retribution," said Perceval, not without a hint of satisfaction.

The initial ascent was easy and the way pleasant. The land was indeed “fat”, as Isembard had remarked. Well-watered by the mountain, the grass was already a rich green and growing well in the deepening spring. A small herd of cattle grazed calmly, nosing about the tufts of miniature purple and white flowers. They lifted their heads to observe the intruders curiously, and a younger one took a few steps towards them, but came no further. The path was broad, meant for the feet of armies, though rutted instead with cloven hoof marks and marked by the odd pile of dung. The horses picked a way for their riders without difficulty.

They climbed fairly rapidly, and soon they could look below them to survey the broad valley out of which they had climbed, and the huge expanse of the lake. A small trail of black moving figures, following the shores, might have been the Franks. They stopped shortly to take their horses off the path to a stream flowing swift and cool from the pass, still bearing the occasional lump of ice. The dogs, too, came bounding over to slurp noisily and shake the cold water free from their muzzles as soon as they were done.

“It is already growing colder,” remarked Helena, as she stooped to fill her own water bottle, “yet at the same time it is brighter and fresher here.”

“We don’t have to share the air with those odorous Franks,” said Caius. “Goodness knows what they like to put in their meat, but it stank.”

“You didn’t complain when that one saved your hide in battle,” said Marcellus. “At least keep your insults for their presence - they’ve earned that.” He gave Caius a friendly punch to show that he was not irate.

“Well, you’re right,” the other admitted “- but they did smell.”

"No more than we will if we don't press on through here," interjected Launcelot, leading the way back to the path.

By the end of the day, they had made it through the entrance to the pass. The horses had begun to tire of the slope, and the riders had been forced to dismount that they might lighten their burdens a little. Soon their own calves were troubled with a dull ache that turned to a fierce burning with every leaden step. Even the stoutest among them was grimacing by the time the ground levelled off and drew them between the arms of the mountain. Only the dogs seemed unfazed by the change in terrain and continued to bound back and forth among the legs of increasingly taciturn horses and men. At Launcelot's command, they halted about half a mile into the pass and paused to stretch and rub their limbs. The sun was dipping over the mountains to their right, and it reflected rose and gold off the snow, making them squint.

"I do not think we can go much further today," reported Paulus to Launcelot and Perceval. "The men need time to adjust, as do the beasts. They have two or three days ahead of them, do they not? Let them rest; we have no pursuers and a few hours will make little difference."

"There is sense in your words," acknowledged Perceval. "I agree - we have entered the pass, and there will be no more steep climbs, if we have been advised aright."

Launcelot nodded. "Tell them to make camp, such as it is."

A little apart from the group, Galahad had spotted something. He crept over to Helena.

"Do you see that deer?" he whispered. Down to their left an animal was grazing. Helena quietly drew an arrow from her quiver and took aim with her bow. The animal moved on a few feet but, unused to humans this far up the mountain, remained unaware that it was a target. Helena loosed her arrow and caught it in the lower neck. It fell and struggled to its feet, but Samson was upon it, dispatching it swiftly with his jaws at its throat. Others of the men, alert to the fresh meal, hurried back down as fast as their aching legs could move to fetch it back to the pass. That evening, they were thankful to save their salt meat for another night and roast small pieces of venison on the ends of their daggers. The dogs, too, were content to gnaw on the carcass, and they added the noise of splintering bone to that of the humans' chewing.

The next day went by without note, except that the air was sharper in their lungs. The pass was not paved, but it had been widened and flattened. Patches of snow and ice sporadically met their horses' hooves, but nothing that yet impeded their path. They made good progress in the daylight hours. The next day seemed fair to follow it, and the party grew quite cheerful. They halted for a meal towards the end of the morning, choosing a rocky spot near a stream that cascaded down in a small waterfall from the rocky cliff above. Beyond that, the snow was thick, and hung over the precipices. Conlaed was bent over a small fire with Caius, attempting to warm some gruel.

"Throw some more faggots on; there's some on my horse."

"We do not know what the next day or so will bring, and wood is getting scarce around here. I think we should save it," replied the monk.

One of the other soldiers approached with a handful of twigs.

"They're a bit green," he said, "but that's the best I can do." He put them next to the small blaze. Caius fed the fire carefully.

"Is it edible yet?"

Conlaed pulled the spoon out of the small metal pot and tasted its contents.

"Almost. We can eat it warm; at least it is better than plain salt pork."

"We don't need hot food right now, anyway, it's getting warmer. Feel the wind coming down?"

Perceval sprung up from where he had been sitting nearby.

"A warm wind?" he snapped. He held his hand up, testing the air. Launcelot leaped up beside him.

"Everyone move!" he barked. "Now!"

"Before we eat?" muttered Caius. "If it's a storm, can't we wait?"

But Conlaed had already kicked in the fire and tossed the contents of the pan out upon the grass. The few things which had been unloaded were hastily packed and they set off.

"Do you think that crevice might be safe?" Launcelot asked Perceval, pointing ahead to a deep open cave carved or worn into the rock face.

"It appears as if it might have been made for shelter, and I cannot see much snow above it," he replied.

"Will someone tell me what's going on?" puffed Marcellus, struggling at the sudden pace.

"A warm wind," said Paulus. "Do you not remember the warning? We could be buried alive in a snowfall if we don't find a safe shelter."

"Has Isembard actually ever seen one of these snowfalls? Why should we believe him?"

As if in answer, a deep rumbling was heard somewhere behind and above them. They kicked their horses forward, and Galahad called sharply to the dogs who were lagging behind and demolishing the last of the discarded gruel. The reverberations grew stronger and a few handfuls of snow skittered off the mountains above to fall about them.

"It's an ele-, an ele-thing!" shouted Caius, kicking his stout horse with such force that it protested. Several of the soldiers paled.

"We can't fight something as big as a hall!"

"Let the horses loose! Maybe it'll eat them!"

Launcelot stopped his own horse to swing round and face them.

"There are no elephants here, just a snowfall that can kill more of you at one time. But I swear, by God's blood, that if I hear any more of this stupidity I will run you through myself and leave you for the snow or an elephant - whichever gets to your miserable carcasses first!"

They were silenced, stung back to reality by his words. Lowering their heads, they pushed forward. The crevice was within a few hundred yards when the ground began to shake. Instinctively, most leaped from their horses and grabbed the reins. It took all their strength to pull the animals into the narrow opening around the boulder that stood in the entrance. Galahad's saddle bag slipped from his horse as he struggled forward. Conlaed, behind him, caught it up as it hit the ground. By the time they had squashed together, the dogs had arrived. They pressed themselves up against the walls. If they had dared let go their reins, they would have put their hands over their ears to stop the roar that enveloped them.

Facing a score of Franks was preferable to this, Galahad thought as he stood beside his father, hanging onto a horse whose every instinct was to bolt into the open. Her eyes were bulging and sweat was running down her neck, despite the cold. Samson pressed up against Galahad's legs, whining softly but more confident in the actions of his master. Great fistfuls of snow and ice came falling, thicker, upon them. It got into the necks of those who had not pulled up their hoods and hit the shoulders of others. The agony of not knowing whether they had found a safe haven or their death was scarcely bearable. Soon the snow was up around their ankles, freezing their feet in their boots, but the equally icy stares of Launcelot and Perceval kept anyone from even contemplating a move.

Finally, when several thought they could hold themselves no longer, the rumblings began to subside and the fistfuls of snow became handfuls and then small bursts. In a few more minutes, it had ceased altogether apart from the faint echoes of the snow which were still bouncing between the mountain walls. The horses eased up on their reins, though they still continued trembling.

"Paulus, you are near the entrance. Go see what lays beyond here," commanded Launcelot. Paulus took a moment to absorb the order, then shook the snow from off his back and moved forward cautiously, shuffling through the snow. Galahad handed his mare's reins to Conlaed and joined him as he was pushing past the boulder. The main path in front of them was covered with a thick layer of snow, but it was still passable. They looked back the way they had come, towards the spot where they had stopped to eat.

"My God," muttered Paulus, so fervently that it had to be a prayer rather than a profanity. There was no longer any trace of the fire, the rocky stream, or the ground itself, for all was blanketed under a rugged heap of snow at least half as tall again as a man. Others came slowly out to join them. Low whistles were heard.

"I'd rather have faced the elephant," said Caius.

"I suppose the Franks saved us twice," remarked Marcellus. "That's a big debt."

"Are you offering to return and repay it now?" asked Paulus. "You are welcome, my friend."

"I'll wait until your hot air melts the snow, thank you."

"When you have quite finished cementing your comradeship, will you help make camp?" asked Perceval. "We should stay here and wait out any changes for the night, at least."

It would have been a far more cold and miserable camp had not each one of the fellowship been aware that he might well not have been alive to suffer it. They spent the afternoon clearing the snow from their shelter, but in the absence of shovels, they were forced to scrape slowly with weapons and utensils.

"We're out of shape," quipped Marcellus, throwing a cooking pot full of snow out into the pass. "You'd think a band of soldiers could make camp quicker with such fine tools." He ducked as Caius flicked a spoonful of ice at his neck.

Not even those sent out to dig along the path for grazing complained of having to work for their own animals. The horses were supplied with a few patches of grass and weeds to supplement the precious store of grain which they were fed. They were left, with the rest of the company, to eat the snow for moisture, for not enough of a fire could be coaxed to melt supplies of water. It was only as the Britons were gnawing their salt meat in the deepening shadows that fell across the crevice that they realised they had not eaten since the day before. Still, few had much appetite.

They brought the horses in, and settled down, man and beast, huddled together for warmth. Galahad sent Samson over to Helena, who had already settled down with the other dog.

"He is your hound," she protested, "and I ask no privilege."

"You are thinner than the rest of us," Galahad pointed out bluntly. "You need Samson, and he will not object."

Helena smiled gratefully and put her arms around the dog's neck, nestling between him and the other. Galahad pulled his new cloak around himself and closed his eyes. All he could see in his head was snow, an expanse of white before his mind's eye. It was going to be a long, cold night.

The final leg of the journey was tough, but not over-hard going for soldiers. The results of the snow fall had been to block the path ahead in places, so that they had to move slowly and dismount to lead their horses over the more treacherous stretches of the pass. The warm wind had soon subsided into a chill air that made them grit their teeth as they marched on. Still, by the afternoon of the second day after their escape, the pass began to decline and slowly widen, and they found themselves descending a slope that merged gradually into the countryside, turning rock and rubble, hillock and scrub, into short, dense grass and the remains of a half-decent road. They stopped at the point where the small stream which had been following them widened into a shallow river, and let the horses drink and feed. They mechanically inspected their mounts as they waited for them to refresh themselves. Marcellus looked up from the back hoof he was examining.

"He needs rest, or he'll go lame," he said shortly. "I can get this stone out, with help, but there'll be a wound, and the cold didn't do it any good."

"Can he make it with a lighter load?" asked Launcelot, scanning the land before them in search of dwellings.

"He'll not make it far, but he'll recover if we get him to shelter. It's a pity to lose such a good horse, but we'll have to exchange him." The horse, as though divining the intent of Marcellus's words, bent his head round and nudged him in the back. The others laughed, and Marcellus slapped him on the flank.

"We need supplies and information," stated Conlaed. "Surely that might afford rest enough?"

"There is a small settlement to the west," said Launcelot, turning back. "It is less than a mile. Can you make it that far with him?"

"You can load up my horse, and I'll walk with you," offered Paulus.

The settlement turned out to be a small farm, tended by tenants of a larger estate. They were not Goths, but rural Romans, and therefore communication was conducted passably well in two Latin dialects. A man was soon called forth to examine Marcellus's horse when he and Paulus came in some way behind the others. He spent a good few minutes admiring it before he could be persuaded to check its foot. He and Marcellus crouched down, muttering together. In reply to a question, he raised his hand, spreading his fingers.

"He thinks it will be five days, maybe a week," said Marcellus, looking back at those who were waiting nearby. Launcelot and Perceval were standing apart, in negotiation with a man who was evidently the head tenant.

"There are no steeds but oxen here," remarked Galahad, "and it looks like there are few supplies that will be useful. But if this is a farm, there must be an estate house within reasonable distance."

Launcelot soon brought them news of the very same import.

"This was a Roman estate, which is now under the lordship of an Ostrogoth. Their master is at home in his hall, about five miles from here." He looked at Marcellus.

"Would you remain here until we send word back to you? I see no dangers among the farmers; I think they are more kindly disposed to us than to foreign masters."

“I’ll see what I can learn,” replied Marcellus, understanding his import.

They were gone within the hour, led rather less than nobly by a cart bearing rushes for the master’s floors. Marcellus bid them a cheery farewell.

“Keep your eyes off the women!” said Paulus, shaking his shoulder roughly but affectionately.

“Well, if it’s only my eyes you’re worried about...” returned Marcellus, grinning his gapped smile. He was still beaming when they set off, evidently not averse to his own private adventure for a few days.

They clipped along behind the cart, which was travelling at an unusually brisk pace. The driver was a thin, impatient-looking man, who drove the sullen ox unrelentingly. He could be drawn little on the subject of his overlord, though the soldiers pressed him. They discovered only that his name was Bedeulf, that he had one daughter and a young grandson, and that he was in the process of rebuilding the Roman villa he had initially destroyed upon gaining control of the lands. The man knew nothing of his king; he gave them a blank look when they mentioned Theoderic’s name.

“Thought we still had an emperor,” he said disinterestedly.

“And there are men under Pelles’s rule who probably think Vortigern still lives,” muttered Conlaed, “but ignorance of politics is not always a sign of lack of discernment.”

“And the humble wayfarer brings the most important news?” finished Galahad, remembering one of his tutor’s old sayings.

“Words of that nature, indeed. I would wager - if I still could - that this taciturn man sees many travellers coming through the pass, and could tell us much of their business, as well as that of his master. We would do well not to offend him.”

Galahad was not sure what they could do to affront a man who would not engage with them, but he did not make this remark to his tutor.

The road that led into the estate had been half-heartedly gravelled, and hooves and wheels crunched across it, through a gate that punctuated a perimeter of crumbling brick and patches of wooden fencing. Towards the back of the courtyard lay a similarly ruined villa. However, this showed signs of resurrection, for men were engaged in refashioning the surviving shell, laying a slightly cruder brick upon the old walls. To the right of the old house, yet a good few paces from it, stood a large wooden hall, more immediately recognizable as the residence of a Gothic lord.

From the hall, a young woman emerged, holding her skirts above the dust of the courtyard. She was flanked by two tall bodyguards, and a bevy of servants trailed at a respectful distance. She looked up at Launcelot and Perceval, her eyes resting on the latter in particular. She said something in a foreign tongue, but the words 'Goth' and 'Roman' were discernible.

"We are Britons, of King Arthur's court," said Launcelot in slow Latin. Her face opened in comprehension.

"You have travelled far, across the Alpes," she replied in the same tongue. "I am Lady Lucilia."

"You are the daughter of Lord Bedeulf?"

Her eyes narrowed a little. "I am his wife," she said simply. "Lord Bedeulf is resting now, but will attend you as his guests later. His daughter is - ailing."

"Forgive us, my lady," said Perceval.

"There is no offence to forgive in unwillful ignorance," she smiled. "If you will care to take refreshment, you may furnish me with information necessary to my lord's understanding of your unexpected appearance so far from your home."

Perceval did not turn questioningly to Launcelot, but, mounted behind them, Galahad could see the slight twist of the shoulders that indicated uncertainty at the situation. Sensing him, Launcelot dismounted, flicking his cloak back from his dagger. The sign read: take care. They allowed their horses to be led away, followed by the dogs and soldiers. The five remaining Britons followed the mistress of the estate into the hall. Inside, a few torches burned low to allow for a dim light, but the fire had long been damped down, and a stale coolness pervaded the air. A table at the end had been set with flagons of wine and small dishes of bread and dried figs. Lucilia bid them sit at the benches. The furniture was old, rich with the patina of age, and carved along its edge with bird and animal motifs. Helena could not help running her fingers along the bestiary.

"It comes from the old house," said Lucilia. "Thankfully not all was lost when the estate was first confiscated by the Ostrogoths."

She was Roman, then, Galahad thought. Probably of an old family, married for political expediency to an aging conqueror. He half-listened to her enquiries, and Launcelot's careful story of their diplomatic mission to Rome. Lucilia, however, attended carefully, nodding.

"There are, of course," she said quietly, "those among the Ostrogoths who do not trust the power of Rome, and seek the ascendancy of Ravenna."

"Our business is not with kings; it is with higher realms," interjected Perceval, leaning forward and looking intently at her. Galahad could see no blush in the gloom, but he saw Lucilia's bosom swell as she drew a deep, silent breath.

"If you come from a land where there is trust amongst peoples, then Britannia is a rare kingdom indeed."

"What is this rare Britannia?" said a thin, rasping voice behind her. Galahad turned his gaze upward to see a wiry, white-haired man standing at her shoulder. His hair and beard were long, and he wore a robe which was meant to be impressive, patterned with knotwork and stars, but which instead hung from his shrinking frame.

"You did not inform me that we had visitors," he continued to Lucilia.

"I was waiting to announce their presence to our lord when he was rested," she replied, without even turning to look at him.

"Forgive me, guests, I am Amara, Lord Bedeulf's advisor."

'Advisor' was a euphemism missed by no one in the company. The man, though of another race, had clearly the marks associated with those such as Merlin - and Galahad flinched when the thought of him brought Nivene to mind - he was a seer, a druid, tolerated superstitiously under a Christian regime that did not like to quite leave all to God's will, but hoped to divine and manipulate omens for its own ends.

"The Lady Lucilia has scarcely finished performing her duties towards us," said Perceval smoothly. "We have been looking, in due course, to discuss our needs with your lord and whomsoever he has chosen as his counsel."

"You may speak with me as with my lord," said Amara, gazing slowly, in turn, at each of them. "One lady amongst you, and your kinswoman?" he said, referring back to Perceval. "This is at least in part an escort?"

"We have already covered our introductions; I am sure you will spare them a third telling and wait on Lord Bedeulf." Lucilia turned to him at last, and smiled pointedly.

"Indeed, when might we expect the honour of an audience?" interjected Conlaed in soothing tones. Launcelot flashed him a glance of gratitude.

"My lord usually arises at this hour. He is probably with his daughter. I shall apprize him of your presence. In the meantime, you have the freedom of our estate."

"You are generous to strangers, my lady," muttered Amara.

"I use discernment," she replied, redirecting her smile towards the fellowship and letting it linger briefly upon Perceval. She bowed her head and left the hall.

Outside, the group walked, apparently somewhat aimlessly, exchanging loaded remarks in casual tones.

"This is a pretty web," said Launcelot in a low voice.

"And a pretty young wife with unsanctioned thoughts," added Helena, directing her comments to her brother.

"Paul was a Greek to the Greeks, and a Jew to the Jew. If we may win our cause by pandering to the weaknesses of others, it is a fair action. And she is a better mark than the old pagan."

"We perhaps speak too hastily," said Conlaed. "We do not as yet know how long are the reins which hold Bedeulf. Let us meet him before we commence a battle on two fronts only."

"We may be on our way within a day," added Galahad, not completely convinced at his own words.

Paulus had approached to report on the reception and findings of the men, and was halfway through a rather mundane account of the stabling of horses when Lucilia returned, shielded by her bodyguards once more. He stepped back, acknowledging her precedence.

"My lord will see you in his quarters. You may follow me." The two guards stood aside to bring up the rear of the group as Lucilia led the party across the courtyard. Galahad considered the Ostrogoth beside him; he was a good head and shoulders above him, and Galahad was by no means a small man, though he lacked bulk. The Lady Lucilia literally watched her back very carefully, he thought.

She led them past the old villa to a cluster of smaller buildings constructed from wattle and logs, like the hall. Sentries stood outside one of the doors. Lucilia waited as they opened the door for her, and she entered, indicating the others to do likewise. Inside, the room was lit by a great many oil lamps, and their varying positions around the walls threw up shadows that crisscrossed along the roof like the old web of a monstrous spider. In front of them, in a large wooden chair beside a bed, sat Lord Bedeulf. He had been a great bear of a man in his youth; that much was obvious. The light fur that covered his torso, too warm for such a spring day, stuck out across broad shoulders that supported a chest which appeared to be caving in on itself. His hair, which remained only at the sides of his head, hung limp, but well-kempt, to his collar bone, and a thin beard trailed down past his neck. He held out a hand whose boney fingers were incongruously decorated with large rings. Launcelot and Perceval bowed briefly, loath to offer more obeisance to one of equal rank, but diligent not to offend, and the others followed suit. As he raised his eyes, Galahad noted that Amara was in the shadows behind Bedeulf.

"My wife tells me that you have travelled from the court of King Arthur of Britannia, and are on route to Rome." His speech was harsh, forced out while he attempted to keep a shortness of breath at bay. As he finished, he wheezed for several seconds.

"Your lady has informed you correctly," replied Launcelot. "We do not seek to impose upon your hospitality, but merely to come to an arrangement concerning supplies before we regain our road."

"There are always arrangements," returned Bedeulf. He focussed, for the first time, upon Helena. "What is the woman to do with your mission?" he rasped.

"She is an emissary from the abbess near Sorviodunum, whom we are escorting to Rome. She is also my sister, the Lady Helena." Perceval spoke up for his sibling, who nevertheless returned Bedeulf's impudent stare with equanimity.

"She's a nun? She has always been a nun - no man's wife or concubine?"

"I have served the Lord and he alone with my body, mind and soul," said Helena.

"You may keep your tongue for him, too, in this place. We do not encourage the Roman ways of letting women think they have an opinion. Lucilia here - she thinks what I think, do you not now?"

"I do not think, unless you bid me do so," she said with trained sincerity.

"Well," Bedeulf said, returning to Perceval, "if she's a holy woman, can she go pray with my sick daughter?"

"I cannot speak for my sister," Perceval returned calmly, "except in that I know she ever fulfills her duties."

"Brother, I will pray with her." Helena turned towards Bedeulf as she spoke, but he did not fully register the defiance, for Amara was leaning over him, whispering in his ear. He looked up at the party for a moment, his eyes alight.

"You will stay, then, until your supplies are readied."

"As we said, my lord," repeated Launcelot, "we intend to come to an agreement with you in a timely fashion."

Beduelf waved his hand dismissively, but his reply was stifled by a cough. Eventually he stopped and took up his thought. "You may have the necessities, and more. We shall talk of the price later." He leaned forward, and a servant placed a large walking stick in his hand. Lucilia came to his side to take his other arm as he pushed himself up, pressing hard upon the staff. He used her to steady himself as he took his first few steps, then he shook her off, though it was clear that it pained him to move unaided.

"I have business to attend to before the night's meal. You are not our only visitors. Avail yourselves of whatever you require." He walked slowly through them to the door, followed by Amara.

"My lady," said Lucilia sweetly to Helena, "will you follow me to meet my lord's daughter? I know that he will desire a swift response to his wish."

"It has been a long journey," said Helena, "but I will pray with a sick woman. However, our Brother here my be of more efficacy than I." Conlaed bowed.

"I could perform certain rites of healing upon her," he offered.

"Most here are Arians, not Roman Christians, or of your Church," said Lucilia. "I doubt that your words would be taken seriously. Still," she added indifferently, "you may come if you will. I am sure that my lord will not refuse any help for his beloved daughter, whether or not it comes from their Church."

"Are those his thoughts, my lady?" asked Perceval.

"To consider any other would be regarded as disloyal," she said coolly. "Now, I will show you where the Lady Hildevara's quarters lie."

"Is she tended by a good physician?" inquired Conlaed.

"Physicians rarely travel to these parts, and the Ostrogoths tend to be suspicious of their ways. She has a nurse, whom I supervise. We do our best, given the capacity we have to act - or trust," she added quietly, as she turned towards the door.

By the time that Helena and Conlaed had returned, the rest of the party had made the best of their situation by at least seeking more substantial refreshments and ridding themselves of the grime of several days' journey. Galahad was inspecting the dogs' paws, thankful that the trip through the mountains had not injured them, when the two drew up near him.

"Did you find aught amiss?" asked Perceval, at his sister's side in an instant.

"I am not sure that anything is aright with this family," said Helena gravely, "but there was no perceivable danger to us, if that is merely your meaning."

"What ails the daughter?" Galahad saw no profit in hiding his curiosity.

"It is hard to say with accuracy, but it is some disease of the flesh - though not leprosy, for there is no whiteness. In fact, it is the opposite - her skin reddens and peels away. She was wearing a veil to meet with us, but I could see the sores visible on her face through the covering."

"Is she dying?" asked Launcelot bluntly.

"As the Lady Helena said," took up Conlaed, "this is a disease beyond our sphere of knowledge, and its fatality is unclear. She was weak, but did not yet have the look of a soul which is moving to the next world. We prayed with her, although I am not convinced her spirit was in a state of grace to receive it."

"Though her illness must have weighed hard on her," said Helena generously.

"And hard on Bedeulf, if it seems that his only male heir is her son, and the child's two guardians are themselves weakened." Launcelot was grim now, digesting the news.

"But what could this have to do with us?" asked Helena.

"I can fathom no logical answer to that, but I know that Bedeulf has placed us into his scheming. I hope we manage to leave before we find out."

If Beduelf's distaste for Roman social customs did not extend to its sound architecture, neither did it encompass its developed cuisine, for the meal that night was undoubtedly Roman in style. Though the partakers sat on benches instead of reclining, they were served several small dishes as opposed to the trenchers of non-Roman tables. Among the dishes placed before Galahad and his companions were quinces stewed in wine and honey, greens glistening in olive oil, sausages fragrant with rosemary and juniper, and fowl roasted in a sauce that Galahad could not fathom, but which was creamy and mild to the taste. Knives and spoons were set by the table, and Galahad, having almost forgotten the culinary lesson he leaned in Londinium, looked to Helena at his side for an indication of how to conduct himself. She noticed his hesitation, and smiled quietly. Without drawing attention to him, she cut the pieces of quince in her dish a little smaller, then used the spoon to eat.

Bedeulf sat in the middle of the high table, with Launcelot at his right, and a young boy at his left. Lucilia sat next to him, and Perceval was placed at her left. The boy did not look comfortable at being seated in the midst of foreign guests; he was attempting to bury his head in his dish unless forced to make a remark by his grandfather. Lucilia made the occasional comment in his direction, but her attention was turned towards Perceval, and Galahad could tell from Helena's somewhat distant replies to his own words that she was straining to overhear their conversation. There was not much that Galahad could glean from his expression; Perceval showed his emotions only to his closest companions, Launcelot and Helena.

Whatever he was saying, it seemed to be enough to keep Lucilia interested, though she kept glancing across to her husband to see if he were observing her. He, however, showed no signs of acknowledging her.

"I am sure that your brother plays a careful game," Galahad whispered reassuringly to Helena. She looked back, startlement in her eyes. She had clearly not meant to let her own feelings show; but she recovered herself quickly.

"Mayhap, my friend. But what game is *she* playing?"

Galahad's answer was interrupted by the arrival of new dishes: nuts, marinated cheeses, small cakes and tiny eggs, accompanied by more of the spiced wine that had seasoned the first course. The food took their attention until the assembled household was near the end of its repast, when Bedeulf struck the table before him with his heavy bronzed goblet. Silence fell. He sat, biding his time, and taking deep, laboured breaths.

"We have this night guests from across the seas, from the realm of the famed King Arthur. We are not unaccustomed to entertaining those who have crossed the Alpine mountains into the domain of our own great King Theoderic, but we greet the arrival of these noble people with especial interest and hope." Beside him, Launcelot slowly but certainly sat upright; Bedeulf's announcement had no relation to their dinner conversation, Galahad surmised.

"We call upon our counsellor and seer to enlighten the company," continued Bedeulf. Amara rose. Further down the hall, the Briton soldiers were on the alert, though they had been obliged, with others, to leave their swords hanging on the entrance wall of the Great Hall. Even Helena's hand went towards the dagger concealed against her thigh.

"Our Lord Bedeulf has ruled these lands illustriously and faithfully for near twoscore years," began Amara in his thin voice. The Ostrogoths raised an acclamation. As it subsided, he spoke again. "While it is universally true that those who give such service are under divine favour, yet forces of evil may afflict a house. It is in the unfathomable illness that has struck his daughter, the incomparable Lady Hildevara, that I have divined a curse laid upon us by the enemies of this house." Several crossed themselves. Galahad began to eye the weapons hanging against the walls. "It is a curse of dark magic and not easily uprooted, but I have looked, as deeply as I may, into the power that attempts to bind this noble family. I have had a portentous dream: I saw that Lady Hildevara would only be cured when a holy and virgin pilgrim crossed the depths and the heights of the land and made a willing sacrifice: her - or his - blood alone can cure."

Perceval leapt to his feet at the same instant that Paulus led the soldiers up from their benches. But Bedeulf had anticipated their reaction: men were in front of the arms before they were barely upright.

"Peace, guests," he said, almost choking with suppressed emotion. "My seer speaks of a willing sacrifice, and not of the life of a holy woman but only sufficient blood to wash my daughter's skin. In return, I assure you, you will go safely on your way with riches which will more than compensate for your - inconvenience."

"You spoke of a willing sacrifice only," said Launcelot coldly, and so terribly that Bedeulf, even surrounded as he was by bodyguards, paled. "If our lady is not willing, then she is not the pilgrim of your seer's dream, and you must allow us to go our way in peace."

The Ostrogoth faced him for some seconds, panting. Galahad wished fervently that the old man would be struck dead at that very moment, and if he had ever learned any of his grandfather's incantations, he would have used them now, blasphemous or not. But instead he, too, stood helpless. By his side, Helena said nothing, her eyes locked into those of her brother, who had willed her into silence.

"You speak sooth," said Bedeulf at last, "but the decision is to be the lady's only. And you are not yet ready to leave; you may take a few days to consider how you might advise her. We can wait."

He sat down, and indicated with a wave of his hand that the meal was to continue. Only after a few minutes' stunned silence did his own people gather themselves and begin to talk in falsely normal voices of mundane matters. The Britons remained mute. Lucilia laid a hand tentatively upon Perceval's arm and said something in a low voice, but he shrugged it off absentmindedly. She frowned momentarily, but then composed herself and turned to her step-grandson. Galahad reached out his own hand and set it gently on that of the motionless Helena. She did not reject him, though she continued silent, communing with her brother across the hall, begging for answers he could not give.

That night, at Launcelot's insistence, the party camped out in the half-finished villa. They chose the partly-roofed atrium for their bedroom.

"It may be colder than the hall, but the company is better," remarked Paulus, as he supervised the arrangements. The men were armed with their daggers, but their swords remained under guard, along with Helena's bow, in the hall. Two of the soldiers were posted as look-outs, that a conference might commence.

"It makes little difference, I know," said Launcelot. "Bedeulf has left us alone to contemplate our situation. Mine is the responsibility. It was madness - blind folly - to walk into this man's demesne without understanding anything of him." He began to pace the room vigorously, as if to wear down his anger.

"Where else could we have gone?" Perceval's voice was coldly logical, but hollow in contrast to Launcelot's passion. "We were debilitated and denuded, and the man is obviously here as a buffer for those who choose to take this pass into Theoderic's lands."

"Self-recriminations are not the issue," interjected Conlaed. "There is only the pressing question of the - request - of the heretic under the influence of the pagan."

"I'll fight my way out with a dagger before I see one drop of our lady's blood spilled," said Paulus hotly. The others agreed.

"We have a few days' grace. If we are careful, we can make it. Most of us have escaped situations of equal evil, and this is a little kingdom divided against itself." Launcelot sounded more hopeful.

"You have not inquired as to my decision," said a small voice. It was Helena.

"Whatever you intend, you must think of our mission," said Perceval, his arm around her protectively. She looked around at the circle of men, then lowered her gaze.

"I do not know," she said simply. "Pray for me."

Chapter Twelve

It was as clear as the dawn which awoke them the next day, breaking in over the walls of the atrium, that they were hostages for Helena's compliance. Nothing was done to hinder their assembling of such stocks as were ready, but extra guards were patrolling the gate and the hall where their weapons lay frustratingly out of reach. Launcelot and Perceval were kicking their heels, mentally and physically, in the dust of the villa, weighing and disregarding plans as they sprung up. Helena was wretched, and Galahad could think of nothing which might raise her spirits.

The dreadful monotony of the morning was broken only by the arrival of a cart into the estate grounds, driven, as Paulus rushed to inform them, by the same man who had conveyed them hither. He was bringing cloth and cheeses from the farm, and this time he was accompanied by a rather stout woman, near his own age, who had an air of congeniality in contrast to her kinsman. Even several extra pounds of flesh could not hide the resemblance between them. If the man was surprised to see the Britons ensconced in such an odd quarters for guests, he did not show it. He approached them, and bowed.

"Sirs, I've news of your horse and man. The animal is nearly healed; a day or so and it will be ready."

"That was swift," remarked Galahad, enough of a horseman himself to understand the matter.

"That would be thanks to my sister there." He indicated the fat woman, who was gossiping with the washerwomen. "She is our healer in these parts, and she sometimes turns her hand to animals, too." Galahad would liked to have asked her secret, but he knew how incongruous such a request would seem at this time. They tried to question the man about Marcellus, but, after delivering his message, he had resumed his taciturn manner, and mentioned nothing other than that the man was well and had, he hinted, eaten more than his fair share of their stores.

Launcelot pressed two small coins into his hand.

"One is for the food, and the other is for not mentioning the soldier billeted with you. Understand?" The man nodded and was swiftly away. He did not return to the Britons; they watched as he delivered his goods and then waited for his sister, who had disappeared. She eventually emerged from the quarters of the Lady Hildevara, and, pausing only to pull her mantle around her head, came striding across the courtyard to where the cart stood ready to leave. Galahad suddenly realized that Helena had slipped out of the villa and was now at the woman's side, delaying her as she was about to climb into the seat beside her brother. Their conversation was brief, and when Helena returned she spoke to no one of the exchange that had taken place. Only at the dying of the day did she raise the matter that remained unspoken on everyone's lips.

"I have decided to comply with the wishes of Bedeulf," she announced to the company. "I can give a little of my blood if he thinks it will heal his daughter."

"It is too dangerous," interjected Launcelot, "and it is but the ravings of a godless pagan priest."

"But perhaps my sacrifice can show them the nature of true Christianity. Perhaps we can persuade them to come into the fold."

"Why do you think that acquiescing to their ways will show them that the truth lies beyond Arius?" It was Perceval, harsh as he had been once before when seeking to bend his sister's will. "No circumstance here demands your blood."

"Already, blood has been shed on my behalf on this quest, and I, too, have taken the lifeblood of men. What is it for me, then, to offer some in return?"

"Is this what it is about? The assuaging of a guilt you suffer? We fought an enemy and received absolution; there is no more need to do penance than there was for the Israelites to pity the enemies they were commanded to annihilate."

"I am not made to serve the Lord with the sword; that is your commission." Perceval and Helena were now oblivious of anyone else, locked in their own struggle.

"You acted under my command. I tell you, it is not a holy thing to yield to their - request. Your mission is to the glory of God in Rome."

"Or is it to the glory of Perceval? Why may I not choose to hear the voice of the Lord for myself? Why may I not, for once, tread a path I, only I, have chosen?"

"You are my sister!" Perceval's voice was choked with rage and despair. He gripped Helena's arms so tightly that Galahad thought they must have pained her, but she made no sound of protest. She kept her eyes fixed on his, smiling softly and tearfully.

"And you are my brother," she whispered. He let his grip fall, and she reached up her hand to gently brush a tear that had fallen down his own cheek.

"She has no hope; the healer I spoke to told me as much. What is it to offer hope and faith to a dying woman? You and I, we have that in our God and each other. Let me do this."

"I cannot expose your life to such a danger."

"How can I die while you live?"

Perceval shook his head. "You must not," he said. The others were not sure to what he was referring, but Helena seemed to understand. She leaned forward and kissed him.

The party was spared the embarrassment of deciding how to proceed by the arrival of Lucilia, who sidled into the atrium.

"My Lord Bedeulf wishes an audience. He intends to demonstrate his largesse were you to aid our family." She could not help staring at Perceval and Helena. "Is there aught amiss?" she asked innocently. "I myself will do all in my power to give you comfort."

Perceval recovered himself. He turned towards her with a smile that made her glow.

"We need nothing. But I am ready, if Lord Launcelot is." They followed her towards Beduelf's quarters.

As soon as they had disappeared, Helena stretched, lifting her arms high over her head, as though she could free herself of her burden. "Come," she said to Galahad and Conlaed, "we must while away our time somehow. Let us explore this villa."

"I would prefer to walk and meditate," said Conlaed. "I will leave the exploration to you young people." He bowed and followed in the direction of Launcelot and the others.

"Well, shall we begin?" Helena sounded falsely bright, but Galahad passed over her tone.

"What are these rooms off the atrium?" he asked, joining in her lightness. They walked softly through the door and found themselves in a small room, half-covered by its tiled roof.

"It looks like the bedrooms in the place at Londinium," he said. "But they had a different word for it. A cubi-" He hesitated.

"Cubiculum," said Helena. "See, its walls are plain and whitewashed. They will not be painted, like those outside."

They looked briefly into the other bedrooms which came off the atrium; they were all partly finished. Then they walked on past the shallow, marble-lined, empty pool in the midst of the atrium and through a narrow passageway into another courtyard. This, however, was only paved around the perimeter, wide though it was. In the centre stood another dry pool, circular this time, with a pedestaled basin in the middle. Helena stepped out into it and peered into the basin. She looked disappointed.

"I thought that there might be a pipe in here, for a fountain," she said. "My home had an old Roman fountain in the garden, but it broke when I was a child. I used to spend hours by myself watching the water spurt up through the mouth of a great stone fish, and cascade down into the pool. Sometimes, when the sun was bright, I could see rainbows sparkling in the air around it. I imagined they were faery folk come to play and laugh with me; I even gave them names. When Perceval and I quarrelled, I would go there to comfort myself until he would come to find me and be reconciled. When it broke, I thought my heart would break with it, I was so young and foolish." She laughed sadly.

"I do not consider it foolish," said Galahad. "Things of childhood have a magic one cannot bear to relinquish." Shyly, he told her of his forest retreat.

"Just before I embarked on my journey to Arthur's court, I walked there again with Samson, as we had done since we were both young. The magic was still there, and I wanted to let it seep into me, to take with me, to give me the belief that I would return to my home. I know not now whether I will," he concluded, "but the memory of that place lets me believe it against all reason."

Helena leaped lightly out of the pond and took Galahad's hand, leading him towards the stately pillars that formed a colonnade.

"Thank you for your confidence," she said. "It is why I always knew we would be friends. We know how to believe - not to have faith, for that is a different gift - but to believe in a good with our whole heart." She let go his hand to stroke a pillar, carved with horizontal grooves.

"I wonder who believes in this?" She mused. "Do you think it is Bedeulf's vanity or Lucilia's homesickness?"

"I think it is Bedeulf's dying bid for power," said Galahad seriously. "He can no longer conquer, so he builds."

"And he fears it will be his only heir, that he and his daughter will die and leave the fate of his grandson in the hands of the Lady Lucilia."

"You think she would murder him? I see rebellion in her eyes - but murder?"

"Bedeulf's people have killed hers and threaten to eradicate their way of life. Would not you be tempted?"

"But is it worth your - health to save him?" Galahad could not say 'life'.

"What are any of our lives worth weighed against another's? We are all equal in the sight of God, and if we can see a good which will benefit another, it behooves us to perform it whatever the consequences, for who are we to hold ourselves above others?"

"Then - then you will do it? But you promised your brother." A look in her face stopped his words.

"Perceval's good is always uppermost in my soul," she said, and, taking his sleeve, pulled him on through the villa.

As the evening drew in, Galahad was sitting with Launcelot, superficially going through the contents of their newly-packed saddlebags, but in reality waiting and praying for a solution to arrive in any way which might be granted. Perceval and Helena had gone for a walk, and none cared to join them. After some time, Perceval returned alone. His face was that of a desperate man.

"Where is she?" asked Launcelot at once.

"She has gone to speak to the nurse of Hildevara. I need your help." Galahad had never before heard him request aid. "I cannot stop her resolve."

"What can we do that you, as her brother cannot?" asked Galahad. But he started back involuntarily as Perceval's visage changed to that of dark despair.

"Whatever you may. You must promise me, as brothers-in-arms, that you will do all. Reason with her, stop her forcibly. Sweet Jesu!" He clutched at his hair. "If any other innocent blood could be offered - but I am a black sinner. I meant to keep myself pure for the Lord, but I failed, once, and there is no regaining of our virginity. It was a moment of lust, a youth and a sweet she-devil of a serving maid. But I swore I would always be the guardian of my sister's maidenhood, that she at least could be dedicated wholly in body and soul to God. Yet - " his voice shrank to a whisper "- I would give that up and take the burden to save her."

Galahad stared aghast.

"You are not asking that we - we take her purity?" he stammered.

"Brother, I will do all for you." It was Launcelot, white and stern. Galahad turned on his father.

"You would rape a nun?"

"I would save a life - by ravishment, if necessary. If you shrink from your sworn bonds, you are not yet a man, my son. Only a true man can take upon himself that evil which effects the good. I will attempt all other means, but if forced, I will do my brother's will."

Galahad was silent, stung to the quick. He watched wordlessly as Launcelot strode roughly passed him and embraced Perceval before leaving the shelter. Perceval turned his face to the wall, ignoring Galahad. He was thankful, for he thought that if he had to say a word, he might cry. He knew why he could not give his all for his comrade, and it was only partly his horror at the idea of raping the sweet Helena. He knew that he would not physically be able to perform the deed, that if she once looked in his face, he would see his father taking his mother, taking her mind as well as her maidenhead. He would see Helena becoming as Elayne, and he would rather she died than drag on her life in that living death.

He did not mark the time that he waited, but it was long enough for him to imagine several disturbing scenarios and then to force himself to rationality once more. Perceval did not stir from his meditations, whatever they were. Galahad hoped fervently that they were not as his own. When he thought that he could abide there no longer, Launcelot returned. He was bearing Helena swooning in his arms, and from his face, Galahad thought for one sickening moment that he had defiled her. But then he saw the blood seeping from her arm, staining her dress. From nowhere, Conlaed and the others streamed in behind him.

"Quickly!" he said, laying her down upon a blanket. Conlaed was tearing cloth as he knelt beside her, and began at once to wrap it tightly around her arm. Perceval joined them, his lips moving wordlessly as he held her head. Her eyes remained shut.

"I was too late. She gave herself to be bled, but they cut a vein."

"By accident?" said Paulus, darkly.

"So the nurse claims."

"Her pulse is weakening," said Conlaed. "Bring me wine, broth, water, anything to strengthen her. We need to keep her fighting." Someone pushed a flask into his hands. Perceval lifted her head, and the monk put the neck of the flask to her mouth. Wine trickled between and down her lips. She coughed and opened her eyes. Seeing Perceval above her, she smiled.

"I love you," she whispered. "I did this for you. Can you forgive me?"

"Hush," he whispered back, pushing her curls, his curls, from her forehead. "There is nothing to forgive. Concentrate on being strong."

"I am so tired," she murmured. "Hold me while I rest." Her eyelids fluttered again. A soldier ran back in with a bowl of broth. Perceval sat her up. The blood had soaked the first bandage, and Conlaed hastily changed the dressing.

"Hold her arm up, and grip the gash closed firmly," he barked at Galahad. He took Helena's arm as commanded, holding it close against his chest, thankful for the permission to touch her, to will his strength into her.

“My lady, listen to me. You need to keep awake, you need to take this broth. It will restore what you have lost.” He held the spoon up to her mouth, but her head tilted back in Perceval’s arm. He put the bowl down and took her wrist, pressing his fingers along the pale blue veins. “I can barely feel a life pulse,” he said. “You must tell her to live, my lord. Perhaps she will listen to you.”

Perceval put his mouth to her ear. He spoke into it words that Galahad wished he were deaf to. Blandishments, pleas, endearments, words so sacredly intimate that they were only meant for two souls joined as one. Still, she did not open her eyes, but her lips quivered, smiled, mouthed the word ‘farewell’. The others turned away as Perceval bent his mouth to hers. When they dared turn back, led by Launcelot, she was lying lifeless in her brother’s arms. He looked up at his friend.

“Help me take her somewhere private,” he said emptily. Launcelot placed his hands beneath her legs. Galahad suddenly realized that he was still grasping her arm. Awkwardly, he laid it down, across her body. His own hand and tunic were dark with her blood. He pressed his hand against his chest as he watched the two men gently carry Helena into one of the bedrooms. When Launcelot returned, Conlaed arose, as if to go to minister to her, but the younger man put out his hand.

“Leave them for now,” he said. He turned around him slowly, looking at the half-finished room. Suddenly, he seized a brick and flung it savagely at the mosaic beneath their feet. The face of a bird scattered into a hundred tiny, multi-coloured pieces. Like her rainbow, Galahad thought inconsequentially. Behind him, Paulus let out a cry of enraged grief and crossed his arms over his head. His fellow soldiers followed him, weeping, regardless of their manhood. Galahad felt something push him in the back. By instinct, Samson had left his forays and returned to the villa. As when he was that twelve-year-old boy, Galahad grabbed the dog's neck and buried his face in his shaggy fur.

He was not aware of how long he cried quietly into Samson's pungent, comforting hair, but he eventually became aware that Launcelot was pacing stealthily towards the bedroom. Suddenly, he heard his father shouting in a whisper, "No!" Instinctively, Galahad leapt to his feet, his face wet with tears which had stuck dog hairs to his cheeks, and came up behind him to look into the chamber.

Inside, Helena lay on a pallet, neatly and serenely, her arms crossed over her. Beside her, Perceval had stripped to his undershirt. He was kneeling, holding his dagger in both hands, his head bent, praying.

"You do not need to do this, Perceval," said Launcelot, choking out the words.

"I failed her," said Perceval, without looking round. "I failed because I was impure. 'If thy right hand causeth thee to sin, cut it off.' I can enter heaven with her if my purity is restored."

"That sin is already repented and forgiven. Do not create a new one. Think of the Grail. Take it for her."

Perceval let out a strangled sob. He raised his hands higher, and Launcelot leaped forward as he brought the blade down. At the last moment, he turned it aside, plunging it into his thigh. He let out a gasp, but was silent. Launcelot knelt by his friend, taking the hilt in one hand, and his head in the other. He pulled the dagger out swiftly, and Perceval winced, but still he spoke not a word. Launcelot took up the discarded tunic and placed it firmly across the wound. Then he pulled Perceval's head down to his chest, cradling him as a mother might cradle a child who had injured itself in play. Galahad watched him rock his comrade gently as the blood seeped through the cloth and ran down his fingers and down Perceval's thigh, watched as Launcelot's tears made an echoing stream down Perceval's golden hair. Once more that evening, he turned away. It was a place for men. It was not for him.

"This was not a consequence foreseen or desired. As one who has suffered himself, I offer my deepest regrets." Bedeulf bent his head to wheeze once more at the effort of speaking.

Launcelot, Perceval and Galahad were in the chieftain's quarters that same night, summoned by several heavily armed guards. They stood in rank, silent, offering neither resistance nor agreement. Bedeulf looked to Amara for assistance. The seer affected a smile of sympathy.

"Your companion embraced a fate which will earn her an exalted place in heaven. Here in our mortal life, we will of course give you a more than adequate recompense."

"We wish to leave, and inter the Lady Helena in a suitable, orthodox resting place," replied Launcelot.

"Yes, yes, I understand. My lord offers these terms: there is a Catholic chapel two miles south of here, on your road to Rome, maintained for those of the Lady Lucilia's family. There is already a sarcophagus available there, and you may find help from the villagers. Three of you will be escorted there in the morning by our men; later, your other men and weapons will be returned. We expect your oath that you will not offer them violence for a deed which only accidentally proved fatal."

"An oath from all of you, mind," added Bedeulf.

"You request our oaths and then treat us as hostages?" said Launcelot, his colour rising. Perceval laid a hand on his arm.

"We accept your terms," he said flatly. The Goth appeared surprised that Helena's brother should be the one to agree. He eyed him narrowly, searching for clues to a plot of vengeance.

"A wise choice," he said at last. "You will get your blood money, and find an ally should you need one on your return journey."

"How, may I ask, is the health of your daughter?" asked Launcelot.

"We cannot tell as yet, but she feels improvement." Amara answered for Bedeulf. "We hold a feast of thanksgiving tomorrow night, for her and your lady."

"We in turn ask to be undisturbed tonight, and to have our requests for our preparations fulfilled."

"Whatever can be achieved - " Amara began.

"Let them have what they want," coughed Bedeulf, "and be done with it."

"Then we shall take our leave," snapped Launcelot. He turned to go.

"My lords, are you forgetting your oaths?" inquired Amara. He stepped back as Launcelot swung round. He spat on the ground at the old man's feet.

"As our lady spilled her blood for you, I will not offer mine, but you have my oath there, in the dust where she will lie, and you will have that of my men. Do you dare ask for more?"

Perceval turned round, limping, and joined his phlegm in the earth. Galahad did the same. Bedeulf said nothing as they exited the room.

In the villa once more, Launcelot briefly told the men of the terms.

"So we wait?" asked Paulus grimly.

“We bide our time - and I want no man to take retribution into his own hands, or to give cause for such a belief.” He glared round at the soldiers who nodded, ashen-faced.

“We must watch with her,” said Perceval. “I will ready her.”

“I have cleaned her wound,” said Conlaed quietly, “and blessed the coins that I laid upon her eyes.”

Perceval took her saddlebag and limped into the bedroom.

“Galahad, I want you and Paulus to accompany Perceval tomorrow. I shall stay to lead the other men.” Galahad faced his father silently. He had not given him a word since the accusation earlier that day. He debated continuing his silence, but at last dismissed the thought as puerile.

“I will do it for her,” he said coldly. Launcelot considered him for a moment.

“I do not deny that I have a hot tongue,” he said, “but I do not speak falsehoods. If you are to lead with us, you must be able to make and act upon the necessary decisions, however heinous.”

“This is not the matter in hand,” replied Galahad through gritted teeth. “It needs no discussion.” Launcelot shrugged and turned to the business of their departure.

Once again it was a night where they slept the sleep of soldiers on a battlefield, snatching rest and watching in shifts. At intervals they left for orders: linen for a shroud; boiling water to dress Perceval’s wound. Conlaed insisted that it be attended to as soon as Perceval left his sister’s room. He made no complaint, but suffered the monk to attend to him, not even registering pain as the bandage was pulled from his wound where it had stuck with the drying blood. Conlaed cleaned it with fresh linen and water as hot as his own hands could stand. He nodded approvingly.

"It is deep, but clean, and already the flesh is knitting. If you give it all the rest you can, it will heal soon." He knew that Perceval was not listening, but he knew also that he needed to emphasize the reality around him.

The only disturbance that night was the arrival of the cart driver from the farm. He respectfully and briefly informed them that his sister was with him once more and that, as she knew the villagers near the chapel, and could lay out a body well, she would accompany them in the morning.

"Though she has a toothache, and will not be able to speak overmuch," he added, not waiting for an answer as he darted out.

Galahad was pleased when the noise of men outside their camp indicated that the first procession was to begin. Perceval and Launcelot bore Helena out on a bier, wrapped in her shroud, the outline of her body only just visible through the cloth. They laid her gently on the cart, which was driven by the courier's sister. The woman's face was bandaged and her head covered; she barely turned to nod at the party. In front of her sat two guards on horseback, and servants held the Briton's horses.

"The dogs go with me," said Galahad, whistling to Samson and his companion. One of the guards began to say something, but the other cut him off, evidently allowing it. Samson sniffed around the legs of the carthorse for a minute, before taking his place beside Galahad. They have found a horse somewhere, thought Galahad, but spent no time on his curiosity.

The guards led the way from the camp, followed by the cart and then the three Britons. The way was dark, and progress slow as the horses carefully picked their path along the road. No one spoke; the body of Helena, dimly gleaming in its shroud in the last of the moonlight, held their tongues.

As the dawn began to rise over the hills, they saw in the near distance the shape of a small church, edged by a short fence where a graveyard must be situated. The cart woman shifted in her seat and scratched her backside. They moved down a gentle slope towards the building. The path narrowed; the two guards in front moved closer together, and Paulus and Galahad were forced to drop back behind Perceval. Suddenly, in a movement so swift it was unbelievable, the cart woman dropped the reins and produced two long daggers from the depths of her clothes. In a bound that belied her bulk, she leapt for the backs of the two guards, stabbing each firmly near the shoulder blades. She rolled to the ground with one, while the other slipped from his horse. In another second, Paulus had leapt from his horse to run to the front of the column, and jumped upon the Goth, sticking his own dagger in the man's throat. He stood up to face the woman, who had dispatched the first guard.

"Marcellus, you dog!" cried Paulus, embracing his friend whose face was now visible as the swathes of cloth had been pushed back from his face.

"Did you think I'd leave you?" he asked.

"But how did you know what was to happen?" asked Galahad, who had come round to catch and quiet the guard's horses.

"I didn't - until I arrived at the estate. I was going to make contact and find a way to free you, but then I heard of this sorry business," he glanced at Helena's shroud and crossed himself, "and it came to me, quick as lightening, that I could travel with you. I'm glad they only sent two."

"Let us convey my sister to the church before we discuss our next move," said Perceval quietly.

"I ask your pardon, my lord," said Marcellus.

"There is no transgression; but we must move."

"Yes, but my lord!"

"Marcellus?"

"The weapons, my lord. They're hidden beneath the cart. The guards were going to leave you to discover them for yourselves."

Perceval almost smiled. "Good work. Now let us hasten; we know not when the remainder of the party will arrive."

Sombreness reigned once more for the short time it took to bring Helena to the tiny church, built with small, neat bricks, in the Roman style. They carried her inside reverently and laid her upon the altar for lack of a table. Perceval knelt to say a brief prayer, the others following suit. Then he took a breath and rose.

"Due rites will have to be postponed. We need to set the ambush for the next escort. Paulus and Marcellus, clear away the bodies."

"We will not have much time to escape," said Galahad. "By the time we have freed the others and made the burial, Bedeulf will have expected his men back."

"That is taken care of," said Marcellus with a hint of pride. "The cart man is going to inform Bedeulf that there is trouble at the farm, and the men took a diversion to sort matters out."

"I've known you for nigh on fifteen years, and I've never seen you use your head like this!" said Paulus, low but admiring.

"It should work for long enough," said Perceval. "They will be preoccupied with the celebrations of this night and are not likely to spare much time for consideration of a few guards."

"Then vengeance has begun," muttered Paulus.

They tethered the spare horses behind the church, but left the cart in view. They found a tinder box and lit a lamp near the entrance, setting one of the bodies in a seat so that it cast a shadow in the doorway. Then they sorted their own weapons out from the pile bundled and tied beneath the cart. It felt good to each man to be in the possession of his own sword once more, the extension of a warrior's arm. After swift consultation, they split to hide in the trees at each side of the road. The landscape was rapidly coming into focus as the sun rose, and there was little natural cover.

"We must strike swiftly," said Perceval as they parted. "There will be no room for mistakes, especially if there are several soldiers."

"I can count on the others to hold their own with us," said Galahad.

"Some may consider themselves under oath," said Paulus.

"Do you?"

Paulus shrugged. "I was sworn not to attack my guards; I only dispatched a dying man. But I did not swear to leave other guards unharmed."

This was the first attack in which Galahad did not feel nervous; Helena's death had left him without compassion for the Ostrogoths. They had, too, a strong element of surprise, and an easy advantage - there were only three guards for the five Britons, as it appeared when they came into view. Galahad waited with Paulus until Perceval's sword flashed a signal in the sunlight, then they surged forward, taking the Goths off their guard and exacting swift revenge.

The Britons under escort were more than glad to see their liberators. Launcelot rode forward to clasp Perceval's arm.

"I knew you would find a way," he smiled.

"The chief thanks goes to Marcellus, our cart woman," replied Perceval. Launcelot saluted his man.

"You cut a fine figure of a matron, Marcellus; we none of us suspected. This will go well for you when we are home."

"And now?" asked Perceval.

"Now we perform rites for your sister. Then - the Ostrogoths will find what it means to have the arm of justice reach from heaven to their heads."

They cradled Helena in a plain wooden sarcophagus which they found at the side of the church. Conlaed spoke a simple service over the body as they knelt before her. There were fewer tears this time, but more resolution in the eyes of the men that her death should not go unmarked. It felt, Galahad thought, more akin to a war council than a funeral.

"Now," said Conlaed, "we should commit this body to the earth. I think there are graves of the religious to the east; we could lay her among them."

"I would not dig a fresh grave if I were you," a voice said behind them. They spun round to see Lucilia pulling a hood from her head. "If Bedeulf discovers that you are the cause of his guards' disappearance, I would not put it beyond him to desecrate her grave in revenge."

"What are you doing here, lady?" asked Launcelot. She pouted.

"That is not the greeting I expected from such an illustrious warrior. I came to perform my Catholic rites of worship, but also to see what had transpired. I had high hopes that you would make good an escape, and I came to lay a request before you." She looked into Perceval's face. "Take me with you. You have seen what my heretic husband can do; what safety have I when the Goths are in the ascendance once more?" She had been pacing closer to Perceval as she talked. Now, she looked up into his face, so close that she might have kissed him. "You understand what it means for a woman to be in mortal danger; take me with you."

Perceval looked at her for a moment, then leaned down, and in a swift movement grabbed her by her hair, pulling her head back to let her stare up into his eyes. She tore ineffectually at his arm.

"I understand," he hissed, "that you are as guilty of my sister's blood as any of those accursed Goths. You were happy for Beduelf and his daughter to commit a deed which would make them loathed. You had jurisdiction over the sick woman's room - you could have prevented the fatal cut." With his free hand he drew his dagger from his belt and ran it lightly along her neck until it pierced the skin. She gasped as she felt the cold metal cut her flesh. Launcelot stepped forward a pace, but did not interfere.

"I could slit your throat and it would be no less than you deserved," he continued, "but this is a holy place, and I will not desecrate it with your blood." He flung her away and she fell against a soldier.

"Guard her while we take conference," said Launcelot. The soldier took her aside, white, and gingerly touching her neck. "We must make plans outside." He glanced at Conlaed. "You know what manner of scheme this must be; blood guilt must be assuaged. You do not have to listen."

"Whatever Bedeulf's sins, he did pay the blood money," began Conlaed.

"And he will get it back when we return. We will not profit from the Lady Helena's death."

Conlaed turned aside. "I will pray," he said simply. The others stepped towards the door. Galahad looked back at his tutor, but he was already facing the altar. He, too, left the church and joined the men sitting on a bench by the door.

"Do you want us to perform an assassination?" asked Paulus coolly.

"No. They celebrate tonight, remember? It is a perfect opportunity."

"Shall we send them to hell in their own flames?" said Marcellus. Launcelot nodded. "Then I think that'll be easy enough. But what about the woman? Should we kill her now?" Several others assented.

"No," said Perceval unexpectedly. "We have one more use for her; she can go with an escort to the nearest monastery and request that they hold my sister, until, if God wills, we can return and take her remains home. Then, the Lady Lucilia can go back to her people for her penance."

"It may be risky," said Galahad.

"True, but I think that a sharp lesson and her dead husband's gold will ensure at least her neutrality."

"I say, kill her," repeated Marcellus.

"We do not fit into her plans of power. It is safe enough. And there are other passes through the mountains."

Reluctantly, agreement was reached, and discussion returned to that night's punitive mission.

"I think that three or four men will be sufficient; we cannot risk more. We are not many, and we are not making any allies in Italia thus far. My son, will you lead them?"

Galahad was taken off guard. He was not accustomed to hearing Launcelot use that term, and he wondered if it was a challenge or an apology. Launcelot's face showed reconciliation, and Galahad hesitated. And then he thought of Helena, laughing, taking his hand, only two days ago.

"I will go," he said firmly.

They set off towards nightfall, Galahad, Marcellus and another soldier. They carried only their weapons and a quantity of rags and oil taken from the church. Galahad had avoided his tutor as much as he could in such a small party; he knew that Conlaed did not approve, but the old man was going against the grain, he reasoned. No one questioned the right of an aggrieved family to seek retribution. He dismissed doubts from his mind.

Even had they not known that a great feast was in the making, it would have been obvious from the activity they found as they crept towards the hall, having left their horses tethered nearby under the watch of a gratefully well-paid and terribly threatened village boy. Servants were staggering across the courtyard from the kitchen area, laden with steaming cauldrons and huge dishes of breads and sweetmeats. A fully-feathered swan sailed by on a silver dish, followed by what appeared to be a pastry menagerie.

The men's enforced stay at the estate had paid off, for they had ready knowledge of the unguarded areas of the perimeter. They had crept in through an unmended gap in the wall and made their way across the rubble of the building site to the villa. The light was too dim to clearly make out any features, but Galahad thought he could feel the dark stains under his feet where Helena and Perceval had shed their blood. He was glad that he had no fear of ghosts, for one might imagine Helena's spirit to be lingering where she lost her life. He noticed that one of the others crossed themselves, though.

"We will stay here until the food has been delivered," he whispered. "Then we split, lay the kindling, and meet by the door."

They waited silently, lest a wind might carry their voices to a sharp-eared servant. When the scurrying had died down, they made their way towards the hall, from where light and laughter were emanating. Marcellus sidled along the wall, and peered in through a small slit.

"The daughter is there," he said. There was a stealthy movement behind him, and he swung round to grab a middle-aged servant who shook silently in his grip.

"You are a Briton?" he whispered in Latin. "You're going to kill them?"

"And you, too," hissed Marcellus.

"Please, I beg. I have no love for them, but there are other servants in there. Let them escape your anger."

"There is no room for mercy, though we might wish it."

"Please, let me get them out. There's only three there now. I swear by Our Lady I'll never tell who did the deed."

"Let him call them at the door," whispered Galahad, coming up behind him.

"We'll all die if these acts of mercy continue," muttered Marcellus. "Well, I'll be by, and I'll slit your throat if you make a wrong move. And you stay here; don't go with them yet. I've a task left for you."

The frightened servant nodded and went to the door, trailed by Marcellus. The others laid the kindling and soaked it and the wooden walls of the hall with oil. In a few minutes, the other servants had slipped out, wonderingly.

"There's work for you in the kitchen; I'll send when we need others with wine," said the first nervously, aware of Marcellus at his back. They trailed back across the courtyard, not unhappy to gain a respite from serving.

An owl hoot sounded: the signal that the other soldier had reached his side of the hall. They struck their tinder, and a fire began to flicker slowly around the edges of the building, gathering pace as the hungry flames caught against the dry walls. The revellers were too deep in their cups to notice until the flames burst through into the hall itself. Cheers gradually turned to shouts and screams. The Britons took up brands lit from the fire, and flung them up onto the roof which, warmed by the central hearth of the hall, was soon bathed in flames which spread down to join the conflagration below. Galahad threw more dry kindling before the door: sticks, rags, straw, anything he could find. At the last, though it took only a few moments, he cast in what remained of the bag of money Bedeulf had given them.

"Let us go," he said, leading the way. Behind him he heard a cry cut short and a thud. He chose not to look back, but he knew that Marcellus had killed the servant.

They made it past the villa and towards the perimeter wall as the courtyard began to be filled with the servants and slaves of the house. Not many were attempting any aid. A few came dragging buckets of water; most stopped at a distance. Galahad might have sworn that one or two threw things onto the flames, but neither he nor his companions paused until they reached their horses where, with a cursory nod to the boy, they were mounted and off as the roof of the hall collapsed behind them, sending a wall of flame into the air that lit their backs as they galloped down the road.

"You need not have done that, Marcellus," he gasped as they rode along.

"I had to; we'll be fugitives from here to the coast if they find out who did this. And if a servant caved in to us, what would he do before a torturer?"

Galahad did not reply. Marcellus was in the right, and yet - he turned his mind to other matters. They were fast approaching the chapel, where the others were waiting, horses saddled.

"Is it done?" asked Launcelot.

"Done well," replied Galahad.

"Then let us be off. If we start slowly your horses can catch their wind."

"The Lady Lucilia?"

"She has helped us, and been escorted part of the way towards her people. Lady Helena is safe at the monastery. Our business here is completed."

Galahad fell in behind his father and Perceval. He did not feel that the business would be finished within himself for a long time.

Chapter Thirteen

The sun was shining gently as they picked up the Mentana Road in their final approach to Rome. This would not have been cause for notice, had it not been that they had spent the past two weeks struggling through torrential rains. The horses and their riders had been almost blinded at times as they pressed on through the rivulets forming around the mounts' hoofs, and on many occasions the men had been compelled to dismount and force their recalcitrant rides over bridges whose surfaces had disappeared under surging rivers. Once again, they were thankful for their Frankish cloaks which not only kept them from being as immersed as fish, but also widened to spread over most of their saddlebags and keep their belongings from being ruined. The dogs, blessed with no such luck, moped along beside them and found their revenge in stinking abominably at night camps, as only a wet dog can.

This was not, of course, to say that the riders had made a dry and comfortable journey. They contended with a constant dampness which either made them sweat and steam uncomfortably or suffer chills which numbed fingers so much they could scarcely hold their reins. It was, as Paulus remarked, the type of weather in which only mad or desperate men would be seen along the road. They were the latter; distrustful of the notion that their deeds at the estate of Bedeulf would not be discovered or suspected, Launcelot and Perceval had urged the company on, hoping to remain well ahead of any messengers. They had avoided the crowded hostels where possible, which were full of diplomats and pilgrims on their way to Ravenna or Rome. The new administrative capital itself, Ravenna, they had similarly bypassed, though their way went dangerously near it.

The rain had left little time for conversation. By day, the men had kept their heads down under their hoods and pushed onwards; at night they were so exhausted by the forced march and the conditions that sleep came as soon as they had consumed their meal. Consequently, each had been left to brood alone. No one but Launcelot dared speak a word to Perceval. The pain which pervaded his whole physique had been so transparently acute that they feared he would shatter if they approached him. For the most part, Launcelot rode silently neck and neck with him, but occasionally he offered a judicious word in a low voice. Gradually, Perceval began to mutter monosyllabic replies, and the pain in his visage lessened by minute degrees. As they reached the approach into Rome, he appeared to have found a resolution in himself, and was steeled to some kind of life without his twin.

Galahad observed this sombre transformation at a physical and mental distance. He, too, was grateful for the pervading rains which for him prevented a confrontation with Conlaed. The act of blood vengeance had torn Galahad between his loyalties for his new and old friends. All his tutor had said to him at their departure from the church was, "Would this be pleasing to the Lady Helena?" The remark had stung his former pupil into guilty silence. He had meditated on these words for much of the journey, but still he found a defence within himself for the enactment of a ritual that predated his own life, even the founding of Conlaed's orders. The death of the servant he regretted, but it had not been his deed. He had pondered, too, the causes of his own response to Helena's death. Had he been driven on by his rivalry with his father, or - had he been in love with her, he asked himself? She had certainly regarded him as no more than a friend, perhaps a younger sibling; her celibacy and her devotion to Perceval had protected her from more complex affections. He had guarded his own emotions, too, and had not questioned why he was drawn to her. He was not even sure what it would mean to be in love. He feared his grandfather, pitied his mother, felt loyalties towards Conlaed and Drystan - but other than that? He could not tell whether he had the capacity for other emotions, or whether what he felt for any one of these constituted a kind of love. Was it the unflinching resolution to do anything for another, as Helena and Perceval, or Perceval and Launcelot? That he did not have, and if the results he had seen were typical, he did not desire it.

Yet here in their sight were the walls of Rome, the great city of God on earth. The sun glinted off its buildings and off the white stone and marble tombs ahead of them, and it gently evaporated the rain from the grass that edged the road, sending up a sweet, green scent. It was impossible not to be distracted from one's selfish thoughts, not to be invaded with excitement at what one might find in the holy city, not to feel that earthly quarrels and sorrows were somehow less important. Inspired, Galahad turned back to Conlaed, who was riding slightly behind him.

"This is the city where the world meets, is it not? Where the nations come together?"

Conlaed smiled quietly and urged his horse level with Galahad's.

"And where there is repentance and reconciliation," he replied. "For us all," he added ruefully. Galahad returned the smile; it was good to be in communication with Conlaed once more.

"I only repent that we didn't execute the Lady Lucilia," muttered Marcellus dourly behind him. "Then we'd not have been force-marched through that flood."

"Marcellus, man, we're facing the holiest city after Jerusalem, can you not turn your heart to it?" Paulus spoke up, goodnaturedly chiding his friend.

"Rome isn't everything to all."

"You are not still dreaming of your plump widow woman?" Paulus managed to elicit a smile from the soldiers at the back of the file, for, in perhaps the only lighter moment of the journey, Marcellus had confessed to an amour with the cart driver's sister.

"Your jealousy is nothing to me," said Marcellus in an attempt to be lofty. A few laughs broke out as they moved on.

Rome may have no longer been the centre of the Roman Empire, but the city proclaimed loud and clear that she still commanded this place in men's hearts. The Mentana road was lined with the white tombs of the wealthy, bearing inscriptions that bade the traveller take note of their inhabitants. Some were almost small villas, with a room in which the families of the deceased could dine sociably with them. ("They really eat with the dead?" Galahad whispered to Conlaed, who replied that it was a pagan custom, but no doubt still occasionally observed.)

The newer, Christian influences on the city were also to be seen in the churches that stood nearer to the walls, encircling the perimeter as if to eclipse the old pagan protection of Rome. Launcelot halted the group by a small church which stood some way before the gate that would take them into the city. By now they were part of a small stream of travellers making their way to and from the old capital. Some were on foot, making pilgrimages and visiting shrines and tombs; they ranged from humbly attired clergy and laymen to well- but sombrely-dressed women clothed in dark colours, their heads covered. Others were travelling on official business and bustled along on horseback or in carriages with barely a glance at the pilgrims or the Britons. Finally, there were those who were riding in a leisurely fashion, richly attired, displaying the wealth of Rome's old families in jewelled collars, the women's elaborate hair styles, and the horses' gleaming apparel.

The men dismounted beside a water trough which was fed by a pipe that trickled a steady stream into the wide basin and then disappeared into a wider pipe which ran towards the church itself. Several of the soldiers stared at it for some moments, unsure whether to entrust their horses to this phenomenon. Perceval, of course, led the way.

"It is only a water system," he remarked quietly, letting his grateful horse dip its head to the cool pool. The others followed suit.

"Are we not going to search out a hostel run by Britons within the city?" asked Galahad. "I hear that there are places for men of all countries."

"We shall abide here a while first," replied Launcelot. "Look around you - there are a myriad of people passing by, and we may find a contact who is of use to us. We shall not appear overly conspicuous in such a cosmopolitan gathering."

So they fed their horses, as others were doing, and certain of the men followed the curious pilgrims and sightseers examining the tombs. Shortly, a middle-aged woman appeared, clad in a simple cloak and tunic, with her hair plaited down her back: a servant, as they judged from the comparisons they had been making. She was carrying a large basket, covered with a cloth. Several of the poorest pilgrims crowded around her, and her short form was practically obscured until the crowd duly dispersed bearing bread and clutching small coins. Marcellus nudged Paulus.

"She's a Briton, surely - look at her face." The woman did, indeed, have the pale skin, light brown hair and firm features common to most of the soldiers.

Conlaed walked forward and bowed. They saw her return the bow, and engage upon a few minutes' conversation. The lightening of her expression suggested to the watching men that she was, indeed, a fellow countrywoman. The monk was swift in bringing her back. She gazed in awe at Launcelot and Perceval who, even after weeks of debilitating travel, still managed to look every inch a pair of noblemen. She curtsied very low and very neatly.

"This daughter of the Church is distributing alms on behalf of her mistress, a widow of our country. She will be very glad to conduct us to her lady's home. Her mistress is in the habit of giving shelter to her countrymen in Rome." The woman nodded vigorously to all of Conlaed's introduction, but remained tongue-tied at the sight of her new charges.

"We are grateful for this opportune meeting," said Launcelot, "but I must beg leave to inquire whether there will be provision for as many as we are."

After a few moments, the woman found her tongue, which turned out to be a rich, southern accent.

"My lady has more than enough room and board for you all. She'll be happy to entertain such guests."

"Did you come on foot?" said Conlaed, switching to immediate practicalities.

"Yes, it can be just as quick here."

"Then you shall ride back with one of us."

The woman blushed. "You mean ride next to one of the men? I'm not sure I could do that."

She was eventually persuaded to ride with Conlaed as a compromise, and the group made the short distance to the gate, the Porta Inomentana, as she informed them. The gate was open wide to allow easy flow of traffic through the city, and the broad road was paved for horses and carriages. Twin towers flanked the portals for protection, and, to their left, the jutting walls of a military base reminded them of the city's might. There was not even a superficial resemblance to Londinium, thought Galahad as he absorbed his surroundings, his mouth set to conceal his astonishment. The area into which they had entered showed a surprising amount of green land within a city, and the street, as far down as he could see, was punctuated by the fronts of rather grand-looking houses.

The serving woman led them a little way down this street, and stopped them in front of one of these very homes. She called to a doorkeeper to take the horses to a nearby stable, and waited as other servants came forth to take saddle bags and belongings.

"There must be many slaves here," remarked Paulus.

"Few slaves pass through our doors," replied the woman. "This is a Christian household, and my lady takes her religious obligations seriously."

The basic structure of the house reminded Galahad uncomfortably of the half-built villa by the mountain pass; he wondered if it would ever now be finished. The atrium of this home, though, was wider, and the mosaics were laid to perfection and gleaming under their feet. The main wall showed an exotic painted scene of musicians, and birds with long, highly-coloured feathers. Along the other walls, sturdy couches were bolstered with embroidered covers and pillows. The men were invited to rest while the mistress of the house was sought. Wine appeared before they had scarcely taken their places, followed hard by the return of the serving woman who had apparently met her mistress on the way to discover the cause of this activity.

Had the men not known that she was a Briton, it would have been difficult to tell. She wore a long, black woollen dress with short sleeves, over which was draped a similarly dark stole, falling effortlessly in perfect drapes around her figure, which, though not slim, was still firm. A veil was attached to a high, curled hairstyle held in place with gold pins that dotted the grey-brown hair; the veil was not over her eyes, but was pinned back, framing a face that showed few lines in its maturity.

"Gentlemen." She held out arms hung with a modest number of gold and glass bangles. "I am Barbara Symmachus Basilius, widow of Petronius Basilius. I am more than delighted to harbor my fellow countrymen, whatever their reasons for coming to Rome, though I hope it may include spiritual edification."

"I am certain that such an omission would be impossible," said Launcelot, bowing. "You possess, if I may be so bold to note it, a very Roman name."

Barbara laughed. "When I first came here, twenty years since, it was too difficult for the citizens to pronounce my birth name - Rieningulid - so my husband insisted I change. I liked the saint's name, and its echoes of 'barbaria', so Barbara I became. The other names, and this good fortune you see before you, came from my second, also late, husband, of the senatorial class. But my story can wait for later. Yours I must have, at least in short to begin with, while lunch is prepared."

She listened thoughtfully as Launcelot explained the bare bones of their story, omitting Helena's role. She said little as she led them towards the rear of the house, to a small room overlooking the garden, where a light meal was waiting to take the edge off their appetites. There was fish, gently fragrant with spices, and several dishes of fruit, set by couches.

"Please," she said tactfully, "sit or recline as you wish. There are no formalities for the lunch hour, and I know that reclining is a custom foreign to many of you. I always sit when alone." She did so as she spoke, and the others followed suit.

"I believe," she continued as they were seated and enjoying food made sweeter by the fact that it was not camp fare, "that it is more than mere fortunate coincidence that you should meet with Agnes, my woman. I believe that it is the Lord's providence. Here at my home you may rest and pursue your business privately. I can give you the breathing space you need to think before you bring your true request before the papal powers - forgive me, but I detect in your narrative facts rightly concealed from strangers."

"You are astute," said Perceval, making the effort to play his role, "and we have told you as much as we are able, though not as much, I trust, as we shall reveal. But why do you, as an obviously faithful daughter of the Church, suggest that our goals are best not unwittingly divulged to its officers?"

Barbara equivocated a little. "We understand the purity and authority of the Church as it has descended through Saint Peter, but we - those who live in its shadow, I mean - are also painfully aware that the flaws of earthly government are not absent from its own."

"You do your countrymen a great service," said Conlaed, letting the matter drop. "Tell me, are there many monastics from Britannia or Hibernia? Any communities, perhaps?"

"You are one of the Scots, are you not? There is still some accent, though I guess you have lived away from your homeland for as many years as I from mine. I see monastics pass through regularly, and you will find many at the Pope's court, bringing missives or hoping for an audience with the Holy Father himself. But, there is one small community, mostly of Brothers from your isle. Scholars to a man. I helped renew their endowment many years back. They are attached to - now let me see - no, I shall have to ask Agnes what church they are near. So many have grown up, it is hard to keep track. I am sorry," she added, looking at Conlaed's quiet face, "I know that you must be eager to meet with your brethren, but rest assured it is but a moment's work to query it; Agnes knows Rome as well as if she had constructed it. She is my right arm."

"Not at all," returned Conlaed. "It is but one of many tasks that await us."

"No, no. You are correct. Connections with fellow religious are important here." She rang a small bell and instructed the arriving servant to fetch the all-knowing Agnes.

"Yes, madam," she answered to the question. "They are just beyond the Porta Aurelia, near the church of Saint Pancras, in that villa that belonged to a consul, the house they say has the oldest fig tree in Rome."

"My thanks as always, Agnes. You shall direct this Brother there as soon as he requests." She turned back to the others.

"Now, gentlemen, are you in haste?"

"We may be," said Launcelot seriously.

"Well, even so, Rome is a large city, and your presence can remain unknown for almost as long as you wish. I suggest that you take the lie of our city, even see some of its sights, and proceed with consideration."

"I've heard," said Marcellus, "that there are great entertainments, in a - circus?"

"The Circus Maximus," laughed Barbara, "yes, there are occasional games, though not as often as there used to be. There are frequent chariot races, though. You could wander over there and see what might be on."

Perceval looked disapproving, but Galahad was secretly glad that Marcellus had asked that question. It was not unreasonable, he thought; they needed some relief from the physical and mental toil of this last leg of their journey. He himself was not averse to seeing some of Rome's great secular sights which Conlaed had described to him from the information passed on by a Welsh monk at Glastonbury who had once made the great journey.

He was paying but scant attention as, the meal nearing its end, Barbara was supervising the practical arrangements for boarding her guests. Launcelot tapped him on the arm, and he looked up apologetically from a dish of figs as his father was saying,

"So you will come with me?"

"Through the city?" replied Galahad, hastily trying to recall what he had only half-listened to.

"Yes. Perceval will go with Conlaed to seek out these Brothers. We can arrange an audience with papal officials, and see something of Rome." Galahad was guiltily grateful that he was spared the more pious expedition.

“And we shall gather local intelligence,” grinned Paulus. “I am sure that my friends here will learn much at the taverns and circus.”

“Indeed you will,” said Barbara, “so it is not an unprofitable idea if conducted with moderation. But although you will not seem out of place as soldiers, or a religious, wandering the city at this hour, it would be more customary for men of higher rank to be at the baths unless they were clearly conducting official business. I can send word to a friend of mine who can lead you discretely through the process; you will not be conspicuously foreign. I also have a more suitable servant whom I can have arrange your audience. He knows the forms for petitioning, and will be able to pave the way for a cordial reception.”

Launcelot’s tentative objections were smoothly but firmly stifled. Barbara, Galahad quickly realised, had a cheerful authority that denied resistence from the stoutest heart. As the other soldiers got ready for a rough wash and a leisurely wander into the city streets, he, his father, and Perceval were soon dispatched with a servant who carried their necessaries, following in the wake of a messenger to their would-be guide.

Galahad decided quite firmly that, sophisticated or not, he was not at all sorry that he had been denied the experience of formal bathing thus far in his life. The prolific nudity did not embarrass him, for he had been used to casual nakedness and sharing bodily functions all his life, from the exhilaration of boyhood swimming to the resignation of cramped camp conditions. Rather, it was the ritual unclothing that unnerved him, the set motions through which he and everyone around him were passing. Some men were engaged in serious business discussions; others were passing gossip and jokes; still others were arguing philosophy or theology; yet all made the same superstitious circuit of the facility. The novelty of the steam room which began their initiation would almost have been entertaining had Galahad not been a little uncomfortable after consuming so many pickled figs earlier that day. They had sat on benches against the wall, sweating gently as their host drove more steam out of a small stove. Accustomed as he was to cold rather than hot temperatures, Galahad revelled in this sensation; the steam caused a strangely refreshing perspiration, different from that induced by work in the rare days of high summer or a long ride.

Their host was a quiet-spoken, middle-aged man named Aurelius, a senator of the old city and vaguely related to Barbara's second husband, "And both of us members of the Symmachi family," he added.

"Relatives of Pope Symmachus?" asked Perceval.

"The same, though not close enough to be guests at his table or expect favours," laughed Aurelius. "Still, blood is a tie, however feeble. Are you ready for the caldarium, the hot room?"

They dutifully, and, in Launcelot's case, a little dubiously, followed him into a room of marble which was bare save for a row of benches and a large tub at the rear, that stretched the full length of the room. Aurelius dropped his towel again and stepped into the water, settling back with a relaxed expression as a deep pink hue rose slowly up his skin. Perceval emulated him without hesitation, leaving Galahad and his father hovering uncertainly at the edge.

"It is not natural," muttered Launcelot, but he imitated his friend after a moment, as did Galahad. They inhaled sharply as the heat of the bath met their bare flesh. They had barely - and gingerly - sat down when a bald, portly man entered and plunged swiftly and cheerfully into the bath beside them, greeting his bathing companions as if they were old acquaintances, which, apparently, only Aurelius actually was. They answered his reply in their best Latin, painfully aware of their accents, though he did not seem suspicious of their foreignness.

"Though you couldn't be those Ostrogoths," he said in a low voice. "You hair's too short, for one thing, and not many of them bathe properly. It isn't manly, they say," and he gave a deep chuckle which was followed by Aurelius's polite, but amused laugh and the grimaces of the Britons, at least two of whom were not at all sure that the Ostrogoths did not have a point.

Just before Galahad was beginning to wonder if he was slowly cooking, Aurelius climbed out of the bath and, calling for a slave, lay down, dripping, on one of the marble benches. He indicated that the others do the same. Slaves entered, armed with glass bottles and what appeared to be small curved knives.

"It is a strigil," whispered Perceval, seeing alarmed faces.

"How is it that you know of this - this effeminate ritual?" hissed Launcelot, lapsing into dialect out of respect for their host.

"There were still baths at Ratae Coritanorum, where I was raised. I attended a few times."

"Are you sure it is Christian?"

For the first time since Helena's death, Perceval smothered a small laugh into the towel he had placed at his head.

"I have learned of no Scripture which forbids it," he smiled. Still, it was only under extreme sufferance that Launcelot permitted the slave to rub oil into his back and then gently scrape away the skin and dirt with the curved strigil.

Just as Galahad, sharing his father's reticence, was beginning to hope it was all over, came the crux of the torture. The portly man raised his head from the bench where he had deposited himself and announced that he had engaged a marvellous new masseur whom he would lend to his friend's companions.

"Just watch what he can do," he said, as the slave came in. He was a burly, hairy man, dressed only in a loincloth. His hands were, it seemed, as large as trenchers. The others watched as he slapped them down upon the stout man, sending flesh quivering away from the point of impact. He then proceeded to massage the man's back. Galahad watched in horrified fascination as the excess pounds of fat were pushed and pulled, just like a lump of dough being kneaded. He did not see how his own wiry frame would survive such a beating. It was too much for Launcelot, who, mindless of the low profile they were supposed to be maintaining, sat up, pulled his towel firmly about him, and, muttering something which quite clearly included the word "sodomite", marched out of the room with as much haste as dignity would permit.

"It is no matter," said Perceval quickly, as Aurelius raised his head. "A warrior does not come lightly to new customs; he is not offended with you."

"Your companion is clearly tense after his journey," said the portly man. "It is a pity he did not stay for the massage. It would have relaxed him. He would have been a new man."

"You are lucky you bypassed the massage," whispered Galahad as they stepped out into the hall and met with a fully-dressed Launcelot. "The cold swim was worth it just to rid myself of the feeling of his hands."

"And about the only worthy aspect of the whole process," he replied. "I had to make a show of moving through it to escape." Still, it could not be denied that, with a thorough cleansing and clean clothes, they had all recovered their bearing as nobles within a great city. Even Aurelius was impressed as he came into the entrance and caught sight of the man whom he had last seen beating a half-naked retreat.

"You will meet with no trouble here," he said, looking at the rings adorning Launcelot's fingers, and the fine, if unfamiliar cut of his tunic. "Barbara instructed me to direct you whither you will, so all my means are at your disposal."

"I expect Brother Conlaed to have marked out our path," said Perceval.

"And since the Lady Barbara's servant is arranging our audience," said Launcelot, "my son and I might make a visit to some sights of Rome. Where might you suggest?"

"You must go to the Capitoline Hill; it is Rome's beginning and her zenith. I will assign you a slave," said Aurelius. "He shall lead you there and accompany you safely back to Barbara's home. Yet, though she is your host, my services and knowledge are still yours as you require."

Outside, Conlaed was waiting for Perceval. Brief, polite introductions were made and thanks given before the men parted on their various missions. Conlaed and Perceval walked with Aurelius a little way down the street, while Galahad and his father were left to order a slave to guide their steps.

Their sojourn in Londinium had scarcely gone unnoticed by anyone, marked as they were by their dress and retinue as men of a royal party. Here, in a crowded metropolis where the rich rubbed shoulders with the poor on the streets, or Gothic warriors and Eastern monks disputed in the shaded gardens, the Britons were at once of such note and least note as gossipping passers-by were inclined to make of them.

"It will not be difficult to hide here; unless there is a good spy system in place," ventured Galahad. They jumped from stepping stone to stepping stone across a road, the mud and rubbish safely below the level of their feet.

"I have no doubt that there is, but whether the city's men cooperate wholly with the Church or the government is a matter in question. I trust we shall be gone before they have discovered all they want concerning us."

In front, the slave turned his steps southwards. The streets were filling after the hour for rest and recreation had passed. They pushed through crowds jostling by a merchant's stall, skirted around several friendly and over-adorned women whose profession Galahad could only guess at, and walked politely but remotely past small groups of toga-clad men finishing business not resolved in the baths. Garlic, perfume and sweat reeled around in Galahad's head, and he was glad to break free a little as they began to make their way up the slope of the hill and towards the temple of Jupiter.

The temple spread itself along the southern summit of the twin-peaked Capitoline, defying travellers to attempt to pass it by. The nearer they came to its many-pillared facade, the further it towered above them, and as they stepped through the portals their necks were craned back in an attempt to assimilate a sense of the building's compass.

"This is not its former splendour, I am told," explained the slave. "It has already been plundered more than once by barbarian armies." He bowed and left them to explore alone.

When they stopped to look forward, it was to be greeted with a monolithic representation of the god Jupiter sitting upon a throne, several times larger than any man. He gazed over their heads, unconcerned with mortal affairs, out across the city which had once worshipped him. The walls which surrounded him were gilded; they were stripped in many places it was true, but still enough remained to give a sense of how the temple must have shone for the citizens who came to ask for aid. Most of the niches and pedestals in the hall stood empty, with only a few urns remaining, monochromatic, ungilded vessels that had not tempted the desecrators from the north. Unspeaking, Launcelot and Galahad walked on through into the two successive chambers, which each contained another image of the king of the gods amidst a tarnished, neglected glory. A few other people milled around, mostly of foreign appearance. Two men in strange, domed headdresses were listening intently to a guide who was gesturing as he explained the surroundings in their tongue. In a corner, a scraggly youth picked at the gilding. No one took any notice. When he had placed a few scrapings in a bag, he moved to the feet of the deity, where a small basket of food had been placed, a last offering. He glanced around, and, catching only Galahad's eye, winked and grabbed an apple. Then he stopped and looked up at the god. After hesitating a moment, he carefully replaced the apple and ran off. Jupiter sat serenely, sending no thunderbolts after the impious beggar child.

Father and son exited the building, still in silence, to walk around upon the steps and see the twin temple of Juno on the other summit, the palaces and mansions which remained around it, and, protecting them all, though little was left to guard, a solid citadel.

"Britannia has nothing compared to this," said Galahad softly at last. "The bones of Rome are more splendid than the living halls of Cataviae or Londinium. It would have taken the wealth of a thousand Arthurs to build this."

"Yet these images are empty," replied Launcelot meditatively. "Even as a child, I heard stories of Rome, and I longed to see its achievements. They take my breath away, though they do not fill my soul. But once, there was a spirit that was Rome, and from here she ruled the world."

"One feels as though she still does," suggested Galahad, looking down at the thriving city below. "Her honour is not yet annihilated."

They climbed down the steps and met with the slave once more. He led the way down the slope. At the foot, Launcelot paused. Galahad stopped beside him. He turned slightly, so that he was only half looking at his son.

"You are correct, I hope," he said. "There are times when you have to judge or honour something or someone not by what they are, but by according to what they stand for, or stood for. Our glory may be tainted, but our spirit is intact. Do you see?" he asked, raising his hand to the capitol.

"I see," murmured Galahad, looking, not at the centre of the world, but at a face handsome and lined, whose eyes showed a weariness with what he was, but whose soul behind them was ready to leap up and reclaim itself.

"I see," he repeated.

When the Britons regrouped at Barbara's villa, it was to find that Perceval and Conlaed were as introspective as Galahad and Launcelot, as a result of their encounter with the Brothers. They answered only briefly that they had received a good welcome, and much information to ponder. The other soldiers had mixed news, though they were decidedly more cheerful than their leaders. Their wanderings had caused them, fortuitously, they said, to convene at the Circus Maximus, where there just happened to be a chariot race taking place.

"It was free - and there must have been thousands of spectators!" exclaimed Marcellus. "There was a famous charioteer from Constantinople, making his last appearance for a while, apparently. The girls were screaming his name all through the race. And what a race it was! That circus is huge, but the chariots flew round as if it were a spitting distance from one end to the other. And I swear they took those corners on one wheel."

"And was it instructive?" asked Perceval dryly.

"Well, sir, we certainly learned about factions: the Blues and the Greens. The people here like to divide themselves over any issue, not just games."

"It is true," interjected Barbara. "Theology, entertainments, politics - sometimes, of course, all three are intertwined in Rome - are the subject of fierce rivalries. It stops civil rebellion."

"They are kept at each other's throats instead?" said Launcelot.

"It looked like it might come to that today," added Paulus. "The charioteer for the Blues cut a corner close to the other's axle - I saw the sparks even though we were far back. Well, the Greens' man cracked his whip and caught him on the ear. At least, that's the shout that went up. Fighting broke out in the front stalls - I even saw a woman hit her neighbour on the ear with a loaf of bread. I suppose it was for the charioteer. The soldiers had to step in."

"And I trust that all of you refrained from the fracas?" asked Launcelot sternly, though none of the men appeared sufficiently dishevelled to warrant deep suspicion. They shook their heads earnestly, then began to relate their oddments of information: random, sometimes interesting, a useful tidbit here and there, but altogether fragmented. Galahad tried to concentrate, but inside he was wishing he had been at the games. The glories of Rome's architecture suddenly seemed to fade in his mind in comparison, though the expression of his father did not.

The next morning, Barbara sent the four men off for the Lateran in good time, fussing over their clothing - tweaking a brooch into place, straightening a tunic, smoothing a stray hair, and all the while dropping hints as to their conduct.

"Look appreciative of your surroundings, but not overawed. The deacon will expect reverence, but not obeisance. Mention the Symacchi connections if you find an opportunity - it cannot hurt. Show the hilt of that dagger, Galahad; the workmanship is worth exhibiting. Don't be mistaken for a divine messenger, Lord Perceval - try to look more human."

"Ah, you should have seen him with longer hair," smiled Launcelot. "Lady, do not fear for us. We have given and received audiences enough."

"Yes, I know. Only, try not to make them suspicious."

"Do you show such care for every group of travellers that passes through your doors?" asked Conlaed mildly. Barbara stopped her fussing for a moment and smiled.

"I have been given a charge to care for all my fellow countrymen, but I see in you a purpose beyond the ordinary. I have a feeling that your mission is vital - and fragile. Now, begone, or you shall find yourselves too late for an audience this day."

With that, she ushered them into the street where two servants were waiting by a carriage. ("I know, I know, but two gives a better show," said Barbara hurriedly.)

In streets already busy with people trying to finish their business within the morning trading hours, a carriage was not a much faster method of travel than being on foot. However, it kept the grime of the road from their feet and garments, and afforded them the possibility of looking around more than they had the day before, though they tried not to catch anyone's eye as they travelled. They had scarcely time to assimilate the villas, shops and public buildings that passed them haughtily by when, rising gently up from the surrounding city was the Caelian Hill, and, atop it, the basilica of St. John Lateran, the residence of the Popes. The men alighted from the carriage in front of a large equestrian statue which seemed to have little to do with the purpose of the palace, though it was a perfect reminder of the military foundation of Rome's might that predated its religious purpose. The servants led them past this and up through a pair of great brass doors into the basilica itself. Galahad's first thought was that Helena would have been gratified to know that her anticipation of Rome's holy splendours were justified. It was indeed the city of God on earth. They were walking rapidly - but the place was so vast that their footsteps seemed barely to cover any ground at all - through a great hall, flanked by double aisles. The columns seemed to reach up to the heavens themselves, and, indeed, the ceiling was painted a symbolic blue. The apse, ahead, was walled with a mosaic, at whose centre was a representation of Christ as a beardless young man, looking somewhat like the Roman busts that Galahad had seen on the Capitol. The Christ figure was surrounded by angels, each turned towards him in adulation. One or two, with their pale curls and angular faces, really did look amusingly like Perceval. He must have Roman blood in him, Galahad mused.

Below the mosaic, in the apse, stood a plain wooden altar, adorned with rather incongruous silver busts. Men and women were lining up under the direction of a monk and taking a few seconds to touch each piece as they were moved along the altar. A man began to kneel to say a prayer, but he was tapped on the back before he had dropped halfway to the ground and sent on his way.

"What is this?" Conlaed asked. The servants stopped to muse for a minute.

"The altar is supposed to be the one used by the first Popes," said one, "and the busts contain pieces of Saint Peter and Saint Paul. Their heads, I think." The four men exchanged looks, but said nothing.

The servants led them to the side of the hall, and through a door into rooms which were evidently of a more private nature. They bowed to a waiting monk and stepped aside for Conlaed to make an announcement of their status and a formal request for an audience. The Roman monk nodded solemnly and took over from the servants, who remained in the entrance room. He led them on through a small hall into an antechamber. They were not the only foreigners waiting there; two delegations, one of representatives from the African churches and the other consisting of deacons from Greece, hovered patiently in the room. The parties nodded and conversed briefly in the universal tongue, each interested in the other but wary of divulging requests as yet ungranted. At intervals, the painted doors before them were opened to briefly reveal the gilded fretwork on the inside, and a delegation was waved in. Left alone at last, the Britons paced the chamber, observing the paintings of the Last Judgement which adorned the walls, "as if they mean to set a particular atmosphere for the audience," Launcelot remarked sardonically.

Finally, a young boy in a black and white uniform, and with hair clipped above his ears, opened the doors and called for the Britons in a high, reedy voice. They entered at a measured pace, Launcelot and Perceval in front. The doors shut silently behind them, and they were in the presence of the deacon appointed to foreign missions. As if to awe visitors by degrees, this room was the most sumptuously decorated of the apartments they had entered thus far. The walls were encircled with a continuous mural whose subjects - scarcely-clad angels and Romanesque patriarchs gleaming in red and gold - fused the old and new worlds of Rome. The light which streamed in from the high, glassed windows was supplemented with lamps set in golden sconces above the paintings. In contrast to the magnificence of the gilded frescos was the deacon himself, a plainly-dressed man, whose apparel seemed a deliberate foil to his surroundings. He was standing by a low chair, with a table at its side, upon which was a pile of scrolls, some half-opened, others still sealed. Surrounding this were other chairs to which the visitors were directed. The deacon waited until they were seated and then sat down himself.

"His Holiness understands that you have letters to deliver from our son at Glastonbury and our daughter, the abbess from the house near Sorviodunum." He reached out a hand decorated with plain gold rings, engraved with images such as the Lamb and the Cross. Conlaed produced the epistles from his satchel and handed them over.

"It is an unusual delegation for the heads of religious houses," the deacon remarked casually and gently.

"We were en route for distant lands, and agreed to stand as guardian for a Sister who was to deliver the words of the abbess, but who tragically passed away before her journey could be completed." Perceval spoke steadily, but his companions knew how difficult it must have been to leave Helena's name and martyrdom unproclaimed in the hallowed dwelling of Peter's successors.

"Indeed? That is most lamentable," said the deacon, pressing his fingertips together, "and I am sure that our Sister's zeal will be accounted to her in heaven. But what business of the Regissimus, our son in Britannia, has brought you thus far?"

Three of the men forced themselves not to betray their secrets by any hint of a glance towards Launcelot, or a nervousness as they waited for him to speak. After a pause which they could not discern as natural or unnatural, he spoke, outlining a pilgrimage to the Holy Land to seek relics on behalf of the Regissimus.

"A pilgrimage in the king's name undertaken by noblemen - the relics sought must be noble indeed. But the decision is fortuitous. His Holiness wishes to underscore what the Regissimus knows, that there are manifold advantages in a closer relationship between Britannia and Rome, and he is always ready to hear delegations from the farther flung parts of Christendom."

"We would not presume to pass through Rome without conveying the respects of our king to his Holiness," said Launcelot levelly.

"I presume you also offered your greetings to King Clovis or King Theoderic? A papal alliance would naturally cement your lord's accords with these princes, especially pertinent, if I may say, in the case of Clovis, his nearest brother in rule. Yet, forgive me, my eagerness to see harmony among God's anointed ones makes me express my fond wishes. These are not the words of our Holy Father, though I am sure that he prays constantly for such a blessed peace."

The deacon smiled and spread out his hand upon the scrolls beside him, looking down at his fine, polished nails.

"The season makes our journey a pressing one, though we did take an opportunity to meet briefly with King Clovis. Our Regissimus seeks only a true faith," added Launcelot with guarded ambiguity.

The deacon turned slightly to face Conlaed.

"We would not forget the devoutness of the Celtic Church, either, or the fact that a religious brotherhood is as desirable as a political one. Your asceticism is to be praised, but I am also certain that if you take some time to study the piety and erudition of our city, you will conclude that we have much to offer."

Galahad looked from the face of the deacon to that of Conlaed. His tutor showed nothing other than an expression of mildness.

"Foolish indeed would be he who considered himself too proud to learn from any fellow man," he answered briefly.

"There is much knowledge to acquire from the Church, and much grace. May I suggest then, that you grant us your presence upon our return, that the Church may examine and bless your treasures in order that they may provide the utmost benefit for Britannia. Of what nature are they?"

Launcelot inclined his head silently for a moment. As he raised his eyes, the others knew the decision and acquiesced wordlessly.

"We do not understand the true nature of that which we seek beyond these shores, but we trust in our commission. We would not omit any duty owed the Church at Rome."

"If that is so, your journey will be a fruitful and blessed one, I am sure."

"Then, as smoothly as if he had but a passing interest in our movements, he returned to the epistles. The abbess is, it seems, not unknown in Rome, and a pastoral letter was promised in swift return. In a few more minutes, we were dismissed with a cordial blessing and ushered out to make way for the next party." Perceval concluded his rendition of their meeting to Barbara over the meal that night. Launcelot's company had been begged by Aurelius for an exchange of politics, and the other soldiers were eating with the servants, whose quarters they were sharing.

"He may have been clothed plainly, but his words were as gilded as the murals around him," added Galahad, pleased at his comparison.

"He is no doubt weighing your designs," commented Barbara. "I trust that you gave a story which can be corroborated. Papal intelligence reaches too many courts for you to travel under different pretenses from place to place."

"I think if we had commenced our journey a little later in the season we would have had papal messengers as companions on the roads," said Conlaed. "By the Lord's design, we have managed to keep a pace or two ahead of everyone."

"How soon do you expect replies?" Barbara turned to the practicalities once more.

"A few days."

"Much can be accomplished in that time - by any party."

"What if the deacon sends ahead to Jerusalem?" asked Galahad, who was tired of listening. "Then we will find a lukewarm welcoming party, no doubt. Our discretion will be of no use and our quest void. I think we should embark at once, regardless of the letters."

"A warrior should know when to be patient and when to strike," admonished Conlaed. Galahad blushed to be corrected in front of a woman.

"I am not unaware of what a good intelligence system can accomplish. It is time for swords to be drawn," he said, a little more hotly than he intended due to the strong Italian wine.

Perceval, seated next to him, leaned over and spoke in a low voice over the rim of his wine cup.

"Meet with Conlaed and myself tonight, a quarter burn of a candle after we have retired. We will have a mystery to show you, one that will change your mind." He said no more, neither enticing nor urging Galahad to accept, but turned back to end the meal with neutral conversation. Like the deacon, Barbara had not pressed them for details of their journey, but she was the recipient of more information than the papal representative, for she persisted in treating them as generously as if she were privy to all their confidences. Still, no one spoke the name of the Grail. Having reached the Holy City, it paradoxically seemed more dangerous to name their aim aloud.

Long after the meal, as the villa settled down to sleep, but for a restless dog or two enjoying the cool air of the gardens, Galahad was in the atrium to meet with the older men, who were ready with cloaks and lamps.

"Is it safe to make our journey known abroad?" he asked, indicating the light.

"Perhaps safer than arousing the suspicion of the watch by sneaking through the streets in darkness," replied Conlaed. "We will use the light while it is advantageous."

He was correct. There were several pockets of respectable company moving to and fro through the streets, making their way home from convivial dinners with friends or assignations with lovers. The three tried to effect the aura of a homecoming, and passed by several watches without arousing suspicion. When they reached the place where the Via Appia met the city gates, Conlaed shielded his lantern from the light and led them through a small opening at the side. As the guard caught sight of his tonsure, he let them pass without comment. They walked along the Appia for another mile or so, passing by more pagan sepulchres of the type they had seen on their entrance to Rome. Some way further out, they began to see small basilicas, richly carved. In the lamplight, which was diffused in the night air, Galahad could see the dim shadows of images he recognised: the Good Shepherd, Mary with the Christ child, angelic figures.

"What are these?" he asked in a low voice, not trusting their privacy even on the open road.

"They are monuments, built mostly near the tombs of the martyrs, some above where they are buried. It means we are close to the entrance we need," replied Conlaed. He veered off the Via Appia and led the way along a smaller path, laid and hardened by feet rather than stone. Eventually, he stopped by another small monument.

"Mind your step," he said. "This staircase is old."

Galahad was about to ask what staircase, but before he could do so, the monk appeared to be sinking methodically into the ground. Perceval followed on, and Galahad hurried after, suddenly uncomfortable about being left behind among these unfamiliar landmarks. He could see the lamp shining more brightly in the confines of the narrow passageway, and he followed it down. The stairs were indeed old, caved in the middle from the tread of thousands of the faithful. The smoothness of the walls, too, were the result of as many pairs of hands groping their way down into the darkness.

At last they ended their slow descent and stood in a small tunnel, dark except for a shaft of moonlight which penetrated through an aperture in the roof above. Galahad surveyed the area illuminated by their lamp. Perceval finally lit his, and the doubled light almost dazzled them for a second. When he focussed at last, Galahad let out a gasp.

"Tombs!" For, around him were several small rooms, in which he could see niches set in the walls, some empty, others closed up with marble slabs or mortared tiles, all, quite clearly, burial places.

"The resting places of the first generations of Christians - here even are martyrs and popes, asleep until the last trumpet," whispered Perceval, with some of the old fire in his voice.

They had almost come to the last room in the group as they spoke, and Galahad paused to look inside more closely. The walls were lined with tombs, and the whole room had been whitewashed. Around the niches were frescos, a little cruder than those he had seen in Barbara's home or at the Lateran, but nevertheless impressive and unexpected. The prophet Jonah was there, praying from the belly of the great fish, one of Galahad's favourite stories as a child who had never seen the sea; elsewhere, seven people were seated round a table on which were placed three baskets of loaves, with others beside them; fishes nearby reminded him of the miracle of feeding the five thousand; in a corner, Moses struck a rock with his staff, and water was gushing forth to aid the Israelites.

"Even in death they preach to us," said Conlaed. "Look - everything is a symbol of baptism, the Eucharist or the resurrection."

"You have not been here before, then? You seemed to know the way so well."

"I memorized it from the description I was given. Still, no words can express what it means to be here. If it were my lot to die far from home, I would pray that my bones could rest with these believers."

They moved on though the passageway. As they walked, the light sprung up and curved around the walls of the old tombs, fading as it reached to the stone ceiling. At the end, a small companion light gradually became visible, half-shaded by whoever was its guardian.

"We are far enough inside," said Perceval in a low voice. "I shall remain to watch the entrance. Listen well, Prince Galahad." He took up position at the curve in the passage, hand on his sword hilt.

Conlaed led the way towards the lamp. The passageway opened into an alcove, where a fellow monk stood waiting calmly beside tombs blocked in with what appeared to be very old tiles.

"Is this indeed the place where he lies?" asked Conlaed, touching the edge of a shelf lightly with his fingertips.

"It is so, and attested by record and tradition," replied the monk in an accent similar to Conlaed's. "His remains were transferred here when the cemeteries were first dug."

"This," said his tutor, turning to Galahad, "is where the scholar and Hebrew, Barnabus, was laid to rest by the descendants of the brethren he converted when Rome was not yet the city of our Lord. It was in his name that this Brother's house was founded as an Order of study."

"The house where you have been visiting?"

His tutor nodded.

"It is a small house, and dedicated to poverty of living, and is thus overlooked by many who seek good only where there are riches. Yet it has in its library and in its scholars a repository of Hebrew and Greek manuscripts and learning that few can equal. It was in the library, upon communing with our good Brother Ebentius here, that he revealed to me a text of Barnabus's life, one which shines a light, if it be true, upon our quest." He nodded to his companion to take up the narrative.

"The blessed Barnabus was acquainted with the first descendants of those apostles who travelled the world with the Gospel, and who had fled Jerusalem when it was sacked by the Romans. The writer claims that many holy relics were saved from the flames by believers who took refuge with other communities of Christians."

"My grandfather was correct?" Galahad shook his head, surprised. "And the Grail?"

"It is not in Jerusalem, so it is asserted, but in a monastery outside Constantinople."

"Then why reveal this to us, and in here?"

"It is not a known theory - even within the monastery. I myself only happened upon the manuscript by accident; it had been caught behind another. This event transpired many months ago, yet I revealed it to no one. I pondered and prayed, and then my Brother arrived, with the pious lord, and it felt as if it were an answer to my petitions."

"Tell him the prayer," said Conlaed, taking pity on Galahad's curiosity for once.

The monk leaned nearer. "I have been here for twenty-five years," he whispered, "and I have seen this city change. It is still the home of the faithful, but it is also a place where the fashionably religious come to visit shrines and relics as one might visit the circus. Worse still, relics here are often plundered - even by monks themselves, eager to bring home a thing of power to their monasteries, and to shine in the reflected glory of what they have stolen. Even as I marvelled at the information I discovered, I was afraid lest the Grail, should it be found and returned to Rome, should be trivialized or stolen. I could not trust even my Brothers with my burden, which has weighed like sin upon my shoulders. But now, you have come, and I see a chance for the Grail to rest in a land where the Church is as yet uncorrupted by earthly wealth and splendour."

"You said that it was a theory only."

"It goes against tradition, it is true, but the manuscript is evidently of some age," replied Conlaed, stepping in. "I have seen it myself. It also contains other facts which can be attested as truth."

"Yes, but -"

"But what?"

"Why chose me to decide? Why not Launcelot?"

"The Abbot did not bless your father as the Grail questor. He blessed you," said Conlaed gently.

Galahad was silent for a moment, feeling foolish. That first night at Arthur's court seemed no more than a dream - he suspected much of it to be no less than a fantasy orchestrated by Merlin, and Pelles from afar- and the ensuing journey had left him believing himself not consecrated, but tarnished and inadequate.

"I do not know that I was given discernment," he said at last, having failed to muster up any sense of his authority. "I would defer to others. If you and Perceval are in agreement, I have no argument. I do not feel that my time has come," he ended, the words ringing somewhat lamely in his own ears.

The two monks, however, seemed satisfied with a humility they heard in his speech.

"Then we shall go, Brother," said Conlaed. "You cannot pretend that your business took you much longer than this. If we do not meet again, our prayers shall join us."

"I thank you. I will let you leave first; I still have some duties among the dead." He bowed.

They retreated quickly and met with Perceval as they made their way back down the passage.

"It is agreed?" he asked. Seeing their faces, he did not need an answer. He resheathed his sword and they left the catacombs quietly. Now the open countryside seemed noisy in comparison with the stillness of those underground tombs. Galahad could hear the bats flitting after the humming gnats and whirring moths, and faint owl calls indicated a wood nearby. Still, they talked only in whispers as they retraced their steps to the gate, and entered with but a brief, polite reply to the guard's enquiry as to the success of their visitation, as such he assumed it to be. Once inside the city gates again, the openness of the streets, with their readily perceived population, relaxed the companions, and offered privacy for freer conversation.

"We must tell the Lord Launcelot. He will be waiting for us if Aurelius has not held him," ventured Conlaed as they were passing a party of young men singing a bawdy chorus.

"And the lady Barbara also," said Perceval unexpectedly. Two heads turned towards him in the dark.

"We will need her aid in our journey, I know," said Conlaed, "but should we entrust her with such a dangerous piece of information?"

"I trust her," said Perceval, "because I know that Helena would have, and she has - had - an instinct for people who were noble of character. It is not too late, I hope, to listen to her."

"She taught us all," said Conlaed, sensitively guarded in his reply.

"Yet she had to die to teach me to look beyond my own creed. I have learned that, even if one holds the noblest truths, one cannot compel others to live by one's beliefs." The sojourn with the faithful dead seemed to have loosened Perceval's tongue. "Barbara's faith and practices may be different, but she has integrity. That should be sufficient testimony for us. It would have been for my sister."

"It is no shame to admit that we cannot understand a lesson when it is first presented to us, nor a person while they live."

"How could I not understand my soul? I knew - and still I did as I did. But," he added pensively, "I believe she understood. I think - I hope - she forgives me."

"The dead know no anger," said Conlaed gently. "What was done on earth matters no more to her."

"Yet what I do will still matter only because of her." Perceval looked away from his companions, a sad smile playing across his lips.

They traipsed back along the few remaining streets in silence once more. In this, they were in keeping with the wearier groups of walkers still straggling the streets, politely evicted by a tired host, or unable to revel any longer. They reached the villa to find Launcelot and Barbara in the atrium, sipping spiced wine and conversing comfortably.

"How was your business?" asked Barbara. "At least, I presume it was business and not illicit pleasures that drove you about town of an evening."

Perceval bowed. "I apologize that we did not make our mission fully known to our hostess, but, if Lord Launcelot is in accord, we are now free to divulge our information."

"I am interested in these new evidences, also," interjected Launcelot, any hint of objection smoothed over by the wine.

They told their tale, briefly at first, and then expansively as they answered questions, chiefly from Barbara. When she had completed her examination, she sat back and swirled her wine in its cup gently and thoughtfully.

"The Brother has a valid point," she said. "In cities, especially this one, there is at once such a capacity for doing good and giving growth to faith, and yet there is also such room for evil to flourish. I would not leave this place, but Rome is no longer a goddess."

"Yet," said Launcelot, "it is easy for a dotard to see that the Church would lay claim to the Grail, and with good argument. Just how much of our conversation with the deacon contained inferences that he grasped? He is a shrewd man, and it is certain that he forced me to reveal more truths than I intended."

"You would be as ignorant as we in that," answered Perceval. "He will obviously suspect that we know the relics we seek are important, but he also believes we are headed to Jerusalem, which is now in doubt."

"Yet even if we escape to Constantinople, what might await us there? Who knows what authority in that city would not be ready to claim such a relic also? The Roman Church has weak links there, but the native Church is powerful." Launcelot began to drum his fingers on the table in an irritated fashion.

"We forget," said Barbara, "that things - wealth, relics - do not matter in themselves. It is how we use them. How would you use the Grail, if it is to be found, if the legend is indeed a fact? To its own glory - or to King Arthur's?"

"You are unafraid to hit the mark, my lady," smiled Launcelot, relaxing for a moment. "It would be a falsehood to say that no honour would fall upon the Regissimus with the chalice in the possession of our isle. Yet our king is also a true Christian soldier. I have no doubt of his piety. In all our fellowship, only our Lord Perceval here surpasses him." Perceval showed no emotion at this praise, but Barbara seemed satisfied.

"When I left the shores of Britannia as a bride, Arthur was only at the beginning of his ascendancy. I had vaguely heard his name from my husband's lips, but we had no conviction that life in our own country would be stable or prosperous. Yet, as the years passed and I harbored many of my countrymen here- and not a few countrywomen, too - I began to realise that far more news of Arthur reached the ears of the people than one would expect, and in those tidings I heard hope and pride. So then," she concluded, "for my old homeland, and its protection amongst pagan kingdoms, I will aid you. What do you need most?"

"Passage to Constantinople," said Galahad.

"Only that?" she laughed. "Shall I throw in a concealed embarkation, a bribed captain, supplies and a Greek-speaking guide? You will need to speak with Aurelius. He has interests in merchant ships."

"We would prefer, for our safety and those of others, that as few people as possible know of our movements," added Launcelot.

"Yes, you still have not told me what transpired on your journey. I am sure it involved bloodshed; it always does with warriors. Aurelius desires my hand in marriage." Barbara ended there by way of explanation.

"Why is it that I have never met a Briton Christian woman who has understood the meaning of female subservience?" asked Launcelot with a twinkle in his eye.

"And how would our Lord's resurrection have been discovered if it were not for women of independent mind?" retorted Barbara. Launcelot knelt and kissed her hand.

"My lady, we are yours to command in Rome - and glad of it." The laughter that filled the atrium was so full and genuine that a sleepy servant poked his head through the doorway to see what was afoot. He shook his head as if used to his mistress's unconventional gatherings, and retreated.

The next morning, towards the end of business hours, they made their way to the house of Aurelius, situated near the city's gardens. It was older and larger than Barbara's home, and the atrium was lined with ivory statues of young women draped precariously in wisps of linen, and bearing fruit or musical instruments on impossibly smooth shoulders. Galahad could not refrain from staring at them as they waited to speak to Aurelius. The master of the house was at the far end of the atrium, talking with several men who were obviously of a lower class than he. At his side was a small table with a coffer, and a slave was counting out money for each man. They were thanking him formally, but not obsequiously, and left soon after, glancing with only fleeting curiosity at the assembled Britons.

Aurelius rose and held out his arms.

"Welcome, friends," he said, "and a ready welcome to you, Lord Launcelot, so soon returned. Let us go into the study; it will be a more private place for our discussion."

They followed him through the atrium into an adjoining room. It was furnished less sumptuously than the entrance hall, but still with great taste. The floor was tiled with a simple red and white checkered pattern, and the walls plainly painted in ochre and white. There was one large writing desk and a wide chair with a cushion. There were also several smaller chairs, and a low couch in one corner. Scrolls sat upright in a cylindrical pot in one corner of the desk, and wax tablets, pens and ink were strewn around it. Aurelius's secretary, a small, bearded man, had followed them into the study, but he was dismissed quietly after he had gathered the chairs together for the guests.

"Now, gentlemen," said Aurelius. "This is not a social call, I presume - unless you are asking me to accompany you to the baths once more?"

Launcelot laughed graciously; he was always able to see his behaviour in its true light after the incident had passed.

“You have guessed aright. Our superlative hostess has presumed upon your own goodwill and sent us hither to request your aid in our departure, which we hope to accomplish as swiftly as may be done without suspicion.”

“Without suspicion? I sense a story about to come forth, and before the evening hour, too.”

Conlaed obligingly repeated the broader points of their tale for the second time.

“And the formidable Barbara thinks I can get you safe passage?”

“I would be happier if you could tell us who has been following us for the last two days,” said Launcelot casually.

“You are discerning,” laughed Aurelius. “Yes, I have had men on your trail, but not to mark you so much as any that were marking you.”

“Were they?”

“A man from the Lateran was interested in your movements, but he was persuaded to seek other quarry.”

“Do you have many spies?” asked Perceval.

“No one in Rome is safe without men who will watch his back, or those of his friends. I did not reveal this to you, because I did not want any among you to walk as if he knew there was protection behind him.”

“That was not an unwise choice,” conceded Launcelot. Galahad noted that he had shown no interest in how the spy had been ‘persuaded’ to refrain from following them.

“But now you need help which is greater than a few hidden bodyguards. We must make, I think, a diversion. Any who are lurking in your wake must know that you have indeed embarked - but not on a ship headed for Constantinople. They must think that you are resolutely headed for Jerusalem, perhaps even follow you onto the boat.”

"Impersonators." Launcelot was not surprised, but he spoke slowly as if he were following Aurelius's train of thought as he commented.

"Might I persuade you to change your clothing with others who could fit your descriptions? I can have you fitted with some Roman armour - much more durable, anyway, if you will forgive me for saying so. This nation perfected the art of war generations ago."

"Would you not be burdened by the deceit?" asked Perceval, with a curious rather than accusatory tone.

"Was not Saint Paul smuggled out of a city in a basket? It is no shame to leave his city in the way he left another."

"You are not the Christians we expected to meet in Rome," said Perceval candidly.

"Then how do you perceive us?"

"You are less pious, yet - you are truer."

"I will take that as a compliment," said Aurelius, "and leave it there."

Chapter Fourteen

It was in the hours before dawn, a few days later, that a small party ushered forth from the house in the street down from the Porta Inomentana. They wore short, Roman cloaks, which hung over a foreign costume. Led by a servant, they disappeared into the darkness, heading for the river.

Some time later, another group emerged, flanked by two dogs. They wore long cloaks, but their boots were Roman, and made the sound of military footwear on the cobbled streets. They took a similar route, and arrived at the river port to see a ship glide silently out towards the dawn.

"Was that it?" whispered Galahad.

"It seems so," replied Launcelot. "It has the marks that Aurelius indicated. It is to meet a ship in Ostia and take on board goods bound for Jerusalem; it is not due to put into any port for several days. Any who followed those men aboard will be marooned for some time."

"Well, I'm glad they didn't get our cloaks," said Marcellus, wrapping his around him. To a man, the Britons had resolutely refused to hand over their most precious article of clothing to their impersonators. "I don't know how the Romans got to Britannia in those flimsy bits of cloth."

"Look - there are our horses," interrupted Paulus. "We'd better get them aboard."

The horses, now knowing full well what a ship portended, were not cooperating with their Roman stable hands, but were pulling at their reins, and snorting loudly, or at least it sounded so in the silence of the emerging day. The Britons hastened forward to quiet them and, after much coaxing, managed to gain control. Launcelot drew the end of his cloak over his horse's eyes and led him reluctantly up the ramp to the ship. The others eventually followed.

"We could have done with your sister's horse," said Launcelot quietly to Perceval. "It was far more obedient, and a good leader."

"It was better left with Barbara," replied Perceval. "There is no use in dragging excess weight and responsibilities with us."

The calls from the sailors rose in the air, as messages were relayed along the small ship. The anchor was weighed and several pairs of oars hit the water simultaneously to guide the ship out of the port and into the current of the Tiber. The men watched as they began to glide downstream, floating by the sights of the past few days, now grey shapes that merged in the mist arising from the river.

"Do you know the legend of Cloelia?" asked Launcelot of those standing around. Galahad did not.

"She was a Roman girl, handed over as one of many hostages in a war with Porsenna centuries ago. They say that she broke her bonds and swam across the Tiber back to Rome."

"That must have been a near impossible feat."

"But she believed in herself as a Roman, and she won through. That is what we must do now."

Galahad was leading his horse carefully up and down a small section of the ship. She had been at sea for some days, but remained unconvinced at the idea of developing sea legs. In fact, none of the Briton's horses had taken kindly to the river journey or the change to a larger ship at Ostia, and they might have proved too skittish to handle on such a long journey had it not been for the presence of two other mounts, hardened by discipline and frequent journeys.

These two, a tall, lean pair, belonged to the charioteer whom Marcellus and the others had seen at the Circus Maximus, performing his final races before setting off for his homeland of Byzantium. Needless to say, the soldiers were elated to have such a companion aboard, although it transpired that his Latin was rather rudimentary, and a Byzantine dialect at that. However, with no duties and only the sea to watch, the men took it upon themselves to extract some exciting stories from the mixture of Greek and Latin he offered when so inclined. Not that he was disposed to be voluble; much of the time, as now, he spent meditating as he stood at the prow of the ship. It took them a week to extract his name - Felix - from him. He was a middle-aged man, with a glossy shock of brown-grey hair which fell to his shoulders. It was kept in place with a thin band that circled his temples; several strands were plaited loosely. His face was clean-shaven and boldly sculpted, and his body had the same muscular angularity. Galahad could understand why he was so popular with the female spectators.

When the charioteer was being taciturn, the sailors were the focus of attention, though Launcelot had warned his men not to interfere with their work. The crew was cosmopolitan, consisting mainly of Greek, Byzantine and Roman sailors, tanned to a uniform tawny hue and bound by a Greek-Latin idiom that resembled that of the charioteer. The soldiers learned a few new songs from the men - though some of the vocabulary was unclear, the intent of the lyrics was not. Conlaed, who had a good knowledge of Greek, claimed that he had never come across certain of the words in his studies. Still, the Britons joined in with choruses as they watched the seamen leap about the ship. They were vastly different in temperament from the stolid channel-crossing sailors of the northern climes. They were lean and weather-scarred, and their shoulders and flanks were knotted from years of back-breaking rowing, yet they displayed a constant lightheartedness in keeping with the warmer weather. They dressed practically for the voyage in tunics and short leggings, and mostly went barefoot for ease in climbing the rigging or keeping a steady footing on deck.

The ship was sailing within sight of the coast, which allowed the curious to keep track of their progress, but tantalized those who were seasick with a constant reminder of the unmoving soil for which they yearned. Caius was as ill as on the previous sea journey, but Galahad found that the Mediterranean seas were kinder to his stomach. They had been skimming the coast of Italia and were moving out to sea to round Sicilia, the island at the edge of the larger land mass. As he stood tracing the coastline, the smell of salt-water mingled with other scents: smoked meat and pickled vegetables. Paulus and another soldier were bringing up their rations, along with a large flagon of wine and the remains of some honeyed cakes. They congregated upwind of the horses.

"This Roman food is all very well," said Marcellus, with his mouth full, "but it'll be good to taste a home-raised rabbit again."

"It'll be good just to get home," remarked another. "But it won't be long now, will it?"

"If God favours us, we will reach our destination soon," replied Launcelot in measured tones, "but as to what adventure may meet us, I cannot say. The way back, at least, should be swifter."

"If your dedication wavers, so will the mission," added Perceval in a warning voice. "The future is not ours to predict."

"Well, I'll predict my future," grinned Marcellus. "I'll take my adventure bringing home a Gothic wife." He leaned back against the side of the ship and closed his eyes, his smile widening as his memories sprung to mind.

Several of the others laughed.

"There are less dangerous ways to warm your bed," said Caius, poking him in the ribs. "Why go back? She'll have taken up with someone else by now - widows can't wait for long, you know."

"Mine will. She swore."

"What, on her husband's grave? How many has she buried, anyway?"

Galahad choked on his mouthful of food, and tried to smother his laugh by pretending to cough.

"Well, at least I have a plan," retorted Marcellus. "What are the rest of you going to do?"

"I think I may retire to Glastonbury," said Conlaed. "I have had more than my share of adventure in this life, and it would be good to spend my last years with my old friends, God willing."

"My wife is good enough for me. I'd a fourth grandchild on the way when I left, too. I'd like to see it," ventured another soldier.

"What will you do, my lord?" Paulus inquired of Launcelot. "Your fame will be great indeed when you return."

Launcelot looked ahead. "I shall do my duty, as always," he said. He did not mention the queen. "But," he added, "perhaps my son shall be at my side, at least until he assumes his northern kingship."

Galahad looked up, startled. Several retorts passed through his mind, to die reluctantly before they reached his tongue.

"Let us see what our adventure brings us," he replied at last. "We have many miles to go together."

The horses sensed the coming change in weather almost before the sailors themselves began to look more concerned. While the latter took the direction of the wind and scanned the clouds, the former became restless and difficult to manage. It was a struggle to get them to take a walk up and down the boards, and the soldiers cursed as they dragged the reluctant animals turn and turn about.

Galahad was standing at starboard, watching the sea. It had darkened slightly, and small, choppy waves were slapping the ship. Conlaed appeared beside him.

"Your lord father was frank last night," he said, "and you were gracious."

Galahad shrugged.

"Do you think of your mother and grandfather?"

"How could I not remember my mother? I pray for her, even though I am not very good at praying."

"She is safe in the Lord's hands - but not only in his."

Galahad turned his head sharply to look at his tutor. Conlaed was unusually nervous.

"There is a piece of news which I have kept from you until the right time. I wanted to be sure that you needed to know your mother was protected. Now, I see that you have such a need."

"What has my grandfather done?"

"He has done nothing; he knows nothing, or did when I departed. Before I left, I performed a marriage between your mother and Drystan."

"Drystan? You married my - sick - mother to him? Did she even know?" Galahad was stunned, yet the blow gave him clear vision. He saw in a flash all the moments, all the remarks, and he understood that Drystan loved his mother, had loved her all these years. He himself respected the man above all others, he admitted freely, but even so, was a horsemaster worthy of a king's daughter?

"She was lucid when she gave consent, but he swore not to touch her as his wife unless she became truly well again. I had to think of her life," Conlaed continued hastily. "With you gone, and Pelles an old man, and an ailing one, though he hides it, anyone might have attempted to take the kingdom. I had to give the Lady Elayne protection, and she understood this. She has a kind regard for Drystan, and his character soars above his station. He was the only one I could trust to fight for her."

The monk laid his hand on Galahad's arm, and the young man did not shake it off, though he did not acknowledge it. He was considering, irrationally, he thought, of the wonder of a love which could wait all those years, which could touch the prize and still not claim it. For a moment, compassion swept over him, for Elayne and Drystan, but for Launcelot and Guenevere, too.

"I do not ask forgiveness now," said Conlaed, "But I hope that you will understand in time."

"Have you told my father?"

"No. I shared this secret with no one, least of all the Lord Launcelot."

Galahad's thought was to go to him at once, to confront him with it, that he might see his reaction and know, truly - what? He was not sure what he wanted to know. Suddenly, as if in response to the revelation, there was a crack which resounded across the heavens. For the moment, his intention was thwarted as a strong cry rose up from the captain. Storm clouds came rolling into view, swifter than Galahad had ever seen. A sailor rushed past, heading for the main sail. Perceval followed on, with Paulus in his wake.

"Galahad, go with that man. Hold the sail as you are commanded." He turned to Conlaed. "You are the right height for the tiller. Go help the helmsman. Do only as the crew tell you," he repeated, breathless, as he raced on to direct the other Britons.

Unhesitatingly, Galahad dropped into pace beside Paulus. Ahead of them, men were untying the ropes which held the main sail to the mast, while one was climbing the pole, loosening bonds as he went. A Greek, pulling taut one of the ropes which held the flapping canvas, yelled something which had no literal meaning to him, but which Galahad instantly knew was a command for them to take his place. The two Britons caught the rope as he let it go, gritting their teeth as it burned their skin before they stopped its progress. Galahad leaned back against the taller man as he braced his feet on the deck. The Greek had run to the centre, ready to catch the sail as it dropped. The man on the mast called out as the canvas began to descend, folding in on itself. But, as it hit the halfway mark, a gust of wind struck it in the fore, pushing it back around the mast. Galahad and Paulus clung to their rope as it strained to leave their grasp. In a moment, two sailors had leaped upon the canvas, forcing it to the ground; others rushed up to roll and tie it safely.

The ship began to lurch as the sea swelled beneath it, and the first wave broke over the stern. A chorus of neighing and barking sent Galahad to the horses. Samson and his companion were weaving in and out of the horses' legs, trying to shelter beneath them. Galahad grabbed the dogs' collars and dragged them towards the hold where he pushed them down. It took some effort to force the reluctant hounds through the hatch; he shoved at Samson's backside, while the dog pushed back, digging his blunt claws into the boards, but at last Galahad managed to unbalance him and send him to relative safety. He quickly tipped the other in and slammed the hatch shut before returning to the horses. Caius was there, with Felix, checking their restraints and shouting words of comfort into ears almost flattened with terror. Another crack of thunder, and the rain fell, with no preliminary warning drops, like a waterfall over their heads. Galahad caught hold of two pairs of reins just as the sea wall rose above all their heads. It was almost impossible to keep the horses steady as the seawater washed over them. Terrified, they fought their bonds, desperate to free themselves and seek their own salvation. It was unnerving for the men, too, to hold their ground, blinded by the spray as hoofs trampled the deck around them. Horses and men gasped in the air between the waves, wondering with each ebb whether it would be their last chance to breathe. A shout in the blindness of the storm told them that another soldier had arrived to aid, and they took heart. Galahad felt his arms becoming numb and he tried to move them without losing his grip. But this had been anticipated. Just as he and others began to feel that they would lose their steeds, Launcelot arrived with other Britons to take their places, not to give rest, but to send them to other tasks.

"Go towards the helm," he croaked, his voice obviously hoarse from giving orders above the storm.

Galahad and the charioteer groped their way along the edge of the ship, slipping in the foam which swirled around their ankles, and swaying with the gusts of wind. Galahad's cloak would have whipped him away like a sail if it had not been too sodden to do more than slap, wet and heavy, against his back. A flash lit the ship before them and, in the grey-blue light, they saw the helm, and the silhouettes of two men braced against it while another was fumbling with a rope which flailed as if it had been a serpent. They came as far round by the rails as they could, and then were faced with the short leap across the deck to the tiller. They yelled their presence, but their voices were swallowed by the wind. Galahad drew himself back slightly, tensing his muscles, and then, in the seconds between gusts of wind, half bounded and half staggered across the planks to fall against the body of his tutor.

"Hold it here," panted Conlaed in his direction. Then he sensed who was beside him. "Hold fast, my son," he reiterated.

"There is another," he called, turning to the figure behind Conlaed. They looked into the darkness to see the other shape lurching towards them. Suddenly, the ship leaped upon a wave and the shadow toppled back towards the ship's side. Another bolt of lightning showed him falling slowly over the edge. From behind Conlaed and Galahad, the second helmsman jumped, the end of the rope in his hand. Galahad recognized the dim form of Perceval, sliding through the water to the rail. Straining forward from the end of the rope, Perceval reached out his free hand towards the arms of the charioteer, just visible as he clung to the rail. In the resuming darkness, the two hands met and a faint noise, discernible even in the storm as the tone of a man who has seen death and escaped, told those waiting that rescue had been accomplished.

In another few moments, Felix, gasping and staggering, was placing his bulk against the tiller as the sailor behind pulled in the rope and resumed his work. For the first time, Galahad realized that the rain was lessening. Several other heads turned upwards told him that the men around him had noticed, too.

The next wave did not manage to crest over the ship but smashed the side, splashing back into the air. Slowly, the darkness of the storm merged into the twilight which had fallen while it had raged. Men's voices became clearer: tired, ragged but jubilant. They had ridden out the danger.

It was some time before an assessment of the storm's assault could be made. All on board were occupied in following the orders of the captain, bailing out water, hanging the sail to dry or taking turns at the oars to set the ship back on course. Although they had given their utmost for many hours, the fact that they had come through intact lent new vigour to their muscles and their spirits; they felt they could work on through the night in the sheer elation of being alive. It even showed in the relaxed, grinning faces of the sea-hardened sailors, who reacted as would the Briton soldiers after a successful battle.

Eventually, the ship was righted as much as possible, lanterns were lit, and the sailors took over their old duties. The Britons gathered near the horses, who whinnied nervously at the sound of men approaching; they had remained skittish and distrustful despite the calming of the weather. Even when they recognised their own riders, they were not overly grateful, remembering their treatment during the tempest. Samson was more forgiving and stuck to his master's heels, determined not to be separated in another storm. Two of the Britons' horses had slight cuts to the legs and neck, but one of the charioteer's pair, less sturdy than theirs, had twisted a muscle in its foreleg. He was engaged in massaging and binding it as they approached and looked up only briefly to nod, though it was not a cursory gesture, but rather an acknowledgment of his debt.

"We were lucky with the horses at least," said Marcellus. "I wouldn't want to trade in steeds who know our arses better than we do."

"What report did you get of the supplies?" asked Launcelot.

"None of our things were washed overboard, but most are wet. Some of the ship's food was lost when the barrels were broken - I think the dogs ate a lot of that." Samson looked up, bloated and unrepentant; his companion was vomiting quietly in a corner. "They're going to have to put into port, but I don't know where."

"We are sailing around the promontory near Corinth now," said Launcelot. "That would be a likely stopping point. I will consult the captain as soon as he is free of these present troubles."

"I'd vote we go the rest of the way on land, if we could," said Caius glumly.

"Actually, it is possible," replied Conlaed. "If we followed the east coast of Graecia, we would be able to cross an isthmus into the Byzantine lands."

"At least we can fight what we come against on dry land," remarked another soldier quietly.

"Our vows were to serve, not argue," snapped Paulus.

"And you will be no safer," remarked Felix, raising his head again. "Give me pardon, but for men who go on land, there are others who attack, who know they are -" he added a Greek word, which Conlaed translated for him, "- thank you - vulnerable, because they chose this way."

"It is true," said Launcelot, "and remember, this captain sails under the direction of Aurelius. It is as much protection as we will receive in this part of the world, perhaps the most we have received in our entire journey. We will disembark at Corinth for a short time, if we can, that much I promise you. But we take our chances with the sea."

Chapter Fifteen

The remainder of the journey was uneventful, with no more squalls to make them question the wisdom of remaining on board. Now that the Britons had proved themselves useful and capable, they were allowed to lend a hand in the running of the ship, which occupied otherwise idle and tiresome hours. Caius even discovered that clambering around on the rigging alleviated his sea sickness, and he was heard to declare, to the amusement of his companions, that he had thoughts of becoming a sailor if he ever grew tired of soldiering.

At last, on a thankfully calm day, the ship glided into the huge bay that served as harbour for the city of Constantinople. Galahad stood at the prow, watching a small set of waves ripple across the water and disappear swiftly into the larger waves pushed out by the vessel, before lifting his gaze towards dry land. Samson stood with him, his massive front paws propped up on the rail and his tail wagging furiously at the sight of a new place to explore. The captain had forgiven him and his companion their opportunistic feast in the hold, but only because Aurelius had promised before the voyage to cover any expenses incurred. For Samson, the sights of the port were irrelevant; he was interested in the land for its own sake, and for the smells that were already wafting on the breeze: fish, of course, but other, unknown foods, and the scents of new animals and people. For Galahad, whose nose could discern only the salt-laced sea around him, it was the scene itself which caught his interest: ships of all sizes anchored around them; sailors black as charcoal or brown as leather; dock men throwing cargo on board ships as easily as he might toss a stone; great, swooping grey and white birds which descended like a conquering army on the spoils cast over the side of a vessel.

Though it was not home to most of those on board, it felt like a homecoming to see dry land and a busy dock. The city was circled round almost as far as they could see with a triple-walled defence, rising in ramparts one behind the other. Not even Rome had been thus protected. Tower after tower punctuated the lines, massive and threatening. The undulating skyline of the city gradually rose above it in places as they approached, dominated by domes of differing heights and girths.

Just as the ship came close to a quay, the shout was given and the anchor dropped. There was a long, gentle tug and the ship strained forward before settling back upon the waves. Galahad was surprised, Samson disappointed. Galahad strode down the ship, rather proud of his now steady gait, to enquire as to the meaning of this stop.

"The captain needs to send a boat to state his business before we can dock," said Perceval, who was patiently studying the pieces in a game he and Conlaed were playing.

"You arose early this morning," remarked the monk. "You must have been eager to be the first to see Constantinople."

Galahad seemed embarrassed. "My mind could not settle," he replied. He was spared further interrogation, for, as he spoke, a small craft was being rowed towards the ship, and the captain came to the rail to meet it as it pulled alongside the larger vessel. The Britons watched as he spoke for some time with the two men aboard. At last they nodded and saluted one another, and then the rowing boat set off once more. The captain shouted to the sailors, who weighed anchor and took up their own positions at the oars.

"There is no choice now, Samson," muttered Galahad, facing the port. "The empire ends here; so does our journey."

Though they had fled Rome in haste, and looked to the end of their quest during the voyage, upon their arrival in Constantinople there was an unspoken agreement for a hiatus, as though they needed to pause for a final breath. In a combination of luck and the hospitality which governed all kingdoms across the West, they were once again provided with a place to stay. Aurelius had mentioned several acquaintances, one of whom turned out also to be an avid supporter of the charioteer. So it was to this man's house, at the edge of the city, that they found themselves bound upon their disembarkation. They found a villa much like those some had lived in in Britannia, or encountered in their journey; a vast walled area which enclosed a house with cloistered walks and formal, symmetrical gardens.

Although the householder, Nicetas, was not a king, his home certainly had the status of a minor court. Besides the usual bevy of servants there was a tutor for his children, a scholar, two priests, and a group of musicians. The teachers and clergymen at least spoke Latin well, but communication with the rest of the household was difficult. Even the master spoke Latin with an accent heavy and unfamiliar to the Britons. His daughter, a girl of about eleven, stood as his translator. She was bright, but not precocious, and was apparently permitted to study with her brothers. Far from being embarrassed about his own shortcomings, her father was instead quite proud of his daughter's accomplishments and allowed her to tag along in his meetings with his guests. It was the custom, he explained, to treat women as intellectual equals in Byzantium.

For the first two days, they fell unresisting into the role of dutiful guests. News from Rome was commonplace, but tidings from further afield were novel, and the Britons found themselves repaying their host's generosity with an exhaustive narrative of the history and reign of Arthur. It was a slow process as the scholar and daughter between them translated questions and answers, but as they struggled, they became more familiar with one another's tongue, until translation was virtually unneeded.

They were sitting in the dining hall at the end of the evening's meal, listening idly to the musicians as they conversed. A servant approached the master of the house and gave a message in a low voice. Nicetas clapped his hands and looked up.

"We have a singer at our door, who begs the opportunity to perform for us. Now you shall hear how we tell tales of our own land."

He nodded to the servant who disappeared briefly to usher in the minstrel. He was a small, portly, balding man, attired in a rather gaudy and incongruous fashion for one of his years. His tunic was sewn from bold stripes of red and green cloth, and a yellow scarf was draped across his shoulders. He bowed low to the host and made an elaborate speech in Greek. Then he walked over to the musicians and they conversed for a few minutes, accompanied by much shaking and nodding of heads and snatches of tunes from both singer and players. Finally, he turned and bowed again, this time to the group in general. The strains of a slow melody began and the singer stretched out his arm and inhaled deeply, swelling his chest. He opened his mouth and, to the astonishment of most in the audience, began to sing in a full, but impossibly high voice. The first song was in Greek, but it seemed to be a tale of love, for the stout little man made each word sound full of sweet yearning, modulating into a poignancy that could only tell of tragedy and loss. As he finished, there was a pause before Nicetas clapped his hands together and cried, "Bravo! But now you must sing in the tongue of Rome for our guests. You will be well rewarded if you please them!"

The singer took a long, musing look at the Britons, then smiled. He indicated to the harpist and intoned a note of middle range. The musician struck a chord and followed with gentle variations of the same key. This time, the singer rendered his story in a voice midway between a chant and a melody, still in the same high tones.

"Far back in time," he intoned, "beyond the memories of our great-grandfathers, there lived a young prince, whose glory was as the dawning sun. The people loved his father as they loved their own, but their love for the prince was illumined with the hopes they saw in him for a glorious future. Yet this prince was not content to bask in the love of his people. One day he went to his father and said, 'My lord, my soul is heavy with melancholy. How can I be fit to be your son when I have not proved my manhood, and shown myself and others that I am worthy to be prince of this country? Send me on a quest that I might earn my fame.'

"'My son,' replied his father, 'the tribulations of this world will overtake you soon enough, and when you ascend this throne, you will find challenges rise to meet you whether you will them or no. Must you seek them before it is your time?' But the prince would not retract his words, and the king, his face grown heavy, spoke again..."

Galahad shifted in his seat as the singer continued, outlining a quest that would take the prince far beyond his homeland and into the realms of strangers. He could sense the pit of his stomach quite clearly; the singer could not have chosen a more admonitory tale had he seen into their hearts. Around him the others began to look uncomfortable, too. They scarcely followed the singer as he carried the prince over perilous seas too seek the helm of a barbaric warrior king, or noticed the prince's triumphs over various cunning and mighty foes.

"...and at the last, as he sailed back with the famed helmet and the bride he had found, he believed he was worthy of his title. He took his final night's rest before reaching the shore, in a silken bed, knowing that the next night would bring him a companion and the sweet joys of marriage. Yet, alas, when he awoke, his bride had vanished, and the helmet with her. Dejected, he tore his clothes and beat his chest. Refusing a horse, he walked barefoot to the palace, only to be greeted by the king with open arms.

"'Do not embrace me father,' he wept, 'for I have failed. I have lost all that I gained, and I shall no longer call myself your son.'

"'Well done, my child,' cried the king. 'Now you are fit to rule! For you have learned humility, the mark of a true man.' With that he waved his hand and the prince's bride came forth from behind a curtain, dressed for marriage and bearing the helmet upon a cushion. The prince acknowledged that he had learned a virtue he had not sought, and pledged to hold it ever as the most important in his life. He wed his princess, and in the feasting gold and spices rained down on the streets for his subjects. In due time they came to the throne, ruling wisely - and humbly - for long years."

The music died away gently, and silence fell over the assembly. The host looked around at the faces of the Britons.

"The money is yours!" he exclaimed to the singer. "You have touched a chord in them. Tell me, friends, are our own stories equal to those of your court?"

Launcelot recovered himself enough to make a favourable comparison.

"What other subject would you care to hear? This man has a store of songs to suit any desire. Do you love war? Magic? Questing? Love itself?"

"Tell us a history," requested Galahad. "One of this country."

"An excellent choice!" beamed Nicetas. His father shot him a look of approval.

After the singer had been handsomely rewarded for showing the best of Byzantine culture, and most of the household had retired, the four Britons gathered in the walled garden at the rear of the house. The moon, high and full, reflected its light off the gilded colonnades, making them glow palely. No one spoke at first, afraid that to name the subject was to admit the possibility that they had come to a point where they had no choice, but that the one they had made might be false. Finally, Launcelot opened their discussion.

"We need to divide men and priorities," he said brusquely. "We must discover the monastery where the Grail should be concealed; we must find a reliquary for its transportation; we must make arrangements for our direct passage from here."

"But if we find the Grail, negotiations may be lengthy," pointed out Conlaed.

"Then we must turn our minds to settling the matter swiftly."

"How swift?" asked Galahad. "Do you mean to steal it?"

"Our mission is divinely defined and backed up with the vision of the monk in Glastonbury. We cannot steal it."

"I remember the vision," said Conlaed. "One of us is not to return. Will that end, then, be in violence?"

There was silence for a moment. This was another question which had remained unaddressed on their journey.

"There has already been a death," said Perceval quietly. "Perhaps my sister atoned for our sinful deeds."

"Sir, I did not imply that the Lady Helena's death was irrelevant, but that she died in another service for her Lord. It seems to me that the vision concerned the principal questors."

"I take no offence. Death in this service would not be unwelcome to me."

"Arthur's kingdom needs you," said Launcelot. "You must look to the future. Think of the life you have saved."

"My face is set forward; if my heart looks back at times, I cannot control it. I am wholly with you."

"That is not a question I need ever ask, or you to answer." Launcelot put his hand upon his comrade's shoulder.

"But the question of our fate is void if we do not discover its destination." Perceval looked to Conlaed.

"I will enquire. We must find the old houses. Once the foundation of Saint Barnabus is ferreted out, there need be no doubt."

"Shall I see whether our captain is outward bound any time soon?" Galahad hated to be penned up, even in a beautiful villa.

"Yes, or get a reliable contact from him, or perhaps our host. We will inform the men tomorrow."

They negotiated the details between them, and, necessary business over, Launcelot and Perceval walked towards their room silently, leaving Galahad and Conlaed behind. The monk looked up at the moon.

"How much may be illumined by such a pale light," he said.

"Father Conlaed," said Galahad. The monk looked at him keenly; his pupil had not used that form of address to him since he was a boy. "I have a confession. I would unburden it to you."

"Your burdens have always been mine."

"It is concerning this journey. You shared a truth with me, and I must return the honesty. When I first left King Pelles' court to find Arthur, the quest of the Grail was already put upon me - by my grandfather. He entrusted me with persuading Arthur to send forth a mission to find the Grail - and to steal it. The first was accomplished for me, but the second I still determined to do. My grandfather gave me a vial of poison; it was his intention - and mine - that I to use it somehow to obtain the Grail, and my revenge. I knew not how I might accomplish this, but I agreed."

"Why?"

"You know my grandfather. Oh, you fear him not, but he had until recently a hold upon me. And more than that, I wanted to discover a way to avenge my mother."

"Yet you changed your mind."

"Yes. I threw the poison overboard as we sailed into the harbor here. That is why I was up before the dawn that morning. I will take the Grail back to Arthur, if we gain it, because I owe more honest loyalty to these men than I have done to anyone in my life. I did not even know how much I truly owed you before I rode as your companion."

"I knew," said Conlaed quietly, "for I discovered the vial in your pack when we were caught in the mountain pass. I did not confront you," he added, seeing Galahad's startled face, "but that was because I knew you would not commit the deed I surmised. How could the events through which we have all passed not change such a resolve? But do you understand your decision? Can you return home now?"

Galahad looked up at the moon, so far away, as far as his home seemed now. "I am not sure. Yet I have my own ally now, in Launcelot."

"Do you love him?" Galahad shook his head in answer.

"No, but I accept him for who he is. I can see what my mother saw, and - I no longer blame them."

Conlaed smiled and put a hand on Galahad's head in a gesture of blessing. "Then you have indeed won a victory over yourself. I have no need to offer absolution."

Galahad was up early the next morning to travel down to the dock. He felt alive and freer since he had confessed to Conlaed. He had shaken off the past, and was beginning to reconcile himself with the present. The future? - that could wait, he thought as he trotted his horse out of the stables, Samson, as always, at his heels. Conlaed had already left for the town to seek news in the churches.

Galahad was just going through the gate when he heard a call, and turned to see his host waving at him.

"I have business at the dock," he explained, "a cargo to inspect. Might I join you?" In his elevated mood, Galahad did not excuse himself. He waited until another horse had been brought and his host had mounted.

They talked of general matters on the journey, of ports in Britannia and the trade that existed there. On this, Galahad's information was a little hazy, but he recalled the merchandise he had seen in Londinium and did his best to describe it. Then, Nicetas began to explain the Greek plays which his children were studying, and which were still performed at the theatre in the city. He was at pains to point out that his daughter was quite as capable of discussing the drama as her brothers. Galahad offered some words of polite but absent-minded admiration, and was relieved to see that they had reached the port.

It took him some while to find the ship on which they had sailed; most of them looked the same to him. Thankfully, one of the crew recognized him from a distance and hailed him. He quickly commandeered a small rowing boat and made his way out to the vessel. The captain informed him that were readying themselves to set sail in a week, when they finished loading the cargo which Aurelius had commissioned him to purchase. He was happy to promise to take the Britons aboard again, and assured him that he had spoken to no one of his passengers, as commanded.

"I'll double my crew for free any day," he joked, patting Samson on the head. It had clearly been a good voyage for him.

Galahad spent some minutes in conversation before leaving the captain to his task. He was rowed back to the dock, where he met up with Nicetas for the journey back.

"You are Lord Launcelot's heir?" asked the Byzantine casually, as they resumed their road to the villa.

"I trace no formal heritage from my father," said Galahad tactfully, "but I am the grandson of King Pelles, whose kingdom in the north has been an ally of Arthur's."

"Indeed? You will be king? I suppose you already have a bride, or one awaiting you?"

Galahad confessed that no such arrangements had been made.

"Then, might I ask that you and your father consider my daughter? Oh yes, she is young, but in a year or two she would be ripe for marriage. You could take her back with you now. Her accomplishments would grace any court; she would soon learn the domestic duties of a new culture, and she is unafraid of adventure."

Galahad almost pulled his horse to a halt in surprise.

"You do not have to give an answer now," his host assured him. "Discuss it with the Lord Launcelot. My dowry would be generous. Speak not of it."

Galahad was relieved at the last remark, for he could think of nothing that he could say in return. He would have to call upon Conlaed to concoct a refusal for him, he thought resignedly.

When he met with his countrymen, he was not able to beg aid immediately, for Conlaed was at the start of reporting his own news, much more satisfactory than Galahad's. The monastery they thought they sought was to the west of the city, close to the shores of the Bosporus. It was, explained Conlaed, a charitable foundation, dedicated to poverty, but not known for its relics. He had not even discovered a rumour of the Grail's existence.

"We shall have to confront them," said Launcelot bluntly. "We cannot send spies, and we cannot make an assault. If they hold the Grail secretly, they have no recourse against an open enquiry."

They set out for the monastery at once; there was no longer a question of measured delays. They were not in fact far from their destination, since their host's estate was on the outskirts of the settled area. They began at a quick pace along the broad byway that connected the city with the estates that lurked just out of its reach. However, it was not long before they began to slow a little as the roads and dwellings dwindled and they found themselves upon a rocky track. They picked their way carefully for about half a mile, until eventually the church building loomed up before them, a structure roughly rotund in shape, about thirty feet high with a conical roof. Not far from it were various smaller buildings, the cells which made up the monastery. A monk, busy scratching the sandy soil of a sparse garden, looked up. He wiped his hands on the rough smock he wore over his black robe, and came forward.

"Sirs, you are welcome to our modest community, though your visit is unexpected."

"We are pleased to meet with you," replied Conlaed. "If you might direct us to your abbot, we would be glad to make our business known."

"You are foreign visitors, I hear by your accent," returned the monk. "I am the abbot, and if you would care to sit outside on such a beautiful day, we can take the benches over there." He indicated in the direction of the church where a few trees stood.

Launcelot and Perceval exchanged looks; it was not an auspicious beginning.

"We had not anticipated such humility of service," said Perceval. "Forgive us for our presumptions."

The abbot smiled, his round face lighting up and his long, dark bushy beard sweeping up off his chest as he beamed.

"We are a small community, and each needs to take a share in the physical tasks. I find, too, that working the land lends itself to contemplation. Our first forefather was a gardener, you know." As he talked, he led them over to some simple wooden benches in the light shade of the trees. The forms had no backs, and they were obliged to sit straight.

"Now, what leads you across the seas to Byzantium? Surely more than a visit to our house?"

"Do you have time for a story, Father?" asked Launcelot.

"Stories shape our lives. There is always time for a tale."

With a nod from Launcelot, Conlaed began their narrative. Galahad was surprised to find himself drawn into a rendition of his own history. Although he was used to hearing sagas that managed to laud the ruler who just happened to be paying the bard's fee, he had never heard himself in a tale before. In Conlaed's rendering, almost musical despite the absence of any instruments, he heard himself, not as he felt he was, treacherous, unfilial and inadequate, but as he was intended to be: single-minded, brave and devoted. He was not at all sure that Conlaed should be painting him thus. Launcelot and Perceval might prove their valour in their demeanor alone, but it must be quite obvious to the abbot that the young man sitting before him was no hero.

As the abbot listened, his beard fell towards his chest again as he lowered his head, taking care to shield his expression. After the narrative drew to a close, he remained silent for some moments. When he finally raised his head to face the Britons once more, his beam was gone.

"You have come a great distance on a slim hope. What makes you believe such evidence, or think that an important relic could have remained undiscovered in such a humble repository?"

"Some might say that your face has just granted us the extra proof we need," said Launcelot smoothly.

"How many know of your journey?"

"Many know of our journey; few know our final destination; our discovery has not been noised abroad."

"You ask a grave question," sighed the abbot at last. "I cannot say that we know of the Grail's existence or whereabouts. An answer would have to be agreed upon by our most holy and learned Brothers. We are all hermits here, and I am abbot only by consensus; I cannot dictate our decisions. If you will return at our bidding, and swear not to tell of our meeting, I in turn will swear by the holy cross that no actions will be taken which are not in your favour."

The four men looked at one another silently before nodding almost imperceptibly.

"We will take those terms," said Launcelot. "We are warriors and servants of Christ. Our word is inviolate."

The abbot rose and bowed, and they reluctantly did likewise.

"We would not keep you from your business," said Perceval, "but might we stop to pray in your church? We should ask for a blessing upon this council."

The abbot's beard, quivering slightly, revealed that he might have liked to deny their continued presence in his grounds, but his mouth assented quietly. He hurried back to the group of huts where several Brothers stood observing the strangers, while the Britons ducked under the door and entered the rotunda. Pacing forward a few paces, they knelt before the altar.

Perceval's head was bowed in genuine prayer, but Galahad could not refrain from studying the worship space. As had been said, no reliquaries were visible; indeed there was precious little ornament. The wall panels were blank apart from a faded painting here and there. A plain wooden altar, its tabletop slightly concave as if it had stood the pressure of chalices over many years, was carved with simple Gospel scenes. A tapestry stood as reredos, a depiction of the Virgin and Christ Child, the gold of their halos a little faded, and a partly patched hole at Mary's elbow, yet no less compelling in the way their faces challenged the worshipper. Galahad stared at the hole as it moved gently in a draft. Suddenly, those around him were rising to their feet, and he hastily followed suit.

"What did you see?" asked Launcelot of the others as they strode back towards the area where their horses were grazing on the rough sea grass. "I detected no obvious closets; there is no place of adoration."

"There is a hidden room," said Galahad. "Behind the altar cloth; I saw a glimpse of wood through the hole in the hanging - it has to be a door or panel."

"Well observed," said Conlaed approvingly, "though it as yet gives no proof that it is where the Grail is concealed - if it is even on this land."

"Whatever the truth, it contains something which they do not want noised abroad," said Launcelot grimly, "and I will have satisfaction." The others stared after him as he marched towards the horses. Then Perceval shrugged and followed on, leaving the other two to catch up as they might.

They spent the evening alone. Nicetas had another dinner engagement, and they had apologized for not accompanying him, but begged their business at the abbey as excuse. His absence reminded Galahad of his proposal the day before, which he repeated rather embarrassedly to his companions.

"She would not be a bad wife," said Launcelot. "Are you sure you should dismiss her so lightly?"

"I have no intention of marrying," snapped Galahad defensively.

"Ever? She's young; you could mould her before you wed. And if your fancy goes elsewhere, she is rich and far from home, and we could find her another choice of husband that would not upset her family."

"That is not the advice I recall you giving at Londinium."

"Perhaps," he admitted. "But duty holds its rewards. You may also find that liking grows where you determine it. Such an education and dowry should be considered carefully."

"I might take her - for Oswald," Perceval added with emphasis.

"Why not keep an option for yourself, Perceval?" asked his friend. "You would form a Christian wifely spirit in her better than any could."

"For someone who has remained unwed himself, you are very keen to advocate that state for others," rejoined Perceval levelly, though with a hint of annoyance in his eyes.

"Soon, you will consider my advice without anger," said Launcelot. "When we have the Grail, you will be consoled and you will think about a new life."

"One without Helena you mean?" flashed Perceval. "I am no longer convinced that we will attain the Grail. Oh, it may be here, but are we worthy? What if, as in that tale last night, the quest is the journey itself? Then, perhaps, we have already failed. We have lied and slaughtered our way across country after country. What do we deserve?"

"Then why did you swear to go on with us in the garden?" retorted Launcelot.

"It is our destiny to take the quest to its end, whatever that might be. I have paid my price, and I have my redemption. I can face anything. Can you?" He arose and strode into the courtyard.

Galahad stared at his father. He was used to the brief, heated debates that occurred between Launcelot and Perceval, but this one had a flavour of ill-will which he had not felt before. Launcelot returned his look.

"Oh, he will forgive me," he smiled, "and we will have the Grail."

“You did not believe so when we set out,” blurted Galahad, irritated himself at his father, and nervous of voicing a truth. “Why do you behave so now?”

Launcelot’s visage changed, to something resembling the look he had for Guenevere.

“When we embarked, true, I was doing no more than obeying orders, dubiously seeking something that would enhance the status of the Regissimus. Yet, as we travelled, and risked our lives for each other and a noble cause, a longing grew in me, to change the accustomed course of my life, to become what I once was. The resolve taunts me, urging me to grasp it and then spurning me just before I possess it. But I know that if I can touch the Grail, I can be cured of this - spiritual disease, that I can give Arthur true service. I will not let this opportunity slip from my grasp, whatever happens. And yes, I too can face my destiny.”

He followed Perceval out to the courtyard, to seek a reconciliation he knew would be forthcoming. Galahad drained his wine glass and sat back. Conlaed, who had been sitting unobtrusively in a corner, took Launcelot’s place beside him.

“Perhaps Lord Perceval is correct in one sense,” he said in a low voice. “The idea of the Grail is certainly tempting their spirits, albeit in different ways.”

“Will the fellowship hold?” asked Galahad.

“I pray so,” answered the monk, “but it will not do so without more sacrifice.”

The summons from the monastery came two days later. They were to meet with the abbot in the late afternoon. Their plans for a possible swift departure had already been put into place, but unfortunately Paulus and Marcellus had already left to undertake some errands in town. Galahad offered to fetch them back; he was, as he pointed out without resentment, not necessary to their plans at the villa, and he had a small purchase of his own that could be accomplished on the way. They agreed, and he set out at once.

The possibilities of what he might meet with that afternoon did not perturb him as he made his way into Constantinople. He knew that he should not feel so absorbed in a secular job, but he had handed over his chances to God, and saw no need to add the endless postscripts of prayers in which Perceval and Conlaed were engaged. Even this long journey had failed to quite cure him of his overriding need for action over contemplation. He had decided that, on his way to fetch the soldiers, he would seek out a wedding gift for his mother, though he knew not when he could deliver it. Drystan would have little to give her, especially if they had to flee Pelles. But then soon, thought Galahad, he would be king and they could live at his court. He had never before contemplated the prospect with any pleasure, but now he saw a purpose in the burden of his birth.

It was not difficult to find the street of Mese, where the permanent bazaar stood. Many of the citizens were making their way in that direction, and soon Galahad had only to follow his senses.

The sounds of chanting grew louder; though Galahad could not understand most of the words, he recognized the tone of merchants gaining attention by singing of their wares. He was accosted before he arrived in the market, with the smell of charcoal laced with meat, perhaps lamb, and onions, along with the spices which had been unfamiliar to him in Britannia, but which had become part of his consciousness as he had travelled further into the Continent and beyond. It was hard to see the stalls themselves at first, hidden from the sun under gently billowing awnings whose vivid reds and blues imitated the equally vibrant clothes of the many people who were mingling along the street as far as he could see. To his left sat a scribe at a slanting desk set upon a trestle, patiently taking down a letter as it was dictated to him by an elderly man. Next to him a cosmetician was holding the hand of an interested lady customer, gently rubbing a salve into her skin while he talked in a tone which suggested he was extolling the beautifying effects of his product. The lady's maid stood by, already opening the purse she held as if she understood that her mistress was a converted woman.

Galahad walked quickly past these; he knew what he was looking for, besides the errant soldiers. Passing by the plates of food stretched out to him and the gems reflecting rainbows of colour into the light that played across them, he stopped at a section where several weavers were plying their wares. The brilliant silks drew his eye, ranging from an ochre as rich as earth to a blue as clear as a perfect sky, but he passed them on, too, pausing at the next stall, which was spread with a selection of fine linens, almost as smooth as the silks, yet crisper, smelling of a purer air than that which pervaded the market.

This was what he wanted, thought Galahad, a gift which was useful, but still beautiful, something which told his mother that he loved her, that he accepted her choice, but that he understood its consequences. When she was not distracted she liked to sew, and he could think of her contentedly making clothes as she sat in the sun outside her dwelling. For a moment, he saw the image vividly, her hands, soft, yet lined as a spider's web, moving across the linens. His attention was drawn back by the strong breath of the weaver as the man, sensing a receptive customer, put his face close and began making comments which Galahad knew were directed towards him, but which he could not understand, given his rudimentary Greek culled from Conlaed and the sailors in the voyage of the last few weeks. He shook his head and began to speak in slow Latin. The weaver smiled and waved his hand over the cloth.

"Very fine," he said, echoing Galahad's language. "You buy for home? Not better anywhere."

"How much?"

The weaver held up a hand. "Cheap, but linens not cheap. Very fine." He named his price. Galahad took a guess at how inflated it was and named another, proportionally lower. The weaver widened his eyes.

"I starve!" he said, and offered a slightly lower deal. In a few minutes they had agreed on a midway price and the linen was being wrapped in a rougher cloth. Tucking it under his arm, Galahad scouted around him for signs of Paulus and Marcellus. He soon spied the incongruous pair: Paulus's tall, dark form was leaning down towards his short, solid comrade, then shaking with laughter as he straightened up. Galahad called out as he approached, and they turned, grinning.

"We did not expect to see you, my lord. News from the mon-". Marcellus stopped as Paulus nudged him.

"Always the diplomat, friend," he said.

"Try saying that next time you've been captured by a band of Goths," retorted Marcellus. "But the question stands, my lord."

"Yes, we are leaving as soon as I return with you. You are needed to arrange our departure."

"So soon? We had hoped to see our charioteer friend race."

"We are no longer on our own time," said Galahad quietly. He turned and began to lead the way through the throng. They had barely travelled the length of three stalls when a female voice addressed them. Galahad turned round. He could not make out her words, but the intent was directed at Paulus. She was smiling and had laid her hand on his arm. Paulus bowed and attempted to gently move his arm away, but her grip was firm. She looked to Galahad.

"You are his master? How much is he? I must have him for my bodyguard."

"I am sorry, my lady, but he is a soldier in a higher service than mine. He must return with us."

"No, no, I insist. I can pay three times his worth."

"I am no slave, my lady," returned Paulus.

"Then you can enter my service freely."

"Lady, I do not understand."

"A man such as you, so tall, so dark, so handsome! I cannot see such a soldier and not have him. I have your price - I have anyone's price."

"Perhaps," said Galahad, "we can arrange a meeting, say five days from hence, when our leaders have discussed this. I am sure..." But he was interrupted by a cry from across the street. A man as stout as Marcellus, but with fat rather than muscle, came pushing his way across the road, drawing the attention of bystanders as he shoved past. Galahad and the others tried to edge away uncomfortably. The fat man confronted the woman, speaking angrily, and she cast some epithets back at him. Then he turned to the Britons.

"Trying to seduce my wife with your filthy bargains! Take that black devil back to his hole and..." He got no further than this, for Marcellus' fist landed squarely in his mouth.

"Fat bastard! You and your whore wife can bugger off now!"

"No!" Galahad and Paulus grabbed Marcellus' arms and swung him round, throwing themselves forward against the marketers. Some stepped out of their way hurriedly, eager not to get involved, but a few, mostly men, blocked their way, not wanting to let such an insult to their fellow citizen go lightly. The Britons put their hands to their swords, which changed the minds of a few. The fat husband had recovered himself. Wiping his bloody mouth on his hand he called out. The three knew it was a hue and cry.

"Meet at the East gate," hissed Galahad. They hit their hands together briefly and then bounded apart. Paulus leaped across a pottery stall, and disappeared into the house behind, much to the astonishment of the stallholder who stood staring after the flying apparition. Marcellus, who knew the length of his legs, ran round a food stall and upset it towards the people who were pursuing him. The yells of the cook and the shouts of the men splashed by hot fat were the only things that followed as he darted into an alley. Galahad saw them go out of the corner of his eye as he set off in a different direction, dodging around another food stall and beginning a weaving sprint that took him towards the gate whence he had come. One of the crowd, a burly youth, began to pace him, looking for a gap in which to cross over. Galahad pushed forward, skimming the spaces ahead. He saw another street, leading in roughly the same direction, and he swerved into it. He was one block of shops down, and far ahead of any pursuers, when a group of soldiers stepped out from a corner. Galahad drew himself up sharply, but he knew that they would see him as a fugitive. Though his lungs were beginning to burn, he swung round towards the opposite alley. Two of the men were upon him instantly, throwing themselves against him. The bundle of linen fell into the gutter and lay there, slowly going brown in the muddy water as Galahad was led away.

The cell in which he was placed was actually more of a room than a prison; at least they recognized a man of wealth over a thief. The foot soldiers had spoken little Latin, and Galahad had had to protest loudly until they brought a sergeant who could speak the tongue well. He had listened, not unsympathetically, to Galahad's pleas of innocence.

"The merchant you insulted is rich."

"I did not insult him. Some subordinates did. I ran because I was pursued, not because I was guilty."

"Well, he needs compensation, if you see what I mean. It's not worth our while to let you go. You're a visitor; he is a citizen. Just tell me where I can find your men, and we can clear it up."

"I do not know for sure," said Galahad truthfully. "I can pay; let him name his price."

"It's more than the money; we need to see the one who assaulted him. He's only in the ranks; turn him over." The sergeant tried to sound reasonable, but Galahad could see that he was slightly irritated; after all, what reason would he have to defend his subordinates? But he could not allow a hindrance to their mission - the mission he himself was supposed to be on at this very moment.

"Let me go free. I had separated from the party, and I was to meet them to find out where to go. If I can find my company, we can resolve this matter. What would it take for you to let me out yourself?"

"Not too much; I've no love for Lord High and Mighty. It would do him good to have one put over on him. He treats us as if we were the dirt on his shoes. But his money has bought men higher than me. You'll have to talk to him yourself."

"Then let me see him."

"He's gone to lunch and the baths. He'll not show up until the end of the afternoon. But if you can tell me where to pick up your man, you can go."

Seeing the answer in Galahad's face, the sergeant shrugged and closed the door. Galahad pounded the wall with his fist. They would be sure not to wait for him to set off for the monastery. Launcelot's words had been too clear: he no longer cared about his son's role. But Galahad wanted to be there. Not because he believed he was chosen - that was a trick of Merlin's, intended for an end he never lived to manipulate - but because, as Perceval had commented, it felt as though it was their destiny to see the quest to its end. He leant his head against the cool wall. Why me, he asked himself? And why now?

He was sitting hunched up on the pallet, watching the sun move into its descending arc through the slit of a window, when the door opened. He sprang up. It was not the merchant, but the charioteer.

"What has happened, friend?" he said.

"How did you know?" asked Galahad, ignoring the question for the moment.

"I was at the baths with my chief patron, who happens to be a rather fat merchant. He told me what happened, and I managed to persuade him that if he wanted my goodwill, he should let me see you. Now come, before he changes his mind."

Galahad ducked under the door and followed.

"I need to get to the monastery of Saint Barnabus, as quickly as possible."

"If it is speed you need, my friend, you have found the right person."

Without another word, he turned and made his way rapidly past the guards and out of the prison. Galahad stepped in beside him, glad to feel a fresh breeze upon his limbs.

"But this is not the direction."

"It is the direction of the stables. We need horses."

Felix moved at a pace somewhere between a walk and a run, a sustainable rate which propelled them swiftly through alleys to the back of a stableyard. He barked in Greek to the groom closest to him, who retreated into the dark stalls. He was soon out with two horses.

"You do not need to accompany me. I know the route," said Galahad. "I would not want to place you in danger or trouble."

"I know a quicker way than you. And you will find I will make you faster." He pulled himself into the saddle, and Galahad mounted the other horse.

"Away!" yelled Felix, kicking the horse's flank with his heels. The mount turned and made swiftly for the gates, with Galahad not far behind.

The road outside the stable was straight and fair, meant for equine travel. They moved quickly for some distance before the charioteer pulled the reins to his left and veered into a side street which came out upon one end of the market. He bounded for the stalls, letting out a deep cry which made the crowd freeze for a moment and then scatter before him. Galahad heard the man's name called out by more than a few people as he raced along behind him, and saw Felix raise his hand without looking for the source of the adulation. He did not have to manage his own horse, but let it follow its master, finding its way sure-footedly across the uneven stones. He leaned forward in parallel with its neck, letting the wind stream over their heads.

They reached the city gate and raced through with a cursory nod to the guards, who clearly thought it an exercise or private race, for they jumped aside, grinning at the champion. The two passed by the side of a few villas and left civilization behind to enter the scrubby pathway that led towards the beach. The air had turned from spicy to salty, and it left its taste upon Galahad's tongue as he breathed hard.

Soon the monastery was upon them. A handful of monks were standing around, not making a pretense of working. They must be awaiting the outcome of the visitation, thought Galahad. He slipped from his horse as it slowed down, and the charioteer grabbed the reins.

"Go friend, I wait," he said, pulling the mounts to a halt.

Galahad did not need to ask where the others were. The nervous glances of the monks, directed towards the church, told him that. He stumbled towards the little, round building. He pushed through the doorway and walked towards the altar, not stopping to genuflect, but crossing himself as he went. The abbot was kneeling by the altar, in prayer. He raised his head at the commotion of Galahad's footsteps and rose to his own feet.

"The vigil has begun," he said, "I do not think it wise to join them. You may disturb the power of the Grail."

"I am part of the fellowship," panted Galahad. "I will claim my place in this quest." He strode on before the abbot could grab him, and, sweeping the wall hanging aside, flung open the little door.

The room was light, much more so than he had expected after the gloom of the church, and his eyes were blinded for a moment. The small chapel was lighted both by a large, glassed dome in the ceiling and by a myriad of lamps which stood in sconces along the wall. Some of them were shielded by stained glass, which made the room glow with a diffusion of colour. There were no seats in the tiny space; indeed, there was no furniture save a small pedestal which was placed so that most of the light came to rest upon it. On this pedestal sat a glass chalice, and before it, Launcelot and Perceval were kneeling, heads bowed.

Galahad stood, not knowing what to do. His sides ached from the race, and he felt sick from fatigue or excitement, he could not tell which. The chalice did not look quite as Merlin had described it. It was silver-stemmed, but a simple, twisted stem rather than an elaborate tree. The cup itself was also unadorned, showing nothing but the light reflected upon it. As Galahad concentrated on it, he thought he began to see it glow faintly in the shimmering air which surrounded it. A faint blue tinge seemed to emanate from it.

Galahad, too, fell to his knees, though not in adoration, but terror. He wanted to speak, but somehow he could not find the words to call out and explain what was before them, what their hopes were resting on. As he knelt, he saw Launcelot lift his head and rise slowly. His father began to pace towards the cup, inch by inch, as if he hardly dared commit the deed.

He cannot, thought Galahad. He is not ready, he cannot die like this.

"Do not!" The words sounded from his lips barely above a whisper. Launcelot did not look back.

Galahad found the strength to rise. He took a shaky step forward, then another, walking inexorably towards the chalice. He felt as though he were choking. He tugged at the neck strings of his tunic, baring his chest, trying to give himself air to breathe and talk. Launcelot was up to the pedestal, and reaching for the cup. Galahad wrenched his arm away, and his father swung round to face him, his eyes aflame.

"Poison!" Galahad croaked.

"It is no poison to my soul. I am ready!" He shook off Galahad's arm, and turned back to the pedestal.

"Do not touch it!" Galahad was wild. He could not force sense into his words, and Launcelot would not read any. He turned round again and shoved his son to the floor. Galahad rolled up against the wall, but sprung up again in a moment. In desperation, he threw himself forward into Launcelot's body. But his aim was not accurate. He caught the pedestal as well. It jerked violently, sending the cup flying into the air. Launcelot took his concentration from Galahad and reached forward as he too fell, trying to catch the chalice. His fingers reached towards it, but Galahad's hand came in front.

"It is my destiny!" he cried. Half staggering, half crawling, he moved a few feet away from his father, and knelt up, looking down at the cup, at what he had done. He tried to stand. He wavered, and, clasping the cup in both hands, he crushed it against his chest as he sank back to his knees, his strength gone once more. What would Conlaed say? Greater love hath no man than that he lay down his life for another. Galahad hung his head, looking at the slivers of broken glass glinting amid the blood that ran over his hands. He began to weep, silently. Perceval was now on his feet, next to Launcelot. They looked down on him; he could feel their presence, but he did not meet their eyes. He thought of Samson, and of going once more with him into the deep forest of his home, into the cool, green canopy of trees and among the musty smell of leaf litter, journeying deep into the peace and darkness of the forest...

They had to wait for a litter to bear his body back to the villa. Felix volunteered silently and rode off, to leave them in private and fetch aid. Galahad's corpse had been carried out of the small room and laid before the altar of the church. The abbot came slowly after them, having assessed the story of those brief moments. He stopped next to Launcelot, by the dais.

"It was not the Grail," said Launcelot flatly. It was a statement, not a question.

"It was the challenge of the Grail. You were warned against its desecration; we let you see it only to adore and take back word. That your young companion should die for it is not of our choosing."

"He died for me, his father." Launcelot placed a hand over Galahad's own. He disturbed the congealing blood, and it trickled slowly beneath his own fingers.

"Then perhaps his quest was victorious."

"Where is it?" asked Perceval.

"I do not know," the abbot confessed reluctantly. "One of my predecessors died without passing on the secret of its resting place. That it was here once is true, and what you saw was blessed with its spirit, intended for true worship and spiritual edification of the faithful. It was no deceit."

"You preach strange truths," replied Perceval dourly.

"And you make strange promises," he returned mildly, looking at Launcelot. When he turned back to Perceval, tears were in the old man's eyes. "We did not intend this," he concluded quietly, "I can only pray that Providence will reveal to us all the purpose in this event."

The body was driven back in silence. When they entered the gates, Samson came bounding up to meet them. He raced around the horses and litter until he spotted Galahad. Leaping into the cart, he licked his face, then began to sniff at the corpse. Suddenly, he sat down. He threw back his head and began to howl. It echoed through the courtyard and up into the air, and brought the household running.

The dog would not leave the body. He followed it to the embalmer's. He watched as the heart was cut out, to be preserved for the journey home. He sat by the vat as the flesh was boiled from the bones and stared dolefully as they were picked out and cleaned before being laid in a casket. Then he followed the men back to the villa, still acknowledging no one, despite kind words and caresses from the soldiers, and a concerned nuzzle from the other dog. Even Conlaed, who had known him from a pup, was not able to elicit a response.

That night, he came into the room where Launcelot and Perceval were sleeping. He pushed open the door and snuffled his way to Launcelot's bed. He stopped at the foot of the pallet, turned himself around a few times and then lay down to sleep. When Launcelot awoke early that morning, unrested though he had slept the deep sleep of grief, Samson sat up and looked him straight in the eye. Launcelot sat forward and reached out his hand. Samson rubbed his head slightly against his palm. The agreement was struck and the burden accepted.

As Conlaed looked over the rail of the ship, making the last, precarious journey across the small channel that separated Britannia from Gaul, he thought back, almost seventeen years now, to that sea voyage from his monastery to the northern shores of the larger island, to shepherd a child who had barely entered into the world. He wondered how he would have felt had he realized that the tutor would outlive the pupil, that he would never see the results of his careful teaching in the life of a man. As he stood, Launcelot came over with Samson at his heels; the dog was rarely more than ten paces from his new master. He leaned on the rail beside him.

"Were you thinking of him?" he asked.

"I contemplated the vision of death perhaps more than anyone in the fellowship," said Conlaed, "but I never let myself imagine that it pertained to Galahad. Even if we possessed the Grail, my homecoming would be empty."

"But where is the Grail?" asked Launcelot, half rhetorically.

"Lost in time," said Conlaed. "I do not think the monks were equivocating. The gift they bestowed in lieu of it was not given lightly." They had not, in the end, left without a relic. The abbot had sent a parcel, which, unwrapped, had revealed itself as a scabbard. The original casing was of ancient leather, but this had now become the lining for a silver outer layer encrusted with stones, from semi-precious topaz and glass to small emeralds and sapphires. It was, he had written, a gift to their king in memory of the young soldier who had offered himself as a sacrifice, and was the scabbard of Simon the Zealot. It was said to protect its user from wounds in battle.

"We will not return in triumph, but it will not be a failure."

"Many will be surprised to see us return at all," said Launcelot. "Perhaps even disappointed."

"I think they will not know us."

Launcelot nodded silently and placed his hand upon the monk's shoulder for a moment, before striding across the ship once more.

Conlaed was not the only one drinking in the sight of Britannia. At the far end of the ship, Metellus was standing, his arm barely able to fit around his stout and beaming wife. He had - to no one's surprise by this time - made it along the dangerous route through Italia to fetch his faithful widow, and married her at the dock before they embarked. At least one happy ending was guaranteed. Nearer the monk, a young girl was also looking towards the shores of her new home. Her face was brave, but her hands shook. Conlaed sent up a short prayer that she would find a new family, just as he had, just as he would. He watched as Perceval joined her and leaned down to say something kind to her. She looked up and smiled. She would survive, Conlaed thought with relief.

He glanced back to the place where the casket sat, next to Helena's coffin. His own bones were weary, he thought, though the flesh upon them had proven its vigour. Too weary to make the journey back up north, though it was his final duty to Galahad. He did not fear Pelles; where many saw a powerful necromancer-king, he discerned a deluded, crumbling old man. From the pallor of his skin, he had been on his way to death when Conlaed left that winter. Yet he owed the boy's mother the truth, and, he admitted, he desired to see whether Drystan's love had effected any cure in her. For the Lady Elayne, he decided at last, he could deliver her son. She and Drystan deserved it, deserved to live their lives in honesty. He would go.

Epilogue

The novice was not a young man; in fact, he was almost past middle age, though still handsome. His hair and moustache, though completely grey, were thick and vibrant; the many lines around his eyes bespoke a mixture of sorrows and joys, of wisdom gained and retained in an active life. It was not unusual for a nobleman to spend his final years preparing for eternity, to live a sedate and slowing life as recompense for the blood he had shed - or ordered to be shed - in the course of his duties. Yet there was a lightness in this man's step as he walked towards the scriptorium, and his shoulders were straight and broad, with no hint of a stoop. He had to bend, though, to get under the doorway. He stood hesitantly on the threshold, looking around into the glow of artificial light which supplemented the waning afternoon sun making its best effort to shine through the lines of windows on either wall. In front of the apertures, the brothers formed their own line at a long table, their sloping desks before them. At the head, a monk was seated before a larger desk, so completely preoccupied in his work that he did not notice the stranger, though he was evidently in a position of supervision over the others.

Halfway down the table, on the right side, another man was standing, peering over the shoulder of a young scribe. He looked up as he heard the novice enter. After a moment his eyes widened, and he smiled, pushing the myriad of lines upon his own face into an expression of gladness.

"Brother Launcelot!" he beamed, walking forward slowly but steadily. "I have waited for your coming since I heard that your request was accepted. I could not have hoped or prayed that our reunion should be so soon."

"Brother Conlaed," said Launcelot, striding forward to catch the older man's hands in his. "Many years have passed since the old fellowship, yet I have missed your counsel and your valour, especially in the dark years." Several pairs of eyes glanced up surreptitiously at this description of the old man who gently cajoled them through their long hours at their writing.

"The years have indeed been long," replied Conlaed, "but all of you, living or at rest, are constantly in my prayers."

"Alas, too many are in the latter category now. Yet we had good times together, even at the end." He trailed off, unwilling to articulate those memories. Yet Conlaed read them.

"Do you want to see the place?"

"May you be spared?"

"In truth I do little but supervise the work nowadays - my eyes tire so easily. Brother Gildas directs the work more closely, and indeed produces his own of uncommon quality and insight. He is working on a history, you know. I think your name will be in it." At the sound of his name, the monk at the head of the table raised his eyes momentarily, but, perceiving that he was not being summoned, returned forthwith to his manuscript.

"He will want to speak with you soon; I know he has questions. But you will get scarcely a word from him until he is ready for your information."

"I have no wish for that sort of immortality any more. If I may lay my body to rest having lived true to my Brothers, it is enough."

"Come, come," said Conlaed, placing his arm on Launcelot's and turning him back towards the door. "The air will do us both good. You sound melancholy. I think that Glastonbury will be a fortunate change for you. The spirit of this place is healthgiving; it has put years on my own life. I may be slow, but I do not ache, not even in the damp winter, and my mind is still clear, a blessing, to be sure."

The two men walked slowly out, leaving many disappointed monks behind. A glare from Brother Gildas quickly sent them back to their tasks. The old companions took no notice of this, but made their way across the courtyard to the small cemetery.

"I do not remember showing overmuch valour," Conlaed said at last, as they reached the first gravestones.

"To defend your comrades, to save their lives in defiance of your own desires, that was courage unappreciated then, though, as I have studied in this life, I saw the cost of your loyalty. You possess an integrity we could have used when the evil times fell upon us."

They halted near the grave of Saint Indracht, but did not look to it. Instead they stared at a newer headstone nearby, a simple piece, smoothed, but not decorated, and carved with plain letters.

"There are few stonemasons to be had hereabouts now," apologized Conlaed, as Launcelot bent down to read the inscription.

"Hic iacet sepultus inclitus rex Arturius in insula avalonia cum Wenneveria uxore sua. Here lies buried upon the island of Avalon the renowned King Arthur with his wife Guenevere," said Launcelot quietly. "So she came here, too. I did not know."

"They bore her body here some two years back. She had made restitution, as we judged, though he did not live to see it. She turned from the Old Ones in the end - yes, I knew of her allegiances - and found a true rest where she had only sought a temporary safety, behind the walls of a nunnery. She deserved to lie by him at the last."

"It was a madness; yet, in those last days, I came to think that the whole world was mad. Why she should cast her lot in with the nephew of the Regissimus, I do not know. Perhaps she saw her death in Arthur's weakening; perhaps it was my fault. If I had not turned from her, not tried to put aside my love and be true to my king, we might still be holding Arthur's realm for him. The Grail changed us, Conlaed. Though we never touched it, it seared our souls." Launcelot knelt by the stone, turning to look up at the older monk.

"Relinquishing your sin did not cause this evil upon our land. Times pass. The Western Empire has crumbled, and many kings fell in its ruins. The Age of Arthur was over, and the treacheries were but servants of a greater purpose beyond their control."

"Then why do we remain, Conlaed? When our children and our loved ones fall before our eyes, why is it our burden to bear the sorrows and regrets? We were raised to be soldiers, you and I, yet we end our days battling our memories."

"If we too were to pass away with the waning of the age, who would hear their song? Who would record their deeds? We live for the sake of the past and the future. I have come to terms with my Cross; here you will find your own strength to bear your part." He looked down kindly at Launcelot and stretched out a hand. "Come, a chill grows in the air, and there are no young bones about this place, either above or below the earth. Gildas has longed to hear you speak of your days with the Regissimus. Let us humour him awhile. Mayhap it will give your heart ease."

The two old men linked arms and walked slowly from the graveyard. Their faces were towards the light of the sinking sun, and it cast long shadows behind them as they went. They passed on by the courtyard and entered the shade of the dwellings; their shadows lingered for a moment behind them, then slipped into the twilight and were gone.

GLOSSARY OF ROMAN PLACE NAMES AND TITLES

Aquae Sulis	Bath
Britannia Minor	Brittany
Camulodunum	Colchester
Castellum Cataviae	Cadbury Castle
Clausentum	Southampton
Civitas Belgarum	South Britannia
Eboracum	York
Hibernia	Ireland
Londinium	London
Luguvalium	Carlisle
Ratae Coritanorum	Leicester
Sorviodumum	Salisbury
Viroconium Cornoviorum	Wroxeter
Comes	Count (high military rank)
Dux Britanniorum	"Duke of the Britons"

Magister militum	"Master of soldiers"
Magistratus	Head of local government
Magistratus Belgarum	Head of area in South Britannia